ROGUE

THE PALADIN PROPHECY

ROGUE

THE PALADIN PROPHECY

Book III

MARK FROST

Random House New York

Text copyright © 2015 by Mark Frost
Jacket art copyright © 2015 by Hilts

All rights reserved. Published in the United States by Random House Children's Books, a division of Penguin Random House LLC, New York.

Random House and the colophon are registered trademarks of Penguin Random House LLC.

Visit us on the Web! randomhouseteens.com

Educators and librarians, for a variety of teaching tools, visit us at RHTeachersLibrarians.com

Library of Congress Cataloging-in-Publication Data
Frost, Mark
Rogue / Mark Frost.
pages cm. — (The Paladin Prophecy ; book 3)
Summary: "Will West and his friends enter the alternate universe of the Never in order to rescue Will's friend and mentor Dave from the dangerous and deadly creatures from beyond."—Provided by publisher.
ISBN 978-0-375-87047-7 (trade) — ISBN 978-0-375-98003-9 (ebook)
[1. Superheroes—Fiction. 2. Supernatural—Fiction. 3. Good and evil—Fiction.]
I. Title.
PZ7.F92164Ro 2015 [Fic]—dc23 2015003959

Printed in the United States of America

10 9 8 7 6 5 4 3 2 1

First Edition

FOR MY SON TRAVIS . . .

ROGUE

ONE

WILL'S RULES FOR LIVING #1:
IF YOU REALLY WANT TO KEEP A SECRET,
DON'T TELL ANYBODY.

"Have you ever tasted champagne, Will?"

"Can't say that I have, no, sir."

Franklin Greenwood gestured to his butler, Lemuel Clegg, who directed one of the uniformed staff members standing by with an open bottle toward Will.

"Just a splash," said Franklin, then leaned over toward his grandson, seated to his right, and winked. "It's not as if we don't have something to celebrate."

"That's right, sir," said Will.

He watched the crystal liquid swirl around the bottom of his glass as the waiter withdrew the bottle. Will raised his drink, imitating his grandfather, and touched the glass to his.

"To the Prophecy," said Franklin.

"To the Prophecy," said Will.

He took a sip and grimaced at the bitter bite of the effervescence. Franklin drained his glass in one greedy gulp and held it out for more. The nearby staff member holding the bottle rushed to refill it, without appearing to hurry.

"I can't tell you what joy these last few months have brought me, Will. I've never wanted anything more than to share with my family the blessings I've worked so hard to create. And as you know, for the longest time I'd given up imagining that would ever be possible."

Will nodded sympathetically, forced another small swallow of the frothy swill down his throat, then set down the glass, hoping he could get away with leaving the rest of it untouched. "I feel the same way."

"Will, this time we've spent together has meant more to me than I can even begin to express. Your willingness to listen and learn without judging, your positive attitude toward our goals . . ." Franklin leaned over and laid a cold hand on top of Will's. "But do you know what has been most gratifying for me? The opportunity to bear witness to your burgeoning talents."

"Thank you, sir."

"I can think of no measurable way to assign a value to that. This is a priceless treasure. After so many disappointments in my personal life, I could never have hoped for more."

"For me, too." Will held his gaze and smiled shyly. "Grandfather?"

"Yes, Will."

"You've told me that, as we get to know each other, you wanted nothing more than to gain my trust."

"That continues to mean more to me than I have words to express. . . ."

Franklin's voice caught in his throat, choked with emotion. Moisture appeared in his hazy blue eyes. He gulped down another half glass of champagne, then took a pocket square from his crested blue school blazer and dabbed away some tears.

"You don't have to say anything, Grandpa. And I only hope that, with all you've seen and heard from me these last few weeks, I've gained your trust as well."

"Yes, of course." Franklin folded and pocketed his hand-kerchief and smiled benignly. "How may I convey that to you, Will?"

"I think I'm ready to hear the whole story."

Franklin considered the request, savored the final bite of his soy-fed Japanese Kobe rib-eye steak, pushed his plate back—another waiting staff member whisked it away instantly—then reached over and patted Will's hand.

"Let's take a walk," said Franklin.

They exited the old, weather-worn castle out a side door that Will hadn't noticed before, depositing them on the less-developed eastern side of the island. The late-summer sun hung low in the sky, shadows edging toward evening. Franklin started down a trim, graveled path that led through manicured gardens. Will kept exact pace with the old man's long, even strides.

"I grew up on this island," said Franklin, looking around as they walked. "My earliest memories are all enmeshed with this place—these trees, the smells, the water, the magnificent views."

"Were you born here?" asked Will.

"Nearby," said Franklin, gesturing vaguely toward the mainland. "Father founded the Center a few years before I was born; I drew my first breath in the small school infirmary that was part of our original campus. All that's gone now, of course. By the time I was a toddler, Father had purchased the Crag and the island from the Cornish family. Everything about the Prophecy and our family's involvement with it starts with Ian Cornish."

"Cornish came to Wisconsin after the Civil War, didn't he?"

Franklin patted Will's arm. "You have been paying attention, haven't you?"

3

"I figured that's why you wanted me to sort through all those old files up there," said Will, nodding back toward the tower that loomed over the castle's eastern half. "To learn about the Center and the Greenwood family tree."

As he glanced up at the tower's windows, Will held up two fingers behind the older man's back, so quickly that his grandfather couldn't see them.

"Indeed. Well reasoned, my boy. Ian Cornish designed and manufactured rifles, cannons, and munitions and amassed a great fortune, as you know, by the end of the Civil War. But he lost his oldest son in the war's final month, and it unhinged the man. He fled New England and settled here, a stranger to this part of the world, half mad with grief, and as a way to assuage his derangement, he put his fortune to frantic work."

"What did he think that would do?"

"In his diaries, Cornish writes of feeling haunted by the restless spirits of the men killed by his armaments—legions of them appeared to him at night, led by the ghost of his own son. Ian believed he was receiving instructions from these spirits about what to build up here . . . and what to dig for down below. And the only way he could find peace was to obey their instructions."

"So that's why he went down into the tunnels."

They passed the small family graveyard that Will had noticed on an earlier visit—his own family's plot—the Greenwoods—and the gravestone of the man walking beside him, Franklin Greenwood, resting below the stone statue of a winged angel lifting a sword to the sky.

"Something was calling him, all right," said Franklin. "But it wasn't the ghosts of dead soldiers—or should I say, that's not all it seems to have been."

"So that's why he started excavating."

"Extending the preexisting system of tunnels and caves under the island, always going deeper, yes. Driven to find something he believed his visions told him waited for him down there. Something he believed would absolve him of his sins and wash away his undying grief."

"And he found it," said Will. "In that lost city down there."

"Strange the ways and beliefs of men," said Franklin. "But sometimes when the mind breaks, and I believe that's what happened to poor Ian Cornish, it can lead you to even greater truths. Like Cahokia."

Franklin paused in front of a small stone mausoleum to catch his breath.

"Although it seems evident that the last of that ancient civilization died or were driven from their home countless thousands of years ago," said Franklin, "some trace of them remained in their lost city—a fragment of their consciousness, I suppose, embedded in a few precious objects they'd left behind."

"Things they called aphotic technology."

Franklin gave him an admiring glance. "You seldom cease to amaze me, Will. You really set your teeth into these research assignments of mine, didn't you?"

"Like you said, never do anything halfway." Will shrugged. "What sort of objects?"

"I'll come to that, but mark my words," said Franklin, raising a finger. "For what he brought back to the human race, Ian Cornish will someday be remembered as one of our most courageous explorers, every bit as important to the story of man as Galileo, Christopher Columbus, or the men who split the atom."

Franklin lifted a small black device from his pocket and pointed it at the stone building in front of them. Carved doors, which had appeared to be purely decorative, pivoted on hidden hinges and with a grind of stone on stone swung open.

Franklin pushed the device again. Just inside the doors, two sleek stainless-steel panels slid apart, revealing the car of a large and ultramodern elevator.

"Allow me to show you," said Franklin, pointing Will toward the car.

Will stepped inside, and Franklin followed. He punched commands into a complex control panel on a side wall just inside the doors. Looking over his grandfather's shoulder, Will watched him enter a specific sequence of numbers. The outside stone doors closed, and the steel panels whispered shut. Will felt a whoosh of air compress around him. They began to descend, smoothly ramping up to what felt like considerable speed.

This is the ground-level entrance to the same elevator we discovered in the hospital a mile down below, Will realized.

"If what he found was so important, why didn't Cornish ever tell anyone about it?" asked Will.

"Oh, but he did," said Franklin. "Cornish had made many influential friends back in his native New England. Chief among them his fellow members in what, on the surface, appeared to be a social or academic club in Boston. Prominent men, pillars of that community, makers of history, all part of an organization rooted in tradition and culture whose origins were bound up with the birth of liberty and freedom in early America.

"But in fact that organization's history ran much deeper than Ian knew, back to the ruling castes and monarchies of western Europe, centuries before our continent was even discovered."

The man took an old-fashioned key from his pocket and held it out on his open palm. It appeared more ceremonial than practical. On its porcelain tab Will saw a three-lettered insignia, intertwined with a ruler and a compass, which he recognized instantly.

"The Knights of Charlemagne," said Will.

"Exactly. Once he revealed this discovery to his colleagues back east, they took tremendous interest in supporting Cornish's work here. A few years later, when the poor man's mental state deteriorated, it was under their supervision that the first meaningful explorations of Cahokia moved forward. Do you begin to see how this all flows together, Will?"

"Yes, sir."

"Ian Cornish's oldest son died in the Civil War, but he also had a *second* son, too young to fight, who knew about Cahokia from the beginning. Cornish initiated the boy into the Knights, and he traveled west with his father when he first journeyed here. This only surviving son of Ian Cornish assumed a key role as the enterprise took shape. And when poor Ian lost what feeble grasp he had on the last of his reason, finally taking his own life, this sturdy young man, Lemuel Cornish, was appointed by his fellow Knights to continue this great work and keep his father's legacy alive."

Lemuel. "Kind of an unusual name," said Will.

"Not for the nineteenth century," said Franklin, looking up at the walls. "I knew him, of course. As did my father. Lemuel Cornish sold us the estate that became the school. But he didn't tell my father anything close to all he knew. He saved that for me."

"Why?"

"Thomas Greenwood—my father, your great-grandfather—was many things. A man of vision, a born leader, and in the field of education nothing less than a prophet. He was also . . . How shall I put this?" Franklin glanced at the ceiling. "You know I'm right, Father—an incorrigible Goody Two-shoes."

Will couldn't help laughing. "How do you mean?"

"Thomas never met a heathen he couldn't convert, a hopeless case he couldn't save, a sinner he couldn't redeem. Goodness, always 'Goodness,' with a capital G. All of human existence divided neatly into black and white, and my father confidently armed with an unshakeable faith in his ability to discern the difference."

Will felt the elevator car vibrating ever so slightly as it began to slow, almost imperceptibly.

"What's wrong with that?" asked Will.

Franklin looked slightly annoyed by the question; the vivid scar tissue behind his ears turned a brighter shade of pink.

"What's wrong, dear boy," said Franklin, meeting Will's eyes with a restrained but reproachful look, "is that such a simple, reductive, dare I say childlike philosophy leaves out all the gray, the in-between, the place where men who learn to actually think for themselves get to decide how to live by their own rules."

The car stopped, and the panels silently slid open in front of Will.

"And that's where most of the interesting things happen," said Franklin.

"Where's Will?" asked Brooke, just entering the suite.

Nick looked up from his three hundredth push-up. "Dinner with Old Man Elliot again."

Nick flipped to his feet and toweled off, pumped, covered with sweat, and grinning at her like he couldn't help it. He couldn't really. Brooke, as usual, looked effortlessly flawless—outfit, accessories, hair, just a hint of makeup, every aspect of her presented self put together like a perfect recipe.

"He's spending an awful lot of time over there," said Brooke as she set down her backpack on the table, then pulled out an appointment book and started writing in it, absentmindedly twirling a stray strand of her golden curls. "What about Ajay?"

"He's still over at the Crag, too, working late, organizing those old whatchamacallit—archives."

"Ar-*kives,* not ar-*chives.* You put *chives* on a baked potato."

"*You're* a baked potato," said Nick, still grinning at her.

Brooke shook her head and laughed, then took a longer, more admiring look at him. "Whatever training program they've put you on is doing wonders for your bod. And absolutely zero for your brain."

Nick turned a chair around and sat across from her, resting his chin on his arms. "Since you're so deeply into playing camp counselor, don't you want to ax me where Elise is?"

"Ax you? All right, I'll *ax* you. Pray tell."

"No clue," said Nick, drumming his fingers. "Why you want to know where everybody is all the time?"

She gave him one of her patented looks of exasperation. "Can't I be curious about my friends?"

She picked up the black phone on the table and punched the lone button. When the operator picked up, she asked, "Would you page Elise Moreau and have her call me, please?"

"What's today's date?" asked Nick when she hung up.

"What does that have to do with anything?"

"You've got your calendar right there in front of you, snowflake. What's today's date?"

"August seventh," said Brooke.

"Oh, that's right," said Nick, snapping his fingers. "It's National Be Curious About Your Friends Day."

She gave him a longer look, and for a moment a flash of malice showed through, before she covered it over. "There must be some way I can unknow you."

"Keep dreaming, darlin'."

Nick watched Brooke as she went back to writing in her book, his smile falling off when she stopped looking his way; then he stood up and moonwalked toward the kitchen, glancing at the wall clock.

"May I offer you a refreshing beverage, Brooksie?" he asked.

"A water would be fine, thanks." Facedown in her book.

"One H-two-O, coming right up."

Ajay slid the last box across the floor, landing it precisely in the only gap in a long row of boxes stacked neatly against the back wall of the circular tower room.

He closed his eyes, put his hands to either side of his skull, and pressed gently. This seemed to help alleviate the pressure that built up during these extensive memorization sessions. Unfortunately, it did nothing for the even sharper headaches that sometimes woke him in the middle of the night.

You're building new neural pathways at extraordinary rates of speed and density. That's how Dr. Kujawa had described the phenomenon to him after the tests they'd recently run. *And "pathways" doesn't begin to do this process justice; you're building superhighways.*

When Ajay looked in a mirror recently, he'd noticed his eyes appeared to have grown larger. His pupils had also become less sensitive to light, almost as if he welcomed it now, because it allowed him to keep them open wider and longer and to see more. He found that he was *hungry* to see more. Most alarming of all, the last time he'd tried on an old baseball cap, the fit was decidedly tighter than he remembered.

He'd decided it was best not to think too much about these things.

Ajay looked at his watch, then hurried to the east-facing

window. He peered down at the path leading toward the shore past the graveyard and quickly spotted two figures moving along:

Will and Mr. Elliot.

Ajay widened his eyes, focusing in on them as he'd learned to do, details accumulating and enhancing the image.

He saw Will glance back toward the tower, reach his arm back, and raise it behind the older man.

Two fingers.

"Good golly, Miss Molly," whispered Ajay in alarm.

He quickly moved to retrieve the knapsack he'd hidden in one of the boxes. Looked at his watch again: 6:50. Ten minutes before Lemuel Clegg would arrive to bring him his dinner.

He removed his small school pager from the bag. The one he'd modified to avoid detection by the school's server network.

"Sensing that he might be less receptive to the actual narrative, Lemuel Cornish never told Thomas about what his father and the Knights had found down here," said Franklin as the doors slid open again. "My father never heard a word about it."

Franklin led Will out of the elevator into a narrow corridor. They hadn't descended all the way to the bottom. This was a level Will had never seen before, built in a style decades newer than the ones in the old hospital, freshly painted, with portraits on the wall, men in nineteenth- and twentieth-century dress who he assumed must have been prominent members of the Knights.

"What kind of a man was he?" asked Will.

"Lemuel? Practical. Levelheaded. He understood only too well how his father had lost his way. That Ian's obsession with what he'd uncovered under these grounds owed more to passion, or madness, than reason. You see, after his initial enthusiasm, Ian gradually became convinced that he'd made a dreadful mistake, that this lost city needed to be sealed off, buried for all time."

"I take it Lemuel didn't see things the way his father did," said Will.

"He was a much more balanced man. Lemuel adopted a curious but cautious approach to the ongoing investigations. It was his idea, for instance, to install those great wooden doors at the mouth of the tunnel. Not to seal anything off, although he let his father believe that was the reason, but simply to prevent any unwanted or accidental entrance."

"Do you know who carved those words on them—*Cahokia* and *Teotwawki*?"

"We don't know exactly when he put the first one there, but we believe carving those words on his son's doors was among the last things Ian Cornish ever did."

"But why did he call it Cahokia? You know about the one in southern Illinois, right?"

"Oh, yes, the Native American archaeological site. Vast mounds of earth, laden with artifacts, evidence of an earlier civilization. French explorers stumbled onto it over three hundred years ago. It's a state park now, complete with guided tours and a souvenir shop, although it wasn't anything close to that organized back in Ian's day.

"But after he paid a visit there, Ian apparently came to believe that his discovery here and that one to the south were part of the same vast underground network of cities. Not a Native American one, mind you, but an even older civilization that the Others constructed long ago beneath the entire Midwest. A conclusion that, in Ian's declining mental state, he believed supported the idea that they had once been Earth's dominant species. Which he in turn interpreted"—he paused and chuckled as he turned to Will with a twinkle in his eye—"as evidence of their desire to take over the world a second time."

"So that's what the second word on the door is about, then," said Will. "You know what that one means, right?"

"Teotwawki. Oh, yes, an acronym: *the end of the world as we know it.* More ravings, but sadly, so it proved to be for Ian. At that point, he had been confined for some months to a padded room here at the Crag, judged a danger to himself. Then he escaped one day and fled down into the tunnels. That's when he carved those letters on the doors with a knife he stole from the kitchen. And then Ian used that same knife to take his own life."

Will paused for a moment. He'd stood in that exact spot, not so long ago. He closed his eyes, sent himself back there, and for a moment touched the overwhelming aura of the poor man's terror and desperation. He shuddered as it ran through him; then he quickly shook it off.

"What about the statues of the soldiers in the tunnel? Did Ian put those there, too?"

"Yes, another folly of Ian's that Lemuel tolerated enough to indulge, even after his father was gone—one soldier for every American war. Sentinels, Ian called them, standing guard against what he feared might one day emerge from down below. I hope you can see by now that poor Ian had some exceedingly strange ideas about *what* he'd found. But he'd also grown far too unstable to come close to realizing exactly *who* he'd found."

"But Lemuel did."

"Oh, yes. And he was also perceptive enough to realize that in order to make the most of it, the Knights would need the help of someone in our family going forward. An ally from the next generation who would appreciate the magnitude, dare I say the magnificence, of what all this could lead to." Franklin glanced over and smiled at Will again. "That's why he came to me."

"But you were just a student here then, weren't you?" asked Will, confused.

"I was twelve," said Franklin.

He stopped before a set of double doors and took out the porcelain key.

"But you see, I was very much like you, Will. I'd discovered the tunnels during my own explorations when I was still in short pants. A boy needs his adventures, doesn't he?"

"I guess so, sir."

"And not unlike Ian Cornish, I found that something down in those caverns spoke to me as well. Not a voice, per se, but a feeling, an emanation that radiated intelligence, mystery, and the promise of something titanic. It was irresistible to my imagination. So I kept venturing back down below, a little deeper each time, until I finally made it to the doors. And that day, as I emerged from the tunnels, I found Lemuel waiting for me."

"Was he angry at you?"

Franklin chuckled. "He tried to make me think so. But after we spoke for a while, he sensed we were kindred spirits. My curiosity was handsomely rewarded. Lemuel began taking me along with him on his trips down below—beyond the doors—showing me, a section at a time, the enormity of what they'd found."

"You never told your father about this?"

"It was a secret only Lemuel and I shared," said Franklin, raising his eyebrows mischievously. "Just as all this will be ours."

He inserted the key into a large rectangular keyhole and turned it. Will heard the lock yield, and Franklin softly pushed the doors open.

A dimly lit carpeted room waited inside. Sleek, spare furnishings, a few expensive-looking works of modern art on the wall. Two leather wing-backed chairs.

Someone was sitting in one of the chairs, turned away from the door; Will saw a thick-soled, old-fashioned black shoe splayed out to the side on the floor but couldn't see the person's face.

"Until one day Lemuel asked me to share our secret with one of Father's colleagues, a faculty member here at the Center, one of my instructors, who'd also taken an interest in me. A man who they knew would appreciate what they'd discovered even better than I.

"You see, Will, from our inception in antiquity, the Knights have excelled at conducting what we would call today 'deep background' on people who are of interest to us. And they couldn't have been more right about this man, or me, for that matter, or the whole situation. It's no exaggeration to say that this pairing became the turning point in our history."

Franklin walked into the room. A sickly sour smell hung in the air, medicinal and threaded with a hint of rot. Will felt a shiver of fear root him to the floor. He forced his legs to carry him forward after his grandfather, toward the man in the chair.

"I'd like you to meet him, too, Will," said Franklin, turning to face him once he reached the other side of the chair.

Will saw an ancient hand rise from the arm of the chair to beckon him closer. Sallow skin hung off the bones, spidery fingers trembled as they waved, fingernails looked like thick yellowed talons.

"Will . . . this is my mentor, Dr. Joseph Abelson."

When Will finally saw the man's face, he nearly keeled over.

* * *

15

The pager buzzed quietly in Nick's pocket as he reached for a water bottle. Screened by the fridge's open door, he quickly slipped out the device and glanced at the message screen.

Go time.

"Holy crapanoly," whispered Nick.

He dropped the pager back in his pocket and took a deep breath as he unscrewed the top of the water bottle. He took a small vial from his other pocket and unscrewed the top. He squeezed the rubber stopper on top, filling it, then drew out the glass vial and squeezed again, emptying the colorless contents of the vial into the water. Nick replaced the cap, pocketed the vial, and grabbed another bottle for himself.

"Here you go, Brooks."

Brooke never looked up as Nick set the bottle of water down on the table in front of her, took a seat across from her, cracked open his own bottle, and drained half of it in a single swig.

"Hot enough for ya?" he asked, then belched.

She finally looked up at him. "If I offer to pay you, will you go away? I can afford it."

"Come on, you oughta know me better than that," said Nick, finishing his bottle in another epic swig. "How much?"

Brooke scowled at him, reached for her water bottle, and looked back at her book. Nick watched carefully as she unscrewed the top, then paused as she finished reading something.

Like he'd seen his friends do, he closed his eyes and tried to send a thought suggestion to her: *Drink*.

"Are you all right?" she asked.

"Yeah, perfect, why?" asked Nick, reopening his eyes.

"Your face was all screwed up, like a baby trying to poop."

Brooke took a long sip of water while slowly shaking her head.

Awesome. The mind thing totally worked. Or maybe she's just thirsty.

"I was just trying to think," said Nick.

"I forgot—for you, that's cardio."

He glanced at his watch.

Seven minutes. That's how long it's supposed to take before it affects the nervous system.

"I'm gonna hit the shower," he said.

"Thanks ever so much for the update," said Brooke, turning away, her face buried back in her book as she took another sip.

Once he was behind his locked bathroom door, Nick answered Ajay's page with one of his own.

Done.

TWO

WILL'S RULES FOR LIVING #2:
YOU CAN'T LIVE YOUR LIFE TWO DAYS AT A TIME.

"Dr. Abelson, this is the young man I've been telling you about," said Franklin, smiling, raising his voice well above a conversational level. "My grandson, Will."

The man's right eye was opaque with milky cataracts. The other had a cold reptilian blankness to it. Wisps of hair clung to his head like cotton candy. The flesh of his face sagged like it was trying to slide off his skull, and the runoff collected in a wrinkled puddle below his chin.

Abelson extended his right hand, mottled and covered with scabs, the fingers bent and twisted like broken twigs. Will reached out and took it. Dry and scaly to the touch, it felt more like a claw.

Will quickly calculated:

This is my grandfather's mentor. My grandfather's at least ninety-five. So somehow Dr. Joseph Abelson—a man who was a contemporary and colleague of Adolf Hitler's—can't be a day less than a hundred and fifteen . . . and maybe even a whole lot older than that.

As Abelson stared at him, a long, dry rasp escaped the man's throat, an attempt at speech that didn't sound like words.

"He says you look like your father," said Franklin with a little chuckle.

And you look like a mummy, thought Will.

"It's a pleasure to meet you, sir," said Will, raising his voice to match his grandfather's level and drawing his hand back.

"As I believe you know, none of the first class of Paladins perished on that 'plane crash' we arranged in '38," said Franklin, then patted Abelson on the arm. "And neither did our teacher. He came back to supervise the program, in the hospital the Knights built for us down below, which you've also seen."

Will couldn't take his eyes off Abelson, who continued to gaze at him with that one unsettling red-rimmed eye. No sense of what he was thinking or feeling registered; that eye looked dead, and his slack face seemed incapable of forming any expression at all.

You're not the only one who can mask his feelings, thought Will as he turned back to his grandfather.

"You weren't even on the plane," said Will.

"No, my father had seen to that—after the interference of his meddlesome friend Henry Wallace. He packed me off to Europe for a few months, and so I missed being part of the program."

"Lucky for you," said Will.

The memory of those pathetic, malformed creatures writhing around, wasting away in the copper tanks down below came to mind. *For the last seventy-five years.*

Will closed his eyes and shuddered.

"Yes, well, we all knew the risks," said Franklin, untroubled. "Those boys all volunteered with open hearts, and not one of them has said they ever regretted it."

Not according to Happy Nepsted, thought Will.

"And although my father had prevented me from participating initially, when I returned to school, the Knights still found a crucial role for me. Can you guess what it was?"

"You were the control group," said Will.

"Precisely, Will. Every worthwhile scientific inquiry requires a baseline to chart any changes in the study group against, and that assignment fell to me."

"But wasn't your father watching you like a hawk, afraid you'd fall back in with them?"

Abelson gave out a small, wheezy gasp and Will realized it might have been a laugh. That's how Franklin seemed to interpret it, and he smiled in response.

"Not during the war years," said Franklin. "Father was far too preoccupied, like the rest of the country. Fighting Fascism, Nazis. Making America 'safe.' Not to mention Father really did believe he'd already expunged the Knights from the Center for good."

"I'm guessing you didn't give him any reason to think otherwise."

"Exactly. I played the perfect choirboy. The next challenge we faced was of our own making. By the time the war was over, as a number of unfortunate issues with the health of our first group began to surface, we'd realized the protocols for the Paladin program would require extensive . . . fine-tuning."

Abelson raised a finger and his tongue rolled around as he issued a few more unintelligible rattles and hisses in Franklin's direction.

Franklin leaned down to listen. "That's right, Dr. Joe," he said, then, interpreting again for Will, "Back to the drawing board *indeed*."

Franklin moved to an opaque curtain covering a space on the wall the size of a medium window.

"But this time we'd found a whole new level of inspiration. You see, by then we'd established stronger and more reliable contact with our . . . new friends from down below, on the other side of the divide."

"But how?" asked Will as he walked over to join his grandfather. "They were all dead by then, weren't they, or banished there—"

"Dead, certainly not, but banished?" Franklin chortled again. "That's only what those preposterous do-gooders who put them there have convinced themselves to believe." He looked at Will sharply. "And you do know who I'm referring to, don't you?"

Will knew he was on dangerous ground here; he tried to maintain a delicate balance of skepticism and light contempt in his response. "I heard they call themselves the Hierarchy. Are those the ones you mean?"

"Exactly so."

"I didn't know they were real."

"Oh, they're real, all right, sorry to say, and full of more self-righteous arrogance and delusional grandeur than you could possibly imagine."

"Who are they?"

"Like our friends, older beings. Far older, from some other realm beyond our imagining, or perhaps, as they claim— I'll reserve my skepticism—advanced souls who've evolved beyond the indignities of physical life on Earth into a more exalted existence. And I suppose it is possible that at one time, in distant ages past, they did serve a useful function for this Earth. Who's to say? Maybe for a period of time they faithfully fulfilled that purpose.

"But once our friends developed into something like their equals, I believe the Hierarchy's pride got the better of them. Instead of celebrating them as peers, they perceived the Others as rivals, and from that moment on, these fools forfeited any claim on their former role as "benign protectors." After that, they engaged in a genocidal crusade to thwart a magnificent race of beings that was guilty of nothing more than realizing its destiny. Which culminated in the Hierarchy's tragic decision to 'banish' the brightest light this world had yet produced."

Franklin's voice trembled with barely suppressed anger and his hands were shaking as he waved them around emphatically. Will had never seen him so wound up.

"Now you and I, we're expected to learn from our mistakes, correct? Well, the norms of human behavior don't apply to our 'lords and masters.' That was only the beginning of their missteps, Will. During our own human history, these fools have made countless blunders interfering with the affairs of men, thwarting our progress, holding us back from reaching our highest potential.

"But the worst mistake the Hierarchy ever made was their first one, and how badly they underestimated the Others they tried to so callously destroy. And soon we will finally make them pay for it."

Will's blood ran cold, but he kept his voice neutral. "I'm not sure I understand. Do you mean your friends aren't actually trapped in—what do they call that place again?"

"The Never-Was? Oh, yes. They were trapped in there all right. Banished. Never to be seen again."

"So how did they make contact with you?"

"In dreams, of course," said Franklin, as if this was the most obvious answer in the world. "To begin with. Both Dr. Abelson and I experienced this, a slow filtering of ideas into our minds. But it took us a while—thick-skulled hominids that we are—to realize these remarkable creatures were reaching out to us through a language of symbols and images, not words—and that eventually led us to what they wanted us to find."

"What was that?" asked Will.

"A more direct way of communicating," said Franklin, grasping a pull string attached to the curtain. "Through the device they'd left behind so long ago specifically for that purpose. They'd designed it as a kind of beacon, like the black boxes in today's commercial airplanes. One that emanated a faint signal that could only be perceived by individuals attuned to its peculiar frequency—the one that Ian Cornish had first sensed when he arrived and searched for down here in vain all those years. The one that Lemuel and Dr. Joe and I finally found."

Franklin pulled the curtain, revealing a window looking into a small adjoining room, about the size of a closet. On an elevated platform sat the object.

It was the ancient brass astrolabe Will had once happened across in the basement of the castle. A larger version of the one Franklin had given him when he'd first revealed his identity— the one sitting on the desk in his bedroom—but an exact replica, as near as he could tell.

"Put those glasses of yours on," said Franklin, placing a kindly hand on Will's shoulder. "And then have another look at it."

Jumping out of the shower, Nick dressed quickly, then grabbed the bag he'd packed with all the items on his checklist. He listened at his door, glancing at his watch. Counting down the seconds to seven minutes. He cracked open the door and peeked out.

Brooke was no longer at the table. Nick's heart skipped a beat; he looked around and didn't see her anywhere. The water bottle still stood on the table, half empty; that meant she'd drunk more than enough to do the job.

Nick cautiously crept through the living room and peeked into the kitchen. She wasn't in there either. Then he noticed the door to Brooke's room hung open a crack.

Nick moved silently across the room. As he was about to nudge the door open, he heard a whisper of movement behind him. Brooke lurched out of the shadows behind the fireplace, extending an outstretched hand at him. Her face twisted in fury and spite, almost unrecognizable.

Don't let her touch you. That's all they'd told him. That was all he needed to hear.

Nick vaulted into a backward somersault, landing on his feet on top of the sofa, then springing off again to the far side, putting the sofa between them.

"Wha' did you do?" she screeched at him, her voice slurring.

"What?!"

Brooke staggered toward him, her motor skills visibly impaired, fighting desperately to stay upright, yelling even louder.

"Wha' the hell did you do to me?"

She tripped and fell over the footstool in front of the sofa, then scrambled after him, pulling herself up onto the cushions.

"I didn't do anything to you," said Nick.

"Don't lie to me!"

Everywhere Brooke touched, every*thing* she touched, wilted and shrank, leeched of color, light, and whatever life or energy it once possessed—blanched, discolored, drained. As she yanked herself up to her feet again, rabid with fury, struggling to find her balance, Nick shuffled back behind the dining room table.

"I don't know what the heck you're talking about," said Nick.

"Yesh you do!"

She lurched toward him again, grabbing on to the top of a

dining room chair to keep from falling. As her fingernails dug into the veneer, a coarse vapor issued from under her hand, and the slat of wood collapsed inward, sending her tumbling toward the table. She landed with both hands on its surface, her fingernails dug in, and then she slipped backward toward the ground, leaving scorched, skidding nail marks and handprints behind.

Nick couldn't see her for a moment. As a precaution, he took two running steps and parkoured around the wall behind him, flipping and landing in the center of the room.

He looked back but didn't see her under the table where he'd just seen her go down. That strange black vapor rose from a variety of places, and the table and chairs looked as if a piano had fallen on them. Nick picked up the small shovel from the fireplace tool set.

"For crying out loud, Brooke," said Nick. "You touch your mother with those hands?"

She rose up suddenly from behind the sofa and leaped at him again, hurling herself through the air between them with astonishing speed. As Nick somersaulted out of her path, he saw the front door fly open; someone entered and pointed their raised right hand at Brooke.

A bright red flower blossomed in the back of her left shoulder. She landed hard, scorching the carpet, then rolled, staggered halfway to standing, reached back, and pulled what had hit her from her shoulder.

A small dart.

She looked at it, uncomprehending, before dropping to her hands and knees and then face-planting on the floor. Dark, acrid vapor rose from the carpet all around the outlines of her body.

"Talk about mood swings," said Nick.

Coach Ira Jericho stood in the doorway, loading another dart into the pistol in his hand.

"Check to see if she's out," said Jericho.

"No way, I'm not touching her," said Nick, still wielding the shovel.

"What, she too tough for you, McLeish? Can't be serious, little bitty thing like that," said Jericho, walking toward her body.

"Little bitty thing? Dude, you didn't see her go straight-up psycho. She's like a hella honey badger."

They both looked down at her, Nick a step behind Jericho, maintaining a safe distance. Head turned to the side, eyes rolled up in her head, Brooke's back rose and fell regularly, deep breaths, totally out.

"Shouldn't we tie her up or something?" asked Nick. "Check that. She'd just melt the rope."

"She won't be doing anything but drooling on the floor for a few hours."

"What'd you hit her with?"

"Enough to tranq a moose," said Jericho, looking at her closely.

Nick leaned in closer, peering at her delicate eyelashes and turned-up nose. "I'm just kinda glad I didn't have to clock her with this shovel. I mean, no matter how mad evil she's gone, she's still sort of my friend, you know?"

Jericho stared at him. "Whatever you say, McLeish. Are you ready to roll?"

"Put me in, Coach."

"Grab your gear. We don't have much time."

Nick grabbed his backpack and the one they'd packed for Will, then joined Jericho at the door.

"Guess I'll have to work through all this emotional stress

down the road," said Nick, taking a last look back at Brooke as they hustled out into the hall.

Ajay took another bite of the ham and cheese sandwich the butler, Lemuel Clegg, had brought him and chomped on another handful of potato chips.

"I can't quite put my finger on what it is," said Ajay, chewing away, "but the sandwich is particularly delicious this evening."

Clegg didn't usually stay and watch him eat—in fact, he hadn't done it since Ajay first started working on the files a month before.

Drat.

"Did you make this sandwich yourself, Mr. Clegg?"

Clegg just stared at him, arms folded, scowling, immune as always to any attempts at charm. The man was so consistently, aggressively antisocial; Will had advised Ajay that the only way to make him leave you alone was to keep talking to him.

"I'm thinking that you may have employed a different condiment this time? Perhaps some diced gherkin pickles or a strategically deployed slice of Japanese daikon?"

Clegg looked at his watch.

Why is he waiting? Does he suspect anything? Have I done something to give away the game?

"I understand your inscrutability perfectly," said Ajay with an agreeable grin. "A master chef never gives away his secrets."

Ajay snuck a look at his watch: 8:10.

If this lummox doesn't clear out of here soon, I'm going to fall seriously behind schedule.

"I'm going to most likely be working quite late tonight," said Ajay. "Mr. Elliot wants me to get through at least two more boxes. So I should probably get back to the task at hand."

Clegg didn't move. Ajay noticed a slight clenching of the

muscles around Clegg's eyes when he mentioned Mr. Elliot's name.

Maybe he's afraid of his boss. Or maybe he's just waiting for the plate.

Then Ajay remembered something he'd read earlier in the day and put the pieces of a small puzzle together.

Wait till I tell Will about this one.

Ajay stuffed the rest of the sandwich—almost an entire half of it—into his mouth and chewed aggressively, then drained the last of his glass of lemonade until it leaked out the sides of his mouth before holding out the empty plate and glass toward Clegg.

"Thans agan fuh suth'a dewicious wepast."

Clegg took the plate and headed for the stairs.

That was it, then. Old Sourpuss just didn't want to make another trip all the way back up here for the crockery.

The pager in Ajay's pocket chirped. He blanched, and his hand instinctively reached to switch it off.

Clegg stopped at the door and turned back to him. "What was that?"

Still chewing, Ajay took out the pager and looked at the message display. "Juth one of my annoying woommates I imagine—yes, it's that knucklehead Nick. Wondering where I am."

"That's not the sound those pagers usually make," said Clegg.

Ajay took a few steps toward him and swallowed hard, forcing down the rest of the sandwich. "If I may take you into my confidence, Mr. Clegg. I took the liberty of adding a specialized ring tone for when my closest friends are trying to reach me."

He waited to see if Clegg was buying it. Unclear.

"I know that moderating school-issued equipment is not

specifically allowed, of course, but I examined the Code of Conduct and couldn't find anything that specifically forbids it either."

"Let me see it."

Clegg held out his hand. Ajay gave it to him, holding his breath, hoping that Nick didn't page him back while he was looking at the screen. If he confiscated it now, a lot more than their whole mission would be compromised.

After a few moments of turning it around in his hands, Clegg gave it back. "Check in with security when you're finished here. They'll escort you to the landing for your ride back to the mainland."

Clegg turned abruptly on his heel and walked out. Ajay waited until he heard the man's footsteps clang all the way down the circular stairs to the bottom; then he turned on the pager to check Nick's message.

On my way.

Ajay checked his watch, sucked in a deep breath, grabbed his knapsack, and headed for the back elevator. When he reached the foyer, he caught a glimpse of himself in a mirror hanging on the wall and stopped.

"Ajay Janikowski," said Ajay softly to his image. "I hope you are fully prepared to stare death in the face and, if necessary, spit in its eye."

The answer to that, Ajay sadly noted, was far from conclusive.

Will slowly took out the dark glasses and put them on after he closed his eyes. When he opened his eyes, he was looking directly at the astrolabe.

The device had appeared inert without the benefit of his lenses, its orbit of overlapping brass loops and rings locked in static positions. Through the glasses, he saw that they were all revolving and rotating independently from one another, but in complex, synchronized patterns. Then a metallic stalk rose up from its center, one of the rings transitioning from a hoop of silver steel into the neck and lethal head of an enormous, metallic serpent. Hooded, like a cobra, with cold, jeweled ruby eyes.

Staring at him. He felt it instantly:

This thing is alive. It's not just a machine; it's one of them, a living device infused with some kind of consciousness from the Other Team.

Will met the thing's eye. He instantly heard thoughts filter into his mind—but not words; rather they were whispers of images, dim and silvery at first, glowing out of the dark, then growing in strength and resolution. He closed his eyes and tried to tune in to what it was sending to him.

Images of the city they'd found, but not the crumbling ruins he'd seen below—this was a thriving community, full of foot traffic and trade; shops, businesses, even a glimpse of the huge cathedral-like building where they'd found the entrance to the passages below. Softly glowing white globes of light suspended in the air above illuminated the scenes like streetlamps.

The creatures inhabiting the city in the vision were all distinctly alien forms, corresponding to the skeletons they'd seen there but displayed here with the variety of size, shape, and coloring you'd expect to find on the streets of any human city. Some were elderly, others clearly children, playing in the streets. No signs of the disorder, violence, or butchery that the vast sacrificial boneyard they'd found beneath the cathedral seemed to suggest was central to their character.

This looked orderly. Socially organized. Prosperous. And the most unexpected word to describe it:

Civilized.

"What is it showing you, Will?" asked Franklin.

"Something I didn't expect," said Will.

The moment he spoke, the images faded from his mind, and he found himself eye to eye with the serpent again. But now he could detect a glimmer of life, or intelligence, in its cold bejeweled eye. It was assessing him, trying to penetrate his mind.

Will took the glasses off. He didn't want to think or feel what this thing seemed to be trying to tell him.

We were a people.

He heard Franklin laugh at something again and looked back to see him leaning in toward Abelson, listening.

"Yes, he has a great deal to learn about our friends," said Franklin. "As did we all once."

Will closed his mind to that troubling doubt, and the trailing questions it raised, and turned back to his purpose with renewed resolve.

"So this thing is what you found down there," said Will.

"That's right," said Franklin. "Hidden in the ruins, concealed from casual eyes. A living artifact that contains the essence of who they are, for whoever might find it. Once we made contact with it, mentally, the emanations slowly led us to its location."

"So most of what you know about them, you learned from this thing?"

"It's the heart of their gift," said Franklin, holding the device in a mesmerized gaze. "Once we learned to align ourselves to it. This requires strict mental discipline; you have to sit with it, spend time in its presence. Express your willingness to bond with it and it will slowly make itself known to you. You'll learn all this for yourself, Will, soon enough."

Will knew exactly what he meant already. Looking at the device, he felt its power even now, reaching out to him, seductive and warm, a pleasant, flattering feeling, like the sight of an old friend's familiar face after a long separation.

"This enabled the Others, with whom we were about to make direct contact, a way to show us who they were and what they had to offer. Dr. Abelson broke through first. He proved particularly adept at amplifying that connection and so he subsequently learned more from them than any of us."

Abelson nodded a few times, or it might have been a tremor, and the right side of his face twitched slightly. Will realized he might be trying to smile. He even raised his arm a quarter of an inch off the chair and gave Will a halfhearted thumbs-up.

"Why was that?" asked Will.

"Technologically, to this day, the Others remain worlds ahead of us, but they could plainly see that Dr. Joe was the leading scientist in our ranks. So our friends graced him with a series of concepts and ideas so advanced none of the rest of us could even comprehend them. But not Dr. Joe. He alone recognized them as world-changing inspirations. And utilizing the tools of the advanced labs we put together for him, the good doctor began to realize and transform these gifts into the wonders we've enjoyed ever since."

"Aphotic technology," said Will.

"Exactly right, Will."

Will summoned up a dose of innocent, boyish enthusiasm. "I'd really like to see them. Could you show some of these things to me?"

A knowing look passed between Franklin and Dr. Abelson.

"I think we might be able to arrange that," said Franklin, hiding a smile. "Come with me, son."

Franklin patted Abelson on the arm and headed for the

door. Will followed, stealing a glance back at the ancient basilisk of a man, still as a rock, watching him with that disturbing fixed eye.

"And I'll tell you how we came to learn about the Prophecy," said Franklin.

Ajay slipped out the side door at the base of the tower. Earlier in the day he had snuck down and disabled the security camera perched on the wall just outside, and he was pleased to see that the cable he'd disconnected hadn't yet been put back into its socket.

Keeping to the cover offered by the trees and lush landscaping, he tried to walk as slowly as he could manage. In case he was discovered, he was prepared to explain to any security personnel who asked that he'd been unable to resist taking a stroll around the island on such a particularly pleasant summer evening.

As long as they don't torture me. I'm fairly certain that I would crumble like a cookie at even the slightest physical discomfort—

The pager in his pocket buzzed, and Ajay jumped about a foot in the air, half landing in some bushes. He looked at the message on the pager:

Waiting.

Ajay snorted in disgust, tempted to respond: *Can't you see I'm doing the absolute best I can, woman?* But he texted back only:

Moments away!

He scrambled to his feet and hurried along the path. As he entered the small graveyard, Ajay caught a glimpse through the trees of a security guard walking nearby. Before he could react, a hand grabbed him by the collar and pulled him behind the hedge around a large stone statue.

Elise shoved him down against the base of the figure. She put a finger to her lips, begging for silence. He nodded. Elise peered around the stone, keyed in on the guard; then, shaping her hands around her mouth like a megaphone, she sent out the sound of an adult's footsteps walking along a gravel path, placing it on the far side of the guard, headed back toward the castle.

The guard perked up and immediately stepped away in that direction.

Ajay's eyes widened. "That's a new one," he whispered, once the guard moved out of range.

"I've had three weeks to work on a few moves," she said. "Follow me."

They crept along the gravel path until they reached the small stone mausoleum. Ajay pulled out another one of the devices he'd been working on.

"Not yet," said Elise, slapping his hand.

"What do we do, then? It's supremely dangerous to just stand out here exposed in the open like this."

Elise glanced at her watch. "We need to get down to the water."

The elevator trembled slightly, building to a greater rate of speed as they descended. Will tried to estimate how far down they were traveling as he listened; clearly they were going far deeper, maybe *twice* as deep than they had dropped already.

All the way down to the hospital this time.

"Consider for a moment, Will, the whole of our narrative," said Franklin, hands folded behind his back, looking up at the ceiling. "The Knights of Charlemagne is an organization that is over six hundred years old, ruled throughout the centuries by the same guiding philosophy. Working always behind the scenes, utterly without interest in fame or glory, invisible to the common man and thus able to apply a consistent moral gravity on the course charted by Western civilization. In this regard, we have no equals in history."

"How did we do it?"

Franklin turned to him, his bright eyes lit up by a believer's zeal. "One reason alone—we never worked for personal gain. The Knights remain single-mindedly focused on the betterment of our race. Recognizing always that the upward development and growth of the human being—our *physical* evolution aside—have always been due, not to the masses but to the efforts of the extraordinary few."

"The tip of the spear theory," said Will, remembering a lecture by Professor Sangren, his history teacher.

"That's exactly right, Will. All meaningful progress in our history has been generated by a select few, the best and brightest of us who make up that sharp point of the spear. My father ascribed to this theory and he was one hundred percent correct about, well, at least this much. And he founded the Center here in pursuit of furthering that goal. I give Thomas all due credit for that, an honorable effort in support of a noble cause.

"But Thomas was not a Knight, and although he was given many opportunities to join them, he refused all their entreaties, dismissing them out of hand. Such was my father's pride, his supreme belief in his own singular vision. As a result, he didn't go nearly far enough to face the rising challenges that lay ahead of us. The Knights believe, correctly, that the human race is headed for self-destruction. Stupidity, greed, lack of foresight, driven and all too easily led by fear—this is humankind's natural state, Will. It's brought down every civilization that's flowered on this earth."

"And you think you can change that," said Will.

"I know we can. Because since the beginning of this new relationship, through the gifts provided by our friends, we possess an opportunity to advance our species, not solely in the social, political, or intellectual arenas, but in *all* of them, and to do so along with our physical development *simultaneously.*

"Nothing like our program has ever been attempted in recorded time. It's never been possible before, because we possessed neither the knowledge nor the adequate scientific techniques. We no longer have to wait for evolution to create a stronger, wiser human being; we can engineer it ourselves."

Will felt a cold chill. He wasn't sure if they'd descended so far underground that the air had cooled.

"As you know, Will, Dr. Joe's first attempts at the Paladin process with my lamented classmates fell short of our expectations—regrettably—but science never makes progress without trial and error."

"What about Hobbes, or Stephen Nepsted?" asked Will, struggling to stay calm. "They weren't both failures, at least not at first."

"No, they were great successes, rightfully celebrated. And their personal achievements provided enough encouragement for us to forge ahead, on a less ambitious scale, until the rest of the means and methods we needed fell into place."

"How long did that take?"

"Nearly forty years. Oh, we had other successes during these lean decades that kept us going. One in particular that we'd asked our friends to help us with—the development of a treatment to halt the aging process."

Will looked at him, puzzled. Franklin smiled at him, anticipating the question Will was thinking.

"Why? Because we knew that in Dr. Abelson we had our greatest chance for realizing our ambitions, but the good man was getting on in years. So our friends bestowed upon us a simple biological technique that slows, and nearly stops altogether, the deterioration of the human body. It turned out to be as simple as flipping off a switch, the one that instructs our cells to stop reproducing. Canceling the organism's expiration date, so to speak."

"And you used it on yourselves."

"Dr. Abelson insisted we try this protocol on him first, of course, and then I volunteered—twenty years after I'd lost my chance to participate the first time. That was nearly sixty years ago, Will. Joe was almost sixty at that time. I was nearly forty. Now I'd say the results speak for themselves, wouldn't you?"

Franklin grinned at him, stretching the skin around his face tight to his skull. Will raised his eyebrows and nodded, wondering what he'd see if he looked at his grandfather through the Grid, choking back his revulsion.

"Mortality for the masses is a blessing. We'd never survive billions of these loathsome *oiks* hanging on indefinitely, draining essential resources from our planet with their hunger for violence and mindless animal appetites. But for those few of us with the intelligence, vision, and will to chart a new course for human history? Death is a seriously stupid inconvenience."

The elevator slowed and came to a quick stop. The steel doors slid open. Franklin led Will out into the space he and his friends had discovered earlier in the year, near the rear of the underground hospital, which was subdivided into two smaller rooms. One was the locked chamber at the far end where the freakish remains of his grandfather's classmates were stored in metallic cylinders.

And the room next to it that held the devices of aphotic technology.

Getting closer.

Out of that room stepped another of Franklin's original class of Knights, Edgar Snow. The man Will knew as Mr. Hobbes and the leader of the Black Caps. Bald, taut as barbed wire, his malevolent eyes gleaming. Will hadn't seen him in weeks. He was supposed to be Franklin's age, but he didn't look a day over forty. And a rock-hard, badass forty at that.

"Hello, Will," said Hobbes with a smile in his surprisingly soft voice.

"Edgar," said Will.

"I asked Edgar to join us so he could show and explain to you how some of our more recent gifts from the Others work," said Franklin.

"Sounds good," said Will blandly.

Will blinked on his Grid and saw the heat signature of three others just outside the door. Two figures followed Hobbes into view a moment later, Todd and Courtney Hodak, the brother and sister freak team. Wearing shorts, T-shirts, and running shoes, taut muscles rippling, their eyes alight with the same dark gleam, smiling aggressively. Will hadn't seen them for a few weeks either.

"If it isn't the Doublemint Twins," said Will.

Franklin got a polite chuckle out of that.

"Hello, West," said Courtney, with slightly less than her usual sneer.

Todd only nodded at him, the hostility in his eyes needing no elaboration.

"Nice to see you guys," said Will.

The last person to step into the room was Lemuel Clegg, Elliot's morose butler.

This wasn't going to be as easy as it looked. And he'd already thought it was almost impossible.

* * *

Ajay pointed out the concealed camera in the trees within seconds of their arrival at the eastern shore.

"Is there a microphone attached?" asked Elise, looking up at it.

"I don't see one from here."

"How close are they?" asked Elise, turning to the lake.

Opening his eyes wide, Ajay quickly scanned the water to the northern side and focused in on some unusual ripples in the water.

"Less than two minutes," said Ajay.

"Let me know when they're about to reach the surface," said Elise.

She moved to the tree trunk, grabbed a branch, and quickly shinnied up ten feet to the camera mounting. The camera sat on a swivel, slowly panning back and forth across a big slice of the lake. She looked down and waited for a signal from Ajay.

He raised his hand. When the disturbance in the water reached within twenty feet of the shoreline, Ajay lowered it.

Elise leaned in toward the device, pursed her lips, and whistled in a low, sustained almost inaudible frequency. The camera emitted a troubled scratching sound as she scrambled its internal electrical signals.

Moments later, Nick rose out of the water. The first thing he saw was Ajay frantically waving him ashore, just outside of the camera's view. Nick quickly sloshed out and joined him at the edge of the woods.

Just behind Nick, something smaller breached the surface. At first Ajay thought he was looking at the head of an otter, but that was obscured a moment later by a burst of turbulence when the shape swelled and changed into that of a man.

Coach Ira Jericho stepped out of the lake and quickly followed Nick into the cover of the trees. Ajay hurried after him, lost in thought, trying to sort out what he'd just witnessed and couldn't let go of. Once they reached the others, Ajay gaped at Jericho, searching for some kind of clarification for something he couldn't compute.

"It's not polite to stare," said Jericho, without turning to him.

"Am I staring? I don't believe so—that is, I didn't intend to stare, if I actually am. I'm not, actually. Now I'm looking over here—"

"Ajay, Coach," said Nick. "Coach, Ajay."

"I haven't had the pleasure," said Ajay, shaking Coach's hand.

"I assume that's why he introduced us," said Jericho.

"Well, yes, because it's highly unlikely we would have ever met on the playing fields," said Ajay. "You see, I'm not terribly athletic."

"Oh, I disagree," said Nick. "I'd say you're *EXTREMELY* terrible at athletics."

"Never mind," said Ajay.

Elise dropped down from the tree and joined them. "Let's hit it."

She led them back through the woods toward the mausoleum, trotting in a low crouch. Jericho jogged alongside her, Nick and Ajay following behind them.

"Have you heard from Will?" asked Jericho.

"Not yet," said Elise, glancing at her watch. "But we need to be next to that elevator when I do."

"Nick, did the others contact you as planned?" asked Ajay.

"First thing this morning," said Nick, glancing at his watch. "The Perfessor said they'd be at the location exactly when they're supposed to be."

"Do you trust them?" asked Elise, glancing back at him.

"I trust him to do what he said they would, yeah, absolutely. Why, don't you?"

"I gave up trusting a long time ago," she said.

"I like the way you think," said Jericho.

Franklin led Will into the device room. Clegg followed while Hobbes and the Hodaks stayed near the doorway. Will put out his stoutest mental defenses and kept as far away from them as he could, closing his mind to prevent any of them from picking up the slightest hint of his intentions from either thoughts, tells, or behavior. He was most wary of Clegg, a man who'd always given him the creeps and who was more than physically capable of giving him trouble.

"We're all blessed, Will, that the Others have been so generous to us over the course of our long and mutually beneficial relationship," said Franklin, his hand trailing over a control panel near the door.

"How so?"

"They've provided us with an abundance of miracles to behold. Since the end of World War Two, Dr. Abelson and the research and development team we've assembled here have turned dozens of their gifts into groundbreaking scientific and industrial patents."

As Franklin spoke, the stark white walls of the room illuminated like a light board. A slideshow display of modern technological advances appeared all around them. Many of the objects looked purely technical and obscure, but more than a few—a fax machine, a microwave, a cellular phone—were familiar, even commonplace, consumer goods.

"You've got to be kidding," said Will.

"Not in the slightest. This was intentional on their part; the commercial exploitation of these more prosaic offerings has resulted in an unlimited source of funding for our more . . . ambitious work."

They approached the two bright steel cylinders in the center of the room that Will had discovered during their last trip down here. Clegg positioned himself just behind Will's left shoulder, in a blind spot.

Maybe Franklin doesn't trust me as much as I thought.

"During the last three decades, they've given us leads to devices more specifically beneficial to our higher ambitions," said Franklin, trailing a hand across one of the smooth, shiny containers.

"Ones that helped you start to realize the Paladin Prophecy," said Will.

"Precisely," said Franklin, then raised his forefinger. "But it wasn't their work alone. I'm proud to tell you it was your father's research that gave us the key to understanding exactly how we could bring our ambitions to reality. In spite of his subsequent betrayal, I give him all credit where credit is due."

"Betrayal in what way?" asked Will as neutrally as he could manage.

"Once he made his breakthrough, I thought Hugh was entitled to know how we intended to utilize it. My hope, my natural expectation, was that he would choose to stand with us as we moved forward, realizing the fruits of his labor together. Your father chose, instead, to run away."

Will noticed a sneering smile cross Lemuel Clegg's face. He wanted to slap it right off him. "Why do you think he did that?"

Franklin's eyes clouded over, and he looked away sharply; apparently this was still a painful, uneasy subject. "Your mother was pregnant with you, Will, at the time. They'd had terrible difficulties conceiving a child over a period of many years. She miscarried a number of times. It was heartbreaking, really. So I . . . I made the decision for them . . . to make them a part of our program."

"At one of these fertility clinics you controlled," said Will.

"That's correct. Not far from here. In Chicago."

"And they never knew what they were getting into?"

Franklin still wouldn't meet his eye; he appeared to be in turmoil, either still angry with his son or with himself about this—or maybe both.

"Not all of the details, no. As far as they knew, this was a conventional clinic, employing the standard protocols for fertility procedures."

Will had to choke back his anger, trying to sound neutral. "Why did you do that?"

"This was my decision, not taken lightly, but without hesitation. For a number of reasons, Will. I thought it would ensure my son's commitment to our cause. I misread him completely. He took my only grandson away from me and hid you from me all these years, living in the shadows like a common criminal."

"You don't think he had a right to be upset?" asked Will, then instantly regretted it.

"He had no right! Not after all I'd been through. He had no right to take you away from me! I could not allow him to do that!"

Will had to turn and look away, struggling to keep his growing fury at the man in check.

"Fortunately, I had others in the family who weren't quite so squeamish about helping me with the Great Work." Will noticed Franklin glance over at Lemuel Clegg with a strange look, which Clegg returned with an intensity of anger and pride that Will could make no sense of.

Franklin walked directly to Will, pleading with him, his eyes red and wild, expecting, as if he deserved one, a sympathetic hearing.

"Why do you suppose I kept searching for you as desperately as I did for all these years? I never gave up hope, Will, that you and I would be reunited. I realized I'd lost your father long ago, but I was not going to lose you!"

After their one fateful encounter six weeks earlier, when he learned he was still alive, Will hadn't seen his father, Hugh, again. He knew he was in some way a prisoner here, forced to work again in Franklin's infernal program. He wanted to grab the old man, right now, force him to tell him where his father was and demand his freedom, but he didn't dare to, knowing he wouldn't be able to hold back his anger. Revenge would have to wait; he couldn't jeopardize what they were about to do now.

Will bit his tongue and turned back to Franklin, determined to keep all emotion from his face. "But what was different this time around? It failed before. How did you know the procedure would work?"

"The irony is that your father's research had provided us with the proper technique," said Franklin, calming down. "And since that time, our friends on the other side have given us the material we needed to realize the program in the way it was intended."

Will kept looking over at Clegg, who reacted strangely whenever Franklin mentioned Will's father. "And all they've asked in return for that is . . . what?"

Franklin hesitated. Will sensed he was about to lie. "Something we never intend to give them, of course. On their terms, that is."

"But they're looking for a way back into this world," said Will. "Isn't that it?"

"Not precisely," said Franklin, raising a finger again, challenging the idea. "They seek *unlimited* passage, the key word being *unlimited*. Our position is slightly different, you see. We believe that their access should be something that we control."

Will tried not to sound too skeptical. "And you really think we have something to say about that?"

"As long as we control these devices," said Franklin, placing his hand on a particular spot on top of each cylinder. "There's absolutely nothing to worry about. They will be allowed back into this world on our terms, and our terms alone."

Both cylinders opened, as Will had seen before. Thin seams appeared and widened vertically along their fronts, until the cylinders opened like doors, revealing a series of shelves. The shelves slid smoothly out as if floating on air, each lined with indented compartments holding a different technological object.

There, in the middle of the tray of the cylinder on the right, sat the gun-shaped object that Will had once seen Lyle use to open a portal to the Never-Was.

The Carver.

Will turned slightly away and closed his eyes for a moment. Concentrating, he located Elise with his mind—she was exactly where she was supposed to be, directly outside the ground-level entrance to the elevator. He sent her the combination to the operating panel that he'd seen his grandfather use to activate the controls.

4951

A few moments later her voice reached back to him: *Got it.*

When he opened his eyes again, Will saw Franklin smiling slyly at him.

"What is it?" asked Will.

"There's one last piece you're going to want to know, Will. But I warn you, you may find it disturbing."

Will waited.

"Once your father made his breakthrough—the development of a technique that allowed us to work directly on the enhancement of human genetic potential in vitro—our dear friends gave us the greatest treasure of all. The one that has made possible the creation of this whole new generation of Paladins."

"What's that?" said Will, turning back to him.

"The gift that made all of you—Courtney and Todd here, the last two classes of Knights and all those to come, your friends, even you, my dear boy—who you are today."

Will saw them all smiling at him. "I'm sorry . . . I don't understand."

Franklin moved closer, smiled, and spoke softly. "The genetic material that, together with all the estimable qualities you already possessed from our family, made you what you are, made you as truly remarkable as you have become—do you see what I'm saying?"

Will felt his mind locking up. Not wanting to believe any of what he sensed he was about to hear.

"Your enhancements," said Franklin, his eyes shining. "Their *bequest*. That genetic material . . . came from *them*. From the Others. Our dream is alive in you, Will. You're living proof. You are my masterpiece."

They heard a jolt from the next room—the elevator starting back up the shaft to the surface.

THREE

Two Months Earlier

WILL'S RULES FOR LIVING #3:
IF YOU HAVE TO HIDE YOUR TRUE FEELINGS FROM
YOUR FRIENDS, THEY'RE NOT YOUR FRIENDS.

On a rooftop of the Crag, Will stood transfixed at Franklin Greenwood's side, staring at his father through thick one-way glass. His father, Hugh Greenwood, wore operating scrubs and was holding a scalpel to Elise's throat as she lay unconscious on an operating table. Mr. Hobbes stood behind Hugh, pointing a pistol at his head.

"That's one-way glass," said Franklin. "He can't see or hear you, Will. And you have my solemn word that if you just do as I ask from this point forward, no harm will come to him, or Miss Moreau, or any of your friends."

"Why should I believe you? Why should I believe anything you say?"

"Because, my dear boy, my name is Franklin Greenwood. I'm your grandfather."

Will didn't hesitate and looked up at him decisively. "I'll do whatever you say."

That single glimpse he'd been given of his father alive would inspire Will, in ways that Raymond would never know. They were both prisoners now, and still in terrible danger, but just knowing his dad was still alive was more than enough to fuel Will's secret rage and keep him going.

That night, lying alone in bed, he'd paged through his father's book of rules, hoping for guidance. On the back cover, written faintly in the margin near the binding, he found a single sentence in his father's hand.

You have to write your own rules now.

His father was right. This was uncharted territory. Will knew he was being watched—even in his own room—so he didn't even dare to write them down. That night he began storing his thoughts away, engraving onto his mind a set of rules that would not only get him through this, but would also eventually allow him to strike back. And he couldn't fight this fight alone. If he gave Raymond or the Knights one single hint that he wasn't playing along, they'd snuff him out like a match.

The next day, pledging loyalty to his grandfather's mad vision, Will persuaded Franklin to spare the lives of Ajay, Nick, and Elise. He even convinced the old man that he could bring them around to join him on the side of the Knights. Franklin seemed to want to believe him. During the following week, he met with each of his roommates briefly in private—except for Brooke, their betrayer, and he'd told no one else about that yet—and made that case, letting them know nonverbally that they were being watched and mustn't say what they were really thinking. All three silently listened, puzzled, but followed his lead.

That was all he'd dared to tell them. Nick, Elise, and Ajay asked no questions and buried themselves back into their busy school routines. Every night, Will went across the lake to have dinner with his grandfather at the Crag. He seemed pleased with Will's cooperation and, so far, with his roommates' compliance.

One night, three weeks later, when Will returned from dinner with Franklin, he found Elise alone in the pod, studying at their dining table. Without even looking up at him, she sent him a thought:

So can they read your thoughts?

Will took off his coat and put his things away without looking at her.

I don't think so, he sent. *But they've put cameras in here. And mics. Everywhere.*

I figured. They don't know that you know, do they?

No.

Let's keep it that way, sent Elise.

Will went into the kitchen to make himself a sandwich. Their communication link was stronger than ever, emotion woven into every exchange. Even their silences were more eloquent than words.

You need to tell me what happened. I don't remember any of it.

They drugged you, sent Will.

Then, as he sat silently eating his sandwich and looking at a magazine, and she sat looking at her book, ostensibly studying, he told her the rest of it. The story tumbled out of him, everything that had happened since they'd been ambushed in Lyle's cave while searching for the Carver. He saved the shocker for the end: The old man they'd come to know as Mr. Elliot was his own grandfather, Franklin Greenwood, the second—and long-presumed-dead—headmaster of the Center for Integrated Learning.

Elise didn't send a single reaction back and kept looking at her book, but he could tell she wasn't actually reading. When he finished, she hesitated for a moment, pretended to write something down, and then finally sent back a thought:

Nice family you got there, West.

Will pretended he saw something in the magazine that made him smile.

I have a plan, he sent.

Great. The last time you had a plan, I ended up drugged like a lab rat, strapped to a gurney, about to lose my vocal cords.

She erased something furiously on her notepad.

I can't guarantee it'll work, sent Will. *I can't even guarantee we'll live through it. But if we don't hit back, and fast, we're going to lose whatever small chance we have.*

What's our other option?

Elise took a drink from her water bottle.

There's only one other way to keep us alive. Give up, sign on to their program, and watch these maniacs destroy the world as we know it.

Elise choked on her water. Will looked up from his magazine.

"You okay?" he asked.

She nodded, coughing, and sent him a thought: *What about your father, Will? If he's here and he's alive, can he help us?*

Will turned the page. *I haven't even seen him again, and I haven't brought him up. I assume Franklin's got him locked down out of sight, in case he needs a trump card to lay on me.*

You're sure Franklin's sold that you've bought in?

I'm working on it. I've got an edge. Franklin's only weakness— aside from the fact that he's a complete raving lunatic—is his attachment to me. He wants to believe me. He's sentimental about family, and I'm the only one left, in his mind, who can fulfill his psychotic, messed-up "legacy."

The front door opened. Nick and Ajay trudged in, set down their bags, grunted hellos, and went to their separate rooms.

When do we tell them about this?

Tomorrow morning, sent Will, glancing at his watch. *Nine o'clock. Bring them with you to Coach Jericho's outside office, the big tree behind the field house.*

Jericho? Why Jericho?

Because he's the only other person on the planet I can absolutely count on. Except for you. I'm sorry I couldn't tell you all this until now, but I had to make sure I was in the clear. I would never have made it this far without knowing you'd be there for me.

He chanced a look up at her. Elise hesitated, then looked away, but what she was feeling came through to him without her having to say a word. The mood shifted when Brooke came through the door, smiling and bubbly, her blond mop piled under a stylish hat. She greeted them both warmly.

"Hey, guys, how was your day?"

"Not bad," said Will.

"Okay," said Elise.

"Good, good," said Brooke, passing them on her way into the kitchen. "Mine was *excellent.* I'm going right in to hit the books—chemistry exam tomorrow. Anybody want anything?"

"No thanks," said Will.

What about her? Elise sent to Will.

Will knew this question was coming and answered carefully:

She doesn't know any of this. I'll explain why tomorrow. And right now I really need to talk to her alone.

"Shoot, I forgot all about that chemistry thing," said Elise, getting up from the table. "I better hit it, too. See you tomorrow."

Elise went straight to her room and closed the door. Brooke came out of the kitchen, eating some yogurt.

"She seem okay to you?" asked Brooke.

"Why?"

"I don't know; she's just been real quiet lately. Something's going on I think."

"Can you sit down for a second?" he asked, moving out a chair for her.

She heard something in his tone and took the offered seat. "What's up?" she asked.

Will looked into her dazzling blue eyes and smiled. She smiled back and patted him on the knee. Will knew she'd betrayed them to Franklin and the Knights. She'd been the traitor in their group all along, since their freshman year, before Will had even arrived at the school. He'd struggled to understand why. His best guess was that her loyalty to family—her diplomat father had been a member of the Knights since his own graduation from the Center—trumped any feeling for her fellow students.

Will had no doubt she was still reporting back to Franklin about them every day. Providing a closer perspective on Will's professed "conversion," looking for any weakness or inconsistencies. Watching him with those beautiful lying eyes.

Will thought: *It takes a liar to know one. It also takes one to fool another.*

"I have to tell you something big," he said in a whisper, "but you have to promise me you won't tell any of the others. You're the only one I can trust."

She furrowed her brow and leaned in. "What is it, Will?"

He let it all tumble out, convincingly, the whole story. How he'd found out who his grandfather was. What he'd learned from him about the Knights. How he'd decided to keep it all from their other roommates.

"But why is that, Will? Don't you think they should know?"

"No. No, we mustn't tell them."

"I don't understand—"

"Because my grandfather's convinced me that I misunderstood what the Knights are all about. All along, from the beginning. I think it's real possible that I . . . was completely wrong about them."

Will watched Brooke struggle to formulate the "right" response, but she couldn't conceal her genuine surprise.

"What makes you so sure?" she finally asked cautiously.

"They have good reasons for everything they've done. I know this sounds crazy, but Franklin's half convinced me that their cause is righteous—"

"*What?*"

"Keep your voice down," said Will. "For real. All they've ever wanted is to protect the future. Our future, Brooke. That's what they're doing here. That's why they did what they did to us, and that's why we are the way we are."

"You can't be serious, Will."

"Look at us, Brooke, at the things we can do. Whatever else you think about them, the Knights' plan for us worked. You can't deny that. The school, all of this, the whole Paladin program is about them helping us reach our potential, for the good of the world. That's been their plan all along."

Brooke continued to feign unease, pressing him for more confirmation about what had changed his mind, but he could see she was having a harder time hiding how happy this made her inside.

"I've been through so much—leaving home, losing my parents. My whole life's been turned over. I think when I got here, I was looking for someone to blame—some way to make the pain go away. I grabbed on to the Knights as an easy way for me to push it all back, pretend it wasn't real. My grandfather's helped me to see that."

It was working. He knew that beneath her practiced levels of deception, this was getting through to her.

"Brooke, I'm not expecting you to believe me on faith alone, and I'm not asking you to. All I'm trying to say is that my grandfather has a vision for me, and I believe in it now. He sees me as a central part of the Prophecy."

She held his eyes, without even blinking. "Why are you telling me all this?"

He looked into her eyes for a long beat and leaned in even closer before he answered.

"Because there's no one else here I trust more. You're the only one who might understand but . . . I'm thinking very seriously about going along with what he has in mind for me."

His heart ached, lying to her face so brazenly. A few months earlier, he'd been more than half in love with her. He had to remind himself, almost continually, that Brooke's betrayal could easily have killed him and all of his friends, more than a few times, and probably had already killed their former roommate, Ronnie Murso.

That lethal memory prompted Will to summon up the thought-form of a thick steel wall shielding his mind as they spoke. He knew that it shut her out completely; all she had to go on was what he told her, and how he sold it. He'd always been good at hiding his feelings, by necessity, but he still couldn't tell if she completely bought it.

To close the deal, he took both her hands in his, his eyes locked onto hers.

"However you feel about it . . . whatever you decide to do, you need to keep this a secret from the others. Is that asking too much?"

She lowered her gaze, simulating a turmoil so convincing that he half hoped it was real. Then she looked up at him, eyes alight with sincerity and confusion.

"I really want to believe you, Will . . . This is so much to take in. Can you give me some time, or is that too much to ask?"

Time enough to go back to Franklin and find out how they wanted her to respond.

"I understand completely," he said. "Take all the time you need."

They both stood and he gave her a heartfelt hug, trying to ignore what the warmth of her body made him feel. As she kissed him on the cheek and went off to her room, Will had few doubts that she'd bought the story. He had a much harder time convincing himself that what she still made him feel meant nothing to him.

After going out for a run the next morning—and using his speed to make sure that no one could have followed him—Will was the last to arrive at Jericho's old oak behind the field house. Coach Jericho, tall and as severe as a blade in his black sweats, quickly led them deeper into the cover of the forest, then kept watch as Will told Nick and Ajay what he'd revealed to Elise the night before.

The moment he finished, Ajay jumped into Will's arms and bear-hugged him. Nick rushed in after him and picked them both up off the ground. Will saw tears in Ajay's eyes, while Nick just kept his closed tight.

"Yes, yes!" said Nick.

"Okay, okay," said Will, the air squeezed out of him. "Don't crush me."

"I knew it, I knew it," said Ajay to Nick. "I told you we could count on him."

"Correction, I told *you* that," said Nick, arguing at close range on either side of Will.

"Baloney, I trusted Will more than you. I never stopped believing in—"

"You're completely cracked, Ajay."

"Nick, I can't breathe," said Will, trying to disengage.

"Don't fight over him, you goofballs," said Elise, prying them apart. "Save it for the bad guys."

"So what are we going to do, Will? How do we respond?" asked Ajay as he finally stepped back. "Are you contemplating a full frontal assault, or something more devious and far less suicidal?"

"Hey, why isn't Brooke here?" asked Nick.

Will glanced at Elise. "I didn't ask her to come."

"So you told her already?" asked Ajay.

"No," said Will, certain his unease was showing. "And it's important that none of us says a word about this to her right now. She's doesn't know, and she doesn't need to know, and it needs to stay that way."

"That's quite a lot to ask us to take on faith alone, Will," said Ajay, puzzled. "Why?"

"Because she can't be trusted." Coach Jericho spoke behind them, startling them all.

"But *why*?" asked Nick.

"*Because*," said Jericho bluntly, "Brooke's been working for them since the moment you all got here. She sold the rest of you out from day one. Her father's a Knight, inner circle, always has been. Like father, like daughter. She went rogue."

Nick was shocked, Ajay looked stricken, and Elise banged a fist into a tree, her face coiled in anger. Will hated seeing them suffer like this.

Ira Jericho stepped closer, his sharp features taut and imperious, staring down at them. "Don't give me that hurt face, West. They need to know. What they don't know *can* kill them."

"Maybe you're right," mumbled Will.

"Why does *he* know about it?" asked Elise, nodding at Jericho.

"I told him first," said Will sheepishly.

"Before *me*?" Elise looked wounded.

"Get over it, sister," said Jericho, giving her his death stare.

"Excuse me?" asked Nick, flaring up in her defense. "You can't talk to her like that."

"From this point forward, nobody here gets to think of themselves first anymore. In other words, you can't be teenagers anymore. You don't have that luxury, and you might never have it again. Will went this whole time without telling you any of this and that saved your lives."

His three roommates glanced at Will, looking slightly ashamed.

"How do you think he managed to do that? Forget about your precious little feelings, and check your damn egos at the door. From now on, if any one of you breaks this trust between you, the rest of you are going to die. Can I make that any clearer for you?"

Elise shook her head, eyes downcast.

After a moment, Nick spoke first. "Wow, Coach, I . . . I didn't even know you could talk that long."

"I realize that you're the track coach here and everything, but if you don't mind my asking, sir," said Ajay. "Who *are* you?"

"Good question. I mean, are you like, what, from the CIA or something?" asked Nick.

Jericho closed his eyes and shook his head, almost

imperceptibly. "In words even you might understand, McLeish: I'm the best chance you have to make it to your next birthday."

"Yeah, okay," said Nick, nodding thoughtfully. "I can work with that."

"I can explain," said Will, taking something from his pocket. "I told you I had a friend who'd been helping me. The one who told me about the portals and the Knights, and he gave me these glasses."

"I take it you're referring to your allegedly dead helicopter pilot?" asked Ajay, looking up and to the left as he accessed his memory.

"That's right," said Will. "Except there's nothing alleged about him. Elise met him, sort of."

"Dave," said Elise.

"And was this prior to or *after* the wendigo yanked Dave into the Never-Was?" asked Ajay.

"After." Elise nodded. "Brooke saw him, too."

"Correct," said Will. "Just before that, Dave told me I was going to meet someone at school who could help me get through this. So . . ."

Will turned to Coach Jericho, holding out his arms as if presenting him to the others. Jericho, playing along, gave him a slight salute.

"Yes, I see," said Ajay. "But if you don't mind elaborating, sir, what exactly is your connection to Will's ongoing . . . situation?"

Jericho sighed and shook his head.

"I do apologize for persisting with my line of inquiry, sir," said Ajay, fidgeting with his hands. "But as our modest little group's unofficial custodian of Keeping Things Straight, it would be tremendously helpful for all of us, really, to have some small notion of how you fit in."

Jericho looked at Will again, who shrugged apologetically. "I guess you ought to tell them."

"First, okay, I've heard all the stories students throw around about me," said Jericho, annoyed. "For starters? I am *not* the great-great-grandson of Crazy Horse."

"Aww." Nick looked disappointed.

"I'm the great-great-*great*-grandson of Crazy Horse," said Jericho, holding up three fingers. "I get pretty chapped you chuckleheads never get that right."

"I *knew* it," said Nick, turning to Ajay, asking for a high five. "I told you, didn't I?"

"And what does this admittedly remarkable family tree of yours mean as far as we're concerned, exactly?" asked Ajay.

Jericho moved to the edge of the deep woods. He spoke softly, barely above a whisper, never taking his eyes off the forest.

"This was our home, for a long time, more than ten thousand years. The stories say that early on my people learned something of what you've all seen down below here."

"What did they do about it?" asked Elise.

"There wasn't much they could do. There was dark power there, but it seemed to be latent, sleeping. So those in my lineage have always been charged with . . . keeping watch, in case any part of it woke up. But that tradition was lost, for a few generations, after my people were moved off the land."

"During which time—making an educated guess—Old Man Ian Cornish and his family came to town," said Ajay.

"That's right," said Jericho.

"And much hilarity ensued," said Elise dryly.

"So, wait, you're telling us you're like the last in a whole line of these shaman dudes," said Nick, scrunching up his forehead.

Jericho turned to look at them, but his voice sounded far

away. "Living on the reservation, they had to hide it to survive. Times changed. Suppress your own talents long enough, gradually they fall away. We moved into cities.

"My grandfather was a car mechanic at a garage in St. Paul. My father ran track in college, then taught social studies at a public school. But they both knew our family's history, and once I was old enough, they told me all about it. How they'd had to keep this tradition hidden for almost a century. Easier to stay alive that way.

"But times were changing again. My generation was looking back at what used to be, realizing how much we'd lost. I was almost your age when I decided to try and train in the old ways."

"How?" asked Ajay.

"Had to track down this crazy old coot. Lived alone in a yurt way out in the Black Hills. Medicine man, about ninety-five years old. Not a healthy ninety-five; he was half deaf, half blind, with skin like an alligator and mean as a snake. A few of my people told me he was the last one left who could teach me to walk the path. Didn't have indoor plumbing or two cents to his name, but I knew instantly he carried himself with more dignity than any man I'd ever met.

"At first he wouldn't even talk to me. Pretended he couldn't hear, kept telling me to leave. So I just slept on the ground, right there in front of his yurt. Took six months to convince him I was serious before he'd say a word."

"So he became your teacher," said Elise quietly.

"And I assume he taught you . . . a number of mythical— that is to say, *traditional*—skills," said Ajay, eyeing the small leather pouch around Jericho's neck. "Shamanistically speaking."

"That's right." Jericho looked up at them again.

"Skills such as . . ."

"After a few years he told me what was down deep below this ground," said Jericho, ignoring Ajay's invitation to elaborate. "And the need for having someone, one of our people, to man this post. He decided that since I'd arrived when I did, it meant I was the one to do it. I've been here ever since, over twenty years."

"Coach," said Nick sincerely, "what you just shared with us is like so totally super-powerful, and I don't even know what most of it means, but personally? All this time I thought you were just like this regular coach dude, and I'm just really way super super super sorry if I was ever a dick to you."

"What do you mean 'if'?" said Jericho.

"Well said, Nick," said Ajay. "Heartfelt and completely incomprehensible."

"You think I enjoy this gig?" said Jericho, looking angry. "Giving up my chance for a normal life, stuck babysitting the spoiled brats of the ruling class so I can keep watch over an old pile of bones?"

"So you're not like bitter or anything, are you, Coach?" asked Nick.

Jericho sighed heavily and leaned back against a tree. "I'm only telling you this because if I don't live through what's ahead of us, I'd like to know that somebody alive somewhere knows my story."

"That's presuming *we* live through it," said Ajay.

"How can we stop them, Will?" asked Elise.

"Yeah, dude, what's the plan?"

"Once I'm sure I've completely gained his trust, I'll get my grandfather to lead me to the Carver," said Will. "I'm going to steal it, and then we're all going in to bring back Dave."

"We're going into the Never-Was?" asked Elise, staring at him.

"Yes."

"Wait, what?" said Nick.

"All of us?" asked Ajay, wincing.

"Don't even start with that," said Nick, holding up a hand.

"Do you have the slightest idea what it's like in that place, Will, or where Dave might be if we get there?" asked Elise.

"Yes to the first question, and as far as I know it's more dangerous than I can even describe," said Will. "No to the second. I have no idea where he is."

"How do we know he's even still alive?" asked Nick.

"He wasn't alive when I met him," said Will.

"Say what?"

"What he means is there's no way they can kill him since he's already dead," said Jericho.

"What he said," said Will.

"But why?" asked Elise, with a penetrating stare. "Why are we trying to find Dave?"

"Because I believe the Knights and the Other Team—those things we saw down below—are about to make their move. They're going to use those monsters to launch a full-scale invasion at us any day now. And by that I don't mean just *us*—I mean our *world*. According to the Hierarchy, these things plan to wipe human beings off the map and take over again, and if they're right about that . . . our best and only chance to stop them starts and ends with Dave."

"What can Mr. Dave do that's so super-special?" asked Nick.

"He can bring the full weight of the Hierarchy down on their heads. He can call in the freakin' cavalry." Will immediately glanced over at Jericho. "Pardon the expression."

"Wouldn't have been my first choice of words," said Jericho.

"Let's call it *Wak'an Tanka*, then," said Will.

"Now you're talking."

"Why can't you warn the Hierarchy yourself?" asked Elise. "What do we need Dave for?"

"I don't know how to begin doing that," said Will. "I don't even know where they are. Dave never told me."

"Dude, just try going outside and yelling."

"Just for the sake of argument, Will, what happens if we *don't* save your old pal Dave?" asked Ajay.

"A seriously above average chance that we'll face the end of all existence as we know it," said Will.

What Will *didn't* tell them, what worried him more than anything, was that he hadn't heard a whisper from Dave for months now, and no matter how hard he tried he hadn't been able to reach him through the mental connection they'd developed. The only reason he believed that Dave could still be rescued was blind faith in the man's ability to survive, but that didn't push the idea that he might be leading them on a one-way mission to disaster far from Will's mind.

"Okay, so providing that we are somehow able to locate and extricate your dear dead friend Dave," said Ajay, pacing with his hands behind his back, "from whatever sorts of dire circumstances may have befallen him in this dreadful other dimension, have you given any thought as to how we're all going to get ourselves . . . back *out*?"

"Yes," said Will. "The Carver. It works both ways, in and out. I think."

"That's a relief," said Nick.

"So just the five of us," said Elise, standing up. "In some lethal, extra-dimensional location, looking for a dead guy, up against a legion of pissed-off demonic beings and their army of monsters."

"Sounds like a fair fight," said Nick.

"Well, if you have anyone else you'd like to bring along," said Will, "I'm open to suggestions."

"We shouldn't take anyone else going in," said Jericho. "The smaller the squad the better. Element of surprise, fewer bodies to keep track off."

"There's a lot we've got to do to get ready for this," said Will. "It's going to take weeks to prepare, in secret. We'll have to be ready to drop anything and go at a moment's notice, and we ever give them the slightest hint of what we're up to we're probably all dead."

That quieted everyone.

"So who's in?" asked Will.

Nick and Elise raised their hands. Then Jericho raised his, which surprised Will. Jericho saw his look.

"Adult supervision is required for any extended field trips," said Jericho dryly. "School rules."

"You don't have to do—"

"Hold on, Will," said Ajay; then he turned to Jericho. "This will most likely require you to use your powers and, perhaps, turn into a bear, yes?"

Jericho looked annoyed. "If I had to guess."

Ajay raised his hand. "If he's in, I'm in."

"One other thing. Even if we make it in, the Knights will probably be ready for us when we come back out," said Will. "Dave told me there's 'no time' in the Never-Was."

"So you think that means we'd come out, back into our world, a split second after we go in," said Ajay.

"Possibly."

"Okay, that's way weird," said Nick, holding his head.

"Oh, really?" said Ajay. "But the rest of this you're okay with?"

"I don't know, time-travel stuff, man, it just puts the zap on my head."

"Then you're right, Will. Coming back out," said Jericho. "That's when we're going to need all the help we can get."

Everyone thought about it for a moment, but no one could come up with anyone.

"At this point, who else can we trust?" asked Elise.

"Well, I got a line on somebody," said Nick. "Maybe more than one person. They're not from the school, though, but their powers are totally awesome. And this one guy just might be able to help us recruit somebody even more important."

"Who might that be?" asked Elise.

"Our old buddy Nepsted," said Nick. "The blob in the tub, the beast from the basement. Who else besides me thinks it's a smokin' good notion to get Moby Squid playing for our side?"

"Who in the world's going to help you do that?" asked Will.

Nick took a ragged and vaguely familiar-looking piece of paper from his pocket, one that looked as if he'd been carrying it around for many months. He unfolded it and showed it to them and Will recognized it immediately: an advertising flyer with garish blocks of print announcing an evening of professional wrestling at a local off-campus venue, featuring five theatrical portraits of the featured headliners.

"Not this again," said Ajay.

"That's right," said Nick; then he pointed to one of the portraits. "And if this dude can't help us get Nepsted to back our play, I'll eat my hat."

Nick led them to a large expanse of degrading asphalt outside of the nearest town, the vast parking lot of an old abandoned factory. Four mobile homes had been parked to form a square, creating an open area inside them where voices could be heard. The RVs looked weathered and road weary, colors faded, paneling stressed with age. They stepped to the closest trailer and knocked, loudly, on the side door. The voices in the back stopped.

Moments later they heard footsteps inside, and the entire caravan trembled with each approaching step. The door opened six inches and a huge square face, framed by a round halo of wild kinky black hair, appeared in the crack, staring down at them.

"What d'ya want, meat?" The man's voice was half rasp, half snarl.

Ajay shrank back slightly behind Nick and Will. "Why would we want meat?" he whispered.

"He didn't ask us if we *wanted* any," whispered Will. "That's what he *called* us."

"I see."

"We need to talk to 'the Perfessor,'" said Nick.

"No autographs today, kids," said the man.

The big man started to close the door. Will stuck his foot in the way.

"We don't want his autograph," said Will. "This is important."

The man looked them over for a longer moment, curious; then he adopted a self-conscious formality. "And whom should I say is calling?" Will heard a note of Brooklyn in his rumbling tones.

"Tell Henry this is about an old friend of his from Flagstaff, Arizona," said Nick.

The man's beady eyes, set deep in his massive skull, narrowed and darted back and forth between Will, Nick, and Ajay.

"Wait here," he said.

The door closed and he lumbered away.

"You know who that is?" whispered Nick.

Will and Ajay shook their heads.

"Dudes, that's the Barbarian," said Nick, barely able to contain his excitement.

Will and Ajay looked at each other and shrugged: *No idea who that is.*

Will gestured for the others to be silent; all three leaned in to listen. They heard the rear door open, then voices in the back, one rising in volume. A moment later they heard the door open again and the crushing footsteps hustled to the door, rocking the whole wagon from side to side.

They took a step back as the door opened all the way. This time the giant man—Will figured him for at least six foot six and well north of three hundred pounds—waved them inside. His black wavy locks shook with every step and fell all the way over his shoulders. He wore no shirt, just swim trunks printed with tropical fish and a pair of flip-flops. His heavily muscled torso was hairless and roughly the color and texture of a buttery tan leather sofa.

The three boys stepped in and followed the man through the trailer to a rear door on the opposite side. He had an oddly delicate habit of shaking his hair away from his face as he stomped. He held the back door open and waved them through.

"After you," said the Barbarian.

They stepped down into the little courtyard formed by the four trailers, a forlorn patch of broken concrete punctuated with spindly weeds. A pale red tent stood in the center of the space, tall and surprisingly spacious. Faint gypsy music played somewhere and the smell of garlic and barbecued meat hung in the air. They stepped to the open flaps of the tent and looked inside.

Plush carpets, pillows, hanging lamps, and throw rugs gave the interior an Oriental atmosphere. Smoke lingered in the air, exotic flavors of incense and spice. A tall, well-muscled woman in a one-piece swimsuit—long blond hair gathered casually on top of her head—stretched out on a tiger-striped divan reading a paperback novel. A table with a big stone chess set, halfway through a game, sat nearby.

A man sat on an elevated chair that looked a little bit like a throne, studying the chessboard, his chin on his hand, legs crossed. He wore a retro Chicago Bulls jersey, red sweatpants, and a pair of classic Air Jordans. He sported a natty goatee and appeared to be about forty. His body was well proportioned but he couldn't have been more than four and a half feet tall. His eyes traveled to the boys as they entered and he waved them forward. He looked bored and relaxed, with a lazy smile, but Will noticed a cold steeliness in his eyes that belied the diffident pose.

"Greetings, sports fans," said the man, his tone wry, his voice full of easy authority and an octave lower than they expected.

"Hello, sir," said Nick.

"Thanks for seeing us," said Will.

They both nudged Ajay, standing between them. "Indeed a pleasure, Mr. Perfessor, sir."

"Do you represent the Lollipop Guild, or is this a visitation from the local chapter of my fan club?" asked the Perfessor.

"Neither, actually, sir," said Nick, then lowered his voice. "Although, if I may, I'd like to inject that I am in fact your biggest fan."

"Interject," said Ajay.

"So to what, then, do I owe the pleasure of your company?" asked the Perfessor.

"Actually, Henry, we have something kind of unusual to share with you," said Will.

At the mention of the name, the Perfessor's eyes flicked over to the languid blonde, who was watching them all intently over her paperback, and she arched one exquisitely shaped eyebrow. Although she hardly seemed to move a muscle, Will saw her body tense and coil; some kind of menace that he had no interest in finding out about radiated off the woman.

"About Flagstaff," said the Perfessor.

"Yes." Will took a photograph from his pocket, a faded and yellowed snapshot. "To be more precise, Mr. Nepsted, it's about your father."

He extended the photograph—a shot of a smiling young couple holding an infant outside a hot desert town hardware store—and the Perfessor's eyes widened as he took it from him. The blonde saw the concern on his face, put down the book, and sat up. The Barbarian took a couple of steps in from the entrance.

"We believe that's you, in the picture," said Will. "With your mother and father."

"My father died in a car accident," said Henry cautiously. "Forty years ago."

"I know that's what you were told," said Will. "But he's alive. And we know where he is."

The man's gaze hardened and flicked around their three faces, settling on Will's. "This is not the kind of adolescent prank I'm going to find endlessly amusing."

"I understand why you'd feel that way," said Will as sincerely and urgently as he could. "But a prank about something this personal is the last thing we would ever try to pull. What we have to share with you is as serious as a heart attack."

"Where did you get this?" he asked.

"Your father gave it to us," said Will. "And we can take you to him."

The Perfessor's eyes flicked over to the Barbarian and the blonde. Will saw him subtly signal them that they could stand down; the conversation would continue.

"Oscar," he said to the Barbarian, "let's not forget our manners. Why don't you bring our guests something to drink?"

"Beer?" asked Oscar.

"Use your head, Oscar," said the Perfessor patiently. "You wouldn't want to contribute to the delinquency of a minor, would you?"

Oscar thought about that, which took visible effort; then he snapped his fingers and pointed at the boys. "*Root* beer."

The Barbarian stomped out of the room. The blonde pretended to go back to her book. The Perfessor gestured for the boys to sit on the pillows in front of his chair, leaning forward with his hands on his knees.

"I'm all ears," he said.

FOUR

WILL'S RULES FOR LIVING #4:
IF ANY TASK YOU UNDERTAKE REQUIRES YOU
TO "DIE TRYING," YOU MIGHT WANT TO
RECONSIDER YOUR PLAN.

Will figured he had about half a minute before the elevator reached the topside level where Elise and the others were waiting. Maybe another two minutes after that for the car to come back down to the hospital. He'd never been worried about Franklin as a physical threat, but he knew that Hobbes, Clegg, and the Hodaks would be a challenge for him to handle alone.

"Perhaps Dr. Abelson's decided to join us," said Franklin, glancing up. "Lemuel, would you see if that's Dr. Joe on the elevator and assist him, please?"

Clegg left the room. Will blinked on the Grid and watched the man's heat signature through the wall as he moved across the space outside toward the elevator. He also picked up that Hobbes and the Hodaks were just outside, watching him closely, so when he turned to glance back at the Carver, nestled in its case, he blinked off the Grid and moved his head slowly, betraying no intentions.

Will heard a low rumble of turbulent sound coming from the other room and wondered if he was somehow tuning in to their thoughts. Franklin had mentioned that the "gifts" he'd been given should continue to develop over time; maybe his power to pick up things from other people's minds was expanding.

"Can you explain to me what these things are for, or how they're used, Grandfather?" asked Will.

"I'd be delighted to, Will," said Franklin, reaching over and tousling his hair.

Will had to exercise every ounce of self-control not to react.

But if he touches me like that again, I'm going to break his arm.

"This metallic cube, here on the right," said Franklin, "I would best describe this as a power source, given to us by our friends, that can be used to awaken some of the creations they left behind."

"What sort of creations?"

"Oh, I believe you've encountered a few of them already," said Franklin, smiling vaguely. "During your ill-advised foray down below."

Will shuddered at the memory of the hideous treelike creatures that had chased them as they made their escape from Cahokia, the ones that pulled themselves out of the ground and came to startling life after he'd seen Hobbes use this very same cube.

"But what are they?" asked Will.

"I might best describe them as . . . forms of artificial life, built for specific purposes and hidden away in important places. Concealed, until they're called upon, as a sort of secret weapon, if you will. Our friends call them sleepers."

"Are you saying they left more of those killer tree things lying around up here?" said Will, pumping up more dismay than he felt.

"No, no, not the ones you encountered before *precisely*," said Franklin, amused at his discomfort. "Similar, to some extent, only in that they're all hybrids—that is to say, genetic fusions of our life-forms with theirs."

"Where are these things?" asked Will.

"They haven't disclosed to us where most of these 'sleepers' are located as of yet, but I'm confident that they've left a goodly number of them behind. Strategically situated near areas where they felt they would eventually be needed, ready to be activated when the moment is at hand. The moment of truth. And I can assure you, Will, that time is drawing near."

Will listened carefully; the faint hum of the elevator had stopped moments earlier, at the top of the shaft. He pictured his friends stepping on board as the doors slid open. He quickly opened up a channel, reaching out to find Elise.

Hobbes is down here. So are the Hodaks and Lemuel Clegg. I'll update you. Be ready.

It seemed an eternity—maybe two seconds in real time— before he heard her answer:

Roger that.

"What about this one on the left?" asked Will as he pointed to a flat, round silver disc, about six inches across, fashioned from some kind of slick advanced polymers.

"Ah, this one's a medical device," Franklin rattled on, full of pride. "Astonishingly effective at repairing human tissue at the cellular level. They work only once but fortunately they're not difficult to produce. I've used them myself, many times, on everything from a sprained ankle to the common cold."

"How do they work?"

"To be honest, we're still trying to find that out ourselves— something to do with how the signal it emits interacts on an electromagnetic level with the bacterial biome of the injury itself. I'd say there's more than a little money to be made with that one, wouldn't you agree?"

Will nodded, countering Franklin as he moved around, stepping behind the steel container in order to put it between himself and the door. He momentarily sent his senses far above and detected the slightest shudder as the elevator began to descend again. He started a countdown in his head for the time it would take to reach them; there was still a lot more he needed to learn from Franklin. A few minutes' worth at least. Will felt his pulse kick up a notch, adrenaline starting to thump through his body.

Franklin glanced back at the elevator, distracted, as he realized it was descending toward them. Will didn't want him thinking about that.

"Now this one I've seen before," said Will, pointing to the device in the center of the shelf's container.

"Yes, I know you have," said Franklin, tapping it with a fingernail. "We call this one the Carver, which I think you know as well."

"That's the one Lyle took."

"Yes. As I've explained, we should never have put our faith in that Ogilvy boy, for any number of reasons."

"I saw him use it," said Will, "but I still don't understand exactly how it works."

Franklin's fingers traced delicately over the Carver's elaborate handle. "It allows us to open a temporary passage, between our world and the space where our friends reside. We've also learned we can use these symbols along the handle here to call certain kinds of their creations over to our side. On an as-needed basis."

Like the ones you sent to kill me in Ojai before you knew who I was, thought Will.

"How?"

"You simply switch it on, here, and point it where you want to create the portal," said Franklin as he picked it up and demonstrated, without actually activating the device. "Like so."

"Isn't that something?" said Will, resisting the impulse to touch, or grab for the device, just yet.

"And then hold on tight. Both hands. I'm told it can deliver quite a kick."

"I'm a little confused, sir. I mean, if they want so badly to find their way back into this world, why don't they just build one of these things themselves and use it to carve a hole over there?"

"That's another astute query, Will," said Franklin, holding out the Carver for Will to look at more closely. "Our friends sent Dr. Abelson the design for this, exactly as you see it here. They depended entirely on our engineering skill to construct it—as with everything else they've shared with us—because they apparently do not possess the technology or natural resources to manufacture anything this sophisticated over there."

"Really? What kind of world are they in?"

"One utterly unlike our own, as I've come to understand it. Primitive, violent, and, what's the word I'm looking for . . . remade in their image? I'm told they've transformed it utterly, which is nothing I'm in any great hurry to personally experience, I can assure you."

"Has anyone from our side ever gone over there?"

"You mean, through one of the passages we've opened?" asked Franklin. "Good heavens no, son. That's an appallingly bad idea."

"Why?"

"We have no idea how we'd be greeted there, to begin with."

"But you told me they were our friends."

"That's our word for it, not theirs. Which doesn't mean there's any certainty they wouldn't treat us with the extreme savagery they routinely demonstrate against each other."

"In other words, you *don't* trust them."

"Let's just say it could prove to be most unfortunate if they ever got their hands on this," said Franklin as he held up the Carver, thoughtfully looking it over as he turned it around in his hand.

Will tried to conceal his shock. This was some of the worst news he'd heard yet. "I had no idea. I thought they were our allies."

"All the more reason for keeping them where they are, don't you think? As I mentioned to you before, we have no intention of ever allowing our friends free and open access to our world."

"But you told me you made a deal to do exactly that—"

"No, no, no—"

"—to help them come back here in exchange for everything they've given you."

"Not in so many words," said Franklin. "I'm not saying they would necessarily agree with our interpretation of the arrangement, but that's not really our concern. We have no contract here. As far as diplomacy is concerned, the only true interest is self-interest. It's called *realpolitik* in our world, Will. Another subject I believe Professor Sangren covered for you."

Will had started a countdown in his head for the arrival of the elevator—less than thirty seconds now—but he pushed past the line of what felt safe to learn a little more now; he wouldn't get another chance. "When you open a passage, what stops them from coming through it whether you want them to or not?"

Franklin chuckled. "Thankfully the passages only last for a short period of time, and as I mentioned, the Carver has the ability to summon only specific variations of their kind. We've never brought through any of their life-forms other than the ones we've called for, and given how briefly the passages exist, there's never time to bring over more than a handful at a time."

"Okay, so what if one of us did go over there?" said Will.

"All you'd have to do to come back would be to carve another hole, on that side, and go through it?"

"Theoretically," said Franklin.

For the first time, Franklin looked at him with concern about the nature of the question itself, but Will was beyond caring what the old man thought now.

Fifteen seconds.

"And where would you end up back on this side? Somewhere close to where you went in?"

"We don't really know, never having tried," said Franklin. "Is there a particular reason you're so interested in this line of inquiry, Will?"

Will blinked on the Grid, took a final look into the room outside, then reached out to Elise:

Hobbes is just outside the door, to the left. Clegg is on the right. The Hodaks are standing together, in the doorway to the storage room. None of them know you're coming.

Then Will turned all his attention to his grandfather. "Yes. Yes, there is."

He reached out and snatched the Carver out of Franklin's hands. The old man stared at him with complete puzzlement, uncomprehending.

Good. He never saw it coming.

The elevator doors in the next room opened. Will covered his ears. A blast of sonic energy that sounded like a revving jet engine issued from inside. Using the Grid, he watched the blast lift Hobbes off his feet and throw him back against the far wall. Will then saw four more heat signatures charge out of the elevator.

In the doorway, the Hodaks looked stunned for a moment before they ran toward the elevator.

Will pushed the button Franklin had showed him on the

Carver and felt it jolt to life in his hand. He had to grip it with both hands to keep it from flying around.

"What in the name of God are you doing, son?" asked Franklin.

"I'm not your son," said Will fiercely.

Franklin looked stunned, unable yet to comprehend the enormity of this blow to his grandiose vision.

Will sent a message to Elise: *In here.*

The Carver's power kicked up to yet another level, and now it required all his strength to hang on. He pointed it away from the old man, and a white-hot beam shot out of the barrel—just as he'd seen it do when Lyle used it in the cave—and appeared to scalpel a hole in the air, welding a slender seam out of nothing. He concentrated on moving the beam slowly counterclockwise, as Lyle had done, tracing the shape of a large circle like the ones he'd seen.

Nick flew by the doorway, tangled up with Todd Hodak in a roiling muscled mass, fists flying. Will heard them hit the far wall with a thud. When he heard the roar of an animal, he glanced out into the next room past Franklin and blinked on his Grid:

As he watched, a tall, thin silhouette quickly morphed and contorted into the outline of an enormous bear. It reared up onto its hind legs, standing nearly ten feet tall, directly in front of Hobbes's glowing shape, mauling the man with both enormous front paws.

Behind him he saw Ajay throw a globe of some kind toward the doorway; it shattered like a water balloon, splashing Courtney's invisible shape with some kind of bright green paint or dye—

Okay, chalk one up for Ajay's idea on how to handle Courtney.

Ajay pointed and fired a second device at Courtney; two

lines, weighted with steel globes at the end—like a bola—flew out, encircled Courtney's stained body, and wrapped around her like hypersonic tetherballs, pinning her arms to her sides. Courtney lurched or fell around the corner, just out of sight.

Correction: chalk two *up for Ajay,* thought Will.

"Will, in God's name, what are you doing?" pleaded Franklin, backing toward the safety of the room's far corner. "What in the world are you thinking of?"

"Just stay out of our way," said Will. "I don't want to hurt you, but I wouldn't mind it that much."

The circle hung in the air, about two feet off the ground, half completed. Sweat dripped from Will's face as he strained to hold on to the Carver bucking in his hands and maintain the round line of the portal.

Ten seconds, he said to Elise.

She appeared in the doorway a moment later, dragging a kicking and screaming Courtney by the hair.

"Give it a rest, bi-yatch," said Elise.

Elise bent down and let loose a concentrated burst of sound that landed like a haymaker to Courtney's chin. Her head rocked back and hit the floor, and she went down hard on the threshold, nearly unconscious.

Ajay stepped delicately over Courtney's green-stained body, lifted the small device that had fired the bola at her, and blew on its barrel like a gunfighter before sticking it back in a pocket of his vest.

"Busted," said Ajay.

The circle was now two-thirds complete, its edges smoldering with an unearthly hot glow.

Help the others, said Will, looking toward Elise.

Elise turned back to Nick as he rolled by the door again,

locked in a clinch with Todd, both of them throwing powerful punches.

"You can't be thinking of doing this," said Franklin, pressed back against the wall. "You can't possibly do something so reckless, Will. You mustn't—"

"You don't get to talk to me anymore," said Will.

"Lemuel!" shouted Franklin.

Lemuel Clegg came running into the room, bleeding from the forehead, his clothes disheveled, and he made straight for Will like a bullet.

Will saw him from the corner of his eye and let go of the Carver with one hand, just long enough to summon up a thick thought-form shield in front of him. Clegg ran right into it, without knowing it was there. He crashed off it and fell to the ground. Elise was on top of him in a second, throwing a punch that knocked him completely out. Will felt the Carver start to buck in his hand and got both hands back on it before it went off course.

"But you can't go in there," said Franklin. "I'm begging you, please, you don't know what you're doing—"

"Shut up or I'm going to aim this thing at you," said Will. "How do you think that's going to turn out?"

"You don't understand—it's not safe!"

"Really? You should have figured that out a long time ago, old man," said Will.

With a sharp burst of flame, the two edges seamed together as he finished tracing the circle. The rim lit up with fire all the way around, the air inside it dissipated, and the milky membrane he'd seen before appeared. Will took his hand off the Carver's control and the power ramped down. He shook out his arms, still buzzing from the device's unearthly power.

Ajay was at his side. Pulling a scalpel from a plastic protector lining his pocket, he waited for Will's signal. Will nodded at him. Ajay quickly ran the scalpel all the way around the perimeter of the portal, slicing effortlessly through the translucent barrier. The membrane fell away in one thin wet slab, opening a window into the rocky, barren plain of the Never-Was that he'd seen only once before, lit up by its poisonous green and lavender skies.

Will looked toward the other room: "NOW!"

He shoved the Carver securely into his pocket as he turned to Ajay. "Are you ready?"

"Why do I always have to go first?" said Ajay, staring apprehensively into the distance.

"That's what scouts do," said Will.

"Me and my big mouth," said Ajay.

He took a deep breath, lowered his head, and stepped through the portal.

"Please, Will!" said Franklin.

He tried to say more but his voice was drowned out by another sonic blast from the next room: Todd Hodak flew past the open doorway as if he'd been shot from a cannon. A loud crash followed as he slammed into a wall, and moments later Nick tumbled into the room. Bruised but otherwise untroubled, he landed on his feet and took in the glowing portal before him.

"Well, that's totally ill," said Nick.

"For goodness' sake, don't leave me in here alone!" Ajay cried from inside, the sound of his voice strangely buffeted by some kind of oscillation.

"Got your back, bro," said Nick.

Nick dove through the hole. Will noticed its edges were starting to flicker. No way to know how much longer it would last before it degraded beyond repair. He saw that his grandfather had slumped down to the ground nearby, eyes wide, clutching his chest, gasping for breath.

Elise, standing guard by the door, tossed Will's backpack over to him, sliding across the floor.

After you. He could hear a slight smirk in her thought.

Will's eye went from the burning circle to the steel locker holding the other aphotic devices. On instinct, he grabbed the flat round disc from inside and shoved it into his bag.

What's that for? she asked.

Tell you later.

"Coach!" Will called out. "Time!"

A blur sped into the room, shrouded in mist, its form changing even as it rushed toward him—not a bear anymore, that much was clear, but the outline of some monstrously big panther or cougar. By the time the shape reached him and slipped through the circle, he recognized it as Coach Jericho.

A moment later, a raging Hobbes rushed into the room with a berserker's shout, his bald head bloodied, his shirt shredded, bleeding from multiple wounds and gashes. Elise stepped in behind him and let out a shout that knocked him to the floor and sent him skidding halfway to the portal. She ran after him, stepped on his back, and jumped toward the weakening flame circle. She reached out for Will's hand; he grasped it and they jumped through together.

Blinding lights and thunderous sounds assaulted their senses. With nothing else to orient him, Will clung to Elise's hand and felt as if they were tumbling into a void.

Behind them, they didn't see Hobbes scramble to his feet and launch himself through the portal, just seconds before the last of the circle vanished from the air with a rattling sizzle.

And he wasn't alone.

FIVE

WILL'S RULES FOR LIVING #5:
HEALING TAKES MUCH LONGER THAN YOU THINK.
THE BIGGEST SCARS YOU CARRY AREN'T THE ONES
YOU CAN SEE.

Will didn't feel them touch down exactly. It felt more like waking abruptly from a dream. He still felt Elise's hand in his, and her face, looking at him, was the first thing he registered seeing. She was moving her lips but he heard only a low, dull hum that obscured everything else.

Can you hear me? he asked, reaching out a tendril of connection, mind to mind.

She stopped trying to speak and squeezed his hand. Neither of them let go.

At least this *still works,* she answered.

He could breathe, but it took some effort; the air felt oppressively hot, humid with some thick texture that pressured his lungs. The space immediately around them slowly dimmed from a bright, blank white light into something close to recognizable shapes, like a camera lens adjusting to bright sunlight as you closed the aperture.

What he saw first: rocks, sharp gnarled formations, towering all around them, run through with shining deposits of phosphorescence.

Above the jagged lines of the rocks, that disturbing violet

and lime-green sky appeared behind the rocks, a turbulent, toxic paint box.

Will looked down. The ground looked hard, black and shiny, as if an enormous explosion had transformed the rock into blasted glass.

They were in a canyon, Will realized, looking up at the spires on either side of them. The air felt still, hot and dry; he guessed the temperature was around eighty. The sky behind the canyon walls came into sharper focus, and it looked similar to what he'd glimpsed before, only much more vivid now that he was here—the air thickly layered with streaks of purple, amber, and a particularly poisonous shade of green. It didn't even look like it could support any kind of life. But they were both breathing.

And they were alone. None of the others—Ajay, Nick, or Jericho—were in sight. Nothing else moving, no sign of life in any direction.

Will glanced over at Elise. She was crouched, scanning in every direction, on high alert. She looked alarmed but not frightened. A badass warrior, alert, capable, and ready to strike, and he felt reassured by her presence, glad she was here with him. Elise sensed him watching and glanced over, arching an eyebrow.

Where do we start, hotshot?

Find the others, said Will.

He reached for the small walkie-talkie on his belt. He stuck in an earbud and flicked on the device, keeping the volume low. He tuned it to the frequency they'd all agreed to use and heard nothing but low static and electronic interference.

"Ajay, Nick, this is Will. Can you read me?" he whispered into his wrist mic, then thumbed through a range of frequencies, hearing nothing but the same static.

She tried her walkie as well, heard the same discouraging static, glanced over at Will, and shook her head.

Gee, that's a shocker, she said. *Our good old twentieth-century American technology doesn't work in an alien, demonic dimension.*

Worth a try, Will responded.

He pocketed the walkie as they moved along but left in a single earbud in case it came to life, on the chance that the high walls of the canyon turned out to be blocking the signal.

Ajay shouldn't be left alone for too long out here. He'll have fourteen kittens.

Yeah. They came across almost together. We'll have to hope Nick or Coach found him first.

Will pointed toward the widening mouth of the canyon. *Let's start this way. I can run ahead and check it out, see if I spot them?*

Splitting up at the first sign of trouble in a place you don't know, yeah, that's a classic, West.

Okay, okay, we stick together.

Like duct tape on superglue.

They walked toward the end of the canyon that looked like the way out. The glassy surface underfoot proved slippery, almost like ice, broken up every few feet by sharp, jutting splinters of rock.

Watch your step, sent Will.

Elise carefully touched one of the jagged splinters as she passed it.

These things are as sharp as a razor. Maybe I should just blast the whole place flat before one of us slips and gets impaled.

And announce we're here to whatever ungodly hostiles might be in the area? That's right up there with splitting up in the Bad Idea rankings—

Okay, okay. We get one stupid idea apiece. Low profile, play it smart.

We'll be fine, sent Will.

But he still felt absurdly exposed, picking their way through this steep ravine. Anyone or anything could be watching them from up in those rocky, broken walls, laden with a thousand hiding places.

Will's hearing had finally normalized, and he noticed a dull flat buzz in the still air that went right through him, agitating his nerves and compounding the oppressive weight of the atmosphere.

As they walked along, Will tried to transmit a mental message to Dave, as he had many times over the last few months, hopeful that it might be easier to reach him now that they were in the same zone. He waited, tried again, but got back nothing in return. He made a note to send out regular transmissions, every few minutes or so, to see if the channel to Dave opened up.

How big do you think this place is? Elise asked.

It could be limitless. I mean, it's not a "place" like we know it, in our sense of the word, right?

Elise looked over at him and squinted. *That kind of makes my brain hurt.*

They drew closer to the wider mouth of the canyon, where a flat plain that looked like a vast, dry, rocky riverbed opened up ahead of them. The shards of sharp rock gradually disappeared from the lowering ground, which took on less of a glassy finish. Will stopped and blinked on his Grid, curious to see if it would function here. The familiar lines and hues of his enhanced sensory vision appeared, but nothing showed up as a heat signature and there were no signs of life. No small animals, no vegetation, nothing.

A strange thought occurred to him, and he shared it with Elise:

It doesn't even feel real. Like the whole place was manufactured and they didn't finish it.

Artificial, she replied. *I feel it, too. It's creepy as hell. I'm really glad you're here with me. I don't know if I could handle this solo.*

You could handle anything.

She looked away, an expression on her face he'd only seen once before. Eyes downcast, blushing . . . Had he actually embarrassed her?

"Let's keep moving," she said out loud. "They've got to be here someplace."

Elise took the lead, striding out five paces ahead of him. She pulled a long serrated dagger from a sheath strapped to her right leg and held it expertly at her side, poised for action. Will blinked off the Grid and followed her.

"I've got a new technique I've been working on," she said, not looking at him. "I think it may be kind of similar to that thing you can do."

"How's it work?"

"I send out these short bursts of sound, fast, hundreds of them in a series, and when they bounce back to me, I process them to—"

"Echolocation," said Will. "Like a bat."

She shot him a snarky look. "Like a *dolphin.*"

"Okay, like a dolphin," he said. "I didn't mean *you're* a bat."

"It works like this," she said, turning toward the open riverbed in front of them.

He couldn't hear any of the sounds she made, but he could see her concentrating intently as her mouth moved silently.

"So?" he asked. "Find any fish?"

"Something's moving," she said as she pointed to their right. "Over there."

Will looked in that direction, and then blinked on his Grid. The ground flattened out in that direction, with nothing immediately visible breaking the horizon. But he picked up a faint heat signature, about human sized, and it was moving rapidly around in the same general area.

"Want me to go check it out?" he asked.

"I can run, too."

They took off in that direction. Will geared down so Elise could run alongside him, but he was still surprised to see that she kept up without much effort.

A small rise in the ground before them prevented Will from seeing what they were headed toward, but in about half a minute they crested the rise and looked down into a small clearing twenty feet below, surrounded by the edge of a forest of strange misshapen trees.

The heat signature turned out to be Ajay, running around the clearing, dodging and ducking and weaving away from what looked like a small dust cloud following him in the air.

"Ajay!" shouted Elise.

He glanced up toward them, frantic and harried, and Will noticed he was wearing his dark glasses.

"They're after me but I can't see them!" he shouted. "Help!"

Will and Elise sprinted down the slope to the clearing and the nature of the dust cloud revealed itself.

Insects, a thick swarm of them, vividly multicolored, the size of large marbles, snapping and swiping at him with rows of vicious barbed pincers. As Will moved closer, he could hear them emit an angry buzz like the high-pitched revving of a thousand model airplane engines.

"Take your glasses off!" Will shouted as they ran.

Ajay stripped off his glasses, looked up, saw the swarm, apparently for the first time, and started running around at twice the speed. "Well, that was the most horrible piece of advice in history!"

A chunk of the swarm broke off from the rest of the cloud and headed for Will, flying right at his face. He saw just enough of the ones in the lead to register they had something like hideous human faces. Without thinking, he summoned up a thought-form in the shape of a large bag, snapped it shut around them, and hurled it down. The insects dropped to the ground at his feet and he stomped on them repeatedly, sending spurts of green and violet fluid shooting in every direction.

Ajay continued to dart and dance around, trying to escape the main body of the swarm. Will saw Elise take in a deep breath.

"Ajay, hit the ground!" shouted Will.

Ajay instantly dropped flat, just as Elise projected out a hard crack of sound that rippled through the air like a cannonball and hit the center of the swarm square on. The bugs scattered, torn apart by the force of the blast that passed just above Ajay's prone form.

Ajay covered the back of his head with both hands, grunting and issuing squeals of distress, trying to squirm himself even flatter to the ground as he felt the dead bugs falling onto him and the ground all around him. As Ajay thrashed, Will walked over and knelt down beside him, patting him on the back.

"Ajay, take it easy . . . Ajay!"

Ajay looked up at him, his eyes manic. "Are they gone? What kind of madness is this? What manner of godforsaken hell have you taken us to?"

"Ajay, snap out of it," said Elise, moving around to his other side, taking him by the arm. "We don't have time for one of your freak-outs at the moment."

Ajay turned his head slightly, saw the bodies of the bugs scattered around him, and looked over at Elise. "Invisible bees the size of atomic jawbreakers, and you don't think I have the right to freak out?"

"You couldn't see them with the glasses on," said Will. "We don't need them here."

"Where are Nick and Jericho?" asked Elise as they lifted him to his feet.

"I have no earthly idea. Nick came through the opening just after me, I thought, but I never saw him. I ended up just over there by that big rock."

"Where'd the bees come from?"

"They came hurtling at me out of a mud hive on the side of the rock that could house a family of rottweilers. How did you two find each other?"

"We were holding hands as we passed through the portal," said Elise.

"How endearingly touching and a happy Valentine's Day to you—"

"Knock it off," said Will. "We came in about a half mile from here, up a canyon around that corner over there. If our distance from where you came in is any indication, the others probably aren't that far away. Our walkie-talkies wouldn't work. How about yours?"

Ajay pulled his from his belt. "I didn't even have time to test it. I've been too busy dancing the hornet fandango."

Ajay flipped the device on, rotating his dial through the full range of frequencies. The static sounded a little more varied than it had in the canyon, with a few spots of quiet, but no more viable than theirs.

"I'll tinker with it and see what I can do," said Ajay, "but I don't think we can expect a normal range of electronic behavior here. This appears to be one place where all bets are off."

Will bent down and picked up one of the dead hornets by a wing and held it up to take a closer look. A two-inch stinger extended from the rear of its fat body—thick, red, and barbed with lethal-looking spikes. The thing's face possessed the same unsettling familiarity to human features they'd noticed before in a few of these creatures; this one's stalked eyes even appeared to include corneas and pupils.

"Another one of their manufactured experiments?" asked Elise, looking at it curiously.

"Building a demonic apiary," said Ajay. "What a fascinating hobby. Why couldn't they just order an ant farm from the back of a comic book like normal people?"

"This is apparently what the Other Team does for fun," said Will. "Create genetically manipulated freaks."

"Oh, you mean like us," said Ajay.

"Yeah, but nowhere near as attractive," said Elise.

"You'd have to ask the other hornets about that," said Ajay, pointing at the stalk-eyed bug. "For all we know, as far as they're concerned this one's probably thought of as a swimsuit model."

Will dropped the dead creature and directed his attention to the sky, turning around to scan the noxious horizon.

"What are you looking for?" asked Ajay.

"There's no sun," said Will. "Even broken up by those shifting clouds, the light's all evenly distributed. It looks like it doesn't come from a single source."

Ajay did a similar scan around the sky. "You're right, Will; I'm not seeing suns, stars, moons, or any other heavenly body."

"How do you even know if it's night or day here?" asked Elise.

"They don't exist," said Will. "Unless somebody somewhere has access to a gigantic dimmer."

"That may be the case, but I know what time it is, to the absolute millisecond, if that's any help," said Ajay, pulling out a digital device. "Check that. It's dead as a doornail—whatever that means. Making a mental note to look up the origin of that phrase."

He showed the instrument's readout to them: all zeros.

"What is that?" asked Elise.

"A clock painstakingly synced to the atomic reference of Greenwich Mean Time, an infallibly precise piece of scientific instrumentation, and it may as well be a counterfeit Swatch bought from a West Indies immigrant in front of a Manhattan bus station. I'm supposing there must be some kind of pervasive, generalized electrical interference in this atmosphere."

"No, it's something else," said Will. "Stranger than that. I don't think we're even *in* time right now. The old man said it, too: Time doesn't exist here."

Ajay looked up, scrunched his eyes shut, and thought for a second. "My brain is growing quickly, but not fast enough to get a firm grip on that idea."

"Let's get on the move, this way," said Will, pointing away from the canyon. He set a quick pace and the others followed, trudging forward. "I think it gets even weirder than that."

"How does anything get weirder than 'outside of time'?" asked Elise.

"Do you have a compass, Ajay?" asked Will. "Not a digital one, magnetic."

"Do you even have to ask?" He pulled a small circular brass compass from another pocket of his vest and looked at it. "Oh my goodness."

He showed them the face of the compass as they stopped for a moment. The needle was spinning around violently, first in one direction, then the other.

"Sick," said Elise. "There's a kind of strange taste in the air. Are you picking that up?"

"Yeah. Slightly metallic," said Will.

"I believe that's ozone in the atmosphere," said Ajay, licking his lips. "That could have something to do with the electrical interference. It may be interfering with whatever magnetic poles are in place here, if there are any."

"I was going for something a whole lot weirder than that," said Will as they started walking again.

"Such as?" asked Elise.

"It's possible this isn't even a real place."

Elise and Ajay looked at each other behind Will's back: *What?*

"What I mean is, maybe this whole environment is just a construct of some kind, like a hologram or an artificial thought-form."

"But certainly that's refuted by the fact that we're here . . . We can see and feel it with all our senses," said Ajay, agitated. "Isn't it? Aren't we?"

"You mean maybe we just *think* we're here," said Elise.

"There might be something to that," said Will. "Dave told me this zone is a prison for the Other Team, for the crimes they'd committed against nature. I got the impression that this whole place was designed or 'built' for that purpose alone."

"But what sort of mind—belonging to what manner of being—could create something so detailed, so complete, so . . . so utterly"—Ajay swept his foot along the ground, kicking up dust—"persuasive?"

"I'm not sure our minds can even stretch out far enough to figure that out," said Will. "But that doesn't mean a being like this couldn't exist."

They looked out at the desolate plain opening ahead of them.

"We already have a word for a mind like that," said Elise.

They looked at her, questioning.

"Hello? *God?*" she said.

Ajay's look turned calm and somber. "Will, tell me again who you believe is responsible for creating this place."

"I never told you the first time," said Will.

"Something, or someone, to do with your friend Dave," said Elise. "Wasn't it?"

"Dave called them 'the Hierarchy.' The organization he claimed to work for."

"And who might they be?"

"He said they're like a kind of gigantic celestial bureaucracy, in charge of overseeing all the different aspects of creation on Earth. Responsible for maintaining every kind of life, people, animals, plants—"

Ajay's eyes looked up and to the left, accessing his memory storehouse. "Yes. A concept that appears in a variety of ancient, esoteric philosophies or teachings. In sacred texts like the Hindu Vedas, and in diverse schools of thought like gnosticism and the kabbalah, or more recently theosophy—which means 'wisdom of the gods'—where this idea is often remarked upon and referred to as part of 'the ancient knowledge.' Do go on."

"Maybe you should tell us," said Elise.

"I'm much more interested in what else this Dave person told you about it," said Ajay. "Who did *he* say these beings were, Will, individually?"

"He didn't talk about them as personalities or people. He

described them by their function, like they're the supervisors or protectors of Earth—"

"As in, highly evolved spiritual beings who have transcended what we would consider personal identities and consequently no longer require physical bodies but who possess the ability to appear in one, or as one, as needed," said Ajay. "Typically, whenever interacting with us mere earthlings."

"More or less exactly like that," said Will.

"Okay, good," said Ajay, looking around.

"Why is that good?" asked Elise.

"It means we have a working theory, however ridiculous and improbable, to explain what the h-e-double-hockey-sticks is happening to us. I feel a good deal better now."

"You are a strange one," said Elise.

"Does that give you any idea about what we're supposed to do next?" asked Will.

"Well, the 'ancient knowledge,' not to mention our own scientific method, would recommend we simply continue to rely on our subjective perceptions of all these uncanny experiences. Observe them accurately and dispassionately, compare notes, attempt to reach an objective consensus and respond accordingly."

Ajay had a faraway look in his eyes, his fingers fidgeted like he was operating an invisible game console, and he was blinking repeatedly, as if struggling with a minor mental short circuit.

"Are you all right, Ajay?" asked Elise.

"I'm not entirely sure. As you know, I've done an enormous amount of reading in the Crag's tower these past few weeks, and while it's actually becoming easier to assimilate all this new information, I feel as if the physical structure of my brain is changing ever more rapidly . . . expanding, if you will . . .

which means goodness knows what as far as the state of my *mind* is concerned."

"I'm worried about you," said Will.

"This isn't an unpleasant sensation by any means, mind you, although to say the entire concept is anything less than seismically unsettling would be a massive understatement."

Elise stopped and took Ajay by the shoulders, looking him straight in the eyes. "Why is this happening?"

Ajay blinked again, seemed to come back to himself, and looked at them both, clear-eyed again.

"We're changing, you see," he said. "We're all changing, each in our own way, and there seems to be very little we can do about it—"

"Why?"

"Because it's part of our 'engineering,' my dear."

Elise looked to Will for confirmation. He nodded.

"So while all of the above should be cause for caution and alarm under the best of circumstances," Ajay continued, "we do at least have the benefit of knowing *why* it's happening."

"Makes sense to me," said Will.

"We also have each other," said Elise.

"Yes. Shared experience, in our case, is of the greatest importance," said Ajay.

"It's the only thing that's going to get us through this," said Elise, looking at them both fiercely.

"By the by, Will, I came across a curious nugget of information in my reading earlier today that you may have some interest in."

"What?"

"A rather delicate family matter—regarding your family. I came across a birth certificate from the early sixties. One that belongs to your grandfather's butler, the charming and effervescent Lemuel Clegg?"

"What about him?"

"It seems he's slightly more to Franklin than a butler," said Ajay. "He's also his son—without benefit of wedlock, that is. Born to a woman who apparently worked on the household staff."

Will rolled that around and found it answered most of the questions he'd had about the man.

"So not only is he Franklin's son," said Ajay, "but he's also your uncle. Named, apparently, after the man your family bought the property from—Lemuel Cornish. Lemuel is not a name that exactly grows on trees."

"I always knew he was a bastard," said Will.

"Well, those two bastards deserve each other," said Elise.

Will and Ajay both laughed.

"And to finally answer your original question about what to do next, Will," said Ajay. "Given that during our shared history you have yet to lead us astray through a variety of equally hair-raising situations, I will continue to defer to your intuitive leadership skills and say, your call, Chief."

Will put a hand on Ajay's shoulder. He appreciated his friend's vote of confidence, but even more the observation confirmed for him something he'd begun to notice in himself, something far less obvious within him that had started to change. Not in an obviously physical capacity like his increased speed, endurance, or self-healing, but a more subtle internal ability he seemed to now possess. It had to do with decision-making, particularly under pressure; he simply seemed to know what to do, quickly, when presented with tough odds and difficult choices.

But what was this? Could he also attribute this to their purely genetic changes? Or was it something more hard fought, less a gift than a skill he'd learned to develop on his own, through practice and experience? Was this an acquired talent, or more a part of his character?

And what do you call an ability like this anyway? Decisiveness? Leadership?

No, another word floated up inside his mind, and the ability *itself* informed him that this word was the right one for the quality he was trying to describe.

Intuition. He was learning a different way to *think*. It didn't involve effort or work or calculation; it had to do with moving his conscious mind out of the way and allowing himself to realize that, in many ways, he already knew how and what to do before he even had time to think about it.

Will looked back the way they'd come and noticed the path they were following had slowly descended down a very gradual grade. The arid, dusty land underfoot had gradually transitioned to hard, packed ground that appeared more like hardened clay. Will closed his eyes and his senses sharpened; he could also feel, and even smell, some moisture in the air.

"There's water nearby," he said.

Ahead, the angle of descent steepened and the path they were on gradually narrowed, eventually rounding a curve to the left and leading out of sight into a valley. The right edge of the path began to drop off into an increasingly deep ravine. For some reason Will found it difficult to see anything else; the rest of whatever else was down below seemed to fade into a vague white haze.

"What can you see down there?" Will asked.

Ajay stepped forward and opened his eyes wide. "There's a layer of mist or clouds . . . it's quite thick . . . and I believe I can make out a canopy of trees just below it . . . tall, a variety of species, a mix I would generally associate with a rain forest biosphere."

"This close to a desert?" asked Elise.

"A very abrupt transition, to be sure," said Ajay.

"It's not any more unusual than the rest of it," said Will.

"No, that part isn't," said Ajay, still staring intently down at the clouds. "What's unusual is that there's absolutely no wind down below and some of those trees appear to be moving."

SIX

WILL'S RULES FOR LIVING #6:
THOSE WHO CAN'T DO, DON'T.

Will was tempted to run ahead and take a look, but staying together won out. He didn't really want to push Ajay too much physically or emotionally—he still seemed too fragile—and he could sense that Elise was even more concerned about him.

The temperature dropped steadily as they continued down the path; by the time they neared the edge of the fog layer, it actually felt chilly. Will stopped just before it. The fog started as abruptly as a curtain ahead of them, motionless, bright white, thick as cotton.

They stared at it apprehensively. "Are you sure this is the way to go?" asked Ajay.

"Something really off about it," said Elise. "It looks like fog but it doesn't seem like fog."

"It's more like . . . an idea of fog," said Will. "Almost too perfect."

"Indeed. There's no aspect of randomness or irregularity," said Ajay. "The signal characteristics of water in its vaporous form."

"What he said," said Elise.

Will reached out to touch the edge of the bank. His hand moved into it effortlessly. Cool and wet. Moisture beaded on his skin. He brought his hand back out.

"Feels okay," he said.

"I already know you're going to ask me to go first, so I may as well save you the trouble," said Ajay, pulling himself up to his full height.

And he walked right into the cloud. After just a few steps, Ajay completely disappeared.

"Don't go too far!" shouted Elise.

"I'm only five steps in," he said. "And I've stopped already. Remain calm."

"Can you see anything?" asked Will.

"I can see the ground at my feet . . . I can see my hand in front of my face . . . and that's about the extent of it."

Will and Elise gripped each other's hand, walked in after him, and were instantly enveloped in the cool, cocooning mist. They took one careful step forward at a time. Will couldn't see his feet *or* their hands.

They bumped into Ajay two steps later, without even seeing him, and stopped.

"Ah, holding hands again," Ajay said just ahead. "Any excuse at all, I see. Honestly, people are going to start to gossip—"

"Shut *up*," said Elise.

"Let me try something," said Will.

He blinked on his Grid: Everything looked as vague and milky as what he could see with the naked eye. No heat signatures or other signs of life in range. Useless. He blinked it off.

"Can't see a blinking thing," he said.

"What now?" asked Ajay.

"There's a cliff with a steep drop to the right," said Will. "Let's find the wall that we know is on the left and stick to it. Elise, grab on to my backpack. We'll go single file."

Elise stepped behind him and took hold of his pack. Will put both hands on Ajay's shoulder as he turned, leading them, and inched in that direction, stretching out his hands.

"I don't feel it yet," said Ajay.

"Wait, I think I can tell you where it is," said Elise.

They halted. Elise stepped out from behind Will and issued a series of small, incredibly fast clicks and whirrs; then she took Will's hand and strode ahead a few paces until she stopped them both abruptly.

"If I'm right, the wall should be six inches in front of us," she said.

Will moved next to her, put both hands up in front of him, then moved them slowly forward . . . and about half a foot later made contact with the rocky wall.

"Ah, echolocation," said Ajay admiringly.

"A useful new tool," said Elise.

"And of course the one time we really need it, *my* one puny power proves *absolutely* useless," said Ajay.

"It's not useless," said Will. "And it's not the only time we've needed it."

"And it's not puny," said Elise. "And it's not the only power you have either, Brainiac."

"Okay, so maybe I was fishing for compliments a tiny bit," said Ajay with a lopsided grin. "Why don't you take the lead, my dear?"

"No, you two should both go first, together," said Will. "Elise on the left, keeping your left hand on the wall. I'll bring up the rear."

Will grabbed both of their backpacks and reconfigured them into the right positions.

"I hope you won't object if *we* hold hands," said Ajay.

"Not unless you do," said Elise, grabbing his left hand with her right.

"At least she can't see you blushing," said Will. "Let's move."

They started forward, one step at a time. Will held on to

their packs and found it a little easier to stay centered if he closed his eyes.

"This is deeply weird," said Elise. "Moving around like you're in the dark with so much light around."

"It's the absence of any variety or texture," said Ajay. "Our eyes can't function properly with the mind unless they perceive some contrast. . . . Hold on, just a suggestion now—do you suppose you could move the fog around at all with sound? Just enough to vary it?"

Will heard Elise send out a variety of sounds as they inched along. Nothing seemed to make an impact on the cloud until she sent out one that sounded like a soft, oscillating war whoop.

"That one," said Ajay. "It's creating ripples out ahead of us, and I can definitely detect a pattern."

Will opened his eyes and looked up. He still couldn't see a thing. He blinked on the Grid again. The faintest vibrating lines showed up in the fog ahead of them, almost forming a path.

"Good work, you two," he said.

They continued on that way for a while, in grim, silent concentration, with Will looking up and using his Grid every hundred paces.

"How far do you think it is to the floor of the valley?" asked Ajay.

"From where the fog started? I'd guess about half a mile," said Will.

"Good," said Ajay, raising something to his face that gave off the faintest red glow. "I started a pedometer at the edge of the cloud, and it looks as if we've traveled about half that distance already."

"Is it just me, or does it seem like the fog's a little bit thinner here?" asked Elise.

"You're correct," said Ajay. "We may be moving toward the bottom of the cloud bank."

"Shouldn't it be thicker at the bottom?" asked Elise.

"Yes, the denser vapor should settle lower down," said Ajay. "But not even the molecules here seem to be performing according to form."

It took a little while longer for Will to notice any difference, but eventually he was able to see his own feet, then the path a few steps in front of them. Something about the appearance of the ground troubled him, but before he could formulate a reaction, both Ajay and Elise slipped, their feet flying out from under them. They fell back on their packs, and because Will was still holding on to them, he slipped, too. The path had turned as slick as the blasted ground they'd encountered in the canyon—and before they knew it, they were sliding down and around as if they were on a well-oiled chute.

"Hold on to each other!" shouted Will. "Stay away from the edge, and try to grab on to the wall!"

But there was nothing to hold on to, except each other. Even as the fog thinned around them, they could see that the entire path had turned to the same glassy texture. The path continued to turn to the left, but the force of their mass was carrying them to the right, toward the edge of the cliff. Will reached down for the knife strapped to his calf and dragged the blade behind him, trying to use it as a rudder to steer them back to the left, but the ground was so hard it didn't even leave a scratch.

Elise quickly twisted her body to the right and sent out a thick stream of sound beyond their hearing. The beam of the sound seared into the path, sending up sparks; she was trying to use it as a friction brake to slow them down, which worked momentarily, but the angle of the path steepened and they continued to accelerate, sliding closer and closer to the cliff edge.

Will could see branches and leaves, a dense wall of green vegetation just beyond the edge, but for all he knew they could be the *tops* of the trees, in which case . . . *bad.*

Ajay went over the edge first. Will secured his grip on the back of Ajay's pack with his left hand, and as he slipped over after him, Will reached back, turned, and slammed his knife into the ground just under the lip of the cliff. The knife penetrated and stuck and he held on and braced himself, as a moment later Ajay's mass loaded down onto his right hand and arm. Feeling the strain with every muscle, Will held on to him with a death grip.

"I've got you!"

"I don't think you—"

"No, I've got you!"

Then Elise slid by right next to him, but she reached up and grabbed on to the edge of the cliff with both hands, dangling just beside him, eyes shut.

"Hold on!" he yelled to her.

"Will, you don't need to—"

"Yes, I do, Ajay. I'm not letting you fall!"

"Look down," said Ajay.

Will chanced his first look down. He saw Ajay hanging just below him, and then, through the thinning fog, he saw what was below him.

Ajay's feet were about three feet off the ground. "You're really starting to crush my fingers."

"Oh," said Will.

He let go of Ajay's pack, and he dropped down onto the forest floor.

"Oh my God, you let go of him?" Elise opened her eyes, looked down, and saw Ajay waving and smiling.

Will held out his right hand. She took it, swung down, and

then dropped to the ground next to Ajay. Will found a foot-hold on the cliff wall, pulled out his knife, and a moment later joined them.

The fog had thinned here to a spectral mist that hung uniformly through the trees, allowing them to see roughly fifty feet in every direction. Ajay scanned the forest all around them.

"Yes. Very much like a rain forest. High canopy. Little vegetation underfoot, a layer of mulch covering the ground, although the air isn't as pungent with the smell of decaying compost as you might expect. Otherwise, textbook rain forest biosphere."

Will blinked on the Grid. No heat signatures showed up anywhere in the landscape around them.

"Except no living creatures," said Will.

"What about the moving trees bit?" asked Elise.

"I don't see anything moving at the moment," said Ajay. "Maybe they were just swaying in the breeze."

"It wouldn't be the first time we've run into 'moving trees,'" said Will, thinking back to the treelike guardian beasts they'd encountered in the underground ruins.

"Which way?" asked Elise.

They both looked at Will. He pointed straight ahead, decisively—for no reason other than that it seemed they expected him to make a decision—and started walking, moving vines and underbrush out of the way, picking out a path between the massive tree trunks.

"I may have to break out my hatchet," said Ajay as he tried his walkie-talkie again: still no signal.

"As long as you don't keep *talking* about it," said Elise.

Will blinked on the Grid again, and this time he picked up some faint flickering heat signatures in the distance. Maybe he *had* chosen the right direction after all: He might have to start trusting this "intuition."

But suddenly the heat readings appeared closer, and not just straight ahead but to either side of them, and now there were clusters of them. Some up in the trees and an equal number at ground level. They were small and mobile, moving or crawling, but when he blinked off and looked around, he saw no animals that matched the profile.

"Are you seeing anything?" he asked Ajay.

"Nothing out of the ordinary. Just flowers. Lots of very pretty flowers. And they're giving off a very pleasant scent. Can either of you smell that?"

"Like gardenias," said Elise.

"My mother often wears a perfume reminiscent of this," said Ajay, sniffing again. "You know that familiar aromas activate an extremely powerful section of the brain strongly associated with memory—"

"Stand still for a second," said Will.

Will blinked the Grid back on, looking up and around, trying not to alarm his friends. There were many more of the heat signals now, and the small shapes were still moving when he saw them from the corner of his eye, but when he looked directly at them, they stopped. He picked out a spot on an overhead branch with a dozen of the shapes on it, waited until they stopped moving, and then blinked off.

Flowers. Small, delicate red and white buds, on a short green symmetrical stalk. Common specimens from a million suburban gardens. Harmless and benign.

"Ajay."

"Yes, Will."

"A while back you told me you were working on a freeze-ray-type thingy."

"Oh, yes. A liquid nitrogen dispenser. Very effective, if I do say so myself."

"Did you by any chance bring it with you?"

"Of course I did, Will."

Get ready to run, he sent to Elise.

She glanced over at him calmly and nodded, then tilted her head toward Ajay.

What about him?

Take him with you. I'll follow.

Say when.

"Could I have it now, please?" asked Will.

Will blinked and turned slowly around. Viewed through the Grid, the shapes were moving again. There were hundreds of them now, massing, crowding in from every direction, above, below, and behind, into his field of vision.

But there was still a clear path straight ahead, through a gap between two huge trees.

Ajay rummaged in his pack for a few moments, then emerged with a short, thick stainless-steel canister that looked like a small fire extinguisher.

"Here you are," said Ajay, handing it to him. "Just switch off the safety—here—point the nozzle, pull the trigger, and it should be good to go. I'm quite pleased with it. What do you intend to use it for?"

Go.

Elise grabbed Ajay's hand and yanked him with her, dashing toward the trees.

"What are you doing, woman?!"

Will switched off the canister's safety and blinked on the Grid again. As one, the massed flowers reacted to their movement and swarmed toward him. A packed wave of the things wriggled rapidly toward him over the ground on stalklike roots, while what looked like a curtain of them swept down from the branches above.

Will realized they'd hooked themselves together using rows of small thorns on their stalks. As they swung toward him, he also noticed their petals hinging back uniformly to reveal a round jagged mouth in the center of each blossom, filled with a circular row of sharp white fangs.

Will quickly pivoted around, pointed the nozzle, and pulled the trigger, shooting a freezing mist into the heart of the descending creatures. When the spray made contact with the flowers, a cloud of vapor erupted and they froze instantly, and when the center of their solidified mass struck his shoulder a moment later, it fractured into a thousand icy shards.

He lowered the nozzle and sprayed all around him as he spun around in a tight circle, freezing the flowers on the ground as they neared him, leaving a ring of tiny statues frozen on the verge of taking a bite out of him.

He felt a bunch of the things scampering along his arms and shoulders, survivors of the curtain that hadn't been hit by the spray, so he shook himself like a wet dog—a hundred times more rapidly—and they flew off him in every direction.

And more kept coming, pouring out of the trees, dropping from the branches, blanketing the forest floor, mindless and hungry. He felt teeth nipping at the cuffs of his pants and shoes. He hit the nozzle again and then took off running after the others, pointing it behind him as he went, trailing the freezing spray behind him.

He blinked on the Grid and spotted Elise and Ajay through the mist, about fifty yards ahead. No sign of more flowers in that direction: They seemed to have all massed back where they'd attacked. Glancing behind him, he saw a large, amorphous red blob of the things still moving after him but slowed by the frozen path he'd left behind.

Will took his finger off the trigger and brought up the

canister, much lighter in his hands; he'd used more than half of its contents by now and decided to hold the rest in reserve. He picked up his pace, dodging through the underbrush, and quickly closed in on the others.

I'm behind you, he sent to Elise.

What else *is behind us?*

Nothing you want to stop and smell. Keep going.

A few moments later he was beside them.

"Oh, Will, there you are," said Ajay, slightly panting for breath. "What seems to be the trouble back there?"

"Carnivorous pansies."

"WHAT! Oh dear God, man—there's one on your shoulder!"

Will looked to his right; one surviving flower had clung to him and, using its thorns like Velcro, had crawled up near his neck, teeth exposed, reared back, poised to strike. Before Will could react, Elise shot out a knifed hand and lopped off its head. Will quickly brushed its body to the ground.

"Looks more like a snapdragon," she said. "Crossed with a crocodile."

"We'll be okay. We can outrun them—but don't look back and keep moving."

"Issues I did not expect to face upon waking this morning: being chased by a rabid pack of carnivorous delphiniums."

"What do you see in front of us?" asked Will.

Ajay peered ahead, trying to hold his eyes steady as they trotted along.

"I think we may be approaching a river, or some kind of moving water."

"I hear it," said Elise.

"By the way, your freeze spray? Aces."

Ajay couldn't suppress a smile. "Oh. Thank you very much."

Thirty seconds later, they broke into a clearing by the sandy banks of a flowing river, about forty feet across to the opposite bank, where the edge of an even thicker forest awaited. Will scanned left and right; there was no obviously easier place to make a crossing, before the river curved around a slow bend in either direction. He glanced behind them again using the Grid; the large red blob of flowers was still at least a hundred yards back in the forest but gaining steadily.

"How do you feel about a swim?" asked Elise.

"To be honest, I'm carrying a large assortment of equipment indispensable to our mission that would not necessarily benefit from complete and extended immersion in any form of—"

"Let me put it a different way," said Will. "*Can* you swim?"

Ajay shifted uncomfortably. "For short periods. In still water. Preferably a swimming pool. With the assistance of a generously sized flotation device, of course, should I require it. Fortunately, I've brought one with me—" He reached back toward his pack.

"Never mind about that," said Elise, dragging him toward the water's edge. "We'll hang on to you."

"Hold on a second," said Will.

He looked out at the river. The current was visibly flowing from right to left, but not dangerously so. But something was nagging at him—*intuition*—to take a closer look. He blinked on the Grid.

He detected a lot of movement in the water, although he couldn't make out many heat signatures—whatever was down there was most likely cold-blooded, schools of small fish, maybe, or whatever passed for fish here. But he quickly zeroed in on three larger stationary heat signatures lurking near the river bottom.

Not cold-blooded. Each one about the size of a car.

"Both of you take a look down there and tell me what you see," he said.

Ajay opened his eyes wide, then squinted, then opened them wide again and glanced up at the misty sky. "I'm afraid the perpetual glare on the water makes it difficult for me to see anything below the surface."

Elise immediately got down on her hands and knees, tied her hair back, and stuck her face into the water. They heard her send out a series of the pulsating echolocation sounds. A moment later she pulled rapidly out of the water, stood up, and backed away, then turned to them, pale and alarmed.

"We are *not* going for a swim."

Will blinked again and immediately caught the signature of one of those large shapes racing up from the depths a split second before it breached out of the water near the shore right behind Elise.

Will saw only rows of eyes, a blunt porcine snout at the end of a brutally ugly gray torso, and a gaping, loose-lipped rubbery mouth. Moving as quickly as he could—as quickly as he ever remembered moving—Will planted himself between the monster and Elise, raised the nozzle of the canister, and sprayed a load of liquid nitrogen straight into its mouth; that part of the thing stiffened and froze instantly, and as it reached the apex of its breach, Elise let out a thumping blast of sound.

The creature's frozen face and head exploded as it hit the ground. What was left of its broken, misshapen body splashed back into the river and sank swiftly out of sight.

Will looked at the others and realized that, like them, he was dripping wet with the spewed liquefied remains of whatever wretched beast had just vaulted out of the river at them.

Ajay, who had received the worst of the drenching, looked

down at himself, shocked and disgusted. "I am more desperately in need of a shower than at any previous time in my life."

Will glanced back at the forest and blinked: The great red blob of the massed flowers was less than fifty yards away and appeared to have doubled in size. He could already hear the creepy whisperings of their stalks shuttling through the mulch.

"Which doesn't change the fact that we still need to get across," said Will. "Fast."

Elise had her hands on her knees, panting for breath; the exertion of that last blast had depleted her for the moment. She didn't look like she could recover in time to do the same to the flowers. And Will realized that meant she might not be able to run for it right away either.

While Will racked his brain for a solution, Ajay unexpectedly waddled toward him—still dripping—and held out his hands.

"Give me the canister," he said firmly.

Will handed it over. "What do you have in mind?"

Ajay looked out at the river. "I can't promise this approach will work, but in my expert opinion, it provides us with the most reasonable probability of success. It also requires that you both follow close behind me in very short order—"

"Ajay—"

"Just this once, Will, please do as I say."

Will studied him. He'd never seen his little friend so determined, and considering he was almost entirely covered with a layer of repulsive slime—a condition that normally would have emotionally incapacitated him—this felt like no time to argue.

Ajay marched to the river's edge. Will took Elise by the arm and helped lead her after him.

"You'll need to stay right on my heels," said Ajay. "With *extreme* alacrity. I can't emphasize that strongly enough. And please make every effort to hold your breath as often as you can in order to avoid the vapor."

"Wait—why is that?"

Fiddling with the device, Ajay ignored the question. "Let's just hope Boy Genius here has left us with enough propellant to make this work."

Ajay pointed the nozzle at the edge of the water and pulled the trigger for a moment. An enormous cloud of vapor erupted and immediately dissipated in the light breeze. As the mist cleared, Will could see that the spray had frozen a foot-wide strip of the river ahead of them. Ajay stepped out onto it, with first one foot, then the other, testing his weight; the ice cracked slightly but otherwise held firm.

"I can't predict how long this will hold, so we mustn't hesitate at any point," he said. "Here goes."

Ajay held the nozzle down right at water level and hit the trigger again. He shuffled forward, bent over, spraying continuously as he advanced, stepping lightly along the flash-frozen surface as it formed. Will steadied Elise as she followed Ajay onto the ice bridge, hurrying out onto the river close behind him.

They kept their heads turned to the right to avoid the continuous shroud of vapor, which drifted quickly to the left on the wind. The ice cracked and fractured with every step they took, sending up small shards of crystals and making strange pinging sounds as the flowing current passed below it.

But Will stayed behind on the shore.

About one-third of the way across, Elise glanced back, saw Will standing there, and nearly lost her balance.

What the hell are you waiting for?

Will waved her on. *I'll be all right. Keep going.*

But Will looked down at the shore end of the ice bridge and saw it was already starting to flake and splinter into crystallized fragments. He swiveled around again; the mass of flowers broke out of the forest behind him, a huge, slow-motion wave of brightly colored mayhem, wriggling forward onto the sand.

Will looked at his friends, now in the middle of the river, then back at the flowers. He started running directly toward the flowers, then turned and accelerated up the beach. If this was going to work, he would need to hit top speed by the time he turned back around and reached the water's edge.

Deep in concentration and still unaware that Will had stayed behind on shore, Ajay continued frog-marching forward. They advanced more than two-thirds of the way across when Ajay paused momentarily to shake the canister, then called back over his shoulder to Elise.

"Running extremely low on refrigerant now. We'll have to pick up our pace!"

"Then go! Go! Go!"

Ajay hit the trigger again, laying down an even thinner layer in front of him as he hurried forward in an awkward trot on top of the freshly forming ice. Elise matched his pace step for step. At this increased speed, the ice hardly had time to form before they passed onto it, and water sloshed almost up to their ankles on every step.

"We may have to swim after all!" shouted Ajay.

When they got within ten feet of the shore, the spray began to sputter as the last of the liquid nitrogen exited the canister. Ajay slowed down, and Elise bumped into him, nearly knocking him sideways into the river.

"Don't stop now—run for it!" Elise yelled.

Ajay vaulted off the last solid piece of ice, into knee-deep water a few feet from shore, and plowed forward as fast as he could lift his legs toward the beach. Elise splashed in beside him, grabbed him by the arm, and pulled him along.

Two steps from the sand, a shadow zoomed up from the depths just behind them. Elise saw it and pushed Ajay forward onto the shore just as another one of the river beasts surfaced behind them, giant mouth gaping.

Elise tackled Ajay, shoving him forward and jumping on top of him, then grabbed on to him and rolled them away from the water's edge. The leviathan flopped down onto the beach just behind them, jaws chomping wetly a foot from their legs. Elise rolled them forward again.

In response, the creature propped itself up on two pairs of thick, ventral flippers under its bloated body and used them to claw through the sand in their direction.

"Good God, it's amphibious!"

"How can you even think of a word like that at a time like this?"

Elise scrambled to her feet and pulled Ajay after her, backing away from the advancing behemoth. As they staggered back, Ajay flung the empty steel canister into the beast's gaping maw, and when the beast crunched down on it, they heard the metal smash and shatter. Whatever small amounts of nitrogen were left inside popped and hissed inside its hideous mouth, which only seemed to make it angrier. It kept dragging itself forward, determined to follow them right into the trees and gaining ground, only a few steps behind them now.

Behind the lurching creature, Elise caught a glimpse of a blur moving on the far side of the river, advancing rapidly toward what remained of the quickly disintegrating ice bridge.

Will had waited until the massed flowers changed course to follow him upstream before he turned around and seriously jacked up his speed. The flowers had spread out to almost the entire width of the beach, so he had to motor straight through the center of the pack, passing so fast that he kicked up hundreds of flowers in his wake. When he drew even with the cloud of vapor in the river, he planted and turned hard left toward the water.

The line of the bridge, sinking in many spots, remained clearly visible because of the vapor, billowing even more abundantly now as the ice decayed. Will took in one last deep breath, jumped off the shore, and darted into the cloud. He felt each step splash down at least an inch before his foot made contact with the bridge, and it bobbed alarmingly each time, but he was still able to push off slightly and keep going. By the time he was halfway across, his speed, declining with every step, had been cut nearly in half.

He wasn't going to make it.

As he calculated how far he'd have to jump to reach the shore, another shadow raced up just ahead of him—the last of the river beasts rising to the surface. It broke out of the water directly in his path, shattering what was left of the ice bridge and rising into the air.

Too late to change course, Will kept going—a hundred calibrations instantly taking place—and he ran three steps straight up the monster's back. Just as it reached the height of its breach, Will planted his last step on top of the beast's head and launched himself into the air, arms windmilling to maintain his balance.

He looked down as he reached the apex of his jump and saw he was headed straight for the second beast, lurching after Ajay and Elise near the edge of the forest. Still in midair as he started to descend, Will pulled the knife from the sheath on his leg.

Elise and Ajay glanced back and saw Will appear, flying

down toward the creature behind them. He landed on top of it and brought the blade down with both hands right between its double rows of eyes. The river beast threw back its head, bellowing in pain as it shook its body, sending Will flying off it toward the trees.

The beast staggered forward two more steps and then collapsed in a sagging, rancid heap less than five feet from Elise and Ajay.

Stone dead. Eyes turning glassy. Thick streams of drool and various other disgusting fluids flowing from the ruins of its cavernous mouth.

Ajay stared at it, wide-eyed and haunted. "Sometimes I really wish I couldn't remember everything."

Elise quickly pulled him away, leading him into the forest. "Come on, we've got to find Will."

"I'm okay! I'm okay!"

They looked up. Still a little stunned, Will sat fifteen feet above them, astride a broad branch, hugging the trunk of what looked like a towering eucalyptus. He disentangled his pack from the tree, climbed halfway down, and dropped onto the path beside them, where both were taking out their canteens. Will pulled his canteen too, and they all took long drinks.

"Still think this place isn't real?" asked Elise.

"We were practically guppy food," said Ajay with a haunted stare.

"I never said that *we* weren't real," said Will between gulps.

"You mean like if a giant hippo-grouper eats you in the forest, but there's no one there to hear it—"

"You still get digested," said Will.

"Moist towelette?" Ajay offered a handful of the sealed sanitary packs to them.

"You actually brought those with you?" asked Elise.

"I've been collecting them whenever I eat at Red Lobster for years," said Ajay, wiping his face with one of the dainty, unfolded wet squares. "I'm fond of Red Lobster, and as you know, I am a firm believer in the Boy Scout Motto." He offered the packs again. "Unless, of course, you'd prefer to bathe back in the river."

They both took a few of the packets, opened them, and cleaned off.

"I believe I know what you mean by that, Will," said Ajay. "There is something oddly . . . I'm not sure what the right word is . . . *rudimentary* about this uncanny place."

"Explain," said Elise.

Ajay opened another napkin and fastidiously toweled off his arms. "Well, for instance, I had no reason to believe the liquid nitrogen would interact that way with the river water. In our world, it wouldn't have transpired quite so . . . advantageously."

"How so?" asked Will.

"The vapor would have cooled the air so rapidly it would displace all the oxygen in the atmosphere, and if we'd inhaled any of it, our lung tissue would have frozen solid. We would have asphyxiated almost instantly."

Elise's eyes opened wide in alarm. "And you went ahead with it anyway?"

"Admittedly, it was a calculated risk—"

"Are you out of your mind?"

"Well, if you'll recall our *exact* circumstances, my dear, it was either find a way to walk on water or get nibbled to death by daffodils."

Elise looked at him with a mixture of astonishment and, Will thought, something close to admiration. "You have got to be the dumbest smart guy in the whole freakin' world."

"We got across, didn't we?"

"Hang on, let him finish," said Will, keenly interested in hearing his friend's conclusion.

"What I mean is," said Ajay, gesturing at the forest around them, "this feels more like someone's *idea* of reality than reality as we know it. It's simpler somehow, or not quite fully worked out. . . . What's the word I'm looking for—rudimentary."

"O-kay," said Elise as she considered the idea.

"It's a genuine puzzlement, and please forgive me for being somewhat less than precise, but I'm still working this through—"

They heard something moving around behind them, a short distance away. More than one thing, maybe many, and they sounded big, moving closer. And then they heard a voice rising above all that, laughing and shouting.

"Yee-haw! Come on now, get along, little doggies! Yah! Yah! Yippy ki-yi-yay!"

They looked at each other.

"That's Nick," said Will.

SEVEN

WILL'S RULES FOR LIVING #7:
SOMETIMES, IN ORDER TO GET COMPLETELY SANE,
YOU HAVE TO GO A LITTLE CRAZY.

As they moved on, Will made another mental attempt to reach out to Dave but again got no response. After hurrying fifty yards farther into the woods, away from the river, they came to the edge of a substantial clearing, covered with tall pale grasses, where the strangest sight awaited them.

Tightly packed together, half a dozen six-foot-tall flowers—at first glance apparently gigantic relations of the tiny ones from the far side of the river—shuffled around in a wide circle, kicking up clouds of dust. They featured the same circular array of vivid multicolored petals. Substantial bloodred stalks, including branches that almost looked like arms, rested on a thick cluster of roots that formed a sturdy base. Closer examination revealed that a rope had been thrown around the whole bunch of them, binding them tautly together; they moved as a group.

Twenty feet behind them, holding the other end of the rope, was Nick. In his other hand, he held a bullwhip, and he cracked it at them whenever they deviated from the circular pattern he was running them around. Each snap of the whip tore a few leaves off the creatures' branches, and they flinched at every blow.

"That's right, keep moving, that's the way to do it. You're gonna be good to go for rodeo in no time—"

They all shouted at once: "Nick!"

He stopped instantly, looked up, saw them, and waved cheerfully. "Hey there, boys and girls, 'bout time you showed up!"

They advanced into the clearing together. The flowers turned toward them as one and reacted hungrily, just as the smaller ones had done, opening their petals to show their teeth and edging toward them.

Nick yanked back hard on the rope and cracked the whip at them, and they immediately retreated.

"KNOCK IT OFF!" Then, turning to his friends, "Don't get too close, *mis amigos*. Two reasons: I haven't completely broken 'em in yet. And they smell worse than camel butt."

Will led the others across the clearing toward Nick, taking a wide arc away from the flowers.

"Where did you come in?" asked Will.

"I landed halfway up a tree, about half a mile over that way," he said, pointing behind him. "Good times."

They reached him and exchanged hugs and back slaps all around, interrupted once, in the middle of hugging Ajay, when Nick had to crack the whip again at his captives.

"Good Lord, that's unsettling," said Ajay.

"Imagine how I felt," said Nick. "These suckers came out of the woods and started sniffing around the tree before I even pulled the splinters out of my rear end."

"We ran into their cousins on the other side of the river," said Elise.

"Little cousins," said Will, holding up his hands to show the size. "About yay high."

"No kidding," said Nick. "Must be way more awesome plant food on this side or something."

"Apparently they're meat eaters," said Ajay.

"Tell me about it. Did you get an eyeful of the teeth on these puppies?" Nick pulled a machete from a sheath on his hip and twirled it around. "I had to seriously slice and dice a crap-ton of veggie buttooski before they'd lay off me. Where's Coach?"

"We haven't found him yet," said Will.

"We've had some fairly eventful encounters with the local fauna ourselves," said Ajay. "Or should I say flora. Come to think of it, they're both, aren't they?"

"Yeah, I don't know what their names are; that's your department. But did I mention there was a zombie-apocalypse-sized pack of these suckers to start out with, like maybe a hundred of 'em, right?"

"What made you think capturing them like this was a good idea?" Elise asked.

"Okay, so I jump down, attack, and I'm smack in the middle of opening my super-sized can of weedwackin' whoop-ass when I start thinking, what the heck, maybe there's some way to make lemonade out of this situation—"

The herded flowers began creeping toward them again. Nick yanked on the rope hard and brandished his machete at them. "I said EASE UP, LOSERS!"

The flowers retreated, cowering and shaking.

"Lemonade?" said Ajay, looking at Will and Elise helplessly.

"You know, like an analogy or whatever. So once there were only these few of the bozos still putzing around," said Nick, lapsing into a lame Western dialect, "I pulled out ma' trusty lariat and went full-on bronco buster on their useless stems; head 'em up, move 'em out!"

"Seriously, Nick, what was your plan?" asked Elise, staring at the struggling flowers.

"Plan?" asked Nick blankly. "I was just killing time, you know, waiting for you guys. I didn't have a plan."

"Of course you didn't," said Ajay.

"But I have been thinking they might make a pretty sick dogsled team."

"There's no snow and they move at about three miles an hour," said Will.

"True." Nick nodded as he considered that for a moment. "Guess it'd depend on how big a hurry we're in, right? And we could still run into some snow, somewhere, maybe. Where are we anyway, like up the Amazon?"

"You've been up the Amazon for years," said Ajay.

"We're in the Never-Was," said Elise.

"Oh, so the portal deal worked? That's super cool. So what do we do now? Man, I sure am hungry. Good thing we brought some grub with us, but I figured we should rationalize it, so I didn't chow down. And I've been looking, but I haven't found anything to eat out here yet. Have you?"

"What were you expecting, a sandwich shop?" asked Ajay.

"Yeah, right, like that's gonna happen, Captain Science. I was thinking more along the lines of some nuts and berries. You know, jungle food."

"Irony is completely wasted on him," said Ajay to Elise, shaking his head.

"Yeah, sure, go ahead and mock me, but if the nuts around here are as big as these petunias, I could live off a single pistachio for a week."

"Unless it eats you first," said Will.

"Interesting," said Nick, lost in thought.

Elise moved a few steps closer to study the captive flowers. They shied away slightly, and when she raised her hand toward them, two of the things opened their petals and let out a kind of hiss at her.

"Back off, sunshine!" shouted Nick, yanking the rope again. "So, Will-Bear, speaking of plans, what's the plan?"

Before Will could answer, Elise spoke up. "They can feel."

"Of course they can feel," said Ajay, wandering over near her but maintaining a greater distance from the creatures. "Galvanic surface responses to stimuli in the plant kingdom is a long-established fact—"

"I'm not talking about *autonomic* responses," said Elise. "I think these things might be sentient."

Nick opened up a package of peanuts from his pack. "Of course they are, babe. They're *walking*, aren't they?"

"She said *sentient*, not *ambulatory*," said Ajay. "As in they appear to be able to walk *and* think. Apparently, unlike you, at the same time."

"Ha-ha. Anybody want a peanut? Honey roasted," Nick offered.

Ajay reached into the bag and took a handful.

"Where are you going with this, Elise?" asked Will, watching the flowers react again as he moved up beside her.

"If they can think, maybe they have memory. Maybe even some kind of ability to communicate—"

"Perhaps even the capacity for language," said Ajay; then, when the others stared at him, "They're interspecies hybrids, clearly, and there's no telling what manner of other being they were spliced with, so I'd say every possibility remains on the table, wouldn't you?"

"You want to *talk* to them?" asked Nick, chewing and chuckling. "What are they gonna tell us? 'Man, my roots are *killin'* me today . . . That was one delicious bug—oh, look, a butterfly!'"

"Nick, did you bring a map with you?" asked Will. "With Dave's or Coach Jericho's location conveniently marked on it?"

"No way," scoffed Nick.

"Then please be quiet while we find out, however strange this sounds, if your new pets can help us figure that out. And keep your whip and machete handy, okay?"

"Can do."

"Thank you."

Ajay popped some more peanuts into his mouth as he studied the flowers. "So what would be the most effective pathway into their consciousness? Provided they do have minds, or at the least, some form of primitive brain."

Will and Elise looked at each other, sharing the same thought.

You want to give it a try? he asked.

You go first, she answered. *I'm still recharging.*

"Keep an eye on 'em, Nick," said Will. "I'm going to try something."

Will moved a couple of steps closer to the creatures. He blinked on the Grid and focused on the flowers. Stripped of their outward visual skins, he perceived them as vivid arrangements of biological systems, life-forces circulating through complex cellular interactions. Recalling an animation from a recent biology class, he thought they appeared to be metabolizing carbon dioxide and expelling oxygen. Just like regular plants.

Except . . .

Will narrowed his focus to just one of the creatures. Behind its petals, and that nasty hidden array of thorny mandibles, Will locked in on a small dense mass about the size of a golf ball. Solid dark green, pulsing with dynamic energy, but also cycling continually through other wavelengths of color—blue, yellow, hints of orange and magenta.

"Nick, wave your machete at them again," said Will.

Nick did. The flowers drew back fearfully, just as before. And Will watched this one's "brain" or central processor flood with varying shades of red and violet as it experienced and reacted to this physical threat.

"Looks like they definitely have some kind of brain," said Will.

"I'm thinking about another intriguing, albeit as yet unproven and decidedly esoteric, theory regarding plant life," said Ajay, looking up and to the left as he accessed the memory.

"What's that?" asked Elise.

"It was a commonly held belief in the ancient world. Associated with more Neolithic cultures, naturally, but perhaps not coincidentally, one that is becoming part of modern scientific discussion, as we've begun to assess aboriginal shamanistic practices through a more modern lens."

"What belief would that be?" asked Will.

"That all plant life shares an ability to communicate non-verbally. By means of what one might call, for lack of a better phrase, a spiritual frequency."

"How does that work?" asked Elise.

"No one knows; it's just a theory. But if it's true, it could mean—"

"It could mean that if you can penetrate the mind of one of these things . . . ," said Elise, moving ahead down the same track.

Ajay picked up the thought from her like a runner taking a baton. "One might be able to communicate with *all* the examples of that particular species, as they could share a sort of—"

"Collective mind," said Elise.

"Exactly!" Ajay continued. "And advancing that logic a step further, one might therefore be able to commune with all plants in general. On some grander mythical plane."

"Sounds like a bunch of hooey to me," said Nick.

"I don't recall asking you," said Ajay.

"I'd say it's worth a try," said Will.

"What should we ask them?" asked Elise.

"Have they seen any tall Native Americans or dead helicopter pilots running around," said Nick. "And where can we get something to eat."

"Really not helpful," said Ajay.

"Actually, it is," said Will. "Give me a second."

Will blinked on the Grid, then closed his eyes and gathered his mental energy into a cloud of intention that he then projected over toward the target flower. Trying not to overwhelm or disable the creature, he tried to first quietly surround its "mind" with the cloud, sending out waves of calming vibration.

He felt the thing relax and the color of its "brain" reverted to dark green. As Will wedged open the connection between them, emotional readings began to slowly come across to him: agitation, spikes of hatred, and a reserve of savage anger, held in check by fear.

He paused, let the thing settle down again, then carefully probed deeper—he realized this process was more than a little similar to what he and Elise could do together and what Lyle had tried to do to him a few times. Project his mind into that of another being, but not invasively, with no intent to hurt or punish the thing, just apply a kind of gentle persuasion and gain access to its innermost thoughts—

Then he felt some last line of resistance give way, and suddenly, somehow, he knew he was inside. The effect was jarring, jumbling, disturbing, an assault on his senses. He was inside an alien consciousness, no part of it familiar or reassuring, and he couldn't find anything to hold on to that helped him understand its architecture or how it worked. Swirling colors and indistinct shapes swarmed all around, so he decided to let go of trying to defend against the experience and flow with it, wherever it led him.

He suddenly felt as if he were tumbling along a swiftly moving underground stream, deep in the dark, and the many shapes appeared now as glints of light strobing on every side of him as he rushed headlong and down. Every instinct in him registered danger, urging escape and retreat. Panic rose in his gut but he wrestled it back down with a single commanding thought:

They're taking me somewhere I need to go.

That helped him cut through the fear. The shapes were acquiring more form and dimension as he traveled, and he felt that speeding or falling sensation gradually begin to abate. The shapes and lights started to linger, acquire more definition, and he realized he was seeing pictures that he might soon begin to recognize.

This is how they think. Not in words but in images.

Then he stopped. Completely still. Cold and cool. He felt, and somehow knew, that he was a long way underground. As he adjusted to the dark, a lambent glow rose from clumps of moss around the room, but he still sensed more than saw a vast root system all around him—huge, gnarled, twisting tubes of organic matter shooting up, down, and out in every direction.

It occurred to him that perhaps he had just "traveled" here along, through, or by way of one of these root tubes. And that he might, if he so chose, be able to similarly move out along any of the countless other tubes that now surrounded him.

And follow them to wherever they might lead, which he sensed could take him to just about anywhere in the Never-Was. He knew there was a word for this, and it floated up in his head . . .

Omnipresence.

Then other images, springing from some defined outside source, began to flow into the stream of his consciousness, and as he filtered them into a more manageable context, he found that they added up to thoughts:

This is "home." This is "who we are." They are "all one." These life-forms share a collective "mind."

So Ajay was right. At this most fundamental level, they were all connected. And he had apparently made contact with its source or center; he imagined that Jericho might call it their "great spirit." Will took a deep breath and decided to lean in a little more firmly, project himself farther, until he reached the point where "they" turned into—

We. We are One.

He perceived this not through words but by means of crystal-clear pictures that conveyed its ideas. Almost like hieroglyphs. Many he didn't know and couldn't at first penetrate their meanings. But he found that the few he could translate came to him without effort, and slowly others began to follow, until a series of more complete thoughts fell into place.

We fear Them. The Ones Above. They are the Makers. The Ones who Came After. After the Beginning.

They Changed Us.

Will decided to ask a question in return, constructing it with the same symbols: *Who are They?*

The images that came back to him depicted the beings they called "Makers" directly—tall, forbidding shapes, monolithic, cloaked in shrouds of darkness, their faces hidden deep in shadow. Groups of them, towering over them with sinister intent. Fear rushed up inside Will.

A wealth of emotion flowed into him—the plants' *feelings* felt less alien to him than anything else about them—and Will realized that he was now receiving the story of their entire existence.

He witnessed their process of creation itself, as these beings moved from an idea of life, a blueprint realized through some mystical means of construction into primitive physical forms that slowly, ever so slowly began to evolve, bursting out of the ground, in light and life and the awakening of their senses, then a long period, through endless cycles of life and death—physically dying but never extinguished, living on through the strength of a kind of enduring spiritual blueprint—a long and peaceful existence.

Then, out of nowhere, a wrenching, violent disruption—he realized the things were being torn away from their roots. Transported into some sterile, completely foreign, largely metallic environment. Deprived of nutrition, water, and natural light, dissected, ripped apart and stitched back together in some kind of hideous, heartless experimentation.

Will felt as if a wave of fire broke over him, with a blast of searing pain that nearly doubled him over. There were no borders between him and these creatures any longer. He felt what they felt, knew what they knew:

They Changed Us.

Something *else* was part of their nature now. Some distinct, unwanted *other*. In that anguish, he felt a strange and powerful pang of kinship to these creatures.

I know how you feel, brother.

And somewhere during that exchange, he also received the clear impression he could open a deeper dialogue with them.

So he asked, this time using pictures of his own, like a one-year-old struggling with the elementary building blocks of language:

Where are Makers?

Immediately the answer came back to him in multiple visions of the Never-Was. A flood of them, streaming in so fast that he struggled to process them coherently.

He saw some kind of vast fortress or city—the word *citadel* came to mind—built on an epic scale, dug into rolling hills in front of a majestic, snowcapped range of craggy mountains. Not remotely like anything they'd seen in the zone so far.

So far, so good. So he asked another.

Where is . . . and then he thought of Coach Jericho, summoning up an image for him.

. . . the Bear Man?

He could almost feel the spirits' collective "mind" calculating—sending out the question as tendrils of thought along its serpentine underground network of roots, moving faster than electricity—and an answer came just as quickly back to him, as an image.

The Bear Man, in a very specific sort of location. And with it, the reassuring idea that it wasn't far away from where they were now.

But not exactly safe from harm. Far from it.

Then one last question:

Where is . . . and he showed them the best image he could think of for Dave.

The Man with Wings.

Again, a pause as the question flowed outward. The image that came back was considerably less encouraging than the last.

The Citadel.

The Man with Wings was inside that citadel.

Will uncoupled his connection to the plant spirit "mind," which had the effect of abruptly letting go of his end of a long, taut rope. He felt himself falling backward, a long, long way, and then he blacked out.

EIGHT

WILL'S RULES FOR LIVING #8:
DO THE RIGHT THING, ALWAYS, AND RISK
THE CONSEQUENCES.

He must have been out for only a moment. Elise's face, looking down at him with concern, was the first sight that greeted him. She saw the experience in his eyes; then he knew that she sensed it in his mind as she caught a taste of where he'd been, a fleeting aura of that strangeness from his communion with that foreign consciousness.

Wow. Ajay was right.

So were you, he replied. *They think, they feel, they share a single mind.*

Remind you of anyone?

Reminds me of a few people I know.

"So, dude, what did Little Susie Sunflower have to share?" asked Nick. "Complaints about the aphids, or how hard it is to find a good dental plan?"

"No," said Will, sitting up, waiting for his head to clear. "But it did tell me where we can find Coach Jericho."

"What, for real?"

"One hundred percent."

"So we were right!" Ajay clapped his hands together and gave Elise a high five. "Collective mind, I knew it!"

For the moment, Will decided not to tell them about where

it had told him they could find Dave. Before he mentioned a word to the others, he wanted to discuss that bad news with Coach Jericho.

But first they had to find *him*, and based on what he'd just seen, they had to do it *fast*.

"Come on, guys, we need to hurry," said Will, rising and shouldering his pack.

Elise and Ajay picked up their packs and trudged after him toward the woods. Nick lingered.

"But what about my big bouquet?" asked Nick.

"Unless you want to be solely responsible for them from here on out, young man, you're going to have to let them go," said Elise.

"It's not really practical right now, Nick," said Will.

"Catch and release, man," said Ajay. "You can always pick another bunch later. Maybe we'll happen across a gigantic vase."

"It's the only humane thing to do anyway, right?" asked Elise, seeing that Nick looked distressed.

"Except most trout don't try to jump back out of the stream into the boat and bite your leg off," said Ajay.

Will looked at the still-cowering flowers. It was hard not to see them completely differently now—as lost and pitiable creatures, their natures twisted into perversions of their original innocent state through no fault, choice, or action of their own.

Like us in more ways than one.

Nick walked over to his huddled, shuddering herd. He actually looked kind of sad. And so, in a strange way, did the flowers, which had seemed so feral and ferocious minutes earlier. They dipped their heads submissively and made no aggressive moves toward Nick as he untied the knot on his rope—

Seeing their behavior and sensing what they seemed to be giving off emotionally, Will recognized with a shock: *These things understand—collectively—what was communicated between us.*

As if they'd heard that thought, the flowers turned toward Will. The colors of their petals subtly changed—similar to the way he'd seen the "brain" phase change between colors—to softer shades and from that and the gentle way the petals undulated he felt something else unspoken pass between them that made him realize something even more startling.

They learned as much about me as I did about them.

Will was reminded that he hadn't yet shared or found the right moment to tell his friends about the final bombshell Franklin had dropped on him: that the source of their own genetic mutations hadn't been culled from any known form of earthly life. The foreign DNA they were carrying around had come from *them.* The Others, the Makers, or whatever they called themselves.

That's why I was able to connect with the plants. They have the Others in them, too.

As he gathered up his rope, even Nick seemed to pick up on the change in his charges. Instead of fleeing from him the moment they were free, the flowers stood right where they were, together, in a group, almost as if they were waiting for him to give his permission.

"You dudes take care of yourselves now, okay?" said Nick.

One of them—Will thought it was the same one that he'd zeroed in on, but he couldn't be sure—tentatively reached out one of its armlike branches toward Nick. Nick, initially puzzled, then realized what it was doing. He reached out and bumped the branch with his fist.

"No hard feelings," said Nick.

The flowers appeared to slightly nod their heads; then they

turned as one and with a pace that suggested a surprising dignity not seen before, moved out of the clearing and back into the forest.

Nick turned back to his friends, gathered up his pack, and joined them as they trotted off in the opposite direction. Elise glanced over at Nick a few times.

"You okay, cowboy?" she asked.

"Maybe," he said. "Yeah, I guess."

"What changed?" she asked.

"I don't know. I know it sounds screwy, but I sort of liked them," said Nick, glancing back toward the clearing as they moved into the woods.

"I know what you mean," said Will.

"And I feel kinda bad now that I had to Benihana so many of 'em back there."

"They were threatening to devour you," said Ajay.

"You know more now than you did then," said Elise, putting a hand on Nick's shoulder. "Don't be so hard on yourself."

"Don't get me wrong," said Nick. "It's not like I've gone vegetarian all of a sudden or anything."

"I'm sorry, were you trying to eat *them*?" asked Ajay, confused.

"The other way around."

"Then I don't understand the reference—"

"What I mean is, it's not like I just turned into some sandals-and-socks-wearing tree hugger or anything. I mean, I'd kill for a good burger right about now."

"What are you talking about?" asked Elise.

"You do realize of course that, biologically speaking, flowers are much more closely related to vegetables than mammals," said Ajay.

"Yeah, well, tell their teeth about that," said Nick.

"I have given that some thought, actually," said Ajay. "Perhaps they were crossbred with some sort of savage omnivorous baboon—"

"You're an omnivorous baboon—"

"Guys, right now we need to focus on where we're going," said Will firmly, pointing ahead. "Instead of where we've been."

"How do you know where we're going?" asked Nick.

"Intuition," said Will.

Ahead of them, where a clear, well-trodden path presented itself through the woods, the landscape was transitioning yet again. Small patches of wispy fog hugged the ground, which grew increasingly damp and yielding. Above and around them Will noticed more and more vines, clusters of strangely glowing moss, and rooted plants sprouting heavy fragrant flowers. The same pale light from above grew dimmer as it filtered through the increasingly overgrown canopy. For the first time they heard strange yowls and cries echoing in the distance.

"Animal life," said Ajay.

"Birds maybe," said Elise.

"Let's hope it's birds," said Nick.

"As opposed to what?" asked Ajay.

"Exactly," said Nick.

"Just curious: Why would you imagine that the birds here would be any less unpleasant and terrifying than the rest of what we've run into?"

"Birds are nice," said Nick.

"We're heading into a swamp," said Will, surveying the horizon. "There could be any number of . . . different kinds of . . . things in here."

The air felt thicker with menace the farther they ventured in, and the path grew more narrow, spongy, and soggy, moisture sucking at their shoes with every step.

"And so your best instinct is to, what, keep proceeding into said swamp?" asked Ajay, wringing his hands.

"The plants said this is where we'd find Jericho," said Will.

"Ah, you neglected to share that small nugget with us," said Ajay. "By all means, if the *plants*—that not so recently tried to eat us—told you that this is where we'd find him, what could possibly go wrong?"

"Give it a rest, Ajay," said Elise.

Ajay gazed around uneasily at the deepening gloom of the swamp. "You know I've always felt that, attacks from animals—or plants, for that matter—notwithstanding, of all the untold terrors waiting to befall one in this, or any other world, quicksand is criminally underrated."

"Get a load of this," said Nick, looking at something a few feet off to the left of the path. "I think it's a wall."

He was pointing at the edge of a straight line of rocks that paralleled their path and gradually rose up out of the murky water. About two inches wide, the line of stones, aged and covered with slime, appeared to be artfully carved and mortared together. The wall continued to slowly rise out of the water and run alongside the path for as far as they could see until it disappeared in the gathering mist.

"There's one over here, too," said Elise.

Will turned and looked where she was pointing, to an identical wall running in the same direction on the right side of the path.

"So apparently this wasn't always a swamp," said Ajay, peering ahead into the mist. "Or someone's gone to an awful lot of trouble to make it appear that way."

"What do you see?" asked Elise.

"Nick," said Ajay, snapping his fingers. "Flare gun."

Within moments, Nick had the gun pulled and loaded. He

knelt, aimed, and fired up a flare on a low arcing trajectory along the path, trying to stay below the crowded canopy overhead. A bright globe of white light blossomed about a hundred yards on, burning through the spotty fog, directly over a startling reveal.

A magnificent ruin rose out of the swamp. The walls on either side of their path jointed into a complex spread of higher stone walls laid out in a dense, geometrically precise pattern that they all could now see.

The building appeared to cover about the size of a football field. The outer walls marched up together, in symmetrical rows of increasing height, then culminated in a solid square tower rising from its center. Brutish vines snaked up and around the rocks almost everywhere, and in many places appeared to have grown right into the walls. In a few places, tall trees had erupted, slow-motion explosions bursting out of the ancient masonry.

"That's where Coach Jericho is," said Will.

"Now you tell us," said Elise.

"Inside?" asked Nick.

"That's right," said Will.

"By any chance, did our vegetative acquaintances download a set of GPS coordinates for you?" asked Ajay. "Pinpointing Coach Jericho's exact location?"

"In the middle," said Will, pointing at the tower. "Down below, in some kind of basement."

A chorus of the same howls and barks they'd heard earlier erupted again. Much closer this time, from straight ahead of them. Inside the structure.

"Sounds like he's not alone," said Elise.

"Yo, I've seen Coach get his full grizzly on, okay," said Nick.

"It's the animals, or whatever else is in there, I'd be worried about."

"That's not the problem," said Will. "From what the plants showed me, Coach was trapped in some kind of pit. With thick bars across the top."

"What?!" said Nick.

"And it was slowly filling with water."

"Why didn't you tell us that before?" asked Elise.

"I told you we should hurry," said Will.

"If my earlier observations were accurate," said Ajay, "a prolonged watery immersion should not present any great difficulty for Coach Jericho."

"How so?"

"Based on what I witnessed this morning, I believe he may be able to shape-shift into some sort of aquatic form as well."

"That's no reason not to hurry now," said Elise, and she started running up the path toward the building.

Will sped up and quickly caught up with her before she reached the outer walls, stopping her in midstride. She tried to shake him off, but he held firm.

"Let Ajay and Nick go first," he said. "Ajay can spot any booby traps and Nick can avoid them. If Jericho's in trouble, we can't help if we get into any ourselves."

She reluctantly waited for the others to reach them. Will repeated his instructions, Ajay switched on his flashlight, and the two boys started ahead of them at a brisk pace, examining the ground carefully as they moved.

The path had gradually risen along with the walls on either side. The earthen path had given way to worn dark gray stone pavers, large slabs a couple of feet square. They stopped just outside the first big row of outer walls. An elaborate carved arch spanned an entrance about six feet across. Ajay shone the flashlight along a series of deeply eroded carvings adorning the arch that might once have been faces. Not human faces, at least not entirely. They were some kind of hybrids, but they were too worn out to identify exactly.

"Remind you of anything?" asked Will.

"The stonework and building style are reminiscent of Cahokia," said Ajay. "Obviously nowhere near the same level of decay."

"They haven't been here as long, right?" said Elise.

"Let's check it out," said Nick.

He passed through the entrance first and the others followed. The walls were higher here, maybe eight feet, and the passage between them more narrow, no more than six feet, leading off in either direction about thirty yards until they reached another wall and a ninety-degree turn. The air was still, humid, stifling, with a sour undertaste of rot.

"Which way?" Ajay asked Will.

"Up," said Will, then looked at Nick.

"Up it is," said Nick.

He trotted back outside the entrance, turned, and sprinted straight at the inside wall. He ran up two steps, then turned, leaped, grabbed the edge of the outer wall, and pulled himself up on top of the arch. He stood, turned, then jumped directly over their heads onto the top of the inner wall, looking all around.

"Whoa," said Nick.

"What do you see?" asked Elise.

"It's a maze," said Will.

"It's like one of those . . . what do you call it," said Nick.

"A maze?" asked Ajay.

"That's it! A maze. It's amazing. Hey, that must be where they got the word from: A-mazing!"

Ajay shook his head at Will. "You had to let him go off on his own."

"Nick, can you see where it leads?" asked Will.

"No way, man, it's a maze."

"Let me rephrase the question: Can you see where it reaches the central tower?"

"Sure thing."

"How far do you think it is from here?"

"I'm gonna say . . . wow, at least a quarter of a mile? This is a helluva of a hella maze. Reminds me of this one they put up in Needham every Halloween, made out of corn, that I got way lost in once when I was about nine—"

"Here's what I need you to do, Nick. Stay on top of the walls, go find that entrance, then work your way back to us and talk us through which way we need to navigate to get there."

"Piece o' cake," said Nick.

"No yelling, just come back and tell us."

Nick gave a thumbs-up, leaped off the wall to the next one over, closer to the center. They heard him moving away, then nothing.

"What else did the plants tell you?" asked Elise, her brow furrowed, staring at Will.

"That was it—basement, pit, bars, water," said Will. "And they didn't *tell* me; they *showed* me. That's how they think, if you can call it that. In pictures. Images."

Elise still looked pissed at him.

I'm not holding out on you, he finally felt obliged to send to her.

How'd you know about the maze, then?

I don't know.

I think it's weird.

What?

You just knowing all this stuff somehow, Elise said. *I just think it's weird.*

You and me both, he answered.

Ajay looked back and forth at the two of them, their eyes locked, staring at each other.

"Is this a private argument, or can anyone join in?" asked Ajay.

"I don't know what you mean—" said Will.

"Don't know what you're talking about—" said Elise.

At that moment, Nick leaped back into view on top of the inner wall, only slightly out of breath.

"We're good to go," he said. "Follow me."

He walked along the top of the wall to the left and they hurried to keep up. When they turned right, and then right again, Nick jumped over them onto the next wall closest to the building. Ajay took a small can of fluorescent pink spray paint out of his pack and sprayed an arrow at every corner that they turned, pointing toward the structure. When Nick questioned what he was doing, all Ajay replied was, "You'll thank me later."

They proceeded that way for fourteen more turns, each time following Nick's directions as he crossed above them to the next wall over.

Will examined the walls as they moved along, most of them choked and almost overrun by a latticework of thick ropey vines. He reached out to touch one of the vines, wondering if any of these had been part of the network that had earlier communicated Coach Jericho's location. He did feel a mild buzz—like a weak electrical field—issue from the vine, but before he had time to investigate further, he heard a voice from above.

"Almost there now," said Nick. "Two more turns and we're at the entrance."

Looking up, Will could see the edge of the complex's central tower rising over the nearest walls now.

"Good work, Nick," he said.

"Stupid maze makers thought they could put one over on us—"

"Stop right there," said Ajay, holding up his hand.

They stopped. Ajay's eyes were fixed on the floor a few steps ahead of them, where it took a left-handed ninety-degree turn. He pointed at one of the pavers.

"There's something wrong with that floor stone," he said. "The one at the right inside corner. There's a suspect notch in it, and a slight gap in the mortaring. I don't recommend that we set foot on it . . ."

Nick picked up a loose stone from the top of the wall and dropped it onto the paver Ajay had described. The rock smashed into the broad stone paver; at almost four feet square it covered the whole width of the passage. The paver hinged open ninety degrees and the rock tumbled down out of sight. They heard the stone banging and smashing off walls for a few seconds and then, from far below, a distant splash.

Will leaned forward over the edge to look down through the opening. "It's not a straight drop; it's carved and sloped, like a slide."

"So it's designed to capture any intruder," said Ajay, "but not necessarily kill it."

"Awesome," said Nick, kneeling on the wall for a closer look. "Want me to check it out?"

"Don't be stupid," said Elise.

"Too late," said Ajay.

"Maybe this is how they got Coach," said Will. "Maybe he's down there right now."

"Hey, Coach!" shouted Nick into the opening.

With a loud crack, the paver stone snapped back into place.

"Really?" said Ajay.

"These clowns are a real pack o' jokers," said Nick.

"What do you think we should do?" asked Elise, looking at Will.

"If Coach is down there, it won't do him any good if we end up in the same fix," said Will. "Can we get around it? Do you see anything else up ahead?"

Ajay turned his attention to the visible pavers on the far side of the trap before the passage turned the corner. "I don't see anything else untoward as far as the floor is concerned. Shall we jump across it? I'm not entirely sure that I can negotiate it myself—"

Before he could say another word, the end of Nick's whip dropped into sight near them.

"Grab on, peewee," Nick said from atop the wall. "I'll swing you across."

"Wait, I'll go first," said Elise.

She moved back a few yards, ran forward, jumped, and easily cleared the hinged stone. Ajay fidgeted in place and swallowed hard.

"You next, Ajay," said Will.

"It's too far for me," he said. "The long jump is not in my skill set."

"No sweat, bro," said Nick. "I'll get you there."

Nick leaned down and dropped the edge of his whip as low as it would go, about to Ajay's knees. He grabbed on to it with both hands, then lifted his feet off the ground, wrapped himself around the whip as best he could, and closed his eyes. Nick swung him back and forth a few times, building momentum, then swung him all the way across the trapdoor. His eyes shut tight, Ajay clung to the whip and swung all the way back to the others.

"You have to let go, numb nuts," said Nick.

"My apologies. I was afraid to look," said Ajay.

Nick swung him back across a second time, Elise grabbed him, and Ajay let go, clinging to Elise just a second or two longer than necessary.

Will loped back down the passage, accelerated a few steps, and easily jumped over the trap to join them. Nick coiled up his whip and walked forward along the wall above them, scouting ahead.

"Turn that last corner and we're in," he said.

The three of them turned left around the final corner, Ajay's eyes focused hawkishly ahead for signs of danger. The three of them stepped onto the next paver together and they felt it give, with a loud thunk, and it dropped, but no more than half an inch.

"I did not see that coming," said Ajay.

"That can't be good," said Elise.

"Don't move," said Will.

Nothing else happened for a moment. But then they heard from nearby an ominous grinding sound, stone on stone.

"Crap on a cracker," said Nick.

"What?" asked Elise.

"Ahead of you," he said.

Four pavers ahead of them, the wall had started to move, a foot-thick block of stone sliding directly toward them, slowly at first but picking up speed. They heard another sound behind them; the trapdoor just around the corner had sprung open again.

"Good golly Miss Molly," said Ajay.

"Nick, you'll have to pull us up," said Will.

"Way ahead of you," said Nick as the end of the whip dropped down to them again. "Ajay!"

Ajay grabbed the end of the whip again. Nick quickly spooled him up to the top of the wall and Ajay scrambled onto his hands and knees. With the moving block of stone now less than two pavers away, Nick dropped the whip down again and Elise grabbed on. He reeled Elise up top as Will backed away onto the last paver before the wall, with the open trapdoor just to his left.

"It's okay; I'll just jump back over it," he said.

But as he turned to make the leap, just on the other side of the trap, another tall stone wall slid quickly across, blocking his way. The moving stone block was less than one paver from him and bearing down.

"Stay there," shouted Nick.

Will looked up and saw Nick in midair, falling down toward him, spread-eagled like a skydiver. He landed with his feet against the wall at Will's back, and he extended his arms out just as the sliding block moved within reach. The full weight of the block hit Nick and he braced himself against it, slowing its advance to a crawl, every muscle straining, a human wedge.

"Climb up onto me, dude," said Nick through clenched teeth.

Will jumped up and grabbed on to Nick's rigid middle, which felt like banded steel, pulling himself up and over his torso.

"Hurry up," grunted Nick.

Will got to his feet on Nick's back, using him as a plank, and stepped off him onto the top of the moving block. From there he jumped over onto the wall where Ajay and Elise were waiting.

"Get out of there, Nick," said Elise.

Nick needed to bend his knees now to stay wedged in between the walls, but he was also no longer trying to hold them apart. He slowly contracted his stance and waited until the walls moved within a yard of each other. Then he pushed off with his feet as he let go with his hands and jumped onto the moving block. From there he scampered onto the top of the inside wall, opposite the others, shaking the tension out of his arms and legs.

"Now I know what a panini feels like," he said. "I shoulda just jumped down the hole."

"No, you shouldn't have," said Will. "And we'd better keep moving."

He led the others along the top of the left wall, while Nick kept pace with them atop the right. They reached the arch above the entrance to the central building together. Larger and much grander than the one they'd encountered earlier, more elaborate versions of the same eroded carved faces and figures they'd seen before spanned the length of this arch as well. Ajay leaned in to take a closer look at them.

"I think some of these are snakes," he said.

"Stop trying to reassure us all the time, will you?" said Elise.

Will knelt down to look at the room below the arch and immediately inside the entrance. A plain, moderately sized chamber, lined with the same stone pavers. A few vines had snaked their way inside but there were no other adornments or features. He saw three staircases, one left and right heading down, and a grander set of stairs straight ahead that led up to a landing and a huge set of double wooden doors, studded with bars and metal rings.

"We need to head down those stairs," said Will, pointing to the set on the right.

"How do we get down from here without spraining all eight of our ankles?" asked Ajay, looking down at the ten-foot drop to the floor.

Before anyone could answer, Nick unfurled his rope, tied one end around the arch, and dropped the coiled end to the floor below. Elise grabbed the rope and shimmied down; then Will and Ajay followed. Nick untied the rope, coiled it back up, and stuck it in his pack; he then swan-dived off the wall, tucked, somersaulted once, hit the ground and tumbled forward, and rolled up into a perfect landing on his feet.

"Show-off," muttered Ajay.

"Like you're not?" asked Elise.

"Not *physically*."

"Which way, Will?" asked Nick, looking at the side staircases. "Right or left?"

Will waited and let the answer come to him. "Doesn't matter. Coin flip. They both lead to the same place."

He immediately started toward the right stairs.

"Actually, science has determined that a flipped coin is not strictly a fifty-fifty proposition," said Ajay. "Surprisingly, the coin will return to whichever side you're holding faceup in your hand before it is flipped, exactly fifty-one percent of the time."

"Fascinating," said Nick, and then he stifled a big yawn.

Will led the way down. The stairs were broad and steep, fashioned from the same smooth stone blocks that had been used to build the rest of the structure. They reached a landing twenty steps down; then more stairs doubled back down the other way. They all reached for their flashlights before they descended the second set; Ajay also fixed a device with a strap around his forehead, like a miner's helmet, and switched it on. Peering ahead, Ajay led the way and they slowed their pace as the darkness grew around them.

"Does any of this seem familiar, Will?" asked Elise.

"Not yet."

"But you're positive Coach is down here, right?" asked Nick.

"More than fifty-one percent," said Will. "Less than a hundred."

They reached another landing. The stairs grew more slippery here, moisture seeping in around the stones, leaving a thin layer of scum or moss on the walls.

"We're descending into the swamp itself," said Ajay, moving his twin beams around to examine everything closely. "There's repulsive muck all over the walls, but a section of the stairs is fairly clean right down the middle, which would indicate they're used fairly frequently."

"Yeah, who wouldn't want to climb down under a swamp?" said Nick. "Fun for the whole family."

"You think the Makers built this?" asked Elise.

"This all suggests a relatively robust and developed social organization or, daresay, civilization," said Ajay. "Well beyond the Neolithic, perhaps shading toward bronze or even Iron Age development. Most likely employing a monarchal system, probably tribal, involving familial lines of succession."

"What are you yapping about?"

"That is to say, I don't believe the Makers created this. But I would venture to say they most likely created the creatures who created it."

As they turned the corner of the landing, Will shined his light down at the third set of stairs stretching before them. Tendrils of slimy moss hung down from the ceiling, some of them clumping together to form thick webs. The air felt oppressively hot and humid here. Multiple sources of dripping water echoed throughout the chamber. Even here, tendrils of the same creeper vines that nearly wallpapered the outside of the structure had insinuated themselves into the nooks and hollows of the walls and stairs.

Looking more closely, Will noticed that a broad middle section of this entire staircase was missing the layer of scum as well.

"Must be a lot of people using these stairs," he said, taking the first few steps down. "Look how clean they are here, same pattern, straight down the middle."

"Strange," said Ajay. "One would think you'd see footprints, or at least some gaps, but it's like they've been swept halfway clean."

"Maybe they got a janitor," said Nick. "Who does a half-assed job."

"Yeah, that's probably it," said Elise.

"What was that?" said Will.

He stopped. The rest of them stopped. Everyone listened. Nothing but dripping water.

"Now I don't hear it," said Will.

"What was it?" asked Elise.

"I don't know, something faint, kind of in the background. Let's keep moving."

They started down a few more steps, nearing the halfway point of the staircase.

"There it is again," said Will.

They stopped again, all at once. This time they all heard it.

Something brushing or swishing along the stone.

Then it stopped abruptly.

"Where's it coming from?" asked Elise.

"I can't tell," said Will. "Could be above or below us."

"It's both," said Ajay.

Will turned to Elise: *Let's check it out.*

You take high, I'll take low, she answered.

He blinked on his Grid and turned toward the landing above, and he heard Elise send out waves of her echolocation patterns toward the stairs below.

Large heat signatures, half a dozen of them, showed up on Will's Grid, faint through the stone but moving toward them, maybe two staircases above.

It's bad, she said. *Half a dozen of them.*

Same here. But half a dozen of what?

Not sure. But I know why the stairs are so clean. They're not walking. They're slithering.

NINE

WILL'S RULES FOR LIVING #9:
TAKE CARE OF THE MINUTES, AND THE HOURS
WILL TAKE CARE OF THEMSELVES.

"Ajay, stand between us," said Will quietly.

Nick put himself between Ajay and the stairs leading up, while Will and Elise took a step down, leaving Ajay in the middle. The sinister sounds—and figures on the Grid—drew closer to them.

"Move down to the next landing," said Will, now whispering. "In the corner, where we can see both sets of stairs."

They edged down the last few steps to the landing and took up position in the corner, looking both ways.

"Am I going to need my hatchet?" whispered Ajay.

"Unless you've got something more effective," said Will, his mind racing to calculate their next move. It came to him quickly.

I'm going to make a run down there and try to draw the ones on that level away from us, he sent to Elise.

Check.

Can you make the ones above us think we're somewhere else? Anything to buy some time?

I'll try. What do you think they are?

I'll let you know. And I'll try to get a line on where they've stashed Jericho. I think he's close.

Got it.

"Ajay, Nick, stay with Elise," Will whispered. "I'll be right back."

Will shined his light down at the next staircase; it turned out to be the last set of stairs, and it emptied out into what looked like an open, flat plaza with the same stone floors. The heat signatures appeared to be on that level, somewhere out in the darkness beyond, still more than fifty yards away. Nick put a hand on Will's arm and clamped down.

"Dude, you sure?" asked Nick.

"Yes."

Will nodded to Elise and turned off his flashlight. As he blinked the Grid back on and took the first step down the stairs, he heard Elise throw a vocalization up and around the corner: a perfect impression of some big cat's echoing, menacing roar. Will looked back in that direction and noticed that the heat signatures above them had stopped.

"Good Lord, that even scared *me*," whispered Ajay.

"Yeah, like *that's* hard," said Nick; then he craned his head around to Elise. "Wait, that was *you*?"

"Duh," said Elise.

Will took a deep breath and flew down the stairs. He stayed to the center, where he knew the footing was good, and once he hit the flat of the plaza, he realized that the stones were clean here, too. Firm traction. Good.

And ahead of him, *lots* of slithering.

He stopped dead, opened his senses to soak up impressions from all around him, and immediately sized up what he was facing:

The plaza, as deep as it was broad, appeared square, and as near as he could tell, it ran the full length and width of the stone complex above. He saw four ways out: the stairs they'd just used, two arched tunnels leading down on the wall to his left, and another staircase corresponding to and identical to the one they'd come down straight ahead on the far side of the plaza.

Some kind of structure occupied the dead center of the room: round, maybe ten feet across, with a wall about three feet high around some kind of opening.

Maybe a pit.

Bright spots of lights—torches, he realized—burned in brackets all around the wall. To the right of the circular wall stood a strange structure, like a slightly angled funnel, that ran from the ceiling and emptied into an opening in the plaza floor.

Maybe the end of the tunnel below the trapdoor they'd encountered above.

Farther to the right stood the only opening along the right-hand wall, a massive archway that led away into an ominous, inky darkness.

Will's eyes picked up movement and more light.

Six heat signatures were sliding past the pit, separating, three moving to either side. One in each group carried a torch. He flicked off the Grid and got his first look at them.

His first thought was *snakes*, but no, they looked too broad and muscular and they had arms holding the torches. They were also all holding weapons, spears and swords and axes, so the word that came to his mind next was *snake-men*.

They were tall, well over six feet, gliding along on thick, powerful trunks that undulated back and forth with a sinuous, nauseating grace.

The hard, gray stalks of their scaled torsos flared up into thick, hooded necks—a cobra look—that thrust their flat, vile heads and sharp faces forward. When they opened their mouths, Will saw fangs and forked tongues. Hybrids indeed, but the question was, with what? Something human was definitely in their features, and it informed their gleaming black intelligent eyes, but Will didn't have time to give it much thought.

He ran straight at them, pushing himself to top speed in a few strides, and the move threw them. They hesitated, some kind of communication passing between them, harsh and guttural barks. Will veered left as he neared them and saw the trio to the left of the wall brace and steady themselves, raising and readying their weapons . . .

. . . and then Will shifted to another gear and blew right by them, guttering the flames of the torches as he passed. The blows they brought down at him hit empty space he'd barely occupied. Will passed by the wall—confirming that it did indeed surround a pit, but he had no time to glance down into it—and didn't slow until he reached the opposite end of the plaza; there, he turned in a wide arc and stopped near the far staircase.

He waited there. The creatures, jabbering at each other, momentarily confused, regrouped into a pack and came after him. They didn't even spread out to try and contain him. No strategy, no sense of shared tactics, just an all-out assault, their eyes glimmering with hate, fueled by a primitive brain-stem rage.

More good news, Will figured: Either they weren't as smart as they looked, or they were used to much more stupid prey.

Will jogged to his left, watching the pack adjust that way; then he feinted more convincingly to his right, and they bit on that move, too. When he'd drawn them far enough toward him, he raced back in a wide arc to his left around them and headed back to the middle of the plaza. This time he slowed just long enough to look down into the pit.

There were bars laid over the opening, a latticework of thick black iron, set deep into the stone wall a foot below the rim. It was pitch-black in the pit, but Will did see torch light glinting off silvery water about twenty feet down, and when he blinked on the Grid he caught a single heat signature moving around.

"Coach, you down there?!"

"Why, were you expecting someone else?"

Jericho's voice echoed up through the stone cylindrical chamber, which Will realized looked like a well. He heard splashing, and when he blinked off the Grid, he thought he saw an arm waving up at him.

"You all right?"

"I'm not hurt, but I'm pretty damn inconvenienced."

A spear zipped right by Will's head—he heard it slice the air—and clattered onto the stones behind him, its iron blade throwing up sparks. Then he heard a lot more slithering. He looked back; the pack was closing on him fast.

"Hang in there, Coach," said Will. "We're coming back for you."

"Well, I don't exactly have anywhere else to go," said Jericho.

Will ran again, back toward the original set of stairs; then he jogged left toward the nearest exit on the left-hand wall, an arch that led somewhere down below. The snake-men tracked his every move and he stayed just enough ahead of them to keep them coming. Twice more they hurled weapons at him—an ax and what looked like a hammer or mace whooshing toward him end over end—and for the second one he had to project out a thought-shield to prevent it from making a serious dent in his head.

I found Jericho, he sent to Elise. *He's down here, like I figured: pit, bars, water.*

That's great, she answered. *Uh, we're a little busy right now.*

He could feel the mental strain she was under coming through.

I'm coming back toward you, Will answered. *Taking the long way around.*

Do what you have to do—

I have a plan.

Of course you do.

Will broke off the connection, let the pack close the gap again, and then sprinted toward the far staircase. This time they were smart enough to spread out behind him, six feet apart, trying to discourage him from turning back. Instead he just ran right up the stairs and stopped on the first landing. He looked back just long enough to make sure they were taking the bait, then ran up to the next landing, and the one after that, and then he was back in the chamber they'd first entered.

He ran straight across to the stairs they'd initially descended, where he paused just long enough to see the creatures crest the top of the stairs behind him; then he headed down.

From below he heard the clash of steel on steel and the grind of steel on stone. He blinked on the Grid and saw a mash-up of heat signatures moving around vigorously.

Nearly there, he sent to Elise. *Bringing more with me.*

Oh for joy, for joy.

Will turned the corner around the final landing. Halfway down the last set of stairs, Nick held one of the snake-men around the throat with his left fist and was punching it repeatedly in the face with his sledgehammer right. The thing was nearly out on its feet. Three more of the beasts were already sprawled out on the stairs, either unconscious or dead, a green sludge flowing from their eyes, nose, and small slits in the sides of their necks that were probably their ears.

"Hey, buddy," said Nick, still throwing punches as Will came into view. "Turns out they're not as tough as they look."

"It's about time!" shouted Ajay.

The last two snake-men had squared off with Elise, with Ajay just behind her. Will could sense that she'd spent a big portion of her reserves already, probably with a blast that took out the three on the stairs.

Ajay was pointing another of his homemade gizmos at the one closest to him. He fired it and a spinning steel disc the size of a circular saw blade flew across and severed its hand. The creature gave out an agonizing bellow as its hand fell off still holding a short sword.

Nick smashed the creature one final time and it slumped to the ground in a limp pile. The last one standing, gripping the stump of its severed hand, turned and tried to slide away up the stairs. Nick followed it up to the landing, pounced on its tail, picked the thing up by the tail, and whipped it around a few times.

At that moment the other group of six snake-men that had been tracking Will turned the corner onto the landing at the top of the next set of stairs. Nick saw them arrive, stopped his spin, planted his foot, and hurled the snake-man through the air at them. The thing's body flew like a Frisbee, whirling and ricocheting violently off the walls, and then it crashed into them.

Will and Elise joined Nick on the landing: Without even thinking about it, Will spontaneously summoned up an image of Lyle Ogilvy in full wendigo form and projected it out at them.

That's a new one, he realized as he watched the image appear and saw them react in fright. *They can actually* see *this one.*

Elise, following his lead—his idea had passed between them without him even having to think about sending it—supplied a convincing accompaniment of the wendigo's horrifying screech.

The six snake-men turned as a group and slithered back up the stairs as fast as their tails could carry them.

"Yeah, you better run!" shouted Nick.

With a warrior's shout, Nick bounded up the stairs after them. Will grabbed his arm, which didn't dissuade him—he was pretty sure Nick was too strong to *physically* stop at this point. So he slipped a thought into Nick's mind, hoping Nick would mistake it as one of his own:

Chasing them would be bad.

Nick stopped and turned to Will.

"Chasing them would be bad," he said.

"I couldn't agree more," said Will.

"Hey, but I got a good name for these ugly bastards," said Nick, turning back and suppressing an impish grin. "*Snake*-ers."

They heard laughter behind them and turned to see Ajay leaning against the wall, doubled over; then he stood back up, laughing so hard he was having trouble catching his breath.

Will shot an urgent look at Elise: *Get him down the stairs. Fast.*

She hurried over to Ajay, put a comforting arm around him, and slowly walked him down to the plaza level. Ajay kept laughing the whole way, gasping for breath.

"I mean it was funny," said Nick, keeping his voice down, "but not that funny."

"He's under a lot of stress," said Will, walking down the stairs after them.

"I guess. To each his own, right? I haven't had this much fun since I snuck into the zoo after dark and jimmied the lock on the monkey house."

"You actually did that?"

"Yeah, well, security nabbed me the second time. Caught a big dose of righteous hell from Pop for that one."

"How'd the monkeys take it?"

"Aw, we got along *great*."

"Why am I not surprised?" said Will as they reached the plaza. "By the way, I found Coach. He's over here."

"Awesome!"

Will jogged past Elise and Ajay—she was whispering in his ear, trying to soothe him, and his laughs had subsided into sporadic giggles—and led Nick toward the circular wall in the center of the space. Nick turned a series of somersaults that got him to the wall just ahead of Will. Nick jumped up onto the wall, leaned over, and peered down through the crosshatched bars.

"Hey, Coach," he said. "How's the water?"

Coach Jericho looked up from below, treading in place. "Why don't you jump in and find out, McLeish?"

Nick chuckled. "Fell for that trapdoor number, huh? Oldest trick in the book."

"We have to hurry," said Will, glancing back at Elise, who was leading Ajay through a series of deep breaths and slow exhales. "Those ones that ran off are probably going for help."

"What, you think there's more of 'em?" asked Nick.

"No, Nick," said Will. "I think twelve of them built everything you see here. This whole complex. All by themselves."

Nick looked around and gave it some thought. "All this? *Nah*."

At that moment, from somewhere way deep on the far right side of the structure, they heard drums. Pounding deep and fast, but with purpose and synchronized rhythm.

Lots of drums.

"See, what'd I tell you? There's *gotta* be more than twelve of 'em," said Nick, slipping off his backpack and taking out his coiled rope. "Don't worry, Coach, I got this."

Then from the left side of the complex, which Will had begun to realize might be even larger than they'd thought, they heard a *second* set of drums.

"That's a call and response," said Ajay, suddenly his calm, rational self again.

Another set of drums kicked in, behind them this time, and a few levels lower.

"They're sounding the alarm," said Will. "Calling in reinforcements."

Nick was securing one end of the rope to the bars near the edge of the wall. "Coach, can't you like turn into an eagle or something and fly out of there?"

"If I could do that," said Jericho calmly, "don't you think I would have done it?"

"An eagle wouldn't fit through the bars anyway," said Ajay.

"Good point. It'd have to be like a hummingbird or a woodpecker or something," said Nick, finishing the knot. "That oughta get the job done."

Nick dropped the rope down through the bars and it unfurled toward Jericho. He grabbed it with both hands and pulled himself out of the water. Nick grabbed the other end and started hoisting him up.

"How is he going to get through the bars?" asked Elise, joining them at the wall and looking down. "They're not wide enough."

"We've been over that already and please leave it to me," said Ajay, rummaging through his pack. "I've brought along a selection of moderately sized explosive charges, and if applied in the proper sequence, I believe I can detonate an appropriately sized hole—"

"I'm pretty sure we won't have time for that," said Will, looking around, his senses tuning in to what was going on in a number of areas throughout the complex.

"I can try, then," said Elise.

"No, Elise," said Will firmly. "You need to save your strength."

Will turned back to the pit and sized up the bars; the two rows formed squares, like a checkerboard, each square less than a foot across. Nick had pulled and Jericho had climbed up to just below the bars. He clung to the rope, shirtless, his taut muscles straining.

"You need to figure this out," said Jericho, looking up at them.

"Coach, you look kind of wrinkled," said Nick, leaning down to look at him more closely. "How long you been in there?"

"And you need to hurry," said Jericho.

"And, dude, no offense, but you don't smell so great either," said Nick. "What is that down there, a sewer?"

"I'm going to bend the bars," said Will. "Stay right where you are, Coach."

"There's something you need to know about these things," said Jericho.

"Give me a second," said Will.

Will closed his eyes, summoned up an extra charge of power from the base of his spine, and felt it ramp all the way up his back, down his arms, and into his hands. He spread his fingers and pointed them at the bars: A thought-form in the shape of a turnbuckle appeared just where he visualized it and he inserted it in between the bars just to the right of where Jericho clung to the rope.

Mentally turning the gears of the turnbuckle, Will focused

and applied its expanding force to the bars on either side . . . and slowly each bar began to give, bending right and left, yielding with a rusty creak.

"What are you doing, Will, and exactly how are you doing it?" asked Ajay, wide-eyed.

Ignoring the question, Will paused to gather his mental energy again, then spent it all in a final burst that wedged the bars another few inches apart until they were nearly touching the next square over. Drained by the effort, Will nearly collapsed onto the wall, and the thought-form between the bars vanished with a snap.

"Give me your hand," said Nick, thrusting his arm down through the opening.

Jericho grabbed hold of Nick's forearm with his hand, let go of the rope, and swung over until he was positioned below the opening.

"The drums stopped," said Elise, looking up and around. "Is that good or bad?"

"I vote bad," said Ajay.

"Maybe their arms got tired," said Will, looking around.

Nick slowly lifted Jericho through the opening. First his head cleared, then the arm Nick was holding. But Jericho's left shoulder bumped into the bars, more than a few inches shy of clearing them.

"Can you make it?" asked Nick.

"Not without dislocating his shoulder," said Ajay.

"Look away for a second," said Jericho sharply. "All of you."

"Why?" asked Nick.

"Don't argue with me, just do it," said Jericho.

"Do as he says," said Will.

Nick and the others looked away. Will closed his eyes but first blinked on the Grid; he had recently learned he didn't even need his eyes open for the Grid to function now. He saw Jericho's heat signature drastically change shape into something short and sleek, about the size of a small dog.

Nick reacted with a start, feeling a radical change in the arm he was holding.

"Dude, what the fritz was that?"

Will saw Jericho's smaller heat signature slip easily through the bars, hop over the wall, and flop onto the ground. Then it almost instantly expanded, in every direction. When Will opened his eyes again, Coach Jericho was lying on the ground next to Nick, panting and shivering.

Nick was staring back and forth from Coach Jericho to his own hand. "What in the name of Carl Yastrzemski was that?"

"That's what I *thought* I saw in the lake," said Ajay, almost to himself. "When he was coming ashore."

"Dude, I felt fur," said Nick, "and . . . and a tiny wet little flipper."

"What's the matter, Nick, haven't you ever held hands with an otter before?" said Elise.

Jericho looked up at her and winked. Elise knelt down and offered him a couple of PowerBars and water from her canteen. Nick untied and recoiled his rope, still shaking his head.

"He's actually, absolutely, positively a real shaman," said Ajay, still almost whispering.

All around them, and much closer, the drums began again.

"What did you want to tell us, Coach?" asked Will.

Jericho took a long pull from a canteen, then wiped the excess off his chin. "They're cannibals."

"Oh, really," said Ajay, looking suddenly woozy.

"Good to know," said Nick.

"How do you know that?" asked Elise sharply.

"They said they were going to eat me," said Jericho, matter-of-factly.

"You could understand them?" asked Ajay.

"They made their intentions perfectly clear."

"So what the hell were you swimming in down there," said Nick, making a sour face and looking at the pit, "marinade?"

"There's no accounting for taste," said Jericho.

"Where did you come into the zone?" asked Will.

"In the swamp," said Jericho, getting to his feet and stretching his long limbs. "Not far from here. This structure was the first big thing I saw. I worked my way toward it, and then—yes, McLeish—I fell through the damn trapdoor. I slid down some kind of slick tunnel that dumped me into that hole. Then the water started pouring in. It's been a fun couple of hours."

"Just curious, how did you *know* they were going to eat you?" asked Nick.

"Let's just say it didn't require a human-to-snake-man dictionary."

"For God's sake, what does that matter?" said Ajay to Nick, annoyed. "The point is if Coach was going to be the main course, now we're all part of the buffet."

"We have to get out of here," said Jericho. "Now."

"Something's coming," said Will, getting back on his feet, his energy feeling more fully restored.

Noise, energy, and bright flickering lights were issuing from the cavernous opening in the wall on the plaza's right side. Will recognized the harsh guttural barks of the snake-men, and this time it sounded like there were too many to count. The drums were moving with them, pounding out an angrier, more menacing beat.

"They're over this way, too," said Elise, pointing back to the stairs.

More lights and the side-winding sounds of approaching snakes were coming down both of the staircases at either end of the plaza.

"Oh my freakin' gawd," said Nick, staring at the large tunnel.

The lights—torches in the hands of dozens of the snake-men—were casting forward onto the walls of the wide passage the wavering shadow of something moving with them. Something at least twenty feet tall and as thick as a towering oak, swaying and bobbing in that same, familiar hideous way.

The shadow of a gigantic snake-man.

"Guess the big dog gets to eat first," said Jericho.

"Check, please," said Ajay.

"That is no dog," said Nick.

"Get ready to run," said Will, lowering his voice. "And do exactly as I say."

TEN

WILL'S RULES FOR LIVING #10:
WHEN VISITING A FOREIGN LAND, IT IS ALWAYS
WISE TO OBSERVE AND ABIDE BY THE CUSTOMS
OF THE LOCAL CULTURE. UNLESS THEY'RE TRYING
TO EAT YOU.

The first war party poured into the plaza from the staircase to their left, twenty-five or thirty of them. Torches held aloft, armored with thick, scaled leather and chain mail and armed to the teeth. A trio of drummers brought up the rear, wearing drums slung around their hips, pounding out a martial beat.

A second party, about the same size, spilled out of the right staircase moments later. All of them looked bigger, tougher, and at least twice as strong as the creatures they'd first encountered. Both parties halted at a single commanding gesture from a leader at the front of each pack, each of them half again bigger, tougher, and stronger-looking than the rest of their platoon—officer-class material.

"They don't look much like the ones we fought earlier," said Elise.

"We probably ran into the types who maintain the temple," said Will.

"Janitors," said Jericho.

"Or the ones who do the cooking," said Ajay, settling in behind Nick.

"Wimps," said Nick, disappointed. "We fought the wimps."

"This is their warrior class," said Jericho.

With a precision that would have rivaled any military, both parties spread out in front of the staircase and took up defensive stances.

"Why aren't they coming at us?" asked Nick.

"They're disciplined," said Jericho.

"Their orders are to guard the exits," said Will, turning back to the large passage behind them. "Keep us boxed in. For the main attack, from there."

At that moment, the larger party broke out of the cavern. There were at least a hundred in this group, urged on by a dozen drummers. More soldiers spread out to either side, where they set up precise formations, weapons poised to advance. Most of them wore shinier armor and carried long, lethal-looking spears, and they held large rectangular shields, like the imperial guard of a Roman phalanx.

Once they were in position, the star of the show arrived, writhing out of the shadows with a supple grace that belied its extraordinary size. Twenty feet seemed about right, thought Will, as tall as a two-story house. Its arms had the size and definition of tree trunks, armored at wrist, bicep, and shoulder with bands of iron. It carried a gleaming golden trident at least twelve feet long and as thick as a flagpole, the business end of each blade festooned at the base with a trio of cruel-looking hooks. A leather-studded hood adhered to its long angular face like a glove, and a round band of what looked like gold circled the crown of its head.

"King Mamba," said Nick.

But Will sensed this fearsome creature didn't rule by size alone, as if that wasn't enough. A foul, keen intelligence radiated from its oval reptilian eyes, which sought them out from across the room, using the force of its gaze as a blunt instrument. A long red tongue slithered out toward them a few times, maybe four feet, tasting the air.

Searching for fear, Will thought. *Like any snake, it can taste it.*

The curve of its long mouth already angled toward a grin, but Will thought it took on an added degree of sneer as it sized them up.

"It's trying to scare us," said Jericho.

"Working," said Ajay, his voice quivering.

The snake king took in a deep breath and flared out its hooded neck with a snap, like a parachute opening.

"I don't suppose you could speak nicely to it," said Ajay, hiding behind Nick. "Like you did with the daisies."

Will did give it a try, sending out a mental probe in the snake king's direction. He saw the monster tilt its head to one side as the probe approached. Curious, momentarily, then annoyed, like it had just noticed a gnat.

The thing summoned up some strange source of eldritch energy. Blinking on the Grid, Will saw a thin veil take shape all around the monster's head like a protective barrier, and then his probe vanished, just as if that gnat had been vaporized by a bug zapper.

"No luck," said Will; then he turned to Elise.

I want you to try something. I know you've never done it before and you probably think you can't pull it off. But I need to ask you to try.

Then he told her what he had in mind. Elise looked at him skeptically.

That's not happening.

Yes, it is. If you can do this, you can do that. You take the one on the right. I'll tell you when.

The snake king raised his trident and issued a harsh stream

of orders to the two war parties. While it continued to harangue them, Will turned to his friends, who were all staring at the giant snake.

"Everybody ready?" asked Will.

"As we're ever going to get," said Jericho.

Will sent Elise another message:

Let 'em have it.

They both turned toward the two war parties guarding the front of the stairs. Both concentrated hard and shot the same thought commands at the leaders of the two packs: images, arranged in specific order, one after the other, like a rebus.

Will saw the thoughts land and take immediate effect. The two captains growled and whipped their heads around from their leader and the humans in front of them to their opposite number in the other war party:

That's your enemy, there. Disguised as some of us. Bad bad. Attack attack. Kill kill.

And other vivid word pictures to that effect.

Both captains pointed at each other, raised their weapons, and charged across the plaza at each other, barking out orders and frothing at the mouth. Shocked, but pulled along by their blind adherence to the chain of command—helped enormously, Will thought, by an almost laughably low threshold of intelligence—both war parties followed, albeit with slightly less enthusiasm than their leaders, at least initially.

Their lingering reluctance vanished the moment the two captains savagely collided with a crash near the middle of the room, their swords clashing and clanging, and both parties tumbled after them into a lethal melee, chopping and hacking at each other. From that moment on, training, instinct, and bloodlust took over.

Elise watched for a moment, then turned to Will with no small amount of amazement.

It worked. I can do it, too.

I told you so.

The snake king stared at this spectacle in astonishment. He'd obviously been expecting them to attack, but in a radically different direction.

"Now," said Will.

Ajay and Nick broke toward the stairs on the left, and Will followed closely behind, skirting the edges of the fight in front of them. Jericho and Elise ran toward the stairs on the right.

Not one of the savages in that scrum in the middle paid the slightest attention to them. As both groups reached the base of the stairs, they heard a deafening shout: the snake king laying down the law. He pounded the staff of his trident into the ground and his shout echoed through the chamber like a crack of thunder.

The shock wave had the desired effect: The two captains and their war parties snapped out of their mesmerized state and stared at each other in amazement, as if to say, *How the bleep did this happen?*

Will pushed Ajay ahead of him to the landing and then hesitated long enough to look back and see the snake king wave his trident forward and shout out another slightly less thunderous command that wasn't hard to translate:

Kill them, you idiots!

The war parties, many of them wounded and limping, refocused their wrath on the two groups of humans who just now were disappearing around the first landing of the stairs and gave chase. Will stayed behind one additional beat as Ajay and Nick ran ahead, just long enough to see the rest of the king's army rush forward from the tunnel with a bloodcurdling cry, all of them now in pursuit, while the drummers charging behind them went into overdrive.

Don't stop for any reason, Will sent to Elise. *Until we're back in the swamp.*

The war parties and the regiment behind them split into two groups to follow them, just as Will had figured they would. He picked up his pace and raced to the top of the stairs just as Ajay and Nick were getting there, Ajay slowing down to reach back and grab something out of his pack.

Elise and Jericho were already waiting under the archway above the passage leading out to the maze.

"Go, go, go!" shouted Will, urging Nick and Ajay along as he came up behind them.

They followed the others through the archway into the maze, but Ajay slowed even more between the stairs and the exit to carefully scatter a few handfuls of small objects he took from a pouch.

"What the heck are you doing?" asked Jericho as he waited by the arch.

"There's no point in bringing these things along if I don't get a chance to use them," said Ajay.

"What are they?" asked Will.

"Explosives, a few shrapnel bombs, some tear gas, and a few that throw out a weaponized spray of hydrochloric acid when you step on them," he said cheerfully. "A real mixed bag of Halloween treats."

Ajay scattered the last of his little booby traps—they looked like clusters of nuts and bolts crossed with multi-colored gumballs—then scampered out under the archway after the others.

"Coach, take the lead. Get everybody past the trapdoor!" Will shouted. "Elise, stay with me."

Will stopped with Elise on the far side of the archway and turned back to the entrance. They tensed and waited until they could hear the clamor and slithering of the approaching warriors charging up both stairways.

"Now," he said.

Will covered his ears. Elise took a deep breath, leaned forward with her arms bent back, and sent a howling shriek through the mouth of the entrance. Will heard and felt it bounce off the stones, echoing back and forth in the enclosed chamber, shock waves reverberating so powerfully that the stones themselves seemed to tremble, and then the sound rushed out through the only places it found to escape—down both sets of stairs. They heard screams and shouts from the stairwells as the shock wave crashed into the leading edge of both ascending columns.

"Now get going," said Will.

"What about you?" asked Elise, bent over and panting for air.

"I'll be right behind you."

Elise squeezed his hand and hurried out into the maze. Will took a few steps after her into the passageway, turned, looked up, and focused his mind on the long snake carving in the center of the immense stone archway. He summoned up another powerful mental charge—shaping it this time into the form of a cannonball—and sent it hurtling at the keystone of the arch.

As the thought-form made impact, the archway reared and buckled at its midpoint. The whole structure trembled and then the artful masonry around it collapsed as the central stone gave way. The entire structure dropped to the ground, raising a cloud of dust and burying the entrance to the building with a thick wall of debris.

Will turned and staggered away into the maze, dizzy and light on his feet. A stream of blood gushed from his nose, and he wiped it away on his sleeve. He wasn't sure if he was feeling the effects of just this particular exertion or if the whole encounter was starting to exact a cumulative toll, but he knew his reserve was close to running out.

From inside, on the far side of the pile of debris, he heard a series of small explosions detonating, followed by a series of screams and shouts of pain and alarm and then the slightest whiff of some acrid gas. The survivors of the sound blast had made their way up into Ajay's Halloween minefield.

Will turned the first corner into the maze and headed for the turn around the trapdoor.

A few turns ahead of him, Elise and Ajay had caught up to Nick and Coach. Ajay was taking a certain amount of pride in pointing out that they were quickly negotiating their way back through the maze by following the fluorescent pink tags he'd left behind on their way in.

"See," said Ajay to Nick. "I told you that you'd thank me later."

At that moment, just as Will was trying to summon up the strength to make the jump across the trapdoor paver, an enormous explosion erupted from the front of the structure behind him.

Will turned back to see debris from the pile they'd created there soaring into the air in every direction—he had to dodge a large block of stone that landed, skipped, and caromed off the wall near his feet, ending up on the next paver beyond him that activated the trapdoor. That was followed a moment later by a deafening bellow of rage, and he realized what had happened.

The snake king had reared up to its full height and smashed through the barricade at the entrance, its head and hooded neck rising up and towering above the walls behind Will, looking around for the intruders.

Jericho and Nick heard the commotion behind them; Nick quickly hopped up on top of the nearest wall, looked back, and saw the giant serpent rise up the maze. The snake king spotted Nick on the wall almost as soon as he appeared and surged forward. But instead of following the winding path of the maze, he simply used the bulk of his enormous trunk as a battering ram and burst through the nearest wall, forging the straightest line between two points and heading right toward Nick.

"Oh, mama," said Nick.

"What is it?" asked Jericho down below.

"King Mamba's coming, and he is royally pissed."

As the snake king passed by, Will tried to blend into the wall behind him, feeling the sharp edge of the network of vines digging into his back.

The rasp of their bark gave rise to an idea that began to take shape in the back of his mind. He now recognized the peculiar itch this feeling generated—*intuition* again—although this time he sensed his mind needed more time to roll it around before it would come fully to life.

But the snake king passed by his position without noticing him, intent on some other target farther ahead in the maze, most likely his friends. Will stepped back, took a running leap, and cleared the open trapdoor. Then he accelerated to the top speed he could manage—dizziness still affecting his balance—and whipped around and through the corners of the maze.

As he rounded the first turn, the gigantic enraged snake smashed through another wall only a few yards to Will's right. Glancing back through the ruins it left in its wake, Will saw the remnants of the king's elite regiment—still at least forty soldiers—picking their way over and through the rubble at the entrance, trying to follow their leader.

A few turns ahead, Jericho called up to Nick, "Draw him away! Don't do anything stupid!"

"Fat chance," said Ajay.

Nick launched a series of insulting gestures and sounds toward the onrushing monster, then scampered away to the right, running along the narrow top of the wall as if it were the middle of a street.

The snake king heard and saw Nick moving away to the right and slightly altered its course to give chase, smashing through another couple of walls in its path.

"Get behind me," said Jericho to Ajay and Elise. "And close your eyes."

"Not that again . . . ," said Ajay.

"Do as I say if you want to live," said Jericho.

They did as he said. The sound and fury that erupted within a few feet of them momentarily rivaled the tumult the big snake was causing behind them. Both Ajay and Elise felt a burst of heat, and then the acrid odor and bristling presence of a wild beast filled the air right next to them. When they opened their eyes, they could hardly see past what appeared to be the world's largest grizzly bear immediately in front of them.

A booming gravelly voice, only remotely recognizable as Jericho's, burst from its jaws with a ferocious growl: "CLIMB ONTO MY BACK! HURRY UP!"

The bear bent down on all fours, immense bands of muscle rippling under its fur. Elise immediately jumped onto him, but Ajay froze, gaping at the bear a moment longer.

"NOW, AJAY!"

Ajay vaulted forward like he'd been poked with a cattle prod. Elise grabbed and pulled him up beside her onto the bear's back, and they scrambled farther on top, just below his shoulders.

"HANG ON! AND KEEP YOUR HEADS DOWN!"

Both of them grabbed handfuls of fur, held on as tightly as they could, and lowered their heads. Nearby, they all heard the giant snake smash through another section of wall; when Ajay turned his head, he could see the top of the thing's body moving off to the right but with only a few sections of the maze left standing between them.

Will raced through the turns behind them, desperately trying to catch up. As he rounded the next corner, he caught a glimpse of the bear with Elise and Ajay clinging to its back as it made the turn and headed around the other way.

Wow, thought Will, not even immune to wonder under this kind of pressure. *Coach went full-on bear.*

Nick didn't turn around until he reached the far right side of the maze with only swamp ahead of him, and when he looked back, he saw the giant snake wading its way through the maze toward him, knocking down one wall after another as it advanced. Nick jumped up and down and waved his arms.

"OVER HERE, SNAKE EYES! COME AND GET ME, YOU BIG, UGLY BASTARD!"

They were in a long section of passageway that faced the swamp, so Jericho—or simply "the bear," as Elise and Ajay both perceived it; it was a challenge to hold the thought of this giant beast as "Coach Jericho" while they were riding on his back—turned and galloped back along to the next turn, then swung around and sprinted toward the wall straight ahead.

Elise raised her head and looked up just long enough to

realize what the bear was about to do and sent to Will, *Oh God, Will, he's going straight through the wall.*

Will spun around the next turn just in time to see the big bear lower his head and smash through the wall in front of him. The stones seemed to more or less vaporize on impact and the bear hardly lost a step as he powered through the gap he had created and headed on the same line for the next wall ahead of them, with Elise and Ajay hanging on for dear life. Will scrambled after them.

At the sound of the bear smashing through the second wall, the snake king stopped and looked away from Nick to his left. Nick saw a cloud of dust and debris rising from that area of the maze. The snake king turned again and focused its fury back in that direction. It picked up speed, flattened another few walls along the way, and raised its trident.

"HEY, FANG-FACE, WHERE YA GOING?" he shouted, then muttered when it kept charging away, "Great, a giant snake with ADHD."

In the wreckage behind the snake, Nick could also now see the remaining soldiers that had followed the big mamba into the maze. About a third of the original force appeared to have regrouped and were rushing through the rubble, trailing their leader by no more than a few seconds now. Larger groups of soldiers were spreading out into other sections of the maze, and he noticed more than a few of them were activating secret passages that let them bypass whole sections of the maze uninterrupted.

"Aw crap," said Nick.

Will continued running behind the bear, cruising over the rubble of the first wall. As he hurdled over the crumbled remains of the second, he realized that the snake king was headed back their way and was only a couple of sections away on his right. For the first time, he was close enough to smell the thing, and it wasn't a scent he would soon forget—metallic, dominated by the tang of rancid blood and the smothering scent of ammonia.

He could also hear the shouts and roars of the trailing soldiers in the near distance behind it and, even more distressingly, all around him. The big snake had taken down so many walls by this point that his minions were quickly closing the gap.

Then the idea that had first taken shape in Will's head back at the trapdoor presented itself, fully formed.

That's it.

He immediately threw a thought to Elise: *Get out of the maze as quickly as you can. Straight line.*

Elise leaned forward and shouted as loudly as she could into the bear's left ear: "WILL SAYS TO KEEP GOING STRAIGHT AND GET US OUT OF HERE FAST!"

"OH, DOES HE?" roared the bear, turning to look back at her. Elise saw that the bear's head was bleeding and bruised in many places. "WHAT DOES HE THINK I'M DOING NOW?"

"I MUST SAY I THINK IT'S AN EXCELLENT IDEA," added Ajay, flopping up and down with every stride like a bull rider coming out of his saddle.

"THEN WHY DON'T YOU GENIUSES TRY SMASHING THROUGH A FEW WALLS?"

"OKAY," shouted Elise. "MAYBE I CAN HELP."

Looking ahead, she saw the next wall in their path fast approaching. Elise focused, drew in a deep breath, and blasted out a cone of sound ahead of them. It cracked the stones and then completely smashed through the wall just as they reached it. The bear lowered his head for an impact that never came; the wall was already gone. As they passed through, the bear threw back his head and Elise and Ajay felt a deep vibration rumbling through the bear's back; they realized the bear was laughing.

But if this is going to work, thought Will, *I've got to get out of the maze, too.*

Will watched them pass through another wall, then dug down deep into his reserves and put on a burst of speed faster than any he'd ever remembered being able to reach before. He shot past the lumbering bear, catching a glimpse of Elise and Ajay gaping at him as if they were a frozen snapshot, and realized he was heading straight at another wall himself with no time to change course. Above him and to the right he saw the snake king out of the corner of his eye, nearly level with them now and only one last wall standing between them.

Just beyond the snake, Will saw Nick rushing toward them along the top of a wall, shouting and waving his arms, trying to pull the snake's attention away from his friends back toward him.

In the passageway just below the wall that Nick was traversing, a group of five soldier snakes turned a corner, slithering in the same direction. They hadn't even looked up and seen him yet.

"Yo, butt uglies!" shouted Nick. "Up here!"

All five soldiers looked up at him together, then stopped and hurled their spears at him. Nick contorted and twisted his body every which way, even doing a stationary somersault, which caused the first four spears to narrowly miss him. The fifth he plucked out of the air by the shaft, twirled around a few times—mostly for show—and shouted back down at the snakes: "Thanks for the spear, suckas!"

Nick resumed sprinting along the top of the wall and hopped over to the next one as the soldier snakes angrily hissed and jabbered, falling quickly behind in the maze. Nick was approaching the snake king's right flank now, and it hadn't spotted him yet . . .

. . . intent as it was on the oversized bear rampaging through the maze below and to its left. As it surged forward, the snake king raised its silver trident and hurled it down toward the bear.

Ajay, glancing back from the bear's back, saw the trident leave the snake's hand and hurtle toward them. Will looked up just long enough to see it coming, too. He jumped, turned his body around, too late to slow down, and in midair pulsed a thought-form at the speeding trident.

"STOP NOW!" shouted Ajay in the bear's ear.

The bear tried to slam on the brakes, but the pads of his feet kept skidding along the smooth pavers. Will's thought-form glanced off the trident, altering its physics just enough to knock it off its deadly trajectory by a fraction of a degree.

Then, in rapid order, Will slammed into the wall ahead of him and dropped to the ground, stunned. The bear finally came to a stop three feet away from him . . . and the three points of the gigantic trident descended just between them, burying themselves deep into the stone.

Will rose to his feet, still wobbly, trying to shake off the impact. The bear looked at him around the shaft of the trident and he heard a deep fun-house version of Coach Jericho's voice boom out of the bear's mouth:

"WHICH WAY NOW, WEST?"

Will's eye was drawn up and behind the bear. The snake king was closing in on them. He quickly turned to the open passage to their left, where he caught a glimpse of one of Ajay's fluorescent pink arrows on the wall.

"That way!" Will shouted.

The bear started running.

"Will, jump up!" shouted Elise.

She held out her hand as they passed and Will took it and swung up to join them, landing alongside them with barely a moment to grab on to some hanks of hair before the bear was sprinting full tilt down the long corridor ahead of them.

Just behind them, the snake king reached down and yanked its trident out of the stones with a yowl. It rose up, let out a furious shout of frustration, and then barked a string of orders down at its soldiers, which were now swarming all over what was left of the maze. The snake king was just about to rush forward and make another stab at the bear with the annoying little creatures on its back when it heard a scream behind it.

That was Nick, running up just behind it on the wall, and he let the spear go as he finished the scream. The snake king whipped around and used its trident like a hockey goalie's stick to harmlessly deflect the spear away. Then it glowered at Nick for a moment, apparently having a hard time believing that one of these puny creatures actually had the audacity to attack it with anything.

"Oh, shit," said Nick.

The king's anger erupted; the snake leaned down, unhinged its jaws, revealing tusk-sized fangs, and roared at Nick with an earsplitting bellow that felt like it was going to melt his face and flattened a few of the damaged walls behind him.

Nick turned and scampered back the way he'd come along the wall toward the right side of the maze. The snake king stormed after him, caught up in a mindless berserker rage.

Elise looked up from the back of the moving bear and saw the snake king moving after Nick. "IT'S HEADING AWAY AGAIN."

"KEEP GOING, PLEASE!" shouted Ajay into the bear's other ear. "THESE ARE MY MARKS ON THE WALL. WE'RE GOING THE RIGHT WAY. TWO MORE TURNS AND WE'LL BE OUT!"

"HOLD ON!" shouted the bear.

Maintaining most of his speed, the bear skidded around the corner, and Will immediately recognized the final corridor and archway ahead of them as the one that would finally take them back out to the swamp.

Except that the far end of the passage was packed with a thick column of angry snake soldiers who saw them and rushed forward, giving out a fearsome war cry, their spears raised to attack.

"DON'T STOP!" shouted Will. "DON'T STOP FOR ANY-THING!"

"IF YOU SAY SO," the bear growled; then he lowered his head and accelerated straight at them.

Will looked over at Elise, hanging on for dear life next to him. *Do you have anything left?*

She looked right back at him with a challenge. *Show me what you got.*

Both turned to face the charging warriors. Will took in a deep breath. He heard Elise do the same.

Will looked up and quickly summoned a thought-form above the corridor: a long flat rectangle almost the exact dimensions of the passageway. Once the projection stabilized, he hurried to "fill" it in with the densest matter he could manufacture.

At the same moment, Elise sent out a narrow, concentrated column of high-frequency sound that poleaxed the warriors' nervous systems. Every one of them stopped in their tracks, half paralyzed, let go of their spears, and grabbed for their ears.

Will dropped his thought-form plank on top of the whole column, which knocked them all to their knees, just as the galloping bear smashed into their forward ranks and carved a swath through the entire company, knocking soldiers aside and bouncing them off the walls like bowling pins. They made it all the way through to the final turn, where they rushed out under the archway and down the path that had originally brought them here, back toward the swamp.

"KEEP GOING," shouted Will in the bear's ear. "TO THE END OF THE WALLS!"

Rising up to look behind them, Elise could see Nick still dodging and dancing around on top of the maze walls as the snake king chased after him.

What about Nick? she sent to Will.

He can take care of himself.

What if he can't?

Will snuck a look back at Nick and saw him hop easily over the snake king's trident as it took a swing at him; then he made a series of rude gestures to the thing's face, which drove it even crazier.

We need to work fast, Will sent to Elise. *Keep those things away from me as long as you can. If this works, I think I'll only need a couple of minutes.*

They had nearly reached the end of the wall, where the swamp ended and the stone path began, and the bear was slowing down.

"THIS IS GOOD," shouted Will.

Will slipped off the bear's back as he came to a halt, landing on the beginnings of the stone path. They were about a hundred yards from the entrance to the maze and none of the soldiers had come out of the entrance after them yet. Elise and Ajay slid down after him, Elise taking a defensive stance on the path between Will and the entrance.

Will moved a few steps away from them, closed his eyes, and knelt down on the stones, in deep concentration.

The bear plopped down on his haunches, shaking his head

a few times, panting for breath, blood running down his face and steam rising off his fur from the exertion.

Ajay couldn't take his wide eyes off the bear, filled with wonder at his size and power, awed by the startling energy his presence radiated.

"Does it hurt?" Ajay asked. "Being in this body, or when you change?"

"YES, IT HURTS LIKE HELL," said the bear, looking at him, exasperated. "YOU KNOW WHAT HURTS MORE?"

Ajay meekly shook his head.

"RAMMING YOUR HEAD THROUGH A SERIES OF STONE WALLS WHILE A BUNCH OF OVERGROWN SIDE-WINDERS USE YOU AS A PINCUSHION."

"I see," said Ajay.

He reached out his hand as if to pet the bear's side, or comfort him.

"DON'T EVEN THINK ABOUT IT," growled the bear.

Ajay pulled his hand back, but he noticed more than a few bleeding wounds in the bear's side and ribs, at least one that looked serious.

"Leave him alone, Ajay," said Elise.

"All right," said Ajay. "But aren't you going to change back now?"

"I FIGURED I'D WAIT A FEW MINUTES. SEE HOW THINGS GO."

"Yes. Good idea—"

Then for the first time, Ajay noticed a thin strap of studded leather around the bear's right shoulder, with a small pouch attached.

"What's the pouch for?" he asked.

"THAT'S WHERE I KEEP MY CLOTHES."

"Oh. Is there a time limit for how long you can stay this way?"

"YES. BECAUSE I GET VERY, VERY HUNGRY. SOME-TIMES SO HUNGRY I CONSIDER EATING CHILDREN."

"Ajay," asked Will, behind him, deep in concentration, eyes closed. "Can you do something to grab the big snake's attention? Maybe pull him off Nick for a minute?"

"I can certainly try," said Ajay, reaching for his pack.

Then Will went deeper inside. Took in a series of expansive breaths until he worked his way back down to the place where he'd first connected with the plants.

An interior location, deep underground.

He felt the same sensation, of the ground dropping away below him, and this time found his way there almost at once, but the space appeared indistinct at first and pitch dark. Moments later, something appeared, swimming up toward him from he didn't know where.

A source of light.

Or maybe, Will realized, it was a being.

It took the form of a round tube, open at the top like a funnel, snaking up toward him out of the ground, or maybe a black void. Oscillating with some kind of electrical force that traveled continually up and down its gently waving length. He studied it; the being didn't seem to be composed of matter at all but was made entirely of energy. Not one that he could identify, like electricity, but more like a spiritual kind.

He knew immediately that it had appeared in response to his reaching out for help. Maybe he'd even invited it to come, although he wasn't entirely sure how he'd done it.

Will transmitted a series of pictures about what he hoped to communicate. He needed their help. The process wasn't easy or quick and he had to concentrate fiercely on each picture, in sequence, as if he were a small child building a sentence. Then he repeated the message, one image after another, finding it slightly easier and quicker the second time around.

The tube stayed right in front of him, weaving back and forth. *Listening* wasn't quite the right word for what it appeared to be doing, but *absorbing* seemed to fit. The edge of the tube folded gently in and out, as if it were taking each image *in*, almost like food.

Then the tube nodded and turned slightly. Four other identical tubes immediately shot up out of nowhere and joined it. All five of them hung in the way before him, swaying in unison. The first tube turned to the others and the others now seemed to "absorb" the message from the first one. He saw energy passing or exchanging between them.

Then the other tubes vanished as quickly as they'd appeared. The first tube turned to face Will again. Once again it seemed to nod.

Then it disappeared instantly as well.

Will opened his eyes. Ajay was standing nearby, holding a flare gun. The bear was still resting. Elise stood on the path, focused on the entrance to the maze.

"I'm ready, Will," said Ajay.

Elise glanced back at him.

Whatever you just did, she sent, *it better work.*

We're about to find out, he answered.

I hope so, 'cause snaky-boys are starting to come around back at the entrance. The whole pack of 'em could come charging out after us at any second.

Will nodded at her. He had to trust this process. He didn't know what else to do. Elise put out her hand and helped pull him to his feet.

"Go ahead, Ajay," said Will. "Fire away."

"I took the liberty, before we left, of slightly modifying the payload," said Ajay. "So, as you'll see, this isn't exactly an ordinary flare—"

"STOP YAPPING AND SHOOT IT ALREADY," said the bear, getting back on his feet.

In the distance to the left, they could see Nick still hopping around from wall to wall and avoiding the snake king's attacks. But he was starting to tire; the swipes and stabs from the thing's trident were getting closer and closer to him.

Ajay pointed the flare gun toward the maze and pulled the trigger. A jet of light arced up over the stone walls and exploded high in the air, just to the right and above the snake king.

A starburst of bright white light immediately grabbed the snake's attention and it whirled away from Nick, looking up at this wonder in the sky.

Will reached out for Nick's mind and sent an urgent message:

Get back to where we first came into the maze. Fast.

Nick whipped his head toward Will and the others, and Will could practically read his thoughts:

Where the heck did that *come from?*

Then Nick noticed that the snake king was distracted by the flare and immediately took off sprinting along the tops of the remaining walls in their direction. The big serpent was so mesmerized that he didn't even notice him go.

As Ajay's flare hung in the air and began to slowly descend, the gloomy perpetual twilight over the swamp turned bright as a desert under a noonday sun. And then this brilliant marvel of light began to change.

At the entrance to the maze, as Elise had warned, the column of snake soldiers had started to trickle out after them again, but now they all quickly turned, stopped, and stared up at the dazzling light show above the maze.

"Wait for it," said Ajay.

Another stage of the flare detonated with a series of loud, staccato bursts, like gunfire. Both the snake king and the soldiers recoiled with fear at the sound. The lights that flowed down from this new eruption organized into an image, in stark white, bright reds, and greens: The gigantic face of an Old Testament deity, bearded and stern, stared balefully down at them. Somehow, a deep rumbling issued from it, as if it were speaking to them—the Voice of God.

Will heard audible gasps from the soldiers near the archways, while the snake king backed away from the image and dropped its trident in fear.

Then, just below the deity's face, a third stage of the flare took shape—the outline of a red neon sign, surrounded by twinkling lights, and then three letters appeared in the middle of the sign, as if an ON switch had just been flipped:

OMG

Elise turned to Ajay. "Really?"

"I couldn't resist," said Ajay.

"How'd you do the voice trick?" asked Will.

"Oh, a timed minor detonation built in by layering the pyrotechnics," said Ajay. "No biggie."

Nick bounded down from the last wall in the maze and splashed through the swamp toward them, just as the dazzling image of the face over the maze began to decay.

The snake king and its soldiers were all still cowering in fear, but there was no telling how long that effect would last once the image disappeared. The snake king reached for its trident again and raised it tentatively, as if to guard itself against the shimmering visage.

"Will?" asked Elise.

"I don't know," he said, looking around anxiously. "I don't know if it's going to work."

"If what's gonna work?" asked Nick as he ran up to join them, shaking himself dry. Then he noticed the bear. "Hey, look at you!"

"CORK IT, MCLEISH," growled the bear.

Then Will heard a strange high-frequency sound rising out of the maze. An eerie keening like a cable being stretched or tightened, or tension gradually ratcheting up through a network of piano wires.

"Ajay, keep your eyes on the maze," said Will. "Tell me what you see."

The sound continued to build until it hurt their ears. Ajay jumped on top of a low stone wall nearby to look back toward the maze and opened his eyes wide.

"What the heck is that?" said Nick, turning back toward the maze.

"Something's moving," said Ajay. "All along the walls—I can't quite make out what it is—"

The bear loped over to him. "HOP ON MY SHOULDER, KID!"

Ajay jumped onto the bear's back and shifted himself onto his shoulder; then the bear stood up to his full height and turned toward the maze. Ajay sat nestled in his right shoulder, as tiny as a doll dwarfed by the giant animal, hanging on to his neck as he gazed intently into the distance.

Above the maze, the last of the flare winked out, and the gloom slowly settled over the swamp again.

"It looks like thousands of snakes, wriggling around," said Ajay, peering intently into the dim distance. "No, wait, that's not quite right—"

"Which part isn't right?" asked Elise.

"They're not snakes; they're the *vines*. They're moving, disengaging from the walls, everywhere . . . they're everywhere."

They could all see some kind of writhing movement throughout the maze now; in some places it was so thick it appeared as if the walls themselves had come to life. Then they started to hear barks and shouts of alarm from the snake-men inside.

"They're attacking—wrapping themselves around the soldiers, taking their weapons—and they're forming webs or barricades at all the exits and entrances, cutting off all the passageways."

Will could now see a latticework of vines spreading out across the entrance to the maze, under the first archway, forming an impenetrable barrier. A couple of snake soldiers threw themselves against it, hacking at it with weapons, trying desperately to cut their way out.

Then the shouts of alarm inside turned to screams and they began to issue from every corner of the maze.

"Oh, good gravy," said Ajay. "This is almost sad. Those repellent reptiles don't stand a chance—"

"What's happening?" asked Nick eagerly.

"I'd rather not go into much detail, if you don't mind," said Ajay, grimacing. "But the vines appear to be able to . . . grow rows of very large, disagreeable thorns, if that makes it any plainer for you."

"Righteous," said Nick.

"OMG indeed," said Elise, looking at Will solemnly.

Will was staring deeper into the maze, where he saw the snake king flailing around wildly, swinging his trident at things Will couldn't see.

"What's going on with the Big Kahuna?" asked Will.

The bear turned slightly, and Ajay shifted his gaze toward the snake king.

"Oh, he's in a serious fix now. He's just dropped his trident. The vines are rooting him to the ground and crawling all over his body, and I mean hundreds of them. He's strong enough to pull some of them off, but he doesn't have enough hands to stop them all. Yes, sure enough, they've got him around the arms now. Pinned them to his sides. Only a matter of time before they—yes, there he goes now. Timber."

The snake king toppled over out of sight, landing with a thud they heard from a quarter mile away.

"The bigger they are," said Nick, "the bigger they fall."

"Or something like that," said Elise.

The screams throughout the maze had all subsided now. But they heard a few last angry bellows from the leader of the monsters before it, too, fell silent.

"Uneasy lies the head that wears the crown," Ajay whispered.

"So that's it, then," said Elise. "We're in the clear."

"Time to go," said Will.

"Hold on, they're not quite finished," said Ajay. "The vines are still moving all around the walls and rocks, everywhere you can see. I'm not exactly sure what they're trying to—Oh, wait, I get it."

"GET WHAT?" asked the bear.

"You'll see," said Ajay. "I don't believe this will take very long."

Moments later, they heard a low rumbling start to build from deep within the maze, but it built quickly into something that sounded alarmingly like a landslide.

"Maybe we oughta move our behinds out of here," said Nick, taking a step back.

"No, it's all right," said Ajay. "Keep watching."

Then they realized that the sound building inside was the crack of breaking stones, thousands of them, all at once, building and building, as if the entire complex before them were being struck with an immense hammer, one blow after another.

The central tower imploded, the remaining walls in every direction collapsing like rows of dominos. Clouds of dust and stone fragments rose everywhere, and when the dust cleared and the echoes of the devastation faded away, all that was left in front of them was an enormous debris field of broken rocks.

The vines had strangled the entire stone temple, and all its carnivorous denizens, to death.

ELEVEN

WILL'S RULES FOR LIVING #11:
IT DOESN'T MATTER HOW YOU DO IT.
IT ONLY MATTERS *THAT* YOU DO IT.

"Well, I'm pretty sure that'll leave a scar on my brain," said Nick, staring at the still-settling pile of rubble.

"You asked the vines to do that?" asked Ajay in amazement from on top of the bear.

"Not in so many words," said Will.

"You think that got them all?" asked Elise, looking around the swamp. "Maybe we shouldn't press our luck and get out of here."

"I don't think we have anything else to fear from them," said Ajay as the bear set him back down on the ground. "Might I suggest we restore ourselves with a bite to eat first and try to get properly hydrated?"

"Yeah, perfect, why not?" said Nick. "There's obviously nothing to worry about here. Let's have a picnic in a frickin' swamp."

"Is it safe, Will?" asked Elise, moving closer to him.

Will blinked on his Grid and surveyed the vast, smoking heap of destruction in front of them. Nothing moved; no heat signatures appeared anywhere in the ruins.

"Right now I'd say this is about the safest place we could find," he said.

"A picnic it is, then," said Ajay, reaching into his pack.

"Although we can do without the ants, please, thank you very much," he said, without trying to imagine what kind of jumbo-sized nightmares *those* might be.

"WAIT HERE FOR ME," said the bear as he stalked off toward a large cluster of mangrove trees.

"Are you going to change back now, Coach?" asked Ajay, taking a few steps after him.

"YES," said the bear without glancing back.

"May I watch?" said Ajay.

The bear turned back, annoyed. "NO, YOU CAN'T WATCH."

"Why not?"

"BECAUSE IT'S SECRET. AND IT'S PRIVATE. AND DID I MENTION THAT IT'S SECRET?"

"You also failed to elaborate on whether there's a time limit for how long you can stay in your different forms."

"AND DID I MENTION THAT IT'S SECRET?"

Ajay stood his ground, undeterred. "Does changing back hurt as much as changing the other way?"

"WORSE. WHY ARE YOU SO DAMN INTERESTED?"

"With all due respect, Coach, how else do you expect me to react? Do you honestly believe I would voluntarily pass up an opportunity to watch a genuine, authentic shaman exercise his ability to shape-shift? Or do you think I've gone quite mad?"

"GO EAT A SANDWICH," growled the bear. "AND MIND YOUR OWN BUSINESS."

The bear stalked off the path, splashed through the water, and disappeared behind the mangrove trees. Ajay watched him go and then reluctantly walked back to join the others, who were laying out their lunch with their backs toward the trees and sitting on the edge of the wall. He sat down to join them, but Will saw Ajay turn and peek back toward the trees a couple of times.

"Ajay," said Will. "Eyes this way."

"Dude, got a rock-solid piece of advice for you," said Nick, chewing a huge bite of his turkey sandwich. "Respect the Bear."

"I do, I assure you. I respect him enormously," said Ajay, taking a sealed plastic container from his pack. "I'm just curious, that's all. Insatiably. About everything. It seems to be another strange side effect of"—he waved his hand all around his head—"all *this*."

"I hear that," said Elise.

"By the way, I could not believe my eyes when I first saw you sitting up on the bear's shoulder," said Nick, and then burst into boisterous song: *"On top of Old Smokey, all covered with—"*

"Hair," said Ajay, anticipating the joke.

"Of course I'm referring to Smokey the Bear." Nick finished the tune, and held out his hand for a fist bump. "Come on, gimme some."

Ajay gave him a halfhearted bump but couldn't hide a smile. He peeled the lid off a plastic container and peered inside. "Well, at least it appears that my quinoa salad survived the trip."

"Whatever 'keen-wa' is," said Nick, "I don't want to know about it."

"What do you think those things were doing here?" asked Elise, looking back at the ruins.

"You mean aside from giving carnivores a bad name?" asked Ajay between bites.

"Why them? Why snake-men?" asked Elise. "What's the point of all this crazy stuff?"

"Don't know yet," said Will.

A sharp cry of pain reached them from behind the

mangroves, then a series of agonized groans that Coach Jericho tried to stifle.

"He wasn't kidding," said Elise.

"Man, he didn't sound like that when he turned into the otter," said Nick, wincing.

"It must be harder to expand than to shrink," said Ajay, chewing away.

"That doesn't make any sense," said Nick.

"It kind of does, if you think about it," said Elise.

Nick thought about it, then shook his head. "No, it doesn't. He's shrinking right now!"

"What difference does it make?" asked Will, annoyed. "He can do it, whatever it is. He told us it hurts, and he said it's secret, so let's just leave it at that for now, okay?"

"Hey, I wasn't the one harassing Coach about it," said Nick.

"I was hardly harassing him," said Ajay defensively.

"Knock it off, both of you," said Elise sternly, pointing a plastic fork at them. "Right now!"

Both Nick and Ajay hung their heads and ate in silence for a while. A few moments later, they heard splashing and looked around to see Coach Jericho, dressed in his black sweats, wading back to them through the ankle-deep water. Will thought about pulling out the silver healing disc from his bag and offering it to Jericho, but he didn't look like he was in pain anymore. He just looked haggard and kind of depressed.

No one said anything when Jericho first sat down to join them, although Ajay was obviously biting his tongue to keep from asking him a thousand questions.

"You hungry, Coach?" asked Will, offering Jericho a sandwich.

"Starving," he said.

"Dude, want me to catch you a salmon?" asked Nick.

Jericho glared at him. Elise punched Nick on the shoulder, hard.

"Ow," said Nick. "Sorry, I couldn't resist."

"And don't call me 'dude,'" said Jericho, biting into the sandwich. "Dude."

"I highly recommend you try the quinoa salad," said Ajay, offering his container to Jericho. "It's an excellent source of protein and carbohydrates. Both of which I suspect you could use in massive quantities about now."

"Thank you," said Jericho, taking it from him.

"To bring you completely up to date, Coach," said Will, taking another big bite of sandwich. "We know where Dave is now."

"Is that right? How'd you find that out?" asked Jericho.

"Same way we found you," said Will.

"He says the *plants* told him," said Nick, leaning in as if it was a secret. "He says he can *talk* to 'em now."

Jericho looked up from his lunch, keenly interested. "Is that true, Will?"

"Well, yeah. Sort of," said Will. "I did communicate with them, but I can't explain *how* exactly."

"Plant spirit medicine," said Jericho.

"What's that?" asked Elise.

"That's how you talk to plants," said Jericho.

"You mean talking to plants is actually a thing?" asked Nick, his mouth hanging open.

"Native people have been practicing it for ten thousand years," said Jericho as he ate. "They say plants have spirits just like the rest of us. Along the way, we forgot that we all speak the same language, once we got 'civilized' and decided we were 'smart.'"

"Smarter than what? Plants?" asked Nick.

"Some of us anyway," said Ajay, glancing at Nick. "And how exactly does one go about doing such a thing?"

"Don't have the slightest idea. I can't keep a house plant alive for a week." Jericho pointed his fork at Will. "Why don't you ask him?"

"I'd be happy to fill you in about that down the road, Ajay," said Will, finishing his sandwich and packing up. "But we have a job to do. Let's move. We can talk as we walk."

"Where are we heading?" asked Ajay.

"Out of this swamp," said Will. "We'll figure the rest out as we go. I don't see any way forward from here, do you?"

Ajay looked around and shook his head.

"So we head back," said Will.

They packed up all their gear, took a last look at what they'd done to the snake-men's civilization, and walked single file out of the swamp along the path they'd followed on the way in.

Ajay and Nick took the lead, then Elise. Will hung at the back to talk to Jericho, who limped slightly and still looked a little worse for wear.

"The thing is, I don't really know how I did what I did back there," said Will quietly. "I talked to a few of them once before we found you. I just decided I wanted to talk to them again, and it happened."

"Good."

Will made sure the others weren't listening; he felt embarrassed to even ask the question but he really wanted to know. "But how *did* I do it?"

"You got out of your own way," said Jericho. "Like I've been telling you for months. It doesn't matter how. Getting hung up on 'how' is just the stupid part of your brain throwing a tantrum because it feels left out."

Will thought that over for a moment. The last of the pavers

had already disappeared underfoot, and they were back walking on dirt again. The swamp seemed to close in around them, the air oppressive and damp. As he looked around at the abundant undergrowth, Will realized he'd never think of plants the same way again.

"Those vines must've really hated the snake-men, too," said Will.

"I don't doubt it. They had their reasons. You just gave them permission."

"Why do you say that?"

"There were big chunks of vines floating around in that soup they had me in. Probably used 'em for seasoning, not to mention firewood, torches, all that stuff."

"So you're saying all this backs up what I got from them, that plants have feelings."

Jericho gazed around at the swamp. "I'm saying I'd go out of my way to make sure we don't do anything that's going to piss 'em off right now. Half the stuff in here looks like it could eat *us*."

"That's truer than you know," said Will. "Coach, I've had this word popping up in my head a lot lately."

"What word is that?"

Will looked at him closely. "*Intuition*."

Jericho looked back at him and smiled slightly. "About time."

"Why do you say that? Tell me. What is it—what does it mean to you?"

"It means you're getting it," said Jericho.

"Getting what? What is *it*?"

Jericho spread his arms out, indicating everything around them. He pointed at the ground, at the trees, at the water, at what they could see of the sky above through the canopy.

"You're saying it's everything," said Will. "And it's every-where. Like the Great Spirit."

"*Wak'an Tanka.* The threads of the fabric that *connects* everything. What we share in common with everything we see and can't see."

"But what does intuition have to do with that?"

"That's your higher mind kicking in. Once you activate your intuition, you're tuning into the fabric. You have your fingers on all the threads. When something pulls over there, you feel it right here."

"But how does it—" Will caught himself before Jericho could even scowl at him. "Hold on, sorry, strike that. What you're saying is that intuition means I'm . . . waking something up. Inside me. Higher mind."

"Yes."

"And that means a different way of thinking. Or knowing. That isn't hung up on 'how.'"

Jericho stopped, put a gentle hand on Will's shoulder, and regarded him thoughtfully. He could count on one hand the number of times the man had touched him before.

"Will, it makes me proud to say that you might just be on the verge of not being a complete idiot."

"Gee, thanks."

"Let's just hope it happens fast enough now to keep the rest of us alive."

Will could see that he was dead serious, underneath the hard time he liked to give him. He could also see that Coach was genuinely concerned; they just might *not* make it through this, unless Will stepped up in some way he didn't even know how to do—

How again. *Damn it.* The habit was so ingrained. He'd really have to work at this.

"One other word occurred to me recently," said Will as they started walking again, trying to keep pace with the others. "I'm not even sure I completely know what this one means."

"Okay."

"*Omniscience.*"

"At least you pronounced it correctly," said Jericho.

"I'm guessing it has something to do with what you said about being aware, except in this case you're aware of everything."

Jericho nodded.

"That must be the end point of this progression, right? So what does it mean if you advance that far? Is that like having *all* your fingers on the fabric?"

Jericho looked up, squinting, considering his answer. No, that wasn't quite it.

"When you reach that point," said Jericho, choosing his words with care, "you and the fabric become . . . indistinguishable."

Will studied him for a second. "Is that where you are, Coach?"

Jericho looked at him like he'd just grown a second head; then he laughed. "Kid, I'm just the messenger. Don't mistake me for the message."

Will's attention was pulled ahead of them; Nick and Ajay had stopped about twenty paces ahead, and they were going at each other again. They were on the outer edges of the swamp, working their way back into the forest they'd left earlier.

"I am telling you, one hundred percent, that this is not the path we came in on," said Ajay. "We came directly out of the heart of that forest, but now it's well off to the right."

"You're cracked," said Nick. "This has to be it. Look around, there's no other way to go."

"Look, I don't know how to explain it, but I promise you the path has changed. It is simply not the same—"

"I wouldn't argue with him about anything he remembers, Nick," said Elise.

"Okay, but how is what he's describing even possible? Are you saying the forest has changed position? I didn't see you spraying leaves on our way in with your little graffiti tag can. How can you be so sure?"

"I don't know how I know," said Ajay, pressing both hands to his forehead. "I just *know*."

Will joined them. "What are you arguing about?"

"Ajay thinks the path has changed," said Elise, standing between them, trying to mediate. "That it's taking us in a different direction now—"

"The path *has* changed," said Ajay. "It's taking us much farther to the left."

"Nick, you're always bragging about your 'most excellent' sense of direction," said Will. "Why don't you stop and think about it?"

Nick nodded reluctantly, turned around, looked out in every direction carefully, and then furrowed his brow. "Okay. Okay, this is freaky. He's right. This isn't the way we came in. I don't even know how I know that either."

Before Ajay could gloat, Elise held up a hand right in front of his face to keep him quiet.

"It doesn't matter how," said Will, pointing ahead. "So we keep going this way, then. Follow the path."

They walked on for another quarter of a mile, at which point they left behind the last damp traces of the swamp and passed through an area of transitional wetlands, where the trees stopped completely. The wetlands ended abruptly as they climbed a well-trodden path up a long, gentle rise covered with native grasses.

Reaching the crest of the hill, they stopped and looked out over the most pleasing and expansive vista they'd yet encountered, a long, wide savannah with softly rolling grasslands, extending out in every direction as far as the eye could see. Although the twilight sky provided no more illumination here than anywhere else, the uniformly golden color of the grasses reflected more of it back, lending an enchanting glow to the landscape and, stirred by a gentle breeze, giving it much more shape and dimension.

"Wow," said Elise. "This looks like . . ."

"Africa," said Will, finishing the thought.

"Or, at least, what you think Africa looks like," she said.

"Everyone stay low," said Jericho. "We don't know who might be able to see us here."

They crouched down, but Ajay kept his head just above the level of the grass, peering outward. He pointed out light shining on water in the distance and identified it as a fairly large lake fed by a small river. Animals appeared to be milling around the water, but he couldn't make out what kind they were.

"By the way, Will, you neglected to mention where the plants told you that Dave might be," said Ajay.

"Like maybe standing in a field of grass, I hope?" asked Nick.

Will got up on his knees and stared out at the golden fields, searching for something familiar, anything that triggered a feeling that they were headed the right way.

"He's in a fortress of some kind," said Will. "Built into the side of a mountain."

"A fortress," said Nick. "Cool."

"I don't see anything like that out here," said Elise.

"Those look like mountains to me," said Ajay, pointing way off in the distance. "Could that be where this fortress is located?"

Ajay pointed beyond the lake, where, only half visible in a misty haze, a stark range of steep mountains spanned the horizon.

"I'm not sure," said Will. "How far away do you think they are?"

Ajay stared off into the distance again. "At least thirty miles from here. Maybe more."

"Maybe fifty," said Jericho.

"I don't know. I wish I could be more sure," said Will, looking at them hard.

"Oh, you can be," said Ajay, taking off and opening his backpack.

"I could maybe run ahead and scout it," said Will. "Wouldn't take me very long."

"Nobody goes anywhere now by themselves," said Jericho.

"That won't be necessary," said Ajay.

From a side pocket he slid out a small, square device built out of hard plastic and lightweight aluminum, about a foot across. At each corner, a small rotor extended out of a round plastic housing. Suspended from the middle of the rig was a compact camera.

"No way," said Nick, laughing. "You brought a freakin' drone?"

"Will asked me to prepare for any eventuality," said Ajay, taking out a pocket-sized tool kit. "So I did."

"We've had zero luck with electronics here," said Will. "You think it will work?"

"I can't guarantee it will broadcast live pictures back to us, which is how I originally designed it," said Ajay, adjusting settings on the camera with a small screwdriver. "But I also built in an analog mode, just in case. And the motor is purely mechanical, no electronics involved."

"Meaning what?" asked Jericho.

"Meaning I can program it to perform a very specific flight pattern. Throughout which it should be able to take a series of reconnaissance stills as it flies to those mountains—I gave it a terabyte of memory—and if it's able to find its way back to us, we should be able to view them at our convenience. Provided, of course, that the batteries don't poop out." He tapped a small flat section on the frame. "I gave it a solar backup panel, but that obviously won't offer much help in a place with no sun."

"You think that thing can make it all the way to those mountains and back?" asked Will.

"All we can do is try, yes?" Ajay finished fine-tuning the controls, gazing out at the distant mountains. "So shall we have a go?"

"By all means," said Will.

Ajay set the drone down in a small clearing. "Once I turn it on and it gets airborne, it should simply follow the flight plan I've programmed."

"Do we have to wait for it here?" asked Jericho.

"No, I assume that we want to keep moving forward, yes?"

Will glanced over at Jericho, who sent back a "your call" look. Will nodded at Ajay.

"Good. So I've programmed it to meet us at a specific spot on the near shore of the lake. In slightly over an hour from now, which is approximately how long it should take us to reach the lake at normal walking speed, which I estimate to be about three-point-eight miles from our current position."

"Where, specifically?" asked Will.

"Near what appears to be a stand of giant gum, or should I say eucalyptus, trees. Gum trees are what they call them in their native Australia."

Everyone looked out toward the lake. They could hardly even see there was a lake from here.

"You'll have to take my word for it," said Ajay. "There are gum trees."

He flipped on a row of switches on the back. The small rotors on the drone spun to life and kicked up some fine dust as it immediately rose six feet in the air and hovered there, as if it were staring at them.

"It will reach a cruising altitude of approximately one hundred feet," he said. "I've equipped it with sensors so it can adjust to changes in ground level, which will keep it flying at roughly the same distance above whatever it encounters."

They all gathered around it to take a closer look.

"You built this camera, too?" Jericho asked, almost as if he was impressed.

"High definition with a powerful long lens, so it should be able to gather a plethora of strong details on the ground for us. And without further ado, switching to autopilot and . . . Godspeed, drone."

Ajay reached out and flipped another switch. The drone immediately soared up out of sight, generating no more sound than a sparrow's wings, and zoomed off toward the lake surprisingly quickly.

"How fast is 'God speed' anyway?" asked Nick.

"Let's move out," said Will. "Single file. No talking, put away anything shiny that might reflect any light, and keep as quiet as possible. Ajay up front. Coach, would you take the back, please?"

They set off down the other side of the rise, following the path through the rolling hills toward the flats of the veld. The only sounds were the pads of their footsteps and the soft breeze stirring the tall grasses.

"If this is kinda like Africa," whispered Nick to Elise, "you think we'll see any lions?"

"If they turned out to be anything like the other critters we've run into," she said, "you'd better hope not."

"Lions are awesome," said Nick. "Elephants are awesome, too."

Elise shushed him.

"But not as awesome as lions," he whispered.

Will glanced over at Jericho as he walked beside him; he bent down to examine some blades of grass, then rolled a stalk of wheat from the end around in his hand. He tasted it, then spit it out. At one point he knelt to gather up a handful of dirt, sniffing it, feeling it with his fingers before holding it to his nose.

"What are you noticing?" Will asked him.

"Things don't feel right," he said.

"In what way?"

"There's a kind of coarseness to the plants, the seeds, even the dirt, and none of them smell right either. They're off somehow. Not strong enough."

"I got the same impression earlier," said Will. "Like it's all some kind of fraud."

Jericho looked at him; he'd found the right word. "Why do you think that is?"

"We've all picked up on it. The whole place doesn't seem exactly real. Fake. Like an amusement park but the rides can kill you. And something's missing."

Just ahead of them, Ajay had apparently been listening and

turned to add, "I've been giving this a lot of thought. It feels akin to what programmers might call a 'sandbox world.' A kind of virtual reality, a simulacrum, or to use Will's word from earlier, a 'hologram.'"

"Keep talking," said Jericho.

"A highly effective and persuasive reproduction of our familiar world at first glance, in every respect, until you examine it down to the granular level. Then it breaks apart; you realize the reproduction only goes so far. It's, as you say, missing something. I'm not sure what it is, a kind of deeper molecular integrity or authenticity."

"I know what it's missing," said Jericho.

"*Wak'an tanka*," said Will.

Jericho nodded. Ajay's eyes lit up.

"Ah, yes, the Great Spirit. So you're saying that what it lacks is a spiritual cohesiveness or sense of wholeness."

"That's why it feels different from our world," said Jericho.

"Exactly! As if this had all been manufactured by someone who had intimate knowledge of the process of creation and had seen or experienced it somewhere but wasn't in possession of the complete or correct formula to re-create it."

"Someone like the Makers, maybe," said Will.

"That's a most intriguing idea . . . ," said Ajay, trailing off in thought as they continued walking. "Let me give that some more thought."

When they reached the crest of the next rise, the last high ground before the path descended to the flats, even more of the golden plain ahead of them came into view. Ajay raised his hand to bring them to a stop, and they all sank out of sight into the tall grass as he continued scanning.

"The line of the river extends for miles in that direction, snaking gently back and forth," he said softly, pointing off to the right. "A wide variety of wildlife is at the water's edge, as you might expect."

"Any lions?" asked Nick.

"No, just many more of the same sorts of nightmarish species that we've previously encountered since our arrival . . . although there is a herd of something that looks quite a lot like zebras . . . except that their stripes are all vertical . . . Oh, I see why now . . ."

"Why?" asked Jericho.

"They're all standing upright . . . on what appear to be kangaroo legs."

"Zeb-karoos," said Nick.

"That's just wrong," said Elise.

"Wait," said Ajay, looking farther off to the right. "There is something else moving out in that direction . . . on the far side of the river . . . It's rather large . . . Ah, yes, it's an extremely large cloud of dust and it goes on for quite a while . . . along a road or a byway of some kind, paved with stone . . . Something appears to be on that road . . . that is to say *traveling* along that road . . . Oh my, oh, dear . . ."

Ajay suddenly sank down to a sitting position, facing them, looking frightened.

"What is it?" asked Will.

"Maybe I'm wrong. I hope so. Perhaps you'd better take a look."

Will retrieved his field glasses from his bag and sat up on one knee. He looked first with the naked eye in the direction that Ajay had indicated until he could vaguely make out a smudge that could be the cloud of dust he'd described. Then he raised the glasses.

It was difficult to see much detail through the roiling dust but as his eyes adjusted, he eventually started to make sense of what appeared to be raising the cloud, and why it extended back so far.

"It's an army," he said.

"That's what I thought," said Ajay.

"For real?" asked Nick.

Jericho asked for the glasses and rose up to take a look; then he moved the glasses slowly back to the left. "They're traveling toward those mountains. That road looks like it runs all the way there."

"What kind of army?" asked Elise.

Ajay, Will, and Jericho answered at the same time: "Monsters."

TWELVE

WILL'S RULES FOR LIVING #12:
IN THE FACE OF OVERWHELMING ODDS,
DO ONE SMART THING AT A TIME.

"What kind of monsters?" asked Nick.

"Listen to me carefully, Nick," said Ajay. "Close your eyes and use your imagination. Picture every sort of terrifying beast that we've encountered so far. Both here and back home."

"Okay," said Nick.

"Now imagine creatures that are many times worse than that," said Ajay. "Larger, more hideous, much more dangerous-looking. And there are thousands of them."

Nick thought about it. "Well, that sucks."

"Do you think they'll spot us here?" asked Elise.

"Unlikely," said Will. "They're making a forced march of some kind. Trying to get somewhere fast."

"Their focus will be on the road," said Jericho, looking at Nick. "I don't think they'll notice us. Unless we do something stupid."

"Would you stop looking at me when you say that?" said Nick.

"Why so many? What do you think they're up to, Will?" asked Elise, rising up and grabbing the binoculars to take her own look.

"Dave told us they were preparing for an attack in here,

remember?" said Will. "An invasion against our world. You heard him, too."

"So he wasn't lying or exaggerating," said Elise.

"Franklin kept dropping knowledge that something big was in the works, too," said Will. "But he also told me that it was nothing to worry about because the Knights were in complete control."

"How'd he figure that?" asked Jericho.

"He said the Others could plan invasions of Earth from now until the end of time, but none of them would ever come to pass because they didn't have the ability to create a way back into our world on their own." Will took the Carver out of his backpack. "Unless they got their hands on this."

They all stared at the device for a moment.

"So using the Carver to cut a hole in time/space back into our world from this side," said Ajay slowly, "is the only way they can possibly get back across to Earth."

"That's what Franklin told me," said Will.

Nick looked around and was the first to express what the others were feeling. "Dude, one question: Then why did we bring it in here with us?"

"We don't know that Franklin was telling the truth or that he even knows the truth," said Will. "What if the Makers have found a way to come across on their own, or they're on the verge of figuring it out?"

"If they're smart enough to create all this . . . ," said Elise, looking around.

"Exactly, then they're probably smart enough to do that. Franklin told me the original design for this came from them, so why couldn't they build another one?"

"Dude, I'm not trying to be Debbie Downer," said Nick, "but we still brought it in here."

"The Carver is the only way to get here, and it's the only way we're going to get back," said Will. "So what other choice did we have?"

"Uh," said Nick, looking around at the others, "not coming?"

"But we need to free Dave," said Will, feeling his own conviction start to wobble. "So he can let the Hierarchy know what's going down and get their help . . . so they can stop the invasion."

"That might not be able to take place," said Ajay slowly, "unless they have the Carver."

"So what's stopping us from using it right now to cut our way back and get the frick out of this unholy mess?" asked Nick.

The question stunned him; Will looked around in dismay. Even Elise looked like her faith might be starting to waver.

"Hold up," said Jericho. "Let me see that thing."

Will handed him the Carver. He weighed it in his hand, feeling its heft. Thinking. They all waited.

"So your old granddad told you this is the only one of these that exists," said Jericho. "Anywhere."

"That's right."

"And this man is—let me see if I've got this right—a grandiose, homicidal lunatic who's spent his whole life selling out everyone around him, and by that I mean not just his own family but also our entire species, in order to realize some fanatical plan of rewriting human destiny. On top of which he holds an unbreakable faith in his own delusional beliefs about . . . pretty near everything."

"More or less," said Will.

Jericho turned to the other three roommates and asked calmly, "Question for you: Who are we going to trust, our friend Will, or his messed-up messianic gran'pappy?"

216

Ashamed, everyone either pointed to Will or mumbled his name.

"I happen to agree with you," said Jericho calmly. He handed the Carver back to Will and said, "You were saying."

Will stuffed the Carver into his backpack, unable to meet anyone's eye for a moment. "So, obviously, we have to protect this thing and . . . not let them get their hands on it. Just in case."

"But just in case they've figured out a way to build another one," said Elise firmly, "we have to finish what we came here to do."

Will nodded.

"Right on," said Nick.

"We'd better move along, then," said Ajay, standing up and shouldering his pack. "Hadn't we?"

"Let's head for the lake," said Will. "We'll try to hook up with Ajay's drone. See what that tells us."

Will set off ahead of the others down the hill toward the plain. Elise was about to walk after him when Jericho nudged her slightly and shook his head.

"Give him a minute," he said.

The others started after him, single file, down the path, Ajay leading the way.

As he pushed ahead, Will ran through all the scenarios in his head, over and over again, from every angle. He kept bumping into the same thorny conundrum:

Did what he hope to accomplish here justify the risk they'd taken? In his urgency to take action, had he led his friends into unspeakable danger? And not just his friends. The stakes soared so high beyond their own dire straits that he couldn't even get his head around them.

Because they didn't get any bigger than this: In his eagerness to do the right thing, had he put the fate of the whole world at risk?

And if that was the case, was he any better, really, than his own bat-shit-crazy grandfather or the Knights of Charlemagne? What if, acting with all the best intentions, he'd actually made the one mistake that could make all of *their* mistakes a reality?

Where is this coming from? How did this happen to me? Is there something in my family's makeup, an arrogance in our bones or blood or DNA, some fatal defect in our way of thinking, that leads us into making these kinds of horrific, destructive choices?

Or does it have more to do with whatever alien genetics they spliced into me?

He found no relief as he rolled the situation around, no easy way out. He was either right or wrong about it, and they'd find out soon enough.

But either way, he knew there'd be a price to pay.

The path narrowed as Will reached the bottom of the final hill and stepped out onto the plains. A narrow path forward appeared through the wild grasses ahead, which grew even higher here, almost to his shoulders. Since they were well over Ajay's head, there was no point in having him go first to scout, so Will stayed at the head of the line. Still brooding, he didn't even look back at the others.

Elise moved up to take the position behind him, watching him trudge forward, his shoulders slumped, weighted down with more than the bulk of his pack.

Don't think you have to do this alone, she sent to him.

I don't.

You didn't force us to come with you. We all made a choice. And nobody regrets it.

No one but me.

He glanced back at her with a rueful smile. Elise didn't have an answer for that. She thought she'd never seen anyone look as lonely as Will did in that instant.

Will, as he had done periodically since they arrived in the Never-Was, turned his eyes forward and sent another mental transmission out to Dave, a sort of broadband telepathic SOS. He hoped with all his being that he'd receive something in return, at least some indication that Dave could still be saved, and if so, that they were headed in the right direction. The creeping fear that he'd led his friends on a suicide mission that might well lead to global catastrophe made him want to crawl out of his skin.

He concentrated fiercely, listening for a response. He hadn't heard a syllable from Dave and didn't honestly expect to hear anything back from him now. But instead of the cold silence he'd gotten up until now, this time he heard . . . something. Not words, or an identifiable voice, or anything that was definably "Dave." It came to him as muted as a whisper on the wind.

He zeroed in on it. More a feeling than a sound. A single blip on a radar screen. But it was something. Then he felt it a second time. And as he tried to place it, as vague as it was, it seemed to be coming from those distant mountains. Not much, but maybe just enough on which to hang a fragile strand of hope.

Behind Will and Elise, Ajay fell back alongside Jericho, talking low and fervently.

"You know, Coach, it's occurred to me that, with regard to our previous conversation, there's an emerging school of thought in quantum physics that may have some relevance here," said Ajay. "A number of scientists are exploring the idea that all of creation, the entire known and unknown universe, might in fact be nothing more than a hologram."

Jericho thought about it. "Guess that isn't any crazier than the idea that the world was created by an all-powerful rock floating in a void."

"A rock?"

"But the rock had nothing to use all his powers on, and he got bored, so one day he opened his veins and his blue blood ran out and created the water and sky, and before he knew it, his body had softened and rounded and he had become the Earth."

"Yes, of course," said Ajay, looking up as he located the memory. "The story of Inyan and the Lakota creation myth."

Jericho looked down at him with mild surprise. "Is there anything you *don't* remember?"

"If there is, these days it's not for very long," said Ajay, almost apologetically.

Jericho looked around at the lifeless, false fields of dry grass and up at the pastel-painted sky. "If this is all a hologram, who thought it up? Somebody still had to put it in play, right?"

"That is the fundamental chicken and egg question, sir," said Ajay, trailing his hand through the grass. "Although it may well be unanswerable for the time being, as far as our version of 'reality' back home is concerned. But it raises an even larger question for me: If our own cosmos is just a construct, or a simulation, some sort of ultimate game within the confines of some limitless, unknowable cosmic mind, then what does that make us? Insignificant pawns on someone else's chessboard? Vague figures in some old god's dream?"

"Why does that worry you so much?"

Ajay looked anguished. "Because if that's true, how does anything in us or around us have meaning? And does it actually really matter what we do about anything?"

Jericho thought about it for a moment. "It matters to us," he said. "It matters right now."

Ajay looked up at him searchingly. "Because if it doesn't, what?"

"Nothing means anything," said Jericho. "So we may as well act as if it does."

"I find that . . . oddly reassuring."

"Remembering a bunch of facts is one thing," said Jericho, not too harshly. "Knowing what they mean is something else."

"Knowing isn't understanding," said Ajay thoughtfully. "Yes. And to that point, there's a relatively obscure school of Tibetan philosophy that believes the true mind isn't even located in the brain. They believe it resides here, in the stomach."

Bringing up the rear, Nick had moved up close enough to hear their last exchange.

"No doubt," said Nick. "I do some of my best thinking with my stomach."

"You mean, as in having a 'gut' instinct?" asked Ajay.

"Right on, man, yeah."

"It's a different way of knowing," said Jericho.

"Exactamundo! Like when I'm super hungry, right, but I don't know what I want to eat at first? Do I want a burger or some wings or maybe a Hawaiian pizza, you know, with pineapple and Canadian bacon, which is so awesome? And when, no matter what, I can't make up my mind, my stomach just seems to know *exactly* what I want."

"Uncanny," said Jericho.

"And yet, hardly surprising," said Ajay.

"And that reminds me: Where do they get that bacon in Canada from anyway? Why does ours come in these bumpy rectangles and theirs is a smooth circle? Do they have round pigs or something? I'm thinking maybe you can clear that up for me, Ajay."

"I'll make a point of looking into it for you," said Ajay.

"That'd be great, thanks," said Nick. "Kind of a mystery, though, isn't it?"

"One of the great ones," said Jericho.

Nick turned a somersault away from them, back toward the rear. "Dudes, it's so weird here. No birds, no bugs, no animal poop anywhere. It's like one big strange amusement park."

Jericho and Ajay looked at each other. Ajay thought Jericho might be on the verge of laughing.

"I'm actually worried about him," said Ajay.

"Why's that?"

Ajay lowered his voice. "Is it possible that he's becoming even dimmer as a side effect of all this?"

Jericho glanced back at Nick. "I look at it differently."

"How so?"

"Maybe, in its own way, his mind is actually a superpower."

"What a bizarre concept. In *what* way?"

"Keeps him in the moment," said Jericho, glancing back at Nick again, who was practicing jumping in the air and spinning around in multiple circles. "Doesn't overthink things. Lets him react to what's in front of him without his head getting in the way."

"And given his particular set of skills," said Ajay thoughtfully, "which depend almost exclusively on instinct, no matter how bizarrely he defines it, that would be . . ."

"Extremely practical."

Will glanced behind him. Only his head and Jericho's extended above the grass line, and the path was just wide enough for them to move along without disturbing the stalks on either side. It seemed highly unlikely that anything could spot them in here.

Which was good, because when Will surveyed the area out

toward the river and beyond, the dust cloud raised by the traveling army appeared much more distinct now, visible to the naked eye. He could also see more clearly how far the column on the road stretched out in either direction; it looked like miles, and there seemed to be no end to it.

Will calculated they'd been walking for nearly an hour when the shores of the lake first came into view. And just as Ajay had envisioned, one of the first identifiable features was a large stand of eucalyptus trees. They would've reminded Will of ones he'd known back home in Southern California, if they weren't at least twice as tall as any he'd ever seen there and streaked with more colors than a rainbow.

The animals along the riverbanks to their right were more visible now as well, most of them segregated by type. Small groups of the strange striped kangaroos Ajay had spotted bounded around. Herds of huge, hoofed cowlike creatures with twisted horns wandered through the shallows.

Will saw a large herd of bright red gazelles lope by, with long, flexible anteater snouts. A pack of vicious hyena-like creatures with eight spidery legs skulked around the margins of the area, looking for prey. Lizards the size of lounge chairs wallowed in the mud just offshore. A floating formation of gigantic creatures he couldn't see well appeared to be lurking just under the surface of the water. A variety of cries, screeches, and calls echoed from the area, like an orchestra tuning up.

"See any lions?" asked Nick.

He had suddenly appeared beside Will and was bouncing up and down, trying to peek over the top of the tall grass.

"No cats yet," said Will. "Keep your head down."

"No birds either," said Jericho, also joining them and looking out.

"We haven't seen a single bird since we got here," said Elise.

"Maybe the Maker dudes haven't gotten around to messing with birds yet," said Nick.

"That seems highly unlikely, from a probability standpoint," said Ajay. "Among the vertebrate tetrapods, they're by far the most widespread and adaptable species on Earth, with over ten thousand identified varieties."

"Meaning?" asked Elise.

"It must be a choice," said Ajay. "For some reason they've been unwilling or unable to work with the airborne portion of the kingdom."

"We need to steer clear of this whole area," said Will, pointing toward the delta. "If we stir any of those animals up, they might notice across the river."

They continued on, paralleling the river but staying within the cover of the grass. As they drew closer to the lake, the grass began to thin out before stopping altogether about fifty yards short of the eucalyptus stand. An entire grove of the giant trees spread out between them and the lake, and beyond them they could see a long white sandy beach.

There were also some things Ajay hadn't seen from a distance and wouldn't have been able to until they got this close, as most of it was hidden by the trees.

A road crossed the plain in front of them, perpendicular to their position, and ran into the grove and through it, all the way to the water, then onto a sturdy wooden bridge that crossed the delta where the river flowed into the lake. A six-foot-tall earthen dam held back the river, just shy of the bridge, allowing a controlled flow of water under the bridge. A cluster of small, trim wooden buildings attended a clearing at the near end of the bridge, which ran a quarter of a mile to the far bank.

"Ajay, take a look," said Will, lowering his voice.

Ajay moved up to the edge of the grass, knelt down, and surveyed the area.

"It appears to be an active campsite. . . . There's smoke rising from a campfire in the clearing between the buildings, at least one of which appears to be occupied. . . . There's a rack outside along one of the walls, containing various weapons, not many but enough to maintain a small outpost or garrison, which I'm supposing this must be. . . ."

"Guarding the bridge," said Jericho.

"A fair assumption," said Ajay, then looked off to his left. "Which would suggest it's of no small strategic importance, since from this vantage point I'm able for the first time to see that the lake stretches out for many, many miles to our left."

"So unless we're planning to swim, this bridge is the only crossing point," said Will. "If we want to get to those mountains."

"It's the only one that I can see."

"Don't suppose you brought one of your inflatable boats with you," said Nick.

"I did not have room for everything," said Ajay. "And God only knows what manner of monstrous leviathans are lurking in that lake."

"Something's coming," said Elise, glancing back toward the road behind them.

Then they all heard it, horses at a gallop, and they quickly stepped back deeper into the cover of the grass. Within thirty seconds, a small party of about ten riders appeared, approaching from the left along the road toward the lake. Their horses were all black, lathered up after a hard ride, oversized, their faces covered by hoods adorned with a single red mark in their center. The party began to slow as they moved closer to the trees.

The riders were soldiers, wearing helmets along with modern-looking, segmented dark armor and what looked like rifles strapped across their backs. They were guarding or escorting two riders in their middle.

One of them, who appeared to be in charge, wore the same armor but not the sleek black helmet the others wore, and Will recognized the man's gleaming bald head immediately.

Hobbes.

The other rider in the center also wore the armor without a helmet. She rode expertly, and a mane of long blond hair flowed behind her in the wind.

"Oh my God," said Elise.

Will's heart sank. It was Brooke.

At that moment, Ajay suddenly looked up and to the right, at something the rest of them couldn't yet see.

"Oh, dear," he said. "Here comes my drone."

THIRTEEN

WILL'S RULES FOR LIVING #13:
READ BOOKS TO GET SMARTER.
READ PEOPLE TO BECOME WISER.

"Nobody move," said Will.

Hobbes, in the lead, held up his right hand and the squad of horsemen slowed to a walk. The road turned from dirt to cobbled stone as it entered the grove, and the sharp clip-clop of the horses' hooves cut through the air. Hobbes suddenly held up a closed fist and the horsemen stopped altogether.

Hobbes turned his horse around and trotted back a short distance to the edge of the trees, his eyes scanning the horizon, including the grass line where the group was concealed.

Had he heard or seen or, worse, used one of his freaky powers to sense some trace of their presence?

Hobbes called back to his riders. He waved most of them on toward the encampment but gestured one of them in his direction. A moment later, Brooke rode out to join him on the road. He spoke to her at length, waving his arm across the horizon back in their direction.

He was asking her if she noticed anything.

Brooke looked out, scanning the same span of space, her eyes moving right past the tall grass, but her look didn't linger or even land on their hiding place.

Kneeling beside him, Will could feel Ajay shivering with

anxiety, but he kept completely silent. No one else moved a muscle.

"How long?" Will whispered. "Before the drone gets here."

Ajay glanced up toward the tree line and opened his eyes wide. "Thirty seconds."

Now Hobbes and Brooke were speaking animatedly, with Hobbes pointing back at the outpost and the bridge as he gave orders. Will couldn't hear what they were saying but it wasn't hard to decipher: This was a hunting party, and they'd decided that the bridge was the best strategic location to wait for their prey.

And their conversation was taking too long.

We need to move them out of here, fast. Will looked over as he urgently sent that to Elise.

Can we suggest that to them?

Not those two. They'll figure out where it's coming from and know we're nearby.

Her eyes darted around, to the encampment ahead, then settled on . . .

The horses, she sent. *I've got hers.*

They each targeted a horse. Both looked wet and lathered after a hard ride. Will sent a series of images to Hobbes's mount: feed and water in the camp just ahead.

Hobbes's horse stamped its feet impatiently and whirled around, but Hobbes kept a firm hand and it didn't break from his control. But Brooke's mount reared and bolted for the outpost immediately. She grabbed the reins and tried hard to break its charge but ended up just having to hang on. Hobbes galloped hard after her, pulled up alongside, and was trying to lean over and grab the bridle by the time they entered the camp.

The other riders had already dismounted, letting their

horses drink at a long trough and setting out bags of feed. Most of them scattered as Brooke's horse charged into the clearing among the buildings.

When Hobbes finally got his hands on the bridle, Brooke's horse slammed to a stop and reared up, and she was forced to jump to the ground mid-rear to avoid being thrown. She landed on her feet, looking furious, and raised her hand threateningly. The horse whinnied wildly, reared up again, and then kicked at her, and Brooke had to quickly back away. Hobbes dismounted and, along with a couple of other soldiers, jumped in to grab the reins. Together they subdued the animal, the soldiers leading it away toward a stable in the compound.

I forgot to tell you, Elise sent to Will. *I speak pretty good horse.*

So I see.

I started talking to horses a long time before we figured out how to do this.

What'd you say to it?

I told him exactly what kind of crazy scary bitch was on his back.

"Here it comes," said Ajay quietly. "Right on schedule."

He pointed up above the tree line. Will picked up a faint shimmer in the air arcing down toward them at a swift rate of speed. He just started to discern the darker outlines of the drone and heard a faint buzz, no louder than an approaching bee.

"Come on, baby," said Ajay. "Come to Papa."

Then, just before it cleared the edge of the tree line closest to their position, the drone clipped a branch, spun around, tumbled forward a few times, and got hung up in the branches.

About fifteen feet off the ground and only twenty yards from the center of the camp.

Ajay quickly pulled the remote control from his pack and

used it to kill the drone's motor. Still dealing with the after-math of the ruckus caused by Brooke's horse, none of the sol-diers appeared to notice.

Only Hobbes looked out that way. And all he saw were a few leaves slowly drifting to the ground. He took a few steps in that direction, but Brooke screeching at some of the soldiers, and operatically freaking out about her horse's meltdown, pulled his attention back to the camp.

"Same old Brooke," said Nick, shaking his head as he watched.

"What's she doing here?" asked Elise.

"Obviously, she's rotten to the core," said Ajay bitterly, glancing at Will. "And has been from the moment we've known her."

"Her father's a Knight," said Will. "He's been part of this all along. That's where her loyalty lies."

"I still can't believe it," said Nick.

"Blood trumps friendship, old boy," said Ajay.

"Doesn't matter what the reason is," said Jericho. "She's their problem now."

"Yeah, well, have fun with that, Hobbes," said Nick, look-ing toward the clearing. "Next time she throws a hissy fit and melts your face off."

"But how'd the two of them get into the zone in the first place?" asked Elise. "If we have the only Carver, and the Carv-er's the only way to come across."

"I don't know," said Will. "Maybe Franklin lied to me. Maybe the Makers have another one."

"Maybe they have one he didn't even know about," said Ajay.

"Or maybe they just followed us in," said Jericho.

"I thought the portals only stayed open a short time," said Elise.

"That's what he told me," said Will. "Maybe the old man lied about that, too."

"At a certain point one has to wonder: Is there anything he *didn't* lie to you about?" asked Ajay.

"It is kind of awesome, though," said Nick.

"What is?" asked Elise.

"Dude, they've got *horses*."

"And so, for the moment, our most immediate problem remains," said Ajay, ignoring him. "How do we get my drone out of the tree?"

"I can climb up and grab it easy if we wait until after dark," said Nick, then when everyone looked at him, "Oh. Right."

"We'll have to wait for them to move on," said Jericho, "or find a way to clear them out of that camp."

"Let's wait awhile," said Will. "Maybe they'll move out on their own."

Jericho immediately lay down, stuffed his pack behind his head, folded his arms, and closed his eyes. "Wake me when you're ready."

"Good God, how can you sleep at a time like this?" asked Ajay.

"This is exactly when we need to sleep," said Jericho, who then appeared to immediately fall into a profound slumber.

"Dude, that's actually awesome advice," said Nick, who lay down near him, put his pack behind his head, and closed his eyes.

Ajay looked at Will and Elise. "Have they both taken leave of their senses?"

"Who knows, why don't you try it?" asked Elise, lying down to join them. "Little rest wouldn't hurt you."

"I'm far too wired," said Ajay. "I feel like I've been up all night after chugging a six-pack of Mountain Dew Code Reds and I'm about to take the SATs."

Nick winked open one eye. "Dude, trust me, one thing you do *not* have to stress about is the SATs."

"Keep an eye on the clearing, then, Ajay," said Will, setting down his pack and lying down as well.

"Good God, man, not you, too."

"Wake me up if they make any moves. I need to think. If they don't, wake me in twenty minutes."

Will closed his eyes, not sure if he'd be able to sleep but grateful for any opportunity to rest and let his subconscious chew on the problem in front of them. Within seconds, he drifted off into a deep sleep.

Ajay started a timer in his head and crouched by the edge of the grass line to watch the camp.

The soldiers cooked something large and ugly on a spit over the campfire. They poured hot drinks into mugs that looked like they were made out of skulls. They ate, they drank, but they talked only a little; high verbal skills did not appear to be on the menu.

Hobbes consulted with one of his soldiers, something like a sergeant by the look of the insignia on his uniform and helmet. Together they examined a large parchment, most likely a map, on the porch of one of the larger buildings, probably a barracks.

A short distance away, Brooke sat by herself on the steps outside another one of the buildings. She looked pale and miserable. One of the soldiers brought her a plate of whatever they'd been cooking. She looked at it—burnt, grisly meat of some kind—made an exaggerated face, took a small tentative bite, made an even more exaggerated face, said something nasty to the soldier, then tossed the plate at him.

"Still the same old Brooke," whispered Ajay.

Fifteen minutes later, Hobbes called the soldiers to order. They brought the horses back around. Hobbes and Brooke mounted up—she took a different horse this time—along with half of the soldiers they'd ridden in with. The rest remained behind with the soldiers from the garrison. Hobbes signaled the party forward and they rode out of camp at a gallop, their mounts' hooves clattering heavily across the wooden bridge.

The sound woke Will immediately, before Ajay could rouse him. He came out of it refreshed and relaxed and knelt next to Ajay, looking at the camp.

"How many did they leave behind?" he asked.

"By my count," said Ajay, scanning the garrison, inside and out, "eighteen."

Will blinked on the Grid; a quick head count of heat signatures throughout the camp arrived at the same number.

"I'd hardly call that a fair fight, would you?" he said.

Ajay grinned.

By now Jericho and Elise had woken up as well. Nick was still snoring slightly. Will nudged him with his foot and he came out of it.

"What's up, Chief?" asked Nick.

"I've got a plan," said Will.

The soldiers around the campfire heard the horses react first, stamping and whinnying in the stable. Something stirring them up like that usually meant animals nearby, sometimes large, dangerous ones. Three of them went inside to quiet them down.

Nick was waiting for them. Three down, fifteen to go.

A few moments later, the rest of the soldiers heard the

approach of some large dangerous animals nearing the outpost. Thundering footsteps, then a series of rib-rattling yowls. Wouldn't be the first time a herd of some wild river animals from the delta wandered into their garrison, and they knew what to do: The soldiers grabbed their weapons and gathered in the center of camp, rifles at the ready, taking defensive positions.

Something ran toward them through the grove from the direction of the road. They couldn't see exactly what it was because it was moving far too fast, but they perceived motion more than they saw it and they couldn't miss a line of dust kicking up toward them. They tried to draw a bead on it and braced for action.

Before they even had time to pull the trigger, the blur raced right past them through the center of camp and toward the bridge. Six of them turned to chase after it, while the others, obeying the orders of their sergeant, held their positions, anticipating an attack from the still unseen, but still heard, large animals, which even now appeared to be shaking the gum trees as they approached from the direction of the river.

The blur turned course away from the bridge at the last moment and veered behind one of the larger buildings in the compound. The six soldiers turned and kept up their pursuit, until a gigantic bear silently leaped out at them behind the building.

Nine down, nine to go.

Their sergeant heard a commotion going on behind the big building that deeply troubled him, and then he heard something else make an odd buzzing sound as it swooped over the heads of his remaining soldiers. When he spotted it, he found even more reason to worry.

Something was falling out of the sky toward them—a ball-shaped object unlike anything he'd seen before—and then the ball exploded or expanded or opened up into something else, somehow turning itself into a large net made out of thin rope. It dropped down over the top of them and immediately tangled up their arms and legs, and the more they struggled against it, trying to free their weapons, the tighter the rope seemed to grip them. They could barely hold on to their rifles.

Then a girl stepped out from behind a nearby tree and walked toward them. A young girl, with long black hair, slight and very pretty, and as he continued to struggle against the netting, the sergeant thought, *The bald man warned me about a girl who could—*

When she was about ten feet away from them, the girl stopped, braced herself, took in a deep breath, and opened her mouth wide.

And that was the last thing any of the soldiers remembered.

They dragged all the bodies into the largest of the buildings, which turned out to be a barracks lined with wooden bunk beds. Each of them took a set of armor off the soldier that seemed their closest physical match. Although they had the expected dimensions of human bodies, when they removed the soldiers' masks, they realized that these weren't men, exactly, but some kind of humanoid hybrids. No two of their faces looked alike. Each had obviously been crossed with some kind of wild animal—boar, jackal, ox, wolf, and to Nick's delight . . .

"Hey, I think this one's part lion," he said.

"Good, so your field trip's complete," said Elise. "Be sure to tell Teacher."

"Whatever. I got dibs on lion dude's armor."

Once they'd stripped the armor off, Ajay helped each of

them fasten it on—boots, leg pieces, a vest, something like shoulder pads, arms and forearms, heavy gloves. It covered them nearly from head to toe.

"It appears to be made from some material akin to carbon fiber or a weapons-grade Kevlar, so that gives the lie to the idea that they're entirely without some access to high-caliber manufacturing."

Ajay picked up one of the weapons.

"And these rifles don't appear to be all that different from a modern M-sixteen," he said, looking down the barrel. "In fact, they may be an improvement."

"Don't shoot your eye out, Junior," said Jericho, taking the rifle from him, checking the magazine, and slinging the weapon over his shoulder.

"What about you, Ajay?" asked Will after they were all suited up.

"Oh, no, none of this gear is going to fit me," said Ajay. "I'm far too small."

"Too bad they didn't cross one of these dudes with a shrimp," said Nick, then, after Elise punched him hard in the shoulder, "Sorry."

"Nick," said Jericho, "help me with the horses."

He hurried off toward the stable and Nick followed.

Will looked down at the faces of the soldiers they'd unmasked, lying in a row. "Reminds me of the animal masks we found near the tunnels. In that trunk that belonged to the Knights."

"Perhaps that's no coincidence," said Ajay.

"Feels like a really long time ago, doesn't it?" asked Elise.

"A hundred years," said Will. "Let's get out of here."

When they walked outside, Will watched Elise as she took the lead, effortlessly slinging her rifle up to a ready position.

He couldn't help thinking she looked completely at ease in that sleek black armor, her inner badass ever closer to finding its fullest expression. She must have felt him watching her, because she turned around and shot him a look.

What do we do with Ajay now? she asked him. *If he's not wearing the armor, they'll spot him right away, but we can't leave him behind.*

Of course not. He's coming with us. We'll figure it out.

If anything happens to him—

Nothing's going to happen to him. Or to any of us. I'm working on it.

So, no turning back.

That's right. Moment of truth.

Time to bust down a few doors, kick ass, and take some names.

You took the words right out of my—

Will realized that Ajay was looking back and forth between them again, eyes wide open, like someone watching a tennis match.

"How long have you known how to do this?" he asked.

"Do what?" asked Elise; then she looked over at Will, alarmed. *Is it that obvious?*

"You know what I mean," said Ajay. "And there's no point in lying to me. Do you realize how many indicators I can spot from just the observation of facial muscles alone when someone's not telling me the truth? Forty-five! How long?"

Elise flicked another glance at Will, looking for guidance. He didn't see any reason to hide it at this point.

"Quite a while now," said Will. "Since last spring."

"Really? How fascinating. I'm astonished you've kept it a secret from me as long as you have. Do you suppose this is another side effect of our genetic birthday bequest?"

"Yes," said Will. "Definitely."

"Yes, of course it is," said Ajay, almost to himself. "Then it should work for me as well. Doesn't that stand to reason? Can you teach me how?"

Will didn't answer. Now he looked to Elise for her thoughts about it.

"It takes a lot of practice," she said.

"I'm nothing at this point if not the definition of a quick study," said Ajay. "Please try, Elise. If nothing else, who knows, it's a skill that may come in handy for us somewhere along the line."

Will agreed and nodded his consent to Elise, where all of Ajay's attention remained fixed.

He wants to try with the pretty girl first, Will sent to Elise. *Big surprise.*

Elise looked away, appearing slightly flustered. Will immediately second-guessed his choice of words. Should he not have said *pretty*? He'd just blurted it out without even thinking about it, since it was obviously such a ridiculous understatement.

"Let's give it a try, Ajay," she said. "And given the state of your brain, I'm thinking it shouldn't be too hard for you."

"Okay, ready when you are," he said.

She directed a thought toward Ajay. He closed his eyes and scrunched up his face, making more effort than he would on a twentieth push-up.

"Don't try so hard," said Will.

"Quite right," said Ajay.

He tried, with just as much effort, to relax. Will watched Elise direct another thought at him, and waited. Ajay shook his head.

"I'm still not picking up a doggone thing," said Ajay, opening his eyes.

"Don't worry about it," said Elise. "This is new to you. It might take a little while."

"But that's just terribly disappointing—"

"Go easy on yourself, pal," said Will. "It's like learning another language, that's all."

"If I can master French in three days, I should be able to pick up this."

"And you'll pick it up fast," said Will, "but we'll have to practice on the way."

Jericho and Nick returned from the stables, leading four fully geared fresh horses.

"Choose your ride," said Jericho.

"Oh, dear, I'm afraid I'm not much of a horseman," said Ajay, backing away from the massive beasts.

"You're riding with me," said Jericho.

"Which one do you want?" Will asked Elise.

She looked them over, then turned to the stable. Will saw her concentrate long enough to send another thought somewhere. Then she put two fingers in her mouth and whistled sharply.

The horse that had nearly trampled Brooke came running out of the stable and trotted right up to Elise, bowing its head and stamping its foot in front of her. A beautiful brute of an animal, gleaming black, with a long shaggy mane and tail and wild, intelligent eyes.

"This one," she said, patting the blaze on its forehead. "We already talked about it."

Ajay leaned in and whispered to her, "It works with *horses*, too?"

"I found this in the main building," said Jericho, holding up a rolled parchment. "Take a look."

"Hey, I almost forgot," said Nick. "I gotta go get the drone."

Nick tied the horses to a rail outside the barracks and ran back toward the grove.

Jericho rolled open the parchment. It was a map, on crisp, thick paper, hand drawn in a variety of colored inks. He set it down on the porch while the others examined it. None of the writing was in any form they recognized as language, but a number of significant geographical features were easy to identify.

"The lake," said Will, pointing to a broad blue swatch across the lower middle of the map. "The river. The bridge. So we're here."

He put his finger down on a representation of the garrison and traced the path of the road along the bridge.

"If we follow this to the other side, it hooks up with that main road, here," he said. "According to this, like you saw earlier, Coach, it runs all the way to the mountains."

Will pointed to a series of wavy thin lines, well to the north and west, a symbol he recognized as the topographical representation of a mountain range's elevations.

"What's this?" asked Elise.

She pointed to the end of the road at a rectangular cluster of six joined hexagons, outlined in black and filled in with red, tucked into the shelter of the mountains.

"I'm guessing that's the Citadel," said Will.

"Where that army is headed," said Jericho.

"And that's where we'll find Dave?" asked Ajay.

"I think so," said Will.

Nick came running back into camp, holding Ajay's drone in one hand.

"Dude, sorry, it took a serious beat-down when it crashed into the trees," he said, handing it over.

They gathered around Ajay as he set the device on the

ground and his busy, efficient hands attended to it. Two of the drone's struts were bent, and one of the rotors was hanging by a wire.

"The bad news is she'll never fly again," said Ajay. "The good news is it appears that the camera survived the crash unscathed."

He removed the camera from its housing and attached it by cable to a six-inch viewing tablet that he pulled from his pack. Holding it up so they all could see it, Ajay flipped a switch and the tablet's screen flickered to life.

"I programmed it to snap a fresh photograph every ten seconds."

He scrolled through the pictures as they all watched; overhead views of the golden plain they'd just traversed, then the stand of eucalyptus trees, the garrison, the bridge. Many fleeting glimpses of the army on the road below followed, although not much detail appeared through the rising clouds of dust because of the overhead angle. But the impressive scale and size of the procession was plain enough to see, and occasionally the top of a rolling siege weapon or the head of some colossal beast poked up above the mist.

After passing across the road, images of a rolling green countryside appeared, sparsely forested, dotted with occasional buildings, mostly farms or small villages.

Jericho picked up the map at that point, and cross-referenced the photos to chart the flight of the drone over the land depicted on the parchment. He traced its path from the highway as the pictures continued, and it drew closer to the hexagons of the Citadel. There the landscape turned gradually more barren as it approached, the green hills giving way to a parched and pitted plain, where the outskirts of a massive temporary encampment began to appear in the pictures.

"Oh my Lord," whispered Ajay.

The army they'd seen on the march was apparently on its way to join an even more massive force that had already gathered there. Judging by the photos, this encampment appeared to go on for a number of square miles outside the front walls of the Citadel, images of which now appeared on the screen for the first time. Segregated regiments of every breed of monster they could imagine covered the field, including a battalion of snake-men they saw clearly in the center of one frame.

"Boy, are those snake-dudes gonna be bummed when they get home," said Nick.

"What this suggests," said Ajay, leaning back as he took it all in, "is that there must be a great number of similar encampments to the one we destroyed throughout the Never-Was."

"That's right," said Jericho.

"Each one stocked with a different kind of monster," said Elise.

"One more frightful than the next," said Ajay. "I predict that my nightmares are now going to have nightmares."

"How big is their entire force?" asked Will. "The size of this whole army, can you estimate it?"

"I would have to say . . . in the hundreds of thousands," said Ajay, staring at the photo. "Conservatively."

Will turned his focus to the walls of the Citadel. They were built or carved from some dark granite, all long lines and sharp angles, and it looked as if the whole structure had thrust itself forward out of the hard black bare mountains behind it. From this overhead angle, it was difficult to determine exactly how tall the ramparts forming its perimeter stood, but judging from the relative size of objects on the ground below, they appeared to be as tall as a skyscraper.

"Remind you of anything?" asked Will.

"The wall," said Ajay, his eyes locked on the picture, soaking in every detail. "The one underground, around Cahokia. The craftsmanship is unmistakable."

"These dudes are definitely really good at ... building really sick stuff," said Nick.

The pictures that followed all picked up pieces of the vast structure as the drone had made its overhead pass. It was hard to get a sense of how large the whole compound was, in part because it appeared to be bigger than anything they'd ever seen before; they had nothing to compare it to.

"Curious ... I don't see any defensive weapons or emplacements," said Ajay. "Anywhere along the walls."

"No need," said Elise. "Who'd be crazy enough to attack a place like that?"

They looked around uneasily at each other.

A wide variety of different buildings had been constructed within the walls, although what purpose they might serve was difficult to determine from the overhead angle. But it was clear that a great deal of thought had been given to the overall layout; the spacing and symmetry made this part of the Citadel look like something out of a storybook about Mount Olympus, a city built by or for gods of antiquity. In the center of what appeared to be the main cluster of those buildings, arrayed around a large open plaza, one particular building stood out, the only one of its kind—a huge circular stone dome.

As Will stared at the dome, he felt something tug at his mind: an intuitive stab of recognition. Twitching like a muscle he was just learning how to use. But this time he recognized it.

"I think he's in here," said Will, pointing to the dome. "I don't know how I know this, but I think Dave is somewhere in this building."

"Well, of course he is," said Ajay, his voice quavering a bit. "Dead center in the heart of the darkness."

"Strange," said Jericho. "Have you noticed a single figure anywhere in sight, on top of or inside the walls?"

"None," said Ajay. "Nowhere. I was about to comment on it myself."

"What do you think that means?" asked Elise.

"One thing for sure," said Will, "whatever this place is, it's not for the army they've assembled out here."

"No, they're just cannon fodder," said Jericho. "Like the snake-men."

"What do you think they're all doing here, then?" asked Nick. "Did everybody just show up for the annual monster jamboree?"

"They're obeying orders," said Jericho. "The Makers raise them like livestock. When they ring the dinner bell, these things come running."

"But why now?" asked Nick.

"If your gods that made you gave you an order, wouldn't you follow it?" asked Ajay.

"I might if they asked me nicely," said Nick.

"That's the reason for the wall," said Jericho. "They don't want to reveal themselves. Whoever's running the show stays inside. Keep out of sight; it's easier to maintain their power over their peons."

"I think you're right, Coach," said Will, tapping the center of the Citadel on the screen. "This is the home they built for themselves. This is where the Makers live."

"Well, I'm guessing there can't be that many of the Maker dudes or you would've caught some of 'em on camera, right?" said Nick.

"Maybe they're just not very outdoorsy," said Ajay.

"If there aren't that many, what do they need all these buildings for, then?"

Will pored over the next series of images. Near the back right section of the compound, once the drone had banked a wide turn and began its journey back toward the grove, it passed over row after row of enormous squat chimney stacks, fashioned from black bricks, dozens of them, each belching a foul stream of multicolored smoke into the air.

"These are their factories," said Will, letting his intuition lead him again as his eyes stayed fixed on the pictures.

"For what?" asked Elise.

"Maybe they make all that 'made in China' junk here," said Nick.

"This is where the Makers manufacture all the things we've seen in the Never-Was. From the ground up—the plants, the animals, their soldiers. They started at an elemental, maybe even molecular level. Earth, water, sky, all of it came from these buildings."

"How do you know that, Will?" asked Ajay.

"This was nothing more than a void zone when they first got locked in here, an empty, blank dimension; that's what Dave told me. Turning it into the world that we've seen is what they've been doing ever since they were thrown in and the Hierarchy slammed the door."

"Sorry for sounding thick about this," said Nick, looking around, "but what would they need all this stuff for?"

"Raw materials. That's what everything we've seen since we got here is for."

"Raw materials for what?"

"For making monsters," said Will. "They created this whole world so they could build, grow, and support an army. The one we're looking at here."

He pointed at a shot of the army in front of the wall. That silenced everyone. They looked at the pictures with a lot more concern.

"And we already know *why* they're doing that," said Elise softly.

"So this is where it all started," said Jericho, pointing at the chimneys on the screen.

"Behold their satanic mills, their infernal labs and foundries," said Ajay.

"Is that from a poem?" asked Nick.

"Part of it. William Blake," said Ajay. "And I'm shocked you recognized it."

"I didn't *recognize* it; it just sounded like a poem."

"This is where all the smoke comes from, then," said Elise, pointing to the chimneys. "All that poisonous stuff choking the atmosphere."

"Yeah, but it makes for some awesome sunsets," said Nick. "That is, it would, if they *had* a sun."

Will looked up at the horizon beyond the mountains. He had noticed it was getting harder to breathe, and as they drew closer to what they now knew was its source, the skies ahead appeared darker and more toxic here than anywhere else they'd seen.

"Wait a moment, what's this?" said Ajay, looking at the screen again.

They crowded around the screen to take a look. After the drone flew past the chimney array, it had taken a single shot of what appeared to be a massive construction site.

"Looks like they're building another smokestack," said Nick.

"No, this one is different," said Ajay. "It's more upright, and they're not framing it the same way. I don't even see any bricks, which is what they used for all the others." He used his nimble fingers to enlarge a section of the screen for more detail. "This is some other sort of structure entirely. As you can see, they've cleared out the whole area around it, and it's near what looks like an entrance in the walls, with a road leading directly to it."

"I don't see any workers," said Elise. "How do you think they're building it?"

"They may be obscured by this," said Ajay. "What looks like scaffolding around the structure."

"Maybe the drone flew over during their coffee break," said Jericho.

The ground around the site appeared to be soaked with some kind of black ooze that sent up thick tendrils of smoke. As Will studied that part of the photo, he felt a sudden chill run through him. He hoped, for once, that his intuition was dead wrong about what they were looking at. He closed his eyes and tried to send his mind closer to what was in the picture.

He suddenly felt like he couldn't breathe. His eyes flew open and watered as if he'd been exposed to toxic gas. He coughed and sputtered, taking a few steps away. Nick followed him, patting him on the back.

"Hey, you okay, Will?"

He snapped back into himself and the poisoned sensation quickly subsided. He nodded and took a long pull of water from his canteen. Elise moved close to him, staring at him with deep concern.

What was that all about? she asked.

Tell you later.

Nick was staring up at the violated skies draped over the mountains. "Man, these Maker dudes better get cranking on some pollution controls, stat, or they're gonna choke this whole place out."

"Dave said that's exactly what happened the last time they were in charge," said Will, putting his canteen away. "Back on Earth. They ruined nature. That's a big part of why the Hierarchy booted them."

"For that, and playing God," said Elise.

"It's a loathsome fiend indeed that fouls its own nest," said Ajay.

"William Blake?" asked Nick.

"No, I made that part up."

"The Makers don't give a rip what they do to this place," said Will, packing up his saddlebag. "It's their sandbox. They built it, and they feel like they can do whatever they want to it to get what they need."

"They never planned on staying here for long anyway," said Jericho.

"Since there doesn't appear to be any time here, as we know it," said Ajay, "maybe that starts with them. Maybe time doesn't affect them."

"Will, the last time you talked to Dave," said Elise, picking up Ajay's thought, "that time I saw him with you, he told us the Makers were assembling all their forces then. That was four months ago."

"In our world, yes, but time is definitely funky here," said Will. "The two places don't sync up with each other at all somehow. That might have been a week ago here, or a day, or even the same day."

"Or it could all be happening at the same time," said Ajay.

"Whoa," said Nick.

"Or maybe there's so many of these things, it took that long just to get them together," said Jericho.

"Whoa," said Nick, more softly.

"Speaking of time and space anomalies, how did Brooke

even get here in the first place?" asked Elise. "I understand how Hobbes could've made it across; he was right there in the room with us—"

"Yeah, but we left Brooke back at the dorm, out like a light, just before we left for the island."

"With enough tranquilizer in her system to keep her down and out for a day and a half," said Jericho.

"I don't know the answer to that," said Will.

"Maybe she healed it right out of her system," said Elise. "Maybe she was on our tail the whole time."

No one spoke for a moment. A more somber mood had taken firm hold. Will took a few steps away from the others, looking out past the bridge. Ajay finished scrolling through the last of the drone's photos as it returned to the crossroads, but by then he was the only one watching them. He quietly disconnected the screen from the camera and stowed them both back in his pack.

Jericho walked out beside Will, respecting his silence as he stared into the distance.

"I figure it's kind of okay," said Will.

"What is?"

"To feel like what's in front of us is five times beyond impossible and we're all going to die really horrible, excruciating deaths."

"Most definitely. You'd have to be crazy to look at it any other way."

"I can't stand it, though," said Will, glancing back at his friends. "Feeling responsible. If that's what's going to happen."

"How would you feel if you didn't do anything?" asked Jericho. "Just pulled out the Carver, cut a hole in the air, and we all went home, called it a day."

Will looked at him skeptically. "We can't do that. Not now."

"That makes it easy, then. The choice is already made. You just have to tolerate the feelings."

"But I'm scared."

"Me too."

Will studied him. "You don't look like it."

"I thought you were the master of hiding your feelings."

"I am, sort of. I had to be."

"Think you're the only one?" asked Jericho.

"No. I just don't feel very brave right now."

Jericho exhaled, almost a sigh. "Brave is just a word we put on someone after they do something the rest of us don't think we'd be able to handle. Trust me, every one of them was plenty scared at the time. They just didn't let it get in the way."

Will studied him. "So being brave doesn't mean you're not scared, then."

"It means you're scared, and you do what you have to do in spite of it. You might want to write that one down."

"Sorry to interrupt." Ajay came up behind them, hesitant to intrude. "We were just wondering, Will, since time in its own strange way appears to be of the essence . . . what are we going to do now?"

Will gave another look at Jericho.

"Saddle up," said Will, and moved toward their mounts. "Ditch the backpacks and load all your gear in these saddlebags. How long do you think the ride to the Citadel will be?"

"Horses are fresh," said Jericho, walking beside him, looking off in the distance. "A few hours."

"But what are we going to do after . . . um . . . uh, *after* we get to the Citadel?" asked Ajay, trailing after them.

"I'll figure that out along the way," said Will.

FOURTEEN

WILL'S RULES FOR LIVING #14:
BEING BRAVE MEANS BEING AFRAID
AND GOING AHEAD WITH IT ANYWAY.

They crossed the bridge at a trot, Will and Elise in the lead, riding cautiously. There were no guardrails on either side and the last thing they needed was for one of the horses to bolt and take someone over the edge into the lake. Will noticed a number of large, ominous shapes swimming alongside the bridge just under the surface as they crossed. Some sort of river beasts, trolling for an easy meal.

None of them wore their helmets at first; Will didn't want to limit anyone's vision if there were monsters around, particularly Ajay's. Nick looked a little uneasy on his horse—he confessed that he'd never actually been on one before—but Will figured his freaky agility would quickly help him learn how to make it work. Ajay rode behind Jericho, his arms wrapped tightly around Coach's waist. He kept his eyes closed until after they'd cleared the bridge.

They passed another small building similar to the ones back in the garrison on the other side, but it had been left unguarded. The road was entirely paved with stone here and ran straight ahead for about half a mile before dropping out of sight down a hill. Will signaled them to halt, waved Jericho to the front, and asked Ajay to take a look ahead. At the coach's direction, Ajay stood up on the back of their horse and steadied himself with his hands on Jericho's shoulders, while Jericho held the animal dead still.

"The road ahead of us is clear to the highway," said Ajay, staring ahead; then he peered to his left. "It's clear, too, for the moment. The back end of the big column is about . . . two miles ahead. They're moving rapidly and I don't see many stragglers."

Will let the thought come to him instead of trying to force it. "We'll cross over and head north of that road for a while, then ride parallel to it toward the Citadel. Once we get close to the highway, put your helmets on."

"What do we say if one of them stops us?" asked Nick.

"Unless you recognize their language, don't say anything. There shouldn't be too many soldiers traveling off the road, but if there are, act like you own the place. Anyone else we run into will just think we're a small squad on some kind of mission."

"But what do we want to make them think we're doing?" asked Elise.

Will glanced at Ajay. "We're transporting a prisoner to the Makers. One of the ones Hobbes has been looking for, the humans that snuck into the zone."

"Oh dear God," said Ajay, sinking back down behind Jericho on the horse.

"That's not *actually* what we're doing, Ajay," said Elise. "You're going to be fine."

"You say that now, but what about when they've got me drawn and quartered over a cauldron of molten slag?"

"Dude, chill," said Nick. "We're not letting anything happen to you now. You're riding with the Bear."

Jericho reached back and patted Ajay on the knee. "Next time, I'll let you watch me change."

"Really? Oh, that would be most excellent."

That prospect seemed to settle Ajay down enough to proceed. Will rode on ahead at an easy canter. The land gradually transitioned from the flats near the water to the gently rolling green hills they'd seen in the drone's pictures. If it was possible to put the reasons why they were here out of his mind, Will thought, he could almost think of this part of the zone as pleasant. Maybe it was just the abundance of green—it was soothing and seemed more like home, even knowing it was all fake. Whatever the reason, he was grateful for every bit of peace he could hold on to right now, and he greedily soaked it in, feeling himself settle down as he rode along.

After Will crested the largest hill, the highway came into view, a long gray ribbon cutting perpendicularly across the landscape ahead. Elise rode up alongside him, looking out at the road.

I'm still working with Ajay on this, she sent to him.

Is he getting it?

A little bit, but more importantly it's keeping his mind off what's ahead of us.

Good idea.

"What do you think their plan is, Will?" she asked out loud, looking off into the distance toward the unseen Citadel. "What did you see in that photo? I know you saw something."

"I can't be completely sure. But if it's what I think it is, what they're planning doesn't line up with what Franklin and the Knights believe is going to happen. At all."

He didn't really want to say any more.

Tell me, she sent.

He could feel her staring daggers right into his mind and knew there was no point in withholding anything from her, especially something as explosive as this. He glanced back and saw that the others were still about a hundred yards behind them.

"I think they're building something that's going to give them their own way back in," he said quietly. "That's what is in that photo. I don't know what it is, exactly, or how it's supposed to work. But my guess is it's going to be big enough to send that whole army across."

He heard her take a deep breath, and when he finally looked over at her, he didn't see the righteous fury he'd expected that news would inspire. She looked vulnerable and frightened.

What is it? he sent.

"I'm looking around at this terrible place, and I'm thinking about that—sorry, I know he's still family—bat-shit crazy old grandfather of yours. And if there's some kind of disconnect between those two sides about what's coming next? My money's on the Makers."

"I think you're right," said Will. "But you're wrong about one thing: He's not my family. You guys are."

Elise looked away, hiding her face. He wondered if she was blushing or embarrassed and if, as usual, he'd said too much.

You okay? he sent.

No matter what else happens to us from here on out . . . She turned and looked at him, a look that pierced him to his core, a look he knew he'd never forget.

I love you for saying that, Will.

She spurred her horse and galloped on ahead, moving as one with the animal, looking like she'd been in that saddle her entire life.

Will kicked up his speed to try to follow but he knew he'd never catch her. He knew she wanted to get to the highway first, and he knew exactly why: to make sure it was safe for the rest of them to cross. That's how she was going to deal with her fear, which was as good a remedy as any, and he couldn't argue with it as a tactic. That warrior side of her had come into such full expression since they'd arrived here that he wasn't even worried about her safety, in spite of what he was allowing himself to feel about her. It was hard to imagine anything she'd find waiting on that road that could pose much of a threat to Elise when her powers were fully engaged.

He also knew how hard it was for her to express anything as tender as what she'd just said to him and that she might feel the need to do something violent in response.

Will turned back to the others and waved them onward. He felt a burst of that same violent impulse erupt inside him; he wanted them all to pick up their pace, confront whatever forces were waiting out there, and get down to it. Maybe it was just the effect of seeing that fire in Elise's eyes, but the way he felt right now, he was ready to take on that entire army and the Makers, and they could throw the damn Knights in as a bonus.

With Will leading them, they reached the road five minutes later where it crossed through a small wood. Elise was waiting for them, standing in her stirrups, a wild look in her eye as she stared ahead down the road.

The bodies of a squad of black-armored soldiers were scattered around the site like broken toys, at least ten of them. A couple of them had been tossed up into the branches of the trees, as if they'd been caught in a hurricane.

"What happened?" asked Ajay.

"They left behind another greeting party for us," she said. "Hiding in the trees."

"Nice work, sister," said Nick. "Next time save a few for me."

"Ajay, can you see how far Hobbes and Brooke or any of the others are ahead of us?" asked Elise.

Ajay popped up behind Jericho on the horse and peered

ahead. "I see a small group of riders on the highway, maybe three miles ahead. It looks like they're hurrying to catch up to the back of the column."

"We'll keep heading this way," said Will, pointing to the north of the road. "Just far enough to get us out of sight where Ajay can keep an eye on the road. But we need to move faster now. Everybody good with that?"

They rode hard and straight, heading north on a diagonal away from the highway, all of them bearing down. Both Jericho and Elise leaned into the gallop, peerless riders, and their horses were so big and powerful they chewed up the ground, pounding ahead. Even Nick—who already seemed to have gotten the hang of basic horsemanship—kept pace with them, using his legs to clamp onto the saddle, whipping the reins back and forth like some cowboy he'd seen in a Western. Will struggled to stay at the front of the pack.

A few minutes later, Will signaled a halt, and although he couldn't see it, Ajay looked back and confirmed that he still had the highway clearly in sight to the south.

"And it's a good thing we crossed when we did," he said, looking farther back to the left. "There's another column moving up from the rear."

"Onward," said Will.

He led them straight ahead at a steady gallop, paralleling the road. The green grass and gentle hills he'd enjoyed ended not long afterward, giving way to a flat hardpan of dirt and blasted rocks. That range of mountains loomed over them off to their right now, and the ground gradually tilted up toward them. These were cold, black, and barren peaks. They projected their harsh weight down on the whole region and looked as if they'd thrust brutally out of the earth in the last hour.

Big round rocks began to dot the landscape, some of them immense, and soon there were so many they had to slow down and pick their way through them. Will was grateful for the cover they offered from distant unseen eyes but the place made him uneasy. He felt like the rocks themselves looked angry, cast off by those mountains as they continued to assert themselves. In the distance, echoing down from the mountains, they could hear what sounded like the grinding and tearing of almost constant landslides, boulders clacking off each other as they tumbled downward in some titanic bowling alley. Will half expected to see a barrage of them come barreling down the canyons at them at any moment.

The sky turned ever blacker as they rode on, the constant twilight they'd grown accustomed to now more like perpetual dusk, a grim shroud drawn over the land. They had to slow their pace to a canter. Jericho took the lead now so Ajay could keep an eye ahead and direct their path forward through the rocks.

As they cleared a dense cluster of boulders, a sliver of light appeared on the horizon, a slight glow that gradually dimmed upward as they rode toward it.

I . . . see . . . campfires . . .

Will heard the words slip into his head. He looked over and saw Ajay grinning at him from the back of Jericho's horse. Will gave a slight shake of his head.

You are *a quick study,* he answered.

I . . . told . . . you . . .

Will glanced the other way over at Elise, riding alongside him, focused grimly on the light in the distance.

He can do it.

I know.

Great work, that's incredible.

I didn't have that much to do with it.

Granted, it's like talking to a two-year-old—okay, the world's smartest two-year-old—but it's still kind of startling.

Be glad, she answered. *We're going to need all the help we can get.*

They soon passed through the boulder-strewn area onto a flat, dry, featureless plain, devoid of growth or life of any kind. Will thought it was as if the Makers had lost interest in creating anything other than utilitarian ground this close to their home, nothing more than a way to get from here to there. They picked up their pace again, the cold glow from the camp cutting through the gloom and lighting up half of the horizon ahead of them.

Ajay abruptly held up his hand and called a halt and they slowed to a trot. Fifty yards ahead, the edge of the plain dropped off abruptly. Will dismounted, handed his horse to Elise, and walked forward until he came within sight of the edge of a cliff. He realized they were on top of a wide bluff, perched over and looking down on a huge, bowl-shaped valley below. The main highway provided the only practical entrance into it, through a narrow neck far below to his left. A similar bluff rose up across from them on the other side of the bowl. Both bluffs ran all the way around the rim of the valley, until they both bumped up against the obstacle that provided its northern perimeter.

The wall.

The photos they'd seen from the drone hadn't prepared them for actually laying eyes on the Citadel. The quality of the construction didn't surprise him—smooth, seamless, brutal, and unadorned—but the scope of the complex was almost beyond imagining. The wall wasn't simply tall; it was hundreds of feet high, blank and oppressive, and it angled slightly forward so that it seemed to exert its own gravity on the valley below.

Will looked back at Elise. *Keep the horses quiet. The rest of you need to see this.*

Elise gathered the horses together and, he assumed, communicated something to them that left them calm and willing to wait patiently. Then she and the others walked up beside Will. The moment they all saw the hellish vision, the entire party immediately dropped to their knees, as much in shock as in an effort to stay out of sight.

That glow they'd seen rose from a thousand campfires. Gathered around them, from wall to canyon wall, the entire bowl was carpeted with a sea of malignant armies. There were many distinct encampments, but from here they all blended together in waves of motion and sound and gleams of dangerous metal, rising from the dread valley.

"Monstrous," said Ajay softly. "Monstrous."

"I don't scare easy, right?" whispered Nick. "But in this case I might have to change my shorts."

"That's part of what those walls are for," said Elise. "To inspire fear and awe."

"Like I said," said Jericho. "That's how they keep the peasants in line."

"At least we have a better idea of what we're up against," said Will.

"Us against *all that*?" asked Nick. "Dude, you need a checkup from the neck up."

The encampment appeared to cover every square inch of the valley, and more regiments of foot soldiers were marching down the road to join them, their footsteps stomping out a martial drumbeat. There didn't appear to be enough room to pitch another tent on unoccupied ground, other than the line of the stone highway that cut through the teeming throng all the way to the walls.

"I see Hobbes," said Ajay.

"Gimme a break," said Nick. "How can you pick out one dude in all that mess down there?"

"He's on that central road," said Ajay, pointing down. "Riding toward the wall, about halfway through the valley. With a much larger escort this time."

"What about Brooke?" asked Will.

"She's riding right behind him."

"Guess there can't be that many blondes down there," said Nick.

"Actually, there is an entire battalion of some kind of creatures with golden hair over that way," said Ajay, pointing to the left near the canyon wall. "Although it's covering their entire bodies."

"Awesome," said Nick, taking out his binoculars. "Sounds like yetis."

"Are Hobbes and Brooke heading toward an entrance?" asked Jericho.

"Yes," said Ajay, creeping forward a bit. "Where, as you might imagine, there is a pair of massively impressive gates set in the wall."

"Yep, definitely yetis," said Nick, looking through the binoculars.

"Would you please try to stay focused," said Jericho.

"Dude, it's *yetis*," said Nick, but then he swung the glasses over toward the gates. "Hey, you're right, I can sort of see Brooke, too. And if you don't mind my saying so, she looks kind of hot in that armor."

Will craned his neck up to see a little better; he couldn't locate Brooke, but he could just make out the shape of the gates, the only disruption in the unbroken smooth line of the walls. He took out his own binoculars and sighted them along the road until he spotted movement. As he adjusted the focus wheel, he caught a flash of long blond hair against dark armor.

Seeing her there, riding into the middle of that darkness, Will's heart sank and questions filled his head. How had he so badly misjudged her? How could she have fallen so far into whatever level of madness was required to put her there in that terrible place at this particular time? What good could she think was ever going to come from what she was doing?

"Are the gates opening?" asked Jericho.

"Not the massive gates themselves," said Ajay. "It appears there's a smaller entrance or door built into them. Wide enough to admit a couple of riders."

"Get me to a church," said Nick, staring through the glasses. "Would you look at those knockers."

Elise punched him on the shoulder. Nick lowered the glasses.

"What?"

"You know what," she said.

"I was talking about the *doors*," he said, offering her the binoculars. "Look for yourself."

"There are indeed two immense rings of steel attached to large plates on the gates," said Ajay. "Which I suppose you could mischaracterize as 'knockers.'"

"See?" Nick asked Elise.

"Although I suspect they're purely ornamental," said Ajay.

"Aren't knockers always ornamental?" asked Nick.

This time Will punched him on the shoulder.

"I wouldn't say that," said Jericho. "Some of those jamokes down there are definitely big enough to use them."

"Knock, knock," said Nick. "Who's there? Boo. Boo who? Hey, what are you so upset about?"

"I am going to throw you off this cliff," said Elise.

"They're riding inside now," said Ajay. "Hobbes, Brooke, and their escort . . . and now the smaller doors are closing behind them."

"So she's inside," said Will.

"So how do *we* get inside?" asked Elise.

Will looked from her to Ajay. Then everyone else slowly turned and looked at Ajay, who finally noticed the attention. He stood up and slowly backed away from the cliff.

"Oh, no. Absolutely not, Will. I'm putting my foot down this time—"

"Come on, buddy," said Nick.

"No! It was one thing to employ me as the basis for a cover story while passing through relatively unoccupied enemy territory, but to ask me to sit on the back of a horse, unprotected, and ride through an assembled host comprising the entire history of human nightmares into God knows whatever worse assembly of creatures might be waiting for us on the other side of those doors, provided we even make it that far? It's not fair no matter how you look at it, and I simply won't stand for it."

Will listened carefully. Heard the tremor in Ajay's voice and registered the terror in his eyes. He glanced over at Elise and first saw and then heard that she was thinking the same thing.

Maybe it's too much to ask.

No maybe about it, she answered.

"I heard that," said Ajay.

Will and Elise glanced at each other, concerned.

Can he bust into our channel already?

"No, you didn't," said Will, calling his bluff.

"Heard what?" asked Nick.

"And if you did, you'd know that I happen to agree with you, Ajay," said Will. "It is too much to ask. We're going to look for another way inside."

"Thank you," said Ajay, taking Will's hand and trying to kiss it. "Thank you thank you thank you."

"But if we can't find one," said Elise, "you're Plan B."

"Then I'll find us another way in even if it kills me," said Ajay.

"Dude, what did you hear?" Nick asked Ajay.

"It's not important."

"Leave it alone, kid," Jericho said to Nick.

They all backed away from the cliff and then quietly walked their horses far enough from the edge to feel they could mount up safely again.

As they started riding, Will stared up at the Citadel, hoping for some kind of inspiration to strike. He felt as close to total exhaustion as he thought he could get. The sight of that army down there coupled with the dread gravity of the wall bearing down on them left him feeling hopeless and afraid. The task ahead seemed more than impossible, more than he could even begin to surmount. He hardly possessed the energy to lift his head and look up at the Citadel. The faint thought that everything in the zone, on some level, might not be real offered the only comfort he could find.

They were much closer to the wall here, and the line continued on past where it bumped up against the bluff for a considerable distance to their right, for at least another mile or more. Will briefly considered trying to send a mental probe out along the wall, to see if he could locate a weakness or opening in the fortress's implacable shell, but the risk of having it run into some force or creature along the way that could sense it and trace it back to him outweighed the benefit. Once an alarm was sounded, they wouldn't be going up against the kind of weak-minded minions they'd dealt with up to this point. They were standing on the doorstep of the darkness itself, and the Makers—or the Other Team, or whatever they called themselves—were just on the other side of that wall. The slightest misstep now would have the deadliest consequences, for all of them.

Will led them along at a walk, trying to keep as quiet as possible. He attempted for what seemed like the thousandth time to reach out mentally toward Dave, hoping they might be close enough to him now to get through, feeling more in need of his guidance than ever. Will summoned up the image of that large dome from the photograph, the place where he'd intuited that Dave might be, and zeroed in on it.

Nothing.

What are you thinking, Will?

Will turned his head to look at Elise but she was looking up at the wall, preoccupied; she hadn't sent the message. Then he realized . . . that was Ajay's voice.

I don't know yet, Will answered.

Before offering any advice of my own—and I do have a suggestion that might be helpful—may I first express my deepest gratitude to you for sparing me from the dim-witted scenario that would have offered me up as bait in order to gain entry to this wretched fortress.

Ajay sounded as clear as a bell now and as crisp as the voice of a postgraduate student, or maybe a professor; the two-year-old had grown up fast.

You already thanked me, Ajay.

But not properly.

Will finally glanced over at him, riding along behind

Jericho, smiling beatifically, his bright luminous eyes shining and opened wider than ever. A radically different quality emanated from Ajay now; he was calmer and centered. He looked much older and wiser than his years, a lot more than he had even ten minutes earlier. The word that came to Will's mind to best describe this new quality was *saintly*.

You've been the truest friend I've ever known, or will ever hope to know. Since the day we met you've helped me in every possible way, far from the least of which was showing me how to find the strength to endure this terrifying transformation we're all undergoing. You've done this more by way of doing than in anything you've said, although your words are always welcome, and I am eternally grateful to you in ways I can't even express, although I remain willing to try—

You're doing a fine job, Will sent back, if for no other reason than to slow down the torrent of words flowing into his head. *I really appreciate what you're saying.*

I just thought that, since I seem to suddenly possess the means to do so in a conveniently private way, I had better seize the moment to say it now. Who knows if or when we'll have another opportunity? The changes are occurring so rapidly now, certainly within me, that I've lost sight of any logical end point, not to mention that after a dispassionate analysis of our circumstances, I can't help concluding that we're nearing some sort of resolution, one way or another.

Let's hope you're right.

The wall looked as if it ran on forever, but the distance between it and the bluff gradually narrowed. Will tapped his mount into a trot and they all picked up their pace. Jericho kept even with Will, so Ajay remained directly across from him, and once they'd made eye contact again, Ajay continued.

I also want you to know that I'll be perfectly at peace with whatever happens to me from this point forward. I'm not afraid anymore. Of this place, or whatever's in there or even of dying. Dying painfully over a protracted period of time I'm not so sure about, but if it was to happen suddenly, I'm more or less sure I can handle it.

I guess I'm glad to hear that, Ajay, but I'm going to do everything I can to make sure it doesn't happen.

Ajay gave him an O-K sign.

Now, with regard to our aforementioned powers, one of the most recent that's developed for me—one that I actually just added to the repertoire within the last few minutes—is that I appear to have acquired the ability to project my mind into places that are far beyond my physical location. I haven't had time to fully test the limits of it yet, of course, but I believe this is traditionally referred to as—

Omniscience.

Ajay smiled at him. *Exactly so. Le mot juste. Have you experienced this one as well yet?*

A little. You're a bit ahead of me on that one, Ajay.

Well, in addition to our own individual abilities, I believe that some of our secondary powers will inevitably begin to overlap. This telepathy, for instance, although I don't imagine that Nick has picked that up yet—

He can receive, but he doesn't know where it's coming from.

I will now politely endeavor to avoid making fun of our muscle-bound friend and change the subject.

Very decent of you.

Anyway, I just sent my mind . . . which is interesting, because since I'm also able to simultaneously still be present here while conversing with you, I believe this puts me well on the way to another arcane ability often referred to as "bilocation." More on that later.

Will glanced back and noticed that Elise was staring at the two of them. She appeared to be sensing their conversation, if not actually able to hear it.

As I was saying, I just sent my mind's eye ahead along the wall and unless I'm very much mistaken—unlikely—there is a second entrance less than half a mile ahead on our left. It's nowhere near as grand as the one we just saw out front, which I think we can safely characterize as largely for show, but it is almost as tall and wide as the other and it appears to be fully functional.

Why didn't you say so in the first place?

Forgive me, you're absolutely right. I should have mentioned that straightaway.

Show me where, Will said.

He kicked up into a canter and Jericho kept pace right beside him, with Nick and Elise right behind. Thinking he'd see it when they arrived, Will was surprised when a series of images appeared in his mind as they rode.

He realized that Ajay was "uploading" a mind's-eye survey of what he'd seen.

And when, five minutes later, they arrived at a particular spot along the bluff where Will knew to stop, having seen the images already, he looked down at exactly the location Ajay had just shown him.

The drop from the bluff to the wall was much shorter here because the ground had risen gradually as they traveled along the wall toward the mountains. No more than thirty feet down, while the wall here was no more than fifty yards from the base of the bluff, where a well-traveled road paralleled the wall.

The passageway, double hinged gates, was neither as tall nor as wide as the one they'd seen in the front, and the road led straight inside.

It was also wide open.

FIFTEEN

WILL'S RULES FOR LIVING #15:
AN OPEN DOOR IS EITHER A GREETING OR A TRAP.
BEST TO DECIDE WHICH BEFORE YOU ENTER.

Elise ordered the horses to stand back in a group and keep quiet. The five of them crept forward on foot to the edge of the bluff and looked down at the gates. The road that entered between them immediately reached an intersection where it branched off to the left. It also continued straight up the rise, where they were stationed, and branched off to the north along the wall, toward the mountains. As they watched, a small train of wagons rolled into view from the north side and passed between the gates into the Citadel. They appeared to be fully loaded with black rocks or coal.

"Raw materials," whispered Jericho. "From the mountains."

"They must have some mines up there," said Will.

"So this must be the service entrance," said Ajay. "I would hazard a guess that the construction project we saw in the photos must be nearby."

The wagons were driven by beaten-down-looking sub-human figures in ragged clothes, and they were waved inside by a platoon of guards at the gates geared up in the same black armor they'd taken off the soldiers at the bridge garrison.

"Dudes, this is like a gift," said Nick, cracking his knuckles.

"Let's do this," said Will.

"Time to bang some heads," said Nick, and then turned a

somersault toward his horse, where he pulled out a spiked mace from his saddlebag.

"Or if you'd prefer to take a more rational approach and put Plan B into action," said Ajay, "under these more manageable circumstances I'm quite willing to volunteer my services."

"That's the spirit," said Jericho, patting him on the back.

"On foot or horseback?" asked Elise.

"Horseback," said Will.

Elise turned to the horses, and they immediately trotted forward. Moments later they were mounted up and slowly making their way down the hill to the gates. Looking ahead, Will saw the first two guards outside notice their approach and call to their superior, a larger grunt who came out of a kiosk on the inside of the wall.

"How would you say the dudes in the armor are different from the freaks camped out back there in front of the gates?" asked Nick.

"They're probably bred for more intelligence and discipline," said Ajay. "Military prototypes."

"Then I say we ride in hard like we belong there and ignore these bozos," said Nick.

"No, they might outrank us," said Will. "We need to talk to them."

"But we don't talk monster," said Nick.

"We'll handle it," said Will; then he turned to Elise and Ajay. "I'll take the big one; you distract the others."

Once they reached level ground, Will led them forward at a trot over the final stretch to the Citadel. By then the sergeant had closed ranks with four other grunts, barring their passage, and he raised a hand to stop them before the gates.

Will raised his hand in greeting and sent words right into the sergeant's mind:

There's no need to stop this party. They're the ones we've been waiting for, the important ones we're supposed to let right through.

The sergeant's eye had immediately gone to Ajay on the back of Jericho's horse, but when Will's message hit him, his brain locked up before he could even ask his first question.

Ajay and Elise looked at each other, nodded, then looked at the guards. Two of the grunts behind the sergeant turned immediately and went for each other's throats. The other two grunts jumped into the fight, while the sergeant tried to break it up. Will was about to ride past, when a crowd of soldiers ran out from a barracks toward the melee.

I'll handle them, Ajay sent to Will.

Ajay pointed a finger at the leader of the second group; he stopped immediately and broke into a strange dance; then the one next to him started dancing along right next to him.

Do you recognize it? Ajay asked Will.

Three other guards started performing exactly the same strange, convoluted, synchronized dance steps, and it spread until twenty of them were moving along, when Will realized:

Thriller?

Correct!

"Welcome to Soul Train," said Jericho.

Suppressing a laugh, Will snapped the reins and calmly led their party through the gates. Between the free-for-all and the bizarre dance number taking place around him, the sergeant never even gave them a second glance.

They turned a corner past the cluster of soldiers into the Citadel. The grounds were muddy and cluttered here, piled high with stacks of supplies, barrels, crates, and various building materials on pallets.

Workers from the wagons they'd seen enter minutes earlier were unloading their cargo of rocks into the maw of a gigantic iron-plated machine that vibrated violently, some kind of pulverizer by the look and sound of it. A steady stream of coal and dust passed out the other end of the machine on a rickety conveyor belt, depositing the end product onto a mountainous pile. From there, a crowd of minions, dusted almost a solid black, shoveled the coal into smaller carts on tracks that then rolled off somewhere deeper inside the complex.

Like the soldiers they'd seen, these workers appeared to be subhuman hybrids, some kind of rudimentary humanoid stock crossed with various beasts of burden and possessing qualities of both. They were apparently bred for strength and stamina, for their misshapen faces looked blank and their eyes cold and vacant. Whatever intelligence they might have once possessed had been bred out of them. As he watched them scurrying fearfully around, Will felt a surge of horror and pity—a slave labor force, in seemingly endless supply, created in some foul factory, treated like animals. There was no reason to treat them in any decent or humane way. If one broke down, you just made another one.

He glanced over at Elise and Ajay. When they looked back, he knew they were thinking the same thing:

They're not all that different from us, she sent.

No, sent Ajay. *They were just designed for more menial work.*

What were we *made for, then?* asked Elise.

As they moved along, sounds of heavy construction filtered toward them: the bang of hammers, rhythmic earth-shaking stomps, and the screech of grinding gears. Will signaled the others forward and they followed the tracks of the coal carts deeper into the Citadel, past storage yards and huge stone, glass, and ironworks. Through the partially open doors of a tall building they saw the red-hot glow of a foundry. Inside it was an immense cauldron filled with molten iron that ran out of a chute. Will looked up and saw choking black smoke billow out of one of those mammoth chimneys they'd seen in the photos. It burned his eyes, and gritty particulate matter cascading through the air choked his lungs.

No one else wearing the black armor seemed to be in this area, and not one of the legions of workers paid them the slightest attention. They rode past the foundry, around the corner of a line of huge sheds, and as the clouds of smoke thinned out, the area opened up in front of them, a vast stretch of empty, desolate space that Will also recognized from one of the photos. They dismounted, Elise instructed the horses to wait for them, and they crept around the corner, hiding behind a pile of supplies to take a closer look.

This was the active construction site they'd spotted, large patches of dirt around it tainted by the black smoking soil that Will had reacted to in the photograph. In the center of that spread of despoiled ground, about a half mile in the distance, hundreds of workers swarmed around a gigantic slab of rock or concrete that appeared to be roughly the size of a football field. Rising from the slab was the central object they'd seen in the photo, which had been impossible to identify from the overhead angle of the drone. But they could see it now.

Two huge and graceful arcs, like crescent moons, rose from two solid, rectangular chunks of hard metal to which they were attached or embedded. Will guessed that the arcs stood at least as tall as a ten-story building. They appeared to be fashioned from the same smooth black adamantine material as the Citadel walls. The arcs were facing each other. Their bases were already connected together, forming the bottom of a circle, and the tops of the arcs were within a few feet of touching each other.

Both arcs were completely contained within a network of

scaffolding that was filled by a milling workforce attending to various tasks on them. Most of the effort seemed to be concentrated near the very top, where materials were being continually raised up on long platforms by block and tackle pulley systems. They saw sparks falling and flashes of light from up near where the points of the arcs were about to converge.

As they watched, one of the workers tumbled off the highest scaffold and hit the concrete pad below with a sickening thud. Not one of the other workers around it paid the slightest attention, walking right past the body where it landed and lay motionless.

"Geez Louise," said Nick.

"So much for a worker's comp claim," said Jericho.

"What is that thing?" asked Elise plainly. "What are they building?"

"It's so obvious. I know exactly what this is," said Nick, squinting at it. "They're building a huge honking big gargantuan . . . circle."

"It's a lot more than just a circle," said Ajay, staring at it intently.

Will noticed another workstation off the right of the concrete slab, under a bank of bright lights. There were a couple of large tents in the area, and inside one of them a group of workers huddled around a large hunk of round metallic housing, attending to some kind of finer, more precise work.

"They're building a Carver," said Will.

"I believe you're quite right, Will," said Ajay.

"That's ridonkulous," said Nick. "You said you had the only one."

"I said I had the only one that we knew about."

"And you also said that Franklin told you that was the only one."

"Franklin probably doesn't know about this one," said Elise.

"But they . . . they can't hold that one in their hand, so how does . . . ." Nick was staring up at the arcs, dismayed. "How could they build one that . . . ? How could they . . . ?"

"It's quite a simple plan, Nick. First they built an army," said Ajay, gesturing back toward the valley. "Now they're building its delivery system."

"But how is this thing supposed to work?" asked Nick.

"Look closely at both sides and you'll notice they're installing a metallic track around the inside edge of the circle," said Ajay, pointing to the arc.

"Yeah?" said Nick.

Will looked closer and noticed the metal tracks for the first time. Then Ajay pointed toward the workers inside the tents.

"Over here they're assembling a sophisticated motorized unit designed to revolve or ride around that track. I believe that within it will be contained the same cutting or carving element yours possesses, and as it travels around the circumference of the circle, it will carve the portal."

"And open the gates of hell," said Will softly.

"And hundreds of thousands of these things show up without warning," said Elise. "All over the planet."

"Blitzkrieg," said Jericho. "Surprise attack."

"Hold on, this bunch of skeevy creepos versus the full might of the U.S. military? Sorry, I'm just not that freaked out about it."

"They don't have only brute force on their side," said Will. "As we've seen, they can go stealth mode, and we're not just talking about our country; the attack could be worldwide. There's a whole lot of damage they could do."

"Destroy communications, take down power grids," said

Ajay. "They would undoubtedly go after leadership targets. Influence and control their minds from a distance. The result could be total chaos."

"So you're saying like a battalion of invisible armed yetis could show up on the White House lawn," said Nick, thinking it through. "I guess that wouldn't be good."

"Franklin also said they've got a bunch of units already in place," said Will. "Hidden away. He called them *sleepers*, ready to be awakened once they start the invasion."

"We also don't know how deeply the Knights have infiltrated political and military infrastructures," said Elise.

"After three generations?" said Ajay. "They may have their hands on the levers of power already. Give the word and they could destroy our ability to defend against them before it even starts."

"In other words, Nick," said Jericho, "once that door's open, all bets are off."

"Okay, okay, you convinced me," said Nick. "Giant Carver bad. Let's take it out."

"How close are they to finishing this thing?" asked Jericho, looking up at the arcs.

"Difficult to determine that precisely without closer examination," said Ajay, his eyes scanning all around the site. "But given their bountiful access to resources and unlimited labor pool, I would estimate that they're no more than a day or two away from completing the assembly and bringing the system online."

"Finally some good news," said Nick.

"That's good news?" asked Elise.

"He said a *day* or two," said Nick.

"On the other hand, time is strangely elusive here," said Ajay. "So who knows what any reference to it ultimately means."

"So why don't we just put the hammer to this thing, right now?" asked Nick. "Bring it down on their freakin' heads."

"I'd like to ask Dave about that first," said Will. "Since we might need his help doing it."

"If we can find him," said Jericho.

"But that's why we're here. First things first. We still have enough time to locate him. Unless anybody else feels otherwise—"

Before anyone could answer, they heard the oncoming stomp of many marching boots. They turned back behind the cover of the sheds and dismounted as a column of black-armored soldiers came into view to their right, marching along the main road toward the site. Hobbes, the only figure on horseback, was at the head of the column, and he barked orders at the soldiers as they drew close to the construction. All the work in the area came to a halt, and the workers on the ground scurried out of their way. At a final order from Hobbes, the soldiers broke ranks and lined up on either side of the arc as they reached the concrete base of the platform.

Will felt a peculiar pressure in his head, not painful but a kind of sensory overload; it sounded as if ten thousand voices were whispering inside his brain all at once. He looked around and saw that the others—with the exception of Jericho—were putting their hands near their ears and reacting in a similar way.

The whispering gave way to a swooshing wind, or Will thought maybe it was more like the sound of waves washing onshore, a hundred of them, all at once. He saw that the line of soldiers was wavering, many of them swaying as if fighting to stay upright. Even Hobbes, who had dismounted near the platform supporting the giant arcs, appeared to be under some kind of extreme duress, bracing himself against its metallic base. Then the source of all this interference traveled into view from right to left along the road, passing between the lined-up soldiers.

The thing stood at least twenty feet tall, like a spike, more thin than thick but still substantial. A long cloak of some shimmering silvery black material completely covered it from its neck to the ground, where it swept along, unsupported by any legs or limbs that Will could see. If it had arms, or even a torso for that matter, those, too, were contained within the cloak. Its head, or where its head should have been, was covered by a drooping cowl that arched up and over from its shoulders, concealing whatever was within in a deep black emptiness.

The sight of the thing filled Will with overwhelming dread and revulsion, jamming his mind with signals he couldn't even sort out. He had to force himself to keep looking at it, and he sensed that the others around him were reacting the same way.

The creature's movements were strange, rhythmic and more than mesmerizing, and it appeared to be floating just above the ground rather than walking on it. The oscillating vibrations they were all hearing and reacting to seemed to be emanating from its center, and as disruptive as it felt to them, it seemed to be far worse for the soldiers and Hobbes, who were much closer to it. A few of the ones on the line keeled over as it passed.

The shrouded figure stopped when it reached Hobbes, just below the arcs, where it appeared to hover rather than stand. Will couldn't hear any of what passed between them from this distance, but the creature definitely seemed to be communicating with Hobbes.

Will gritted his teeth against the mental interference and whispered to Ajay, "Can you see anything?"

Ajay leaned forward, blinking repeatedly to fight off the static, studying the two of them.

"It's an inspection," he whispered. "It's come to check on

the progress. Hobbes looks harried. This thing frightens him. He doesn't like being near it."

They finished their brief conversation and the figure floated slowly away from Hobbes. As they watched, it took a slow turn around the entire base of the circle, apparently examining it up and down. Another worker fell off the scaffolding about half-way to the top and fell to the ground near the creature; it never even reacted, floating right over the corpse.

During which, Will noticed that Jericho didn't seem to be suffering any of the same debilitating effects the rest of them were feeling.

"You don't feel what we're feeling from this thing?" Will asked him softly.

Jericho shook his head. "I don't know if that's good or bad," he said.

"That's one of them," said Will. "One of the Makers."

"I kind of figured that," said Jericho.

"Why are we feeling it and you're not?" asked Elise.

Jericho turned to Will. "I think you know the answer to that."

Elise turned to Will. "What?"

"We're connected to it," said Will reluctantly. "Coach isn't."

"Connected to it how?"

Will looked at them; they were all turned to him now. He didn't see any way to avoid telling them and, at this point, couldn't think of a valid reason not to.

"These things, the Makers . . . they're the source for the genetic material that Franklin . . . used for the Paladin Prophecy," said Will.

The other three roommates stared at him, blank and uncomprehending.

"The DNA that the Knights used when they messed with

us . . . or depending on what you believe, what these creatures compelled the Knights to do."

"You're saying that the Makers gave the Knights some of their own genetic code?" asked Ajay.

"Exactly right."

"And that that's what the Knights used for those in vitro procedures, long ago in Hobbes's and Nepsted's day and again when they revived the program?"

"Yes."

"Are you sure about that?" asked Elise.

"No question about it," said Will. "We didn't get all this stuff we can do from random animals or other people. It came from them."

"Shut your mouth," said Nick.

"I'm not making this up, Nick," said Will. "Franklin told me so himself."

They were each managing the shock in their own ways. Ajay seemed to take it in stride, processing it so quickly and logically that the information seemed to bypass his emotions. Nick just kept shaking his head, his jaw set, refusing to believe it. Elise looked like she accepted it, and it wound her up into a cold fury.

"Like we needed another reason to hate him," she said.

"So now we know how and why this has happened to us," said Ajay, taking it in stride.

Nick stood rigidly, shaking his head, every muscle in his body tensed and straining. Tears flowed down his cheeks. "You shoulda told us. You shoulda told us, Will."

"Why? What good would it have done?"

"At least we would have known . . . what kind of freaks we are. Like those poor bastards in the tanks we saw down in the hospital . . ."

Elise put her arms around him and said something softly into his ear. He shook his head, resisting, and then finally let her comfort him.

"It doesn't change anything, really," said Ajay, looking at Will, his eyes shining. "And given the inherent difficulty of what we're here to accomplish and who we're up against, one might actually interpret it as good news—"

"Will," said Jericho.

Will looked at Jericho, then turned to see what he was staring at so intently.

The Maker had moved to the edge of the concrete pad closest to them. Standing upright and alert, it was even taller than it had looked before, swaying in midair.

And it was looking in their direction.

Will blinked on the Grid and saw a plume of energy erupt from the Maker's cowl and fly right toward them. He didn't have time to determine the nature or intent of the burst.

"It knows we're here," he said, pulling everyone back around the corner of the nearest shed. "Get the horses."

As they scrambled away, Will turned back and instinctively threw out a thought-form shield before turning the corner. A second later, the energy from the Maker slammed into his shield, and the pile of supplies they'd been hiding behind exploded with a flash, debris raining down on the shed's roof.

Will followed the others around the corner as the horses came up to meet them and they all quickly jumped into the saddle.

"We're making straight for that dome," he said. "Follow me. Don't stop for anything."

"I know the way," said Ajay.

Will spurred his horse and galloped away and the others followed. He didn't understand what Ajay had meant, until an image appeared in his mind:

An overhead map of the Citadel.

Will recognized it as a composite assembled from all the photographs taken by the drone.

I memorized the grid, naturally, and thought it might be useful to send to you, Ajay sent.

You have no idea.

Will blinked, turning on the Grid again, and then he just seemed to know how to integrate Ajay's image into a kind of transparent heads-up display that appeared in front of his line of sight.

I've even taken the liberty of plotting a course to the dome from our current location.

A bright point of light appeared in Will's display, and it moved with them, charting their progress along a glowing line that flowed around and between the many buildings ahead of them until it reached the dome.

Ajay, you're better than GPS.

Using Ajay's system to guide them, Will led them out of the construction area, never slowing, the four horses' hooves hammering down narrow alleys and careening around corners. The few workers they encountered jumped out of their way or were sent flying. It was darker in this convoluted nest of structures; what little light was left in the sky barely slipped past the tall buildings surrounding them. Will stole a glance back and didn't yet see any signs of pursuit from the construction site. Elise and Jericho moved up to flank him, riding just behind him, with Nick bringing up the rear, arms flailing and elbows flapping as he spurred his mount along.

Elise, take out anything that comes at us. A lot of side streets coming up. No telling how quickly they'll spread the alarm.

I'm on it.

Following the route Ajay had plotted, they turned a corner that took them out of the haphazardly plotted warren of side streets, down a long stretch of empty road between high buildings, and under and through an archway into an entirely different section of the Citadel. Will recognized it immediately as the classical section of buildings they'd seen in the photographs.

The roads broadened into an orderly plan of smooth, brick-paved avenues, where the architectural style arrayed around them looked like a college campus built on a gargantuan scale. Most of the buildings sported immense columns across portico entrances, fashioned from the same shade of gray granite. Every inch of it was constructed with a cold, calculated symmetrical perfection, immaculate and completely devoid of any signs of life.

Will wondered if anything went on inside those buildings, any life at all, or if it was all for show. The shape of it seemed vaguely familiar in a strange way, until he realized that it reminded him of the ruined city they'd found under the Crag. That made perfect sense: The same creatures had built both places; why wouldn't they duplicate the layout if this was their idea of home? But would the Makers look like the skeletons they'd seen down there? The creature they'd just encountered at the arcs didn't conform to those dimensions. Maybe after ages in this strange place they'd evolved into something else entirely?

Will followed Ajay's map onto one of four diagonal avenues that branched off from a large circle with a dry lifeless fountain in its center. Still no sights or sounds of anyone pursuing them, which troubled Will almost more than an actual pursuit would have. What were they waiting for? He didn't see any chance that they could've gotten away clean. The Citadel was only so big and there were only so many places to run.

The avenue led them into a massive rectangular plaza, surrounded on three sides by variations on the rows of columned buildings they'd seen throughout the district. On the side of the plaza farthest from them, set atop a plateau at the end of a tall set of broad flat stairs, stood the round domed building from the photograph. A large covered porch projected out in front of its entrance, with a row of columns supporting either side.

"There it is," said Will, urging them forward.

He blinked away Ajay's map overlay but kept the Grid on, scanning for signs of life as they thundered across the plaza, the horses' hooves echoing spookily around the vast empty space. Will kept scanning; at least five other equally large avenues emptied into the plaza and not one of them yielded a single heat signature.

Do you see anything? he sent to Ajay.

I'm afraid I'm too busy clinging on to Coach for dear life at the moment.

"Don't stop!" shouted Will to the others. "Ride right up the stairs!"

Will spurred on his mount, snapping at the reins and urging it up onto the stairs. The risers were broad and flat, altering the horses' gait but hardly slowing their speed. The stairs seemed to go on forever—there had to be well over a hundred of them—but Will didn't slow until he reached the top, and then raced across a wide, flat patio to the edge of the porch.

He leaped off his horse and sprinted toward the tall set of double doors straight ahead.

"Keep an eye out! And keep the horses close! Bring the saddlebags!"

The others dismounted behind him. Ajay looked back toward the plaza and as Elise gathered the horses, the others followed Will.

"Anything back there?" Will shouted as he got to the doors.

"Nothing yet," said Ajay.

Each door sported a long, thick, vertical iron pull. Will stopped and gripped one of them, then paused to catch his breath. Nick and Jericho ran up beside him, and he waited for Ajay and Elise to join them. The horses gathered in a group under the porch nearby.

"If there's any of them in here, we go in swinging," said Will.

They all looked at him, waiting, eager, ready to engage. No one looked frightened, not even Ajay. Their readiness filled him with confidence and pride.

"Whatever happens from here," he said, "it's been my privilege to call you my friends."

He pulled on the handle, and the door moved toward him. Immensely heavy, it pivoted almost effortlessly on some concealed hinging and opened.

They stepped into a circular atrium and the door whispered closed behind them. There was dark marble flooring underfoot and scaled-down decorative columns distributed around the perimeter. The space was lit softly and evenly from some unseen sources. A dozen symmetrical niches held large urns or statues of abstract shapes. Their footsteps echoed sharply as they crossed the marble floor.

There were no other doors.

"What the heck . . . ," said Nick.

"Spread out," said Will. "Look around. There's got to be another way out of here."

"It must be a puzzle room," said Ajay, his eyes wide open, moving toward one of the niches.

"Don't anybody touch anything," said Elise. "I'm looking at you, Nick."

Nick withdrew his hand as he was about to put it on one of the statues. "Okay, okay. So what do we do?"

"Let Ajay figure it out," said Will.

Which took him all of about thirty seconds. He walked once all the way around the room, looking at each of the statues in the niches. Then he made a second trip and touched a particular part of each statue in a certain way, ignoring the urns altogether. Moments after he touched the last one, they heard a series of gears engage all around the edges of the room, then one large clunk and the entire floor began to sink, smoothly and evenly.

"How'd you know how to do that?" asked Nick.

"It was exceedingly obvious," said Ajay.

"Not to me."

"I'd explain, old boy," said Ajay, "but I'm afraid you'd find it quite tedious."

"You share their DNA," said Jericho. "He's tapping into what they know."

Ajay smiled enigmatically. "Something like that."

The walls turned into a circle of blank black stone around them as they descended past the room's floor level, and the only light now was what reached them from the atrium above. The group instinctively moved together into the center of the floor, looking up and outward in every direction. As the light faded, Nick pulled a flare out of his bag and ignited it, holding it aloft.

"They had one of these elevators at Cahokia, too, remember?" said Elise.

"From the cathedral to the boneyard," said Nick. "Good times."

"That was a rattletrap," said Will. "It didn't look like this."

"They appear to have improved their technology in the interim immensely," said Ajay.

"Yeah, smooth ride," said Nick. "I just hope we're going the right way."

"I think you can count on that," said Will. "It only goes one way."

"Not necessarily," said Nick. "I think it probably comes back up, too."

Ajay sighed and looked back up at the receding atrium, which had almost disappeared from sight.

"Another fifty feet or so," said Ajay.

"Get ready," said Will.

The elevator's speed began to ease. As they continued to descend, a faint light source appeared from one side, revealing a gap in the round stone wall.

They all turned to face it.

SIXTEEN

WILL'S RULES FOR LIVING #16:
WHEN YOU REACH THE END OF YOUR ROPE,
DON'T HANG AROUND.

The elevator floor settled to a silent stop. No one moved for a moment. Through the tall broad gap ahead, they saw a passageway of smooth black stone, at least thirty feet high and about ten across. A short distance ahead, it curved around a corner, where a faint light source sent out a constant pale blue glow. Will felt fresh air circulating around them, cool and slightly moist. It was so quiet he could hear his own heart beating.

"Lead the way," said Jericho.

Will stepped cautiously down off the marble floor into the passageway and the others followed.

Nick turned back to the elevator and held up a hand. "Stay," he said firmly.

"Keep the flare at the back," said Ajay. "I'll see more without it."

Without being prompted, Ajay took the lead, trailing a hand along the wall as he walked forward at a measured pace. Will and Elise followed close behind him. Ajay reached the curve and started around the turn.

Elise glanced over at Will.

Should we try to find out what's ahead of us? I can echolocate; you can use the Grid.

Before Will could answer, Ajay's voice broke into both of their minds:

It would be best if you let me handle this for the moment, he sent. *And, yes, I can hear you both now.*

Will and Elise looked at each other.

"He's changing a lot faster than the rest of us," she whispered. "Does that worry you?"

Will raised a finger to his lips, but nodded.

Ajay's voice continued in their heads:

Looking back, it occurs to me that something within the Never-Was has been conspiring to bring us here since the moment we arrived. The way that paths appeared before us, the landscape changing to encourage our following a certain direction. As if the environment itself was guiding us along, guiding our progress to this point. I wonder if you might have any theories about that?

Will considered it for a moment before answering. *I can only come up with one.*

I'm most interested to hear it.

Dave.

Interesting. I suspect we're about to find out if you're right.

Will watched Ajay's hand trail along the wall, his nails lightly scraping the concrete. They walked for what seemed like a long time before Ajay "spoke" again.

That glow is emanating from a large and rather peculiar source in a large room at the end of this passageway. I'm not detecting the presence of any of the Makers, or hostiles of any kind for that matter, at least for the moment.

That's good to know, sent Will.

And you might as well have Nick leave the flare here in the passage. We won't be needing it where we're going.

Will turned to Nick and gestured for him to leave the flare.

He tossed it back around the turn, which allowed them to realize that the blue glow from ahead had brightened to the point where it offered enough light for them to see all by itself. Will locked eyes with both Jericho and Nick and knew they were preparing for battle.

The curve of the hallway finally ended in another straightaway and some thirty steps beyond that it came to an end and emptied into the space Ajay had mentioned.

The room had been chiseled or hollowed out of that same black stone, rough-hewn and circular, with a high rounded ceiling and walls. In the center of the room, suspended six feet off the ground in midair by no apparent means of support, was the source of the blue light: a gigantic pale blue gemstone, multifaceted, as if cut by a precision jeweler. It was at least twelve feet tall and half as wide. The blue light radiated from it steadily, bright enough while they were this close to it to cast their shadows behind them.

After a few moments, they all shielded their eyes from it. The light was strange. It did more than just fill the air around them; it almost had texture, and if you stared directly at the center of the gem, its intensity was nearly blinding.

Despite that, Will felt some other quality inside the light, something familiar and comforting but also a little terrifying. A feeling that he'd been missing for a long time.

"What is this?" asked Elise.

"Some kind of power source maybe," said Jericho.

"Or maybe it's like the secret gizmo the Makers all worship or something," said Nick. "Their big sacred whatchamacallit."

"No, that's not it," said Will.

Will reached into his bag for something he hadn't needed since they got to the Never-Was: his dark glasses. He slipped them on and now could look directly at the gem. The lenses cut the intensity of the light and allowed him to see what was right in front of them.

"It's a prison," he said. "Dave's in there."

Suspended inside the jewel, in his full angelic gold-white platinum armor, feathered wings spreading out behind him, his gleaming sword pulled halfway out of the sheath on his belt, was Dave. His image was fractured and multiplied by the many facets of the jewel, but Will could still make out the ferocious expression flash-frozen on his face, as if he'd been attacked unaware and then captured and cast inside this bizarre container all in the blink of an eye. He looked paler than Will remembered, and the scars on his face even more vivid, like a figure in a wax museum.

Both Ajay and Nick pulled out their dark glasses, put them on, and looked up at the jewel.

"No way," said Nick. "That's *Dave*?"

"That would explain why you haven't heard from him," said Jericho.

"This must have happened right after we talked to him," said Elise. "He said they were onto him, remember?"

"Yup," said Will.

"Dude, you never told us Dave was a freakin' angel," said Nick.

"I don't know if he's an angel," said Will. "He prefers the term *Wayfarer*, or that's what he told me they call themselves."

"How can he breathe in this thing?" asked Nick.

"He doesn't need to breathe," said Will. "At least I can't ever remember seeing him breathe."

"He's dead, remember?" said Elise.

"Right. So angels are dead, then."

"He's not an angel," said Jericho.

"He's a Wayfarer—and according to him, Wayfarers are dead," said Will.

"Right. So Wayfarers don't need to breathe, then, 'cause they're ghosts."

"Will you give it a rest?" asked Jericho.

"Yet another confirmation that I'm evolving," said Ajay, examining the jewel closely. "I'm not finding Nick nearly as irritating as I usually do."

"Well, I gotta say, for a dead angel dude," said Nick, "Dave looks like a total badass."

Will handed his glasses to Elise, and Nick gave his to Jericho so they could take a look.

"Unbelievable," said Jericho.

"Said the man who can turn into a bear," said Nick.

"I just have one suggestion," said Elise.

"What's that?" asked Nick.

"We'd better bust him out of there, fast, 'cause I think I just heard that elevator start up again."

Will streaked out into the passageway and came rushing back a few moments later.

"Uh, you're right," he said.

"What do you have in mind?" asked Jericho as he handed the glasses back to Will.

Before the words were out of his mouth, Nick had run halfway up one of the walls, sprang off it, somersaulted in midair, and planted both feet into the center of the gemstone with a thunderous stomp.

He dropped straight to the ground and landed on his feet. The jewel didn't even budge.

"Derp." Nick shrugged. "Worth a try, right?"

Ajay moved directly underneath it to examine the gem more closely, looking up as he held on to his dark glasses.

"This is far too strong for simple physical attacks to do any damage," he said. "Although it's definitely artificial, whatever substance this is shares molecular similarities with diamonds—"

"Hold on, you can see *molecules* now?" asked Will.

"Oh, yes, and as a result, I believe I may have identified a very slight inherent flaw that could leave it vulnerable to extremely high vibration or—"

"Sound," said Elise, stepping forward and dropping her saddlebag. "You show me where."

"How long will it take?" asked Will.

"Difficult to say ... but I believe we might just have a chance to crack this, Will," said Ajay, getting down on his hands and knees and examining the gem from directly underneath. "Although it is certainly not going to be a piece of cake."

Will handed his dark glasses to Elise. "Wear these. Nick, Coach, come with me," he said, heading back to the passage. "We'll have to hold off whatever's coming down on that platform."

Will led Nick and Jericho and they ran back down the passageway toward the platform. Will blinked on the Grid as they advanced; nothing showed up ahead of them except the penumbra of the flare Nick had dropped on the ground.

"Grab your flare again, set it wherever you need it to see," said Will.

"You better go ahead," said Jericho, stopping with a dour look. "I promised the kid he could watch this time."

He trotted back down the passageway toward the gem room, calling Ajay's name.

"He's gonna get his bear on," said Nick, glancing after him and whispering to Will. "And Ajay's gonna watch."

"Coach is a man of his word."

"That oughta keep Boy Genius humming for a while," said

Nick as they walked on around the curve. "Something kind of wild's going down with Ajay, dude."

"You think?"

"He's like mutilating right in front of our eyes."

"Mutating."

"Right."

"Be thankful for that. We need Ajay five-point-oh if we're going to get through this in one piece."

Nick picked up the burning flare where he'd left it and considered it for a moment. "You know, I'm actually thinking it might be better to stub this one out and fire one smack at 'em with the gun the second they drop down. That should blind 'em good. What do you think?"

"Wait a second—was that you thinking strategically?" asked Will.

"Ajay said we're all mutating, right? Maybe I'm getting smarter."

"Not exactly the area where I was expecting improvement," said Will.

"Maybe I'm about to become a total freakin' expert on strategery."

They heard a series of grunts and groans from the passageway behind them, a few gasps from Ajay, the sound of armor hitting the ground, then the thump of heavy padded feet and the bear trotted into view.

"WHERE'S THE DAMN ELEVATOR?" he asked.

"Here comes Grumpy," said Nick.

Will moved to the end of the corridor, stepped into the shaft, and looked up. "It hasn't started down yet." Will heard a high-pitched hum begin behind them and glanced back toward the gem room. "Give a holler when it does. I'm going to check on the others."

Will sprinted down the passage and reached the inner room within seconds. Ajay stood a short distance from the gem, holding a laser pointer, directing its red beam at a spot just under the jewel's lower left corner. Elise stood a few feet to Ajay's right, arms spread and tensed, palms up. Her face clenched in a fierce mask of concentration, her mouth forming a small O, directing a beam of sound just beyond Will's hearing at the spot where the laser hit the gem. At the point of impact, a thin thread of smoke began to rise, and when Will looked closer, he saw that it also kicked up a faint cloud of powdery dust.

Is it working? Will asked Ajay.

In principle, he replied. *Whether it will work in* fact *still remains to be seen.*

"IT'S COMING!" Jericho's voice rumbled from down the passageway.

Let me know, sent Will.

Will sprinted away, and seconds later joined Nick and the bear inside the elevator shaft, both looking up.

"It just started," said Nick.

Will could hear the mechanics of the elevator engaging above them, and when he blinked on the Grid, he picked up the shape of the platform dropping steadily toward them.

It was packed from side to side with multiple heat signatures.

"HOW MANY?" asked Jericho.

"Dude, you might want to keep your voice down," whispered Nick.

Jericho swatted him with a paw, knocking Nick a few feet sideways.

"Hey!"

"There are a lot of them," said Will softly. "Move back into the passageway."

They stepped back into the hall. Nick stubbed out the lit flare on the wall, plunging them into darkness; then he pulled out the flare gun and popped a white phosphorous packet into the chamber.

"Light 'em up the second they touch down," whispered Will.

They waited. It was cool in the passageway, almost cold, and shot through with subterranean damp, but Will felt sweat start to trickle all over his body. He blinked on the Grid again and watched the platform glide down into view. Many of the heat signatures were large and bulky, but none of them were twenty feet tall, and he didn't sense the same discomfiting presence of a Maker he'd felt at the arcs.

The elevator came to a stop.

Nick pointed the flare gun and fired. Nick, Will, and the bear shielded their eyes. The flare ignited, exploding inside the elevator with a cacophonous blast and erupting with bright white light, revealing that the entire room was chock-full, shoulder to shoulder, of large, threatening, black-clad soldiers. And all of them—with the exception of a few who were either too smart or too slow to not look up at the source of the sound—were disoriented by the explosion above their heads for a long dangerous moment.

They were also all blinded temporarily, and as they staggered around, the next thing any of them saw was a gigantic bear rearing up on its haunches and rattling the walls with a ferocious growl. The bear's girth filled nearly the entire gap between the elevator and the passageway, and as it swiped its massive paws repeatedly, the front row of soldiers saw their armor torn and rent by its lethal claws. Panic spread quickly through the front ranks as the vanguard tried to push back to the rear to get away and the ones in back tried to push ahead of them to attack the bear.

The few that made it that far were subjected to more

thrashing from the bear and a flurry of fists and feet from a compact whirling cyclone that appeared to the bear's right. Flesh yielded, armor cracked, bones snapped with every blow, and the panic that had begun in the front now became a general alarm. A third attacker then darted through their midst—dealing damage, knocking weapons from their hands, upending the wounded—but it moved so quickly they couldn't even see it. That doubled their already widespread terror, rendering the few who remained upright too shaken to function, many of them dropping to their knees.

Will slowed down long enough to let the last two who were still standing see him—both reacted as if a phantom had just appeared—before Nick leaped in to knock them out with a roundhouse kick. Then both Will and Nick stepped calmly off the platform and stood behind the bear.

Thirty motionless, groaning bodies—armor shredded, weapons broken—piled around the elevator floor.

A few moments later they heard the gears engage and the platform climbed out of sight. Nick pretended to push a button, "operating" the elevator.

"Ding. Next stop, third floor," said Nick. "Sporting goods, patio furniture, and ladies' lingerie. Buh-bye."

Nick waved at the rising platform.

"DON'T GET COCKY," growled Jericho. "NEXT TIME WON'T BE SO EASY."

"Coach, why so hangry all the time? Does somebody need a snack?"

"I'll be right back," said Will.

He sprinted back down the corridor to the other room. Elise had edged a few steps closer to the gem, still pounding her sound stream into the corner of the jewel, her face drenched in sweat, bracing her body against her mounting fatigue.

Her sound beam had opened a tiny crack at the lower left corner of the jewel, and a continuous cloud of dust billowed out from the contact point. Ajay had positioned himself right next to it, watching the beam work through his glasses.

How much longer? Will asked Ajay.

Can you buy us a couple more minutes?

I guess we'll have to.

Moments later, Will rejoined Nick and Jericho, who were both looking up the shaft.

"Something's going on up there," said Nick. "You can hear 'em moving stuff around."

"Probably removing the bodies," said Will.

"IT'S COMING DOWN," said Jericho as he heard the gears engage again.

"What do we do this time?" asked Nick.

"Step back a little farther," said Will. "We can't surprise 'em anymore. Let's see what they come back at us with."

They retreated farther into the darkness of the passage and waited. Will blinked on the Grid and looked up. Plenty of heat signatures on board again, riding toward them, but a lot more variety in their shapes and sizes, most of them big. And they were bringing their own light source this time; it lit up the whole platform with a ripe glow.

"They're sending monsters," whispered Will. "Wait till we get a look at them; then I'll give the word."

They waited ten long seconds before the platform sank into view. Full of close to twenty monsters this time, unarmored, but they didn't look like they needed any; these were dark and scaly creatures, reptilian in some major part of their makeup. Two of the biggest and ugliest of them—giant toad-faced men, is how Will described them in the brief moment he had to look at them—stood right in the middle and up front and appeared to be on fire. Then Will realized they were somehow lit from within, and a few moments after they touched down, both unhinged their enormous jaws and each belched out a fireball the size of a bale of hay directly at where they were standing.

Reacting instantly, Will focused hard, ramped up the power that shot up his spine into his mind, and instantly projected out a thick, transparent thought-form shield, just in time to cover the entire opening of the passage.

The fireballs hit the shield and exploded on contact; a few licks of flames leaked out around the edges, heating up the passageway around them, but the majority of the blast blew back into the elevator, setting most of the monsters on fire.

Will struggled to hold up the shield, as many of the minions on fire hurled themselves at it, issuing a cacophony of horrific howls and screams. Will felt the shield weakening, and the two fire-toad creatures opened their jaws and expelled another volley of flame. Once again the fireballs hit the shield, set the rest of the monsters who were clawing at it ablaze, and burned the ones that were already lightly toasted to a crisp. Will slowly sank to his knees, nearly overcome by the effort—and the stench of all those burning bodies—but he kept the shield intact for a few more moments.

The platform began to rise again, with all the monsters now consumed in flames turning their wrath on the fire-toad men that had ignited them, a hellish vision of mayhem.

"Now there's something I'm not gonna forget very soon," said Nick, watching the burning mass.

"I'LL SAY THIS," said Jericho. "TACTICAL GENIUSES THEY'RE NOT."

As soon as the elevator was out of sight, Will sank to his hands and knees, gasping for breath.

"You okay, buddy?" asked Nick, kneeling down beside Will.

Will nodded, still unable to speak.

Are you there yet? he sent out to Ajay.

You might want to come back here for this part, Ajay replied. *And bring the boys.*

Will dragged himself to his feet. He'd have to walk back this time.

"They need us," he said.

Nick took Will by the arm and helped him along, while the bear loped ahead. By the time they reached the back room, the crack in the jewel had spread into a fissure that snaked out and up the entire left side. Will put his glasses back on; inside, Dave hadn't moved a muscle, still frozen in the same position.

Elise looked like she was on her last legs, shaking and pale, soaked in sweat, but still pounding her sound beam onto Ajay's target. The process generated enough energy and friction that the whole jewel was now throwing off an enormous amount of heat; the entire chamber felt at least ten degrees hotter than when they'd arrived. It was also a whole lot louder, the beam and the jewel giving off an eerie, high-pitched, piercing vibration that assailed their senses. Ajay stuck earplugs in his ears, examined the jewel all around the crack, sweat dripping down his face, and then squinted back at Will through his dark glasses.

We're getting closer, he sent. *But I don't know how much longer she can keep this up.*

Is Dave going to cook in that thing?

You've got me there. As you said, it's difficult to know how anything we do to it might affect a ghost physically.

Will wanted to suggest that he take a whack at it, but he was still holding on to his knees, trying to catch his breath. He didn't feel any stronger at the moment than Elise looked.

I'm trying to remember . . . , Will sent to Ajay. *Isn't there a point in cutting a gem where it's weakened enough that you can split it with a single blow?*

Yes, it's called cleaving, *but they use computers and 3-D modeling for that now. It's tremendously complex, particularly with larger stones, and you usually need a diamond to cut a diamond—*

But we have you, sent Will, and then he looked over at Nick and Jericho. *And them.*

Ajay hesitated for just a moment. *I've got an idea.*

He stood up and moved toward Elise, avoiding the beam, waving his arms at her. She was so intent on her job that she didn't see him until he was standing right beside her and yelling.

"You can stop now! YOU CAN STOP NOW!"

When she didn't react, Will sent her a thought: *Hold up. We'll take it from here.*

That got through to her. She slowly lowered her arms, cut off the sound beam, lost her balance, and fell backward, and Will was right there to catch her. The tone from the jewel slowly rang out, echoing around the chamber.

Elise looked exhausted and dazed, near tears. "I didn't do it. I couldn't do it."

"You did great," said Will, kneeling beside her. "Ajay will take it from here."

"Get this armor off me. I'm burning up."

He unfastened the back of her chest piece and she peeled it off and tossed it away, along with the arm guards. He gave her a drink from his canteen and she drained it empty, then sank back into him. She felt small in his arms, reduced by the effort she'd spent. She nestled into him, for once accepting the comfort he was only too glad to offer. He didn't want to let go of her.

Ajay was huddling with Nick and the bear on the other side of the room. They were asking questions; then they both nodded in agreement. They started across the room, while Ajay moved in to take another close look at the jewel, where smoke and dust were still rising from the fracture they'd widened.

"Somebody needs to listen for the elevator," said Will, almost absentmindedly.

"Okay," she said, looking up at him without even a glance toward the passageway. She turned, reached up, and touched his face tenderly.

"You look tired," she said.

"You look . . . tired, too."

Ajay cleared his throat, and they both looked up; neither had noticed he was now standing right next to them.

"Terribly sorry to interrupt," he said kindly, "but I think you might want to ease back a few feet. In case this works. Or in case it doesn't."

Will lifted Elise to her feet and they helped each other to the entrance of the passageway. Will listened for the sound of the elevator but didn't hear anything.

He turned back and saw that, across the room, Nick was strapping on a second larger helmet, on top of the one he was already wearing. The bear was pacing back and forth restlessly, working himself up into some kind of agitated state.

"What are they going to do?" asked Will.

Once the helmet was secured, Nick gave Ajay a thumbs-up. Ajay returned it.

"You'll see," said Ajay.

Ajay stepped away from them and directed his red laser dot at a point in the middle of the fracture.

Nick and the bear spotted the target, looked at each other, and nodded. Nick ran back to the far end of the room, while the bear sat on his haunches about halfway between Nick and the gemstone. Then Nick sprinted forward, leaped up, and turned a somersault like he was vaulting over a pommel horse just as he reached the bear, who reared onto his hind legs, put both paws on Nick, and whipped him toward the jewel, which added a turbo boost to his momentum. Now traveling through the air at a tremendous amount of speed, Nick stuck his arms at his sides and lowered his chin.

Nick slammed into the jewel headfirst, right at the target, a human missile. A cloud of dust exploded around him, and Nick appeared, cartwheeling out of the top of it, and then he crashed into the wall behind the jewel.

The others hurried forward, Ajay taking the lead. They waved away the smoke and saw that the fracture looked about the same size as before; the gem was still intact.

"Did we get it?" asked Nick.

"Not quite," said Ajay.

Nick climbed to his feet, a little wobbly. He unstrapped the top helmet and stared at it; the entire crown had been smashed in.

"Whoa," said Nick. "Good thing I was wearing two."

"Now what do we do?" asked Elise.

"WANT US TO TRY AGAIN?" asked the bear.

"You might want to ask *me* first," said Nick.

Before anyone else could respond, they heard a loud constant ringing from somewhere inside the gem, and as they watched, small spidery lines spread out from where Nick had crashed into the central fracture, spreading quickly in every direction all around the stone. The cracks deepened, the ringing intensified, and the rock began to crumble, small chunks falling away, then larger ones, disintegrating before their eyes, until with a final bell-like peal, the whole mass of the gemstone dropped to the ground and shattered.

Dave was left lying flat on his back in the smoking debris,

and the moment he made contact with the air, he reverted from angelic form to the more or less human biker appearance that Will had always known him in: military boots, leather pants, air-force flight jacket, and shades. He didn't move at all and he didn't appear to be breathing, but then Will couldn't recall if he'd ever noticed Dave breathing, or if he even needed to.

"So is he still dead?" asked Nick, staggering in behind them. "Or is he like *really* dead?"

Nick pushed past them and leaned down to take a closer look. Dave's shades suddenly tilted down his nose, and he looked right up at Nick with his spooky pale eyes.

"Why don't you poke me with your boot and find out, Jasper?" croaked Dave.

Nick fell backward onto his rear end. Will dropped down on his knees next to Dave.

"For crying out loud, you scared the crap out of us," said Will.

"That was the last thing on my mind, I assure you," said Dave.

Will offered a hand to help him up.

"Not so fast, mate," said Dave, still not moving any part of his body. "Machinery's not quite up to speed. Don't have both hands on the wheel just yet." Then he spotted Elise and it seemed to perk him up. "Ah, you brought one of your buttercups with you. Always was partial to brunettes myself. How's tricks, kitty cat?"

"News flash—it's not the sixties anymore, Rip Van Winkle," said Elise, bristling. "And I'm not a kitty cat."

"How long have you been in that thing?" asked Will.

"No idea," said Dave.

"How'd they catch you?" asked Will. "I thought they couldn't see you."

"They used some kind of beast that could track me. Weeks on end. Cornered, outnumbered, outgunned. I flashed into Wayfarer form for a final stand but the last thing I remember was reaching for my sword; then it was lights-out. Thanks for springing me."

"We estimate that you've been trapped here for at least five months, Earth time," said Ajay, creeping in for a closer look. "Will organized this expedition into the Never-Was to find you."

"I remember you. You're the smart one," said Dave.

"The pleasure is entirely mine, sir," said Ajay with a modest bow.

Then Dave looked past Ajay: "Say, mate, what's up with the bear?"

"He's my track coach. Usually. Coach Jericho."

"He's a shaman," said Ajay.

"Never a dull moment. How's it goin', mate?"

The bear raised a huge paw in silent greeting. Dave nodded his head slightly, the first movement he'd made.

"Can he talk?" whispered Dave.

"WHAT DO YOU WANT ME TO SAY?"

Dave grinned. "Now that's what I love about this job; you see something new every day."

"This . . . is . . . awesome," said Nick in a hushed voice.

"Are you going to be all right?" asked Elise.

"To be honest, love, I haven't felt this badly used since my chopper went down," said Dave. " 'Course, that was with the whole weight of the chassis pinning me to the turf, although I didn't feel it for long, as I expired within moments."

"So you *are* dead," said Nick.

"And come to think on it, all things considered, I feel slightly better than that. A bit of feeling starting to creep back to the extremities." Dave started to slightly wiggle the fingers of his left hand. "How much time have we got?"

"Not long," said Will.

"What's the situation?"

"Not great."

"The Makers have constructed a portal device the size of the Lincoln Tunnel," said Ajay. "And it's about to come online."

"And that invasion force you spotted is parked right outside the walls," said Elise.

"That's seriously bad news," said Dave.

"So what should we do about it?" asked Will, taking out the Carver. "That's what we need to know from you, because I could use this and spring us all out of here. We'd be right back at the Center."

"And wouldn't that give you sufficient time, then, Mr. Dave, sir, to alert the Hierarchy?" asked Ajay optimistically. "So they could swoop in and put an end to all this?"

"Timing might work, or it might not," said Dave, "but this ain't the sort of mission you cut corners on, kids. Where is this portal gizmo?"

"Eastern side of the compound," said Will.

"Your instincts were good, Will," said Dave. "Take that target out and we'll set them back years, maybe even for good. I'm halfway back on my feet; just give me a couple more minutes here—"

"Did anyone else just hear the elevator?" asked Elise, looking up alertly.

Will turned to the passageway. He hadn't heard the elevator, but when he blinked on the Grid, he picked up a small solitary figure moving steadily down the hallway toward them. Then he heard footsteps.

"Somebody's here," he said.

Everyone but Dave jumped to their feet and readied themselves for a fight. Jericho padded toward the passageway to block the way in, but before he got there, someone walked a few steps into the room and stopped.

"I'm not here to hurt anyone," said Brooke, holding up her hands, looking directly at Will.

"Tell that to the sofa you murdered," said Nick.

"DON'T YOU TAKE ANOTHER STEP!"

The bear reared up on its haunches and roared right in Brooke's face. She didn't even flinch.

"Dude, do not let her touch you!" shouted Nick.

"Ah, it's the blond dolly," said Dave. "I was about to ask you where she was."

Will turned to tell Dave to keep quiet—and realized that he was no longer visible. Then he heard Dave's voice in his head again.

"It's all aces, mate—she can't see or hear me," said Dave. "Seems I've still got a touch of the old whiz-bang. If you can handle Miss Congeniality for a sec, I'll be back to full strength in a few shakes."

"It's okay, Coach," said Will. "We'll talk to her."

Jericho, looking as skeptical as a bear could manage, stood back down but stayed at striking distance between Will and Brooke.

"Thank you, Will," said Brooke quietly.

"What do you want, then?" asked Will, unwilling to meet her gaze, trying to keep the anger he felt raging inside him from his eyes.

"I know what you must be thinking," said Brooke, earnest and calm. "All of you, about me. And I'm not going to tell you that you don't have every right to feel that way."

If all three of us focus on her at once, Elise sent to Will and Ajay, *we can probably blow her head right off her neck.*

Will glanced over. Elise was making no effort, or was completely unable, to hide her fury at their former friend. Exhausted as she was, the sight of Brooke was still enough to kick up Elise's deepest reserves, and Will could see she was getting ready to launch an attack. If she was aware of it, or the thought even troubled her, Brooke gave no notice and simply stood her ground.

Let's all remain calm, Ajay responded. *At least hear what she has to say first.*

There's no point. She's just going to lie some more—

But maybe she'll say something inadvertently useful to us, Ajay continued. *Please, Elise. We need to be mindful of the situation and not let our feelings run away from us.*

Will saw Elise give the slightest indication that she'd stand down, for the moment. He exchanged a quick look of relief with Ajay; he wasn't at all sure he'd have been able to dissuade her.

"Say what you want to say," said Will.

"They don't want to hurt you," said Brooke, looking at each of them.

"Oh, yeah? Well, they got an absolutely hilarious way of showing it," said Nick. "How'd you get here anyway?"

"I followed you to the Crag," she said. "After you drugged me. And by the way, that really hurt my feelings, Nick."

"I'll give you something that hurts more than your feelings," said Elise, stepping toward her.

"Easy." Will put a hand on Elise's shoulder. "Go on, Brooke," he said.

"They know who you are, Will, and they know what you are to them." Then Brooke corrected herself. "What *we* are to them. All of us."

"You mean . . . genetically," said Ajay.

"That's right."

"Interesting approach," said Dave, and Will noticed that his voice seemed to be coming from somewhere else in the room; Dave could move again. "Correct me if I'm wrong, but since we last laid eyes on each other, I'm getting a notion you might have had a teensy falling out with blondie bits here."

"What do they want from us?" Will asked Brooke.

"They want a chance to explain to you what they're doing here," said Brooke. "And why. They believe you'll feel differently about it once you hear them out."

"So they sent you in to sucker us out into the open, is that it?" asked Elise bitterly. "Bat your eyes at the boys, turn up the fake sincerity, and assume we'd still fall for your act. Try selling it someplace else."

Brooke turned to Elise. Tears filled her eyes, and her voice broke. "I know you can't forgive me for what you think I've done. I don't expect you to. But you have to believe me . . . I'm just . . . trying to save your lives now."

Will felt his heart surge, and for just the briefest moment he did believe her, before he slammed that door shut. Without looking at him, he sent a message to Ajay:

Is she lying?

Yes and no. It's complicated, he replied. *She may well be lying but apparently she believes what she's saying. That's one of the most interesting characteristics of the sociopathic personality, by the way, but I can't say for certain that she absolutely fits the diagnosis. And that's the bow tied onto the horns of our dilemma, isn't it?*

Will didn't know what to do.

"She'll ask you about me next," said Dave, keying in on what Will was feeling so accurately it made him wonder if Dave could hear their telepathic conversations. "That is, if they sent her down to scout out the situation."

For the first time, Brooke's eyes drifted to the shattered remains of the jewel behind Will.

"What happened to your friend?" asked Brooke. "What was his name . . . was it Dave?"

"You know what to say, mate," said Dave.

Will was encouraged to see that Dave was standing for the first time, leaning against the wall over near Jericho; if he wasn't one hundred percent yet, he was trending toward ninety.

"Dave didn't make it," said Will.

"What happened to him?"

Will added a little extra emotion to sell her on the lie. "As soon as the rock broke open, he . . . he just disintegrated . . . like he wasn't even there."

"I'm so sorry, Will," said Brooke sincerely. "I know he meant a lot to you. I'd heard that he was down here, but I didn't know how to help him."

Laying it on a bit thick, isn't she? sent Ajay.

Brooke took a single step toward them. Everyone else, except Will and Jericho, took a step back.

"What do you think you should ask her now, my young friend?" asked Dave.

"I'd like to know how you think you can help us," said Will to Brooke.

Dave gave him a thumbs-up.

"If you'll come with me now, I can promise you safe passage," said Brooke. "They won't hurt you, any of you. They just want to explain. Quietly and calmly. Then you can decide for yourselves."

"What, to sell out the rest of the human race, like you did?" asked Elise.

Brooke paused. Will noticed the slightest flutter of anger or frustration behind her eyes before she clamped it down and put up the peacemaker mask again.

"I think it would be best for us to share and examine *all* of our feelings," she said. "Together. After you're given the benefit of having all the information."

Will decided to send a message to Brooke, just to make sure she couldn't tune in to how the rest of them were communicating, with a few words he knew she wouldn't be able to stop herself from reacting to.

Unless, of course, she really had turned into a completely irredeemable psychopath. Or been one all along.

I still love you.

Brooke didn't blink or react or even flick her eyes toward Will. He felt relieved, in more ways than one.

So far, so good.

Now he sent a message to Elise. *If we're going after that portal, first things first: We need to get out of this hole safely. We're going with her.*

Elise responded without looking at him. *You're crazy. She'll get us all killed.*

If she makes the slightest move, against any of us, you've got a green light to take her out. And we'll all help.

You won't need to. One wrong move and I'll blast her brain to soup.

With my blessings.

"It's not just my decision," said Will; then he turned to the rest of the group. "What do you think, guys?"

Say yes, he sent to Ajay and Nick.

"Yes," said Nick. "And I don't have the slightest idea why I'm saying that."

"Yes," said Ajay.

"Okay," said Elise.

"Coach?" asked Will.

"Say yes," said Dave, leaning in toward the bear.

"WHATEVER YOU SAY," said Jericho, glancing to his left, annoyed, which led Will to wonder if Coach could actually see Dave at the moment.

"Lead the way, Brooke," said Will.

Brooke clasped her hands together and closed her eyes in an effective simulation of deep emotion. "I'm so grateful that you're willing to listen to me."

"Just keep your hands to yourself," said Nick. "No touching."

Brooke made a refined gesture for them to follow and led them down the passage toward the elevator. She held up one hand and a perfect sphere of pale white light appeared around it, lighting their way.

We're not the only ones still evolving, Ajay sent to Will. *I'm getting a very strong intuitive sense that she's much more powerful than she appears.*

Let me know if you notice anything else, sent Will.

They walked quietly behind her. Will watched Brooke closely, the elegant sway of her body, her long blond mane bouncing slightly with every step. Even in the depths of the Never-Was, her hair looked perfect.

Dave appeared, walking beside Will, watching Brooke as well.

"Didn't figure that one for the treacherous type," said Dave.

"Join the club," whispered Will.

"Best keep a close watch on this one, mate, not that that's rough duty under any circumstances," said Dave. "Things are about to get messy."

SEVENTEEN

WILL'S RULES FOR LIVING #17:
KEEP YOUR FRIENDS CLOSE. KEEP YOUR ENEMIES
IN A BAG AT THE BOTTOM OF THE RIVER.

Brooke led them onto the waiting elevator platform. As soon as they were all on board, the gears engaged and they ascended. Brooke stood in the center. The rest of the group deployed around her in a full circle; all of them turned toward her, watching her raptly.

Brooke clasped her hands together, holding the ball of light she'd generated like a baby bird, and looked up toward a point on the wall above their heads, not focused on anything in particular, smiling blankly. It reminded Will of smiles he'd seen on political wives standing next to their husbands at public events. He realized it was probably a look Brooke had learned from her mother.

Dave walked over next to her, studied her, then walked around her, giving her the once-over from every angle. Brooke never gave the slightest indication that she sensed his presence.

"What are you doing?" asked Will quietly.

"I'm looking for where she keeps the darkness," said Dave.

"Did you find it?"

"Oh, it's there all right, but it's way down deep. I mean, like the bottom of a mine shaft deep. She's a gnarly piece of work, this one, mate."

"Did you ask me something, Will?" asked Brooke, directing that spooky smile toward him.

"I said how did you find us," said Will.

"I just seemed to know where you were," she said. "I've always felt we had a special connection, Will."

Brooke looked back up again. Light began to seep in from the room above. They were getting close.

Behind her, Nick stuck his finger down his throat and mock gagged.

"Not much longer now," said Brooke to no one in particular.

She turned her hands over and the globe of light she'd been carrying gently popped and disappeared. The elevator slowed for the last few feet and clicked into place with a slight whoosh as the floor leveled into the foyer. The room was completely empty, just as they'd left it, but that didn't mean much in the Never-Was. Will blinked on the Grid and confirmed they were alone.

"This way," said Brooke.

She made her tour-guide gesture again and walked toward the doors. They swung open ahead of her, like doors at a supermarket, and she walked through.

Did you do that? Elise asked Will.

Will shook his head.

"That was me," said Dave, appearing outside, holding the doors open as Will walked past him. "Old habit. A gentleman always opens the door for a lady."

Brooke led them out from under the portico onto the broad patio in front of the dome where they'd left the horses. As she passed the animals, they stirred and whinnied nervously. The stallion that Brooke had ridden earlier reared up as if he was about to strike her.

Brooke turned toward it, hands up, instantly ready to defend herself, but Elise reacted more quickly, making a small gesture and sending a thought that instantly backed the horse down. It trotted away from Brooke, around to where Elise was standing. It nuzzled her arm and she patted his muzzle, calming him further.

Brooke papered over her anger, painted that bland smile back on again, turned, and continued walking toward the stairs.

Horses don't lie, sent Elise to Will. *They don't even know how.*

Keep them close by and ready, Will responded.

"You're not even going to believe this," said Dave.

Dave popped into Will's vision, standing about twenty yards ahead of them at the top of the stairs, looking at something down below. Will blinked on the Grid, and at first couldn't comprehend what he was seeing: The entire plaza at the foot of the stairs appeared as a sea of red. Ascending the stairs toward them was a line of towering figures, seven of them, at least twenty feet tall, moving slowly and steadily in sync.

Stop at the top of the stairs, Will sent to Ajay and Elise. *Not too close.*

Then he gave them a few instructions. Ajay handed Will something from his pocket.

"Can they see you?" asked Will quietly.

"CAN WHO SEE ME?" Jericho, padding along next to him, replied.

"I wasn't talking to you," said Will.

"Who *are* you talking to, then?" asked Nick, walking on the other side of Will.

Jericho shushed him, which sounded more like a growl.

"Like I said, they can't see me, mate," said Dave, looking down at the top of the stairs. "Not unless I'm in Wayfarer form. Your move now. Following your lead."

Will whispered a few words to Dave, then turned to the others. "I'll say when."

"When what?" asked Nick.

"When it's go time. Don't show them you're frightened."

"Show who?" asked Nick.

"Them." Will nodded toward the stairs.

Brooke stopped at the top of the stairs and turned to face Will and the others. They walked a few more steps forward until the plaza below came into their view: The entire space was filled, to the margins and beyond, with a mix of the black-clad guards and a varied assembly of the battalions they'd seen outside the walls.

Thousands of monsters.

Will sensed movement on their level, turned, and saw that to the left and right of their position more guards and creatures were rushing into position on either end of the broad veranda, forming a line at least ten figures deep that cut off any possibility of retreat.

"And them," said Will.

He nodded toward the seven Makers floating into view up the stairs toward them. They at first appeared to be nearly identical, but the robes they wore were each of a slightly different hue, and their shapes and postures varied even more noticeably; taller, shorter, more fluid, less graceful. The hooded cowls of their robes concealed their faces. He wasn't entirely sure how—something about its posture—but Will recognized the one just to the right of center as the Maker that had spotted them at the construction site. The taller one next to it, in their middle, possessed an unmistakable aura of authority, and its regal bearing radiated an oppressive sense of power.

"Diapers don't fail me now," said Nick.

"HOW'S THE PLAN WORKING SO FAR?" asked Jericho.

"Ask me in a couple of minutes," said Will.

The Makers floated up and swayed to a stop at the top of the stairs, spreading out in a half circle around Brooke. The one Will took to be their leader hovered just behind her; it leaned over slightly and appeared to be conversing with Brooke, who was doing most of the listening, although Will didn't hear any words. Dave blinked out from his spot near the steps and then reappeared between Will and Jericho.

"Recognize any of these mugs?" asked Will.

"I never got this close before," said Dave; then he gestured toward the one leaning down toward Brooke. "But I'd take that one for the big enchilada."

"Dad?" asked Nick, starting toward the one in the center, holding out his arms. "Is that really you? It's me, Nick."

Elise pulled him back by the collar.

"What do you think, Ajay?" asked Will.

Ajay's eyes were huge and shining, darting around, taking everything in. Will was pleased to see that he didn't appear the slightest bit frightened.

"Astonishing," said Ajay quietly. "Their minds are extraordinary. The most advanced computers we haven't even contemplated yet can't touch the level of complex intelligence I'm sensing."

"Why are you whispering?" asked Nick, whispering.

"I believe there's a good chance they could pick up on anything that passes between us telepathically. That's why it's best we speak aloud, in which case there's a good probability they can't hear us very well if we keep our voices down."

"But wouldn't that be true of anybody?" asked Nick.

"LET THE GROWN-UPS TALK."

"Can you tell what they want?" asked Elise.

"Not in the slightest. This is somewhat difficult to convey, but they seem to have moved beyond what we would normally think of or recognize as 'thinking.' "

"Oh, no, that makes perfect sense," said Nick. *"Not."*

"By that I mean they don't pair emotions with their thoughts, and they're not connected to or driven by them. It seems they may not even possess feelings at all."

"Of course not," said Elise. "That makes it so much easier for them to annihilate things."

"There's something indescribably . . . remote about them. I don't know how else to describe it. It's as if they aren't all here."

Will looked over at them and got an idea. "I can work with that." He leaned in and whispered the idea to Ajay, who raised his eyebrows in interest.

"I will certainly try, Will," he whispered.

"Just let me know," said Will. "I'll try to keep 'em busy until then."

"Of course, Will. And, failing that, I suppose we can console ourselves with the idea that we're making history here, my friends. Face to face with the first truly alien race."

"THAT WON'T BE MUCH COMFORT IF THEY FLATTEN US," said Jericho.

"So let's hit them first," said Elise.

"Soon," said Will. "But not yet."

Brooke appeared to finish her "conversation" with the central Maker. She turned back to them and took a few steps in their direction.

"They'd like to speak with you first," she said to Will.

"That's all of what Tiny just said to you?" asked Nick. "Take me to your leader? It was yapping at you for over a minute."

"Come with me," said Brooke, holding out her hand to Will. "I promise they won't harm you."

"Don't do it," said Elise.

"Or at least don't hold hands with her," said Nick.

"Ready?" said Will to something behind him.

"I'll be right behind you, mate," said Dave.

"Everyone else stay here," said Will.

He winked at Ajay, then walked forward but didn't take Brooke's offered hand. Brooke withdrew it with only slight embarrassment and moved along with him. Will didn't look at her once.

"I didn't believe it at first either, Will," said Brooke intimately. "I do so understand how you feel, but I've learned that they truly do wish us well and I believe them. Your grandfather was right about them—"

"You can stop talking now," said Will.

For the first time, a flash of genuine anger cut through her moony, placid exterior; her cheeks colored and her eyes turned steely.

"You are a very naughty girl," said Dave, appearing right behind and speaking in her ear.

Brooke didn't react. And she covered her anger in a quick transition to hurt feelings.

"I suppose I deserve that," she said.

Will paid no attention to her and kept his eyes on the chest of the Maker in the middle, ignoring the cowl. He blinked on the Grid as they slowly advanced. Then he looked at each of the Makers in turn. He noticed a couple of things he was expecting to see, and one thing he didn't see that confirmed what he was thinking.

He stopped ten feet away from the one in the center. All of them swayed gently, like boats moored at a dock, bobbing in the water. The one in the center hovered forward a few feet and raised its arms grandly and looked like it was about to say something important, and so did Brooke—maybe to translate for it—but Will spoke up first.

"You're probably wondering why I've called you here today," said Will in a loud, clear voice.

Neither Brooke nor the swaying Makers responded; somehow, they looked surprised.

"I know, I know, you think you're running the meeting, and why wouldn't you? You're used to having it your way; I get that. I mean, look at all you've done with this place. Amazing work, truly, an almost completely real fake reality. Populated with all these perfect idiot minions you've put together, hanging on your every word. Congratulations. Must be a really powerful feeling. Godlike, even. Well, not quite, but close, no doubt about it. You are definitely a force to be reckoned with."

"I like where you're going with this," said Dave.

"Will?" asked Brooke.

"So, given that we've got a strand or two of your precious DNA wired into our systems, it's perfectly understandable that you'd assume we'd be totally fascinated with what you'd want to tell us. That we'd be more than eager to help you with whatever you've got in the works. I understand why you'd feel that way. You've learned how to be extremely persuasive with most ordinary humans."

"Will—" said Brooke.

He held up a hand to silence her. Will glanced back at Ajay, who was staring intently at the Maker, his fingers forming a funnel around his eyes. Concentrating fiercely.

Not yet, Ajay sent to Will.

Will summoned up a life-sized thought-form of the living snake astrolabe and projected it onto the ground between them.

"You found out, early on apparently, that sick little toys

like this one can bend people's will in your direction. And that showering humans with a steady stream of your technological 'gifts' just about closes the deal on buying their loyalty. So you decided, based on your experience—correct me if I'm wrong—that the rest of us must be easy marks, too: greedy, selfish, and stupid enough to hypnotize if you dangle enough bright shiny baubles in front of us. Make it Christmas every day of the year and we'll go rogue and stab everybody in the back, even people we care about, and especially people we don't—"

"Will, what are you doing?" asked Brooke.

"Shut up, Brooke," said Will. "And I'm not going to tell you again."

Her eyes flashed again as she dropped all pretense of civility and looked nakedly furious. She stormed toward him and her right hand shot out, glowing a poisonous shade of green, reaching to touch him. And hurt him.

Dave snatched her by the wrist—she still couldn't see him—and she couldn't for the life of her figure out why her hand suddenly wouldn't work.

"Can't drain the life out of something that's already dead, ducky," said Dave in her ear.

Will turned to the Makers again. "But that still wasn't enough to buy you the ticket home you've been looking for. So you thought, what if we give a few of these lesser beings the ultimate gift, a piece of *us*. Slot that software into some human hard drives and we'd grow up to be just like you. New and improved humans, more powerful and willing to do exactly whatever lamebrain thing you told us to, like your legion of homemade knuckleheads out here. We could have saved you so much trouble, if you'd only bothered to ask. Any parents would've told you that raising a kid doesn't work out that way, nature over nurture. We're all stubbornly, willfully determined to be nothing other than who we are. And we happen to be at an age where the absolute *last* thing we want to do . . . is what our parents tell us."

Even if they didn't understand all his words, Will could see that his intentions were getting through loud and clear: The lead Maker hovered in place, looking increasingly agitated.

"Are you crazy? Stop it! Stop it right now!" Brooke struggled and screamed like a banshee, but Dave had her by both arms now, and her strength was no match for his. "What are you doing?! They're going to—"

Will summoned up a thought-form of an elaborate muzzle, sent it shooting toward her, and smacked it right over Brooke's mouth, stifling her instantly.

Behind him, Elise couldn't hide a smile.

"So, no, we're not the least bit interested in whatever you want to tell us about your crazy-pants plans for taking over the planet again, or any part of what your reasoning behind all this twisted Shinola might be. We're not going to help you with one damn bit of it no matter what you do to us or who you think we are.

"We're not your children. You didn't raise us. Our real parents weren't close to perfect, but with the exception of the pretty one here whose parents washed her brains for you, they got one thing completely right: They taught us to think for ourselves. And that's bad news for you boys from clown town."

Dave chuckled. Brooke twisted and screeched but couldn't free her hands or get a clear word out past the muzzle. Will glanced back at Ajay, who was still staring at the Makers.

Almost, sent Ajay.

Will walked back and forth in front of the Makers now, taunting them as he counted out the reasons on his fingers:

"You can't buy us with money, and we don't want power,

not the kind you want, and we don't care about eternal life, you morons. We're kids; we think we're going to live forever. We just want the freedom to be who we are. We wouldn't even want to live in your pathetic idea of a world. It's all fake anyway. We like ours just the way it is. So that's the heart of your problem right there—we're not buying anything you've got to sell."

Behind him, Ajay lowered his hands from his face, breathing hard from exertion.

Got it, he sent.

Will pulled Ajay's laser pointer out of his pocket and waved it around like a gun. For the first time, the Makers actually seemed frightened. When Will blinked on the Grid, he saw just what he expected to see inside the robes—swirling, agitated colors. A couple of them even started to edge backward toward the stairs. It was starting to make sense to him.

"We are, in fact, your worst nightmare."

Will flicked on the laser pointer and the harmless red beam shot out of the barrel. He held on with both hands as if it were bucking around, pointing it at the ground in front of him— where the red line moved across the stone of the portico toward the stairs, slicing his own thought-form of the snake neatly in half, heading toward the Makers.

All of them raised the arms of their robes and emitted a series of high-pitched screams—apparently attack signals for the masses assembled all around them and in the plaza below. A cry rose up from both groups and they surged forward from every direction toward their position at the top of the stairs with a deafening battle cry.

"NOW!" shouted Will to his friends.

He summoned another thought-form in the shape of a hook and sent it shooting toward the Maker in the center. He manipulated the hook to grab the edge of the robe and yank back on it.

At the same moment, Elise sent a blast of sound toward the three Makers to the right of center, Nick launched himself toward two of the figures on the left, and Ajay fired a bolt from a small handheld crossbow directly at the last one on that side.

All four attacks landed simultaneously—Nick flew right through the two he'd targeted and landed, somewhat puzzled, on the stairs below—and all seven robes collapsed.

They were empty. No creatures or Makers. There was nothing underneath them but air. A loud gasp rose from the lines of monsters running toward them from below and behind them. The entire wave halted at once, in shock at the sudden disappearance of their leaders.

Everyone but Ajay and Will seemed surprised, but nobody looked more astonished than Brooke. She stopped struggling in Dave's grip and stared at the last robe as it fluttered to the ground.

"Dude, we vaporized 'em!" said Nick, grabbing one of the robes.

"They weren't even here," said Will.

"What were they?" asked Elise.

"Thought projections. Like what I can do. At least now I know where I got it from."

"No wonder they seemed so remote to me," said Ajay, stepping to the nearest robe.

"Dude, how did you know that would work?"

"I didn't feel threatened by their presence, not like we did by that one at the arc. And when they reacted to the laser pointer like it was a weapon, I got the idea maybe they weren't actually seeing it up close."

"So you weren't even sure?" asked Elise.

"Not a hundred percent."

"I'm confused," said Nick. "But I'm used to that."

"WHERE ARE THE REAL ONES, THEN?" asked Jericho.

"About half a mile from here," said Ajay. "I was able to trace back the flow of mental energy from these shells to a building on top of that rise."

He pointed toward a structure poking over the top of the ring of buildings around the plaza that looked like the Parthenon.

"That doesn't even matter now," said Will.

"It does if they decide to come after us," said Elise.

"Oh, they will," said Will. "We'll just have to be quicker."

"So, but wait, what do the *real* ones look like?" asked Nick.

"Oh, they're hideous, mate, truly vile," said Dave, appearing to them all again, still holding Brooke in a vise grip as he marched her over to them. "Trust me, some things are better left unseen—"

"MEANWHILE!" shouted Jericho.

He pointed back to the horde of guards and monsters who had regained their courage and slowly begun creeping toward them again across the vast portico and up the huge flight of stairs behind them.

"Get the horses," said Will. "We've got to kill that portal."

Elise whistled for the horses. They raced over and stopped beside them, and Elise grabbed their bridles.

"I'm going to need my hands free for this," said Dave, glancing back at the army on the stairs. "What do we do with this one, then?"

Brooke looked up at Will helplessly, pleading, still unable to speak because of the gag. For the first and only time since he'd known Brooke, her elegant composure seemed completely destroyed. Something looked broken behind her eyes.

"Let me," said Elise.

"No soup," said Will.

"I wasn't going to use my voice for this," said Elise.

She walked over and punched Brooke in the jaw. Her eyes rolled back and her knees sagged, and as she fell over, Nick moved in to catch her.

"That wasn't very nice," said Nick.

"Neither is she," said Elise.

"Well, we can't just leave her here."

"Bring her with us," said Will.

The horde had crept within a hundred yards of them now, closing in from every direction. All of a sudden, they broke into a run, the sound of their battle cries rising into a steady din.

"MEANWHILE!" shouted Jericho, even louder.

Will pulled something from his pocket and tossed it to Dave. He caught it and looked at Will with a sly smile; it was the pair of black dice he'd given Will just before he'd been pulled into the Never-Was.

"Now we're cooking with gas," said Dave.

He shook the dice around and they transformed into a shining silver key in the shape of a lightning bolt. He "turned" the key.

His fearsome gleaming red Prowler instantly materialized around him, with Dave in the driver's seat. Everyone stepped back as he gunned the engine and its unearthly throttle roared.

"Who's riding with me?" Dave asked.

"I call shotgun," said Nick.

He tossed the unconscious Brooke over his shoulder and

jumped into the front seat. Her head bounced off the back of the seat.

"Oh," said Nick. "Sorry."

Elise and Will jumped onto their horses.

"We'll ride behind you," said Will.

"Aren't you going to change back?" Ajay asked Jericho, holding the other bridles.

Jericho looked around at the advancing forces. "MIGHT BE BETTER IF I DIDN'T."

"Shake a leg," said Dave.

"But I can't ride by myself," said Ajay, looking nervously at the horses.

Jericho sighed and knelt down. "HOP ON, KID."

Ajay glanced back at his horse for a moment and Jericho knew what he was thinking.

"I AM NOT WEARING A SADDLE."

"I wasn't actually going to *ask*," said Ajay, and he jumped onto Jericho's back.

"Stay close," said Dave.

Dave gunned the Prowler, laid down a circular patch of rubber as he spun it around, and then roared straight off the portico, careening and bouncing down the endless flight of stairs. Will and Elise galloped down after him, close enough to feel the fiery exhaust shooting out of the Prowler's tailpipes. Jericho lumbered along right behind them, Ajay bending low and hanging on like a jockey, clinging to his fur.

As they started down the stairs, Ajay looked behind them and saw the first line of attackers crest the stairs and pour down after them, hundreds of guards and creatures, trailing them by only twenty yards. Many threw weapons—knives and axes and tumbling maces—and Ajay ducked as they flew all around and past them. More than a few bounced off Jericho's thick hide.

"I really shouldn't be doing this without a helmet!" shouted Ajay in Jericho's ear.

"LIVE A LITTLE!"

"Dump blondie in the back!" shouted Dave to Nick. "Then fasten your seat belt. I'm gonna need your help!"

Nick turned around and deposited Brooke into the tiny backseat, where she folded in neatly, her limp body jumping around with every violent bounce. Nick nearly flew out of the car as he turned back around, but he grabbed on to the windshield, flipped himself back into the seat, and strapped himself in.

"Dude, I just gotta say, awesome wheels!"

"They'll do in a pinch!"

Dave pointed toward the dashboard directly in front of Nick and it dropped open, revealing a panel of buttons and pulls. Dave pointed at one of the pulls.

"When I give the word, pull that gizmo there—Not yet!"

"Sorry—"

"What did I just say?"

"You said pull the gizmo—"

"When I give the word! And not *that* one, *this* one!"

"Sorry, Dave—"

"Hang on!"

The Prowler roared down toward the even bigger wave of onrushing attackers from the plaza. Dave gunned it again as they came off a step and grabbed some air, soaring up and then arcing down, directly toward the front of the crowd.

"Now! And don't let go until I tell you!"

Nick pulled the lever. Twin blasts of frigid liquid ice flowed out of two nozzles that popped out of the Prowler's front bumper. The substance hit the front line of the mob and instantly froze them solid. Then it kept pouring, freezing the monsters below and then laying down a thick layer of ice over their heads about the width of a two-lane road. Dave punched the accelerator, the twin exhausts spit fire, and they soared over the front line of the mob.

The Prowler landed on the ice with a jolt and skidded dangerously sideways into a full 360—spraying out a circle of ice around them—before Dave fought the wheel and brought the car back under control. He feathered the throttle again and sped along on top of the ice as the nozzles kept spraying and paving the way just ahead of them.

Just behind them, Will and Elise led their horses into a jump that carried them over the front of the army that hadn't been frozen. They landed on the icy road, skidding and whirling for a moment, until they regained some traction and sprinted after the Prowler, their mounts' hooves digging divots in the ice.

Jericho jumped last, and as he made the leap, the wave of attackers just behind them crashed into the wave of attackers in front of them. Jericho cleared the scrum and landed up on the ice, skidding for a good fifty feet and spinning around a few times, coming very near to the edge. Ajay closed his eyes and hung on, shouting like he was riding a roller coaster, until he felt the bear stabilize and start to run again.

"Are grizzly bears comfortable on ice?" he shouted into Jericho's ear.

"NO. POLAR BEARS ARE!"

"Sorry, stupid question!"

They were halfway across the plaza when Dave glanced back and saw that they'd outrun the rear ranks of the army; they were regrouping and running after them along the elevated ice highway, but he'd opened up a quarter of a mile lead. He looked over at Nick, holding the pull with both hands and staring at it like his life depended on it.

"You can let go . . . YOU CAN LET GO NOW!"

"What? Oh. Sorry, dude. I was concentrating."

Nick let go of the pull. The nozzles stopped spraying and retracted into the bumper, and the Prowler skipped off the last of the ice back onto solid ground. Dave throttled down to a stop and waved the others up to join him.

When they saw Dave give the signal, Will and Elise, in tandem, directed their mounts off the ice and onto the plaza floor. They spurred ahead and quickly caught up to the waiting Prowler. The bear and Ajay trailed close behind them.

"Follow us!" shouted Will. "We know the way!"

"Roger that!" shouted Dave.

Elise took the lead this time, Will following close behind. She drove her horse out of the plaza and onto the road they'd taken on the way in, with the Prowler and Ajay and Jericho, who was starting to labor, bringing up the rear.

"I hope I'm not proving too much of a burden, Coach!" shouted Ajay in his ear.

"ENDURANCE . . . IS MY . . . AREA OF . . . EXPERTISE!"

"I mean, considering that you're a bear versus an obviously supernatural vehicle and two magnificent steeds in peak condition," said Ajay. "I think you're doing remarkably well."

They were moving into the roundabout near the fountain, where they'd first entered the classical sector. Ajay looked back and saw the leading edge of their pursuers just exiting the plaza.

"We've already built about a two-minute lead!" he said, reaching into his pack. "Let's see if I can pad it a little!"

Ajay scattered the last few handfuls of his homemade explosive devices along the road behind them.

Will kept his eye on Elise, just ahead of him, as she led them through the gate of the classical section back into the working quarter. His biggest worry now was whether he could keep up with her.

Do you remember the way? he asked.

Of course.

Will glanced back and around them. The streets here were completely deserted.

They must have pulled all available forces to the plaza, he sent. *To spring the trap.*

Guess we should feel flattered, if they thought they needed all that to stop us.

Somewhere far behind them, they heard a series of explosions. Will thought they sounded familiar.

Ajay? he asked.

Yes, that was me.

We're going straight at the portal. Don't stop for anything. Here's what we're going to do when we get there.

He explained, telepathically, to both Ajay and Elise. By the time he was done, Elise had led them back into the dense warren of narrow streets around the storage sheds. As they turned a corner, Will caught a glimpse of the top of the giant portal over one of the roofs.

There was still no sign of pursuit from anywhere in the sector, and when they turned the final corner into the open construction area, the arcs appeared to have been left completely unguarded. But the work had continued, at a frantic pace; the tips of the arcs were now joined, forming a completed circle, and a battalion of workers were nearly finished attaching the large metal housing that contained the cutting element to the track inside the bottom of the arcs.

Now Will took the lead and spurred his horse across the wasted barren fields toward the arcs. Elise stayed right on his heels. When the worker drones heard the Prowler's throttle as

Dave roared up behind them, they dropped what they were doing and scattered in every direction. By the time Will dismounted at the base of the arcs, they'd all cleared out. Elise jumped down beside him, and they went to work immediately, pulling material from their packs. The sight of the completed arc up close made Will question his plan; it looked as solid and substantial as that big archway in St. Louis.

As Dave skidded to a stop beside them, Nick hopped out of the Prowler and joined them. Dave kept the car idling, flashed out of sight, and then instantly appeared next to the others at the arch.

"I don't know what you hit her with," said Dave to Elise, pointing at Brooke in the back of the Prowler, "but Sleeping Beauty's still in dreamland."

"Two years of repressed rage," said Elise.

"Where's Coach and Ajay?" asked Will.

"Thought they were right behind me," said Dave.

Moments later, the bear loped into view around the final shed, laboring, moving at no more than an unsteady trot.

We're here, we're coming! Ajay sent to Will as he waved from atop the bear.

Elise immediately hopped onto her horse, Dave popped back into the Prowler and gunned the engine, and they both raced out to meet them. Elise pulled Ajay off of Jericho and onto the back of her horse, and after a brief animated conversation, the bear climbed up and stood on the front seat of the Prowler. Moments later they all arrived back at the base of the arcs.

"We have about three minutes," said Ajay, jumping down and looking up at the completed portal. "I see they've made quite a bit of progress. Amazing what you can accomplish when time is fungible."

"Running some recon, be right back," said Dave to Will, and then he disappeared.

The bear dragged himself out of the Prowler and plopped onto the ground, sitting up, too exhausted to speak. As they gathered around, he made a gesture asking for water. Nick pulled out his canteen and poured the entire contents into the coach's upraised mouth.

"You okay, Coach?" asked Elise.

The bear nodded, gasping for breath. Still groggy, Brooke briefly raised her head from the rear of the Prowler and saw the bear sitting right next to her. The bear snarled. She passed out again, wilting back down onto the seat.

"He kept telling me about his conditioning," said Ajay, "but the ursine physique is not ideally suited for long-range exertion."

"Now you know how your team feels when you send 'em up Suicide Hill," said Nick.

The bear swatted the empty canteen out of Nick's hand. "WHAT'S THE PLAN?" he finally said.

"Blow this thing up," said Will, nodding at the arc. "Get out of Dodge."

"The explosives are in my pack," said Ajay without moving.

Will noticed Ajay looking intently back toward the compound in the direction they'd come.

"What's wrong?"

"I may have slightly overstated how much time we actually have."

"Elise, get started on the housing. Nick, give her a hand," said Will, then moved over to Ajay and asked quietly, "What are you seeing?"

"I believe the Makers are coming," said Ajay, not taking his eyes off the horizon. "The real ones."

Will peered out that way but couldn't see anything yet. Jericho had gotten back up on his four feet and padded over to them, looking at the portal.

"HOW ARE WE GOING TO BRING THIS DOWN?"

"Come with me," said Ajay. "I'll need your help."

He hurried off with his pack to where the arcs attached to their huge metallic bases with thick iron brackets studded with massive rivets. Jericho trotted after him. Ajay began fastening small packs of plastic explosives to remote detonators, then had Jericho stand on his hind legs and stick them at strategic spots on the upper ends of the brackets.

Above them, Nick vaulted onto the top of the metallic housing on the track, a shielded silver rectangle about the size of a Volkswagen bus. He located a seam and after a few punches and kicks pried it open, then peeled it back, revealing a solid complex block of futuristic circuitry and indecipherably advanced electronics. Elise looked up at it from below.

"What should we do with this?" Nick shouted to Will.

"Trash it," said Will.

Nick gleefully went to work mauling and ripping and yanking the rest of the shell off the machinery. Once the interior was exposed, Elise started sending small well-placed blasts of sound that obliterated its large swaths of circuitry.

Dave reappeared next to Will, looking concerned. "How much longer is all this going to take?"

"I don't know, a minute?"

Dave looked out at the still-open field in front of them. "We don't have that much time."

"What should we do?"

"Carve a hole with that thing and get you all out of here," said Dave. "Right now."

"What about you?"

"I'll stay and do my job."

"But I'm an Initiate, right? I thought it was my job, too—"

"It's not your job to die."

Dave meant business; Will had never seen or heard him so serious.

"I want to finish what I started," said Will.

"There's no time to argue about it—"

"I'm not arguing."

Will stared him right in the eye.

Dave grinned. "Just making sure, mate," he said.

They heard them before they saw anything, a series of death-rattle screeches that filled the sky, strumming some primeval chord that rent fear deep into brain and bone.

"Here they come," said Ajay.

Everyone turned to look. Seven dim shapes cut through the gloom hanging over the walls, then slowly revealed themselves as seven long slithering bodies gliding toward them on leathery wings.

Winged serpents with sleek toothsome heads and gleaming, slick silvery-scaled bodies. Seven armored riders astride them, each twenty feet tall, and every bit as hideous as their mounts, fleshed-out versions of the reptilian skeletons they'd seen in the catacombs below Cahokia.

"May I present the Makers," said Dave.

Nick and Elise jumped down from the destroyed housing to join them.

"That's why we haven't seen any flying things," said Will to Nick. "They kept the skies for themselves."

"These dudes look somewhat scarier than those empty robes," said Nick.

"You think?" asked Elise.

And then all around them, from out of the warrens and

around the sheds and down the main road leading to the gate, it seemed the entire army they'd seen assembled before the walls double-timed into view, filling the horizon before them in every direction. Will noticed Hobbes, on horseback, leading the front line of the forces at a gallop.

The Makers flew in low over their troops, circling once, urging their army toward the arcs.

"So what's the plan, Stan?" asked Nick.

"Ajay?" shouted Will.

"The charges are set," said Ajay, running over to join them, with Jericho trailing.

"CAN WE GO NOW?"

"I've got the detonator here," said Ajay, holding up a small remote. "But I strongly recommend that we move out of the way first."

"Cut the hole, Will," said Dave, drawing out his long sidearm.

Will put his hand on the Carver in his pocket, then noticed Brooke stirring again in the back of the Prowler down below.

"Nick, get Brooke," he said.

"Seriously?" asked Elise.

"We're not leaving without her," said Will.

"I picked a bad day to forget my asbestos mittens," said Nick.

He dove off the base of the arcs, tumbled to the Prowler, plucked Brooke from the backseat, tossed her over his shoulder, and carried her over to them.

"Go on, Will," said Dave. "Cut it now."

Will took out the Carver but didn't switch it on yet. As Dave strode forward to the edge of the base, Nick ran past him with Brooke, jumped up, and set her down against the base near the others. She had come around again. The thought-form gag had disappeared but she still couldn't speak. When she looked up and saw the Makers flying toward them, she looked absolutely paralyzed with fear.

"Don't tell me," said Elise to Brooke. "You never saw what they actually looked like."

Brooke shook her head.

"And you didn't know what they were really going to do."

Brooke nodded quickly and repeatedly.

"Don't touch anything," said Will, right in Brooke's face.

"We need to move at least another twenty-five feet to our right," said Ajay quietly.

"Not too fast," said Will.

They began to slowly sidestep, away from where Ajay had set the charges on the bracket. Brooke saw them moving, got up, and stumbled after them, terrified of being left behind.

The Makers glided in ahead of their army. They stopped and hovered about fifty yards ahead of the front line, their mounts creating a foul wind with their beating wings. Their leader, the one in the middle, touched down while the others remained airborne.

The lead Maker was, not surprisingly, the biggest and ugliest of the bunch. What they could see of its body appeared to be a festival of rot, layered over with boils and mobile infections. Its face was hidden behind a slitted iron mask, and considering how hideous the rest of it was, Will considered this something of a blessing.

The lead Maker pointed a hand at them and spoke in a grinding, completely indecipherable tongue. Its voice was punishingly loud, like a dinosaur scratching its talons on a blackboard, echoing off all the surfaces around them. The roommates covered their ears as they moved. The Maker finished its threat and waited for a reaction—presumably groveling and abject surrender. Instead Nick stepped forward, grinned, and gave it a friendly wave.

"And a very pleasant BUENOS NACHOS to you, too, lady!"

The Maker seemed baffled by this response, tilting its head to look at him like a dog hearing an unfamiliar sound. Nick turned a few somersaults to catch up with the others, while Dave walked straight to the edge of the base and shouted, "Remember me?"

He raised his sidearm and fired a beam of light that hit the Maker's iron mask and pinged off. Enraged, the Maker raised the crooked metallic stick it was carrying, pointed it at him, and fired a blue ball of blindingly fast energy from its tip.

Dave instantly transformed into his twenty-foot angelic self, raised his gleaming gold-white sword, and deflected the blue ball of energy away harmlessly. The Maker stared at him, furious.

"Get a load of him," said Nick, staring at Dave.

Will and Ajay pulled Nick around the back edge of the right arc.

"I'm cutting the hole now," said Will, flicking on the Carver. "Ajay, blow the charges."

"What about Dave?" he asked.

"Don't worry about him," said Will. "He's dead."

All seven Makers simultaneously raised staves and sticks and fired various kinds and colors of vicious charges at Dave. He held up his sword, shouted something, and a bubble of light appeared all around him. All their energy bolts ricocheted off the bubble and blew up wherever they landed, including a yellow one that hit the base and sent the roommates ducking for cover.

Will pointed the Carver at the air: Ajay pushed the plunger. The charges all around the bracket at the bottom of the left arc detonated—not an overly impressive explosion, given the size of the arcs—but one that sent a hail of rivets and shrapnel at the Makers, plunking a few of them, which irritated them further.

A moment later the thick plate of the bracket fell off and hit the metal base with a resounding clang. The entire left arc wobbled, ever so slightly.

Will took his finger off the trigger of the Carver and stopped to look at the arc. They waited. The archway continued to wobble, swaying a little bit more forward and backward each time, which slowly pried apart the rivets joining the arcs up top. They heard the metal groaning but the arc still didn't topple.

"Come on," said Ajay. "I worked out all the physics. That should have supplied more than enough propulsive force."

Another wobble back and forth but the arc still didn't fall. Will switched off the Carver.

"Give it a push," he said to Elise. "Forward."

Elise and Ajay ran around the back of the arcs into position. He pointed out the precise spot on the arc that she needed to hit. She took in a series of deep breaths, getting ready to unleash a blast.

"You'll have to time it just right," said Ajay, looking up at the swaying structure. "At the apex of the forward lean. I'll say when."

The lead Maker raised its metallic stick again and gave an order in that terrible voice to the forces behind him. As one, the entire army started running forward across the fields toward the arcs, raising their voices in a single deafening shout.

"There they go again," said Nick.

"WHAT A BUNCH OF IDIOTS," said Jericho.

Dave jumped down from the base to the ground in front of the Makers—who all raised their sticks again to attack him—but before they could get off another round, he plunged his sword into the ground, creating a massive shock wave that sent out lines of explosive force in every direction. The ground erupted along every one of those lines, under the Makers and their army, blowing massive numbers of them up into the air.

"Now!" shouted Ajay.

Elise let loose a concentrated blast of sound at the wobbling arc as it teetered forward, applying just enough power to push it past the tipping point.

At that moment, one of the lines of force from Dave's sword slammed into the base of the left arc, nudging it backward. That countered the vector forces pushing the arc forward and kicked the bottom of its base backward as the top tumbled. The left side pulled the right side along with it and now they both cascaded down, the entire structure coming apart at its seams as gravity applied an accelerator.

The arcs crashed down into the field, falling past the Makers and dropping onto the heart of the advancing army. Will saw the largest intact section of the arc fall directly onto Hobbes, who stopped just long enough to look up and register what was about to happen. The concussion as the arcs hit the ground created a shock wave that sent the Makers and their serpent mounts tumbling into the air again. Dust, dirt, debris rose up and obliterated Will's view of the field with a massive plume. Everything in the field—including Dave—disappeared.

"OH, NO," said Jericho.

Will saw where he was looking and took off ahead of the others, reaching them almost instantly. Under a constant shower of dust, gravel, and small stones, Elise and Ajay were both lying on the ground behind the sheared-off base.

Will threw himself to the ground beside them. He couldn't tell where they'd been hit, but they were both lying still—bruised and bleeding in a number of places—and neither of them appeared to be breathing.

The worst thing, by far, was this: Their voices were gone from his head. Stilled. He couldn't hear or find them.

He didn't know what to do. He felt like the arc had landed on him. He couldn't tell how much time went by.

"That thing," said Jericho, who was standing over him now, in human form. "That thing in your pack."

"What thing?"

"The disc," said Nick, who was suddenly standing next to Jericho.

Will looked at his pack, beside him on the ground. The words made no sense—he didn't even know what they meant—but he picked up the pack and emptied it on the ground.

He saw the disc hit the dirt and remembered. Round, silver, six inches across.

The disc he'd taken from Franklin's display case. The healing disc.

He picked it up, turned it around, looking for some kind of switch. Why hadn't he taken the time to ask the old man how it worked?

He pressed it as hard as he could with both hands and the thing hummed to life, pulsing with energy. Then he looked down at both his friends, cold and inert, lying a few feet apart.

Franklin's voice echoed in his head: *It's astonishingly effective at repairing human tissue at the cellular level. They work only once but fortunately they're not difficult to produce.*

"What are you waiting for?" asked Nick.

"It's no good," said Will.

"Why, what are you talking about?" said Jericho. "Use the damn thing."

"It only works once," he said; then he looked up at them. "Who do I use it on?"

Neither of them knew what to say.

"Ajay," said Brooke.

She knelt down next to him. Calm and clear, she looked him directly in the eye.

"Use it on Ajay, Will," she said.

Solemnly focused, Brooke laid both of her hands on Elise, cradling her head. Unsure of how to make it function, Will laid the disc on Ajay's chest. He felt the thing fill with energy, then distribute it out into Ajay's body. He directed his mind into the disc and let his intuition guide him, moving the disc around to the various injury sites—there were quite a few—and waiting for feedback from the disc to guide him on how to deploy it.

It took minutes, not seconds, and he knew it was a race against time. He blinked on the Grid and watched the energy moving into and through Ajay, fighting the injuries, winning some battles, failing others. He paid particular interest to Ajay's head, knowing that he was watching him fight for his life.

When he sensed the disc was running out of juice, Will added some of his own, any way he knew how and a few he just guessed at. He looked up, desperate, and his urgency got through to the others. Jericho knelt beside him and laid his hands on Ajay as well, and then Nick did the same, and then he realized Brooke was there, placing her hands on top of theirs, and Elise was stirring behind her on the ground, breathing again, color returning to her face.

Just then the disc went dark and cold in his hands. Out of power. Will tossed it aside. Everyone stopped. For a long moment, Ajay still looked lifeless . . . and then he took a breath and opened his eyes and saw his friends looking down at him.

"I can't even begin to tell you how interesting that was," said Ajay.

Dave appeared beside them, back in human form again, battered and bruised and limping.

"Bloodied and beaten but these drongos are resilient, I gotta give 'em that. They're regrouping, and they're pretty sauced about it—Skizzers, mate, don't tell me you didn't cut the hole yet!"

Will tossed him the Carver. "Knock yourself out."

Dave switched on the Carver. Will pulled Ajay into his arms and held him for a while and by then Nick had gently carried Elise over to him. When Will put his arms around her and felt the warmth of her body and caught the scent of her hair, he didn't think he'd ever be able to let go.

He saw Brooke over Elise's shoulder, sobbing and saying how sorry she was to anyone around her. Mostly Nick, who was holding her—in a forgiving way—and who was apparently the only one interested in listening.

Standing nearby—standing guard—Jericho took out a handkerchief. He apparently had something in his eye.

EIGHTEEN

WILL'S RULES FOR LIVING #18:
ALL YOU NEED IS LOVE. AND SOME FRIENDS
YOU CAN TRUST. AND A LITTLE LUCK DOESN'T
HURT EITHER.

August 31

Dear Dad,

I've been meaning to write you for way too long now.
I don't know where you are, obviously, so I don't know if
you'll ever see this, but should you ever find it, or if it
finds its way to you, I wanted you to know what happened.

I know the whole story now. Why you ran from the
Center, the reasons you hid me, why we lived the way we
did, and why you never told me the truth. I was angry
and confused about it a lot of the time, growing up. I got
pretty good at hiding my feelings then, but I'm sure you
must have sensed it. Then again, you also had plenty of
reasons not to call me on it.

I felt even more messed up about it when I found out
who you really are. All I can say now is, after getting to
know your father, Franklin—I can't bring myself to call
him my grandfather—I don't think I would have done
anything differently myself. You did the best you could
in a crazy situation.

After they took you in Ojai, I saw you only that one time at the Crag—when he was using you to get me to do what he wanted, just as he was using me to do the same to you. I don't even know if you saw me then. And I haven't seen you since. But I'm choosing to believe you're still alive, somewhere, just like I did after the plane crash.

Hope is the last thing you can afford to lose, right? I think that was one of the best Rules you gave me. Thanks for those, by the way. They really got me through, more than you'll ever know.

I've got a great group of friends here—really "talented" ones, like I am, in a lot of different ways, but you know all about that. It's not the talents that make them special, although that certainly makes all of us unusual. It's not random bits of bizarre DNA that make them great, either. It's the content of their characters.

For instance: They could've used a hundred excuses to back down when I asked for their help, but they never hesitated. We took the fight right to Franklin, the Knights, and the Makers before they could do any more damage. Turned out we had to go into the Never-Was to finish that job, and we tore it up one side and down the other. No brag, just fact. Those creeps won't be making any more runs at our side of the fence for a long time.

When we came back out—five weeks ago now—nothing was how we expected it to be. Franklin had told me that if I used the Carver, we'd come back into our world only a second or so after we'd left. Like most everything else in his life, he got that one wrong, too.

Almost ten days had gone by. Franklin was long gone, and so were all of his Knights cronies on campus, including the man who owned the Crag, Stan Haxley. Nobody's seen or heard from any of them since.

We had another group of friends cover for us while we were in the Never-Was. A traveling troupe of pro wrestlers that my buddy Nick found. One of them was "talented," too—turns out he's the son of a guy you used to know as Jolly Nepsted, the boys' locker room attendant at the Center. I'm guessing you probably know his story; he was one of the first Paladins, in Franklin's group way back when. Anyway, reuniting Nepsted—who'd become a friend of ours—with his son . . . well, when we saw how that turned out, it made everything else we had to go through seem worthwhile.

There was a knock at the door. Nick stuck his head in.

"Dude, we're waiting for you," he said. "Dinner at the Rathskeller, and Ajay's buying. He just cashed his first check for one of those gizmotrons he cooked up in the lab. And Coach is coming, too. I just heard from him."

"Give me five minutes," said Will, chewing on the end of his pen.

"And get this: Coach is bringing his *wife*."

"Coach is *married*?"

"Who knew?"

"I can't even picture it. All right, get out of here, let me finish—"

"Five minutes, you promise?"

"Yes!" Will tossed a barrage of throw cushions at the door—without using his hands.

"Don't make me send Elise in after you," said Nick, then closed the door.

Will started writing again.

It's hard to say what's going to happen next. First semester of our junior year starts next week. The good news is, as far as we know, nobody else on the Center's staff or faculty seems to have been mixed up with the Knights. The few kids we knew were involved either already graduated or suddenly "transferred" over the summer. Or so we're told.

That includes Brooke, our roommate whose parents were long-time Knights, but Headmaster Rourke has stepped up to the plate big-time in her case. Brooke's father, the former ambassador, has suddenly been called to some distant, undisclosed location on "diplomatic assignment"— and if you believe that, I'd like to sell you shares in this new thing I've invented called the Internet. Mr. Rourke has arranged for Brooke to be "studying in Europe" while her family's away, which means stashing her out of the Knights' reach so they can't put her brain through another wash cycle. She'd pretty much come out of that tailspin since we got back, I'm happy to report. If the Knights have any desire to live, they'd better not mess with her again.

Which leads me to admit that we don't completely know how much trouble might still be left out there. The Center seems safe for now, and we're bonded for life, my friends and me. I'm good with that. While we're here, we're keeping an eye out for other "talented" individuals who come along. There could be a lot more of them out there— Franklin kept the Prophecy program going for at least six years that we know about—and we think the Center still has all those kids on their radar.

Another knock at the door and Ajay stuck his head in—his even bigger head, which seemed to have grown another hat size since they'd returned.

"I've been experiencing some fascinating insights about a great number of subjects," said Ajay. "One of which I'd like to share with you, if you have a moment."

"Ajay, everybody's bugging me to get ready to go out." Then Will saw how disappointed he looked. "All right, lay it on me."

"Write this down so you don't forget it."

"Okay, okay."

Then Will wrote down what Ajay told him, word for word.

"Now, did anyone mention to you that I'm buying dinner?" Ajay asked.

"Yes. Nick."

"The money was deposited this afternoon directly to an offshore account I've created." Ajay grinned.

"Why offshore?"

"My father calls it 'walking around money.' A rainy day fund, completely untraceable. So you may rest assured, Will, that whatever good deed we next decide to undertake, as a result of my newly inspired tinkering, we will have at our disposal, as Nick would say, a crap-ton of capital. Sorry, I won't keep you another moment."

Ajay left and closed the door.

In the meantime, we're keeping it all on the down-low around here. We like the idea of just being regular students for a while. None of us really knows how that feels, after all.

By the way, I'm writing down my own rules now. I think that's something you encouraged me to do, right? Someday I hope I get a chance to show 'em to you, Dad. I'm not giving up on that. If I've learned anything from my friend Dave—I'll try to explain him someday, but that'll take a while—it's this:

WILL'S RULES FOR LIVING #19:
DON'T EVER GIVE UP ON ANYBODY.

Something dropped heavily onto Will's desk. Startled, he looked over from the bed where he was propped against the headboard. He got up and walked over to see what it was.

A pair of dark glasses was lying there. Wayfarers, sleek and metallic. And next to them a key—a really strange-looking key, gleaming silver, crooked and old-fashioned, like one you might use on a castle door.

With it was a note, the size of a formal invitation, on creamy white stock with a gold band around the margins—real gold, it seemed. When he picked it up, he heard Dave's voice as the following words appeared on the paper:

> *Dear Will: As mop-up operations in the n-w near*
> *completion, I am delighted to inform you that, after*
> *a thorough review of your recent performance by*
> *the Hierarchy's executive committee, you have been*
> *promoted to level one clearance, effective immediately.*
> *Cheers, mate, you're a Wayfarer.*
>
> > *Your pal, Dave*
>
> *P.S. As I may have mentioned, first perk of the job is you*
> *get to pick your vehicle. Choose carefully!*

Will tried on the glasses, and then picked up the key.

The door flew open with a powerful gust of wind, blowing everything in the room around like in a storm. Will had to brace himself to keep from losing his balance—

And the next thing he knew, Elise was in his arms, wearing her sly grin, looking and feeling and smelling better than anyone had a right to, and as the wind abated, she kissed him softly on the cheek.

"Everybody's waiting," she said, and then kissed him for real. "What's the holdup, West?"

"Tell the gang we'll be a little late for dinner." He kissed her back. "We'll meet 'em at the restaurant."

"What did you have in mind?" Her eyes narrowed playfully.

Will held up the key and grinned.

"We're going for a ride."

WILL'S RULES FOR LIVING #20:
(from Ajay) It is our rarest possession, more precious than any treasure from nature, God, or man. It cannot be bought, sold, traded, or stolen. You only have so much of it, and you never know when it will run out, so you mustn't waste it or just let it pass or, heaven forbid, ever try to kill it.

IT IS TIME. SPEND YOUR TIME WISELY.
FOR IF YOU CAN MASTER THIS ONE
SIMPLE AND ELUSIVE SKILL, MY FRIEND,
YOU WILL FULLY AND TRULY BE ALIVE.

Dad's List of Rules to Live By

#1: THE IMPORTANCE OF AN ORDERLY MIND.

#2: STAY FOCUSED ON THE TASK AT HAND.

#3: DON'T DRAW ATTENTION TO YOURSELF.

#4: IF YOU THINK YOU'RE DONE, YOU'VE JUST BEGUN.

#5: TRUST NO ONE.

#6: REMAIN ALERT AT ALL TIMES TO THE REALITY OF THE PRESENT. BECAUSE ALL WE HAVE IS RIGHT NOW.

#7: DON'T CONFUSE GOOD LUCK WITH A GOOD PLAN.

#8: ALWAYS BE PREPARED TO IMPROVISE.

#9: WATCH, LOOK, AND LISTEN, OR YOU WON'T KNOW WHAT YOU'RE MISSING.

#10: DON'T JUST REACT TO A SITUATION THAT TAKES YOU BY SURPRISE. *RESPOND.*

#11: TRUST YOUR INSTINCTS.

#12: LET THE OTHER GUY DO THE TALKING.

#13: YOU ONLY GET ONE CHANCE TO MAKE A FIRST IMPRESSION.

#14: ASK ALL QUESTIONS IN THE ORDER OF THEIR IMPORTANCE.

#15: BE QUICK, BUT DON'T HURRY.

#16: ALWAYS LOOK PEOPLE IN THE EYE. GIVE THEM A HANDSHAKE THEY'LL REMEMBER.

#17: START EACH DAY BY SAYING IT'S GOOD TO BE ALIVE. EVEN IF YOU DON'T FEEL IT, *SAYING* IT—OUT LOUD—MAKES IT MORE LIKELY THAT YOU WILL.

#18: IF #17 DOESN'T WORK, COUNT YOUR BLESSINGS.

#19: WHEN EVERYTHING GOES WRONG, TREAT DISASTER AS A WAY TO WAKE UP.

#20: THERE MUST ALWAYS BE A RELATIONSHIP BETWEEN EVIDENCE AND CONCLUSION.

#21: FORTUNE FAVORS THE BOLD.

#22: WHENEVER YOUR HEAD IS TOO FULL OF NOISE, MAKE A LIST.

#23: WHEN THERE'S TROUBLE, THINK FAST AND ACT DECISIVELY.

#24: YOU CAN'T CHANGE ANYTHING IF YOU CAN'T CHANGE YOUR MIND.

#25: WHAT YOU'RE TOLD TO BELIEVE ISN'T IMPORTANT: IT'S WHAT YOU *CHOOSE* TO BELIEVE. IT'S NOT THE INK AND PAPER THAT MATTER, BUT THE HAND THAT HOLDS THE PEN.

#26: ONCE IS AN ANOMALY. TWICE IS A COINCIDENCE. THREE TIMES IS A PATTERN. AND AS WE KNOW . . .

#27: THERE IS NO SUCH THING AS A COINCIDENCE.

#28: LET PEOPLE UNDERESTIMATE YOU. THAT WAY THEY'LL NEVER KNOW FOR SURE WHAT YOU'RE CAPABLE OF.

#29: YOU COULD ALSO THINK OF COINCIDENCE AS SYNCHRONICITY.

#30: SOMETIMES THE ONLY WAY TO DEAL WITH A BULLY IS TO HIT FIRST. HARD.

#31: IT'S NOT A BAD THING, SOMETIMES, IF THEY THINK YOU'RE CRAZY.

#32: EVEN THE SLIGHTEST ADVANTAGE CAN MEAN THE DIFFERENCE BETWEEN LIFE AND DEATH. NEVER GIVE IT AWAY.

#34: ACT AS IF YOU'RE IN CHARGE, AND PEOPLE WILL BELIEVE YOU.

#35: TRYING TIMES ARE NOT THE TIMES TO STOP TRYING.

#40: NEVER MAKE EXCUSES.

#41: SLEEP WHEN YOU'RE SLEEPY. CATS TAKE NAPS SO THEY'RE ALWAYS READY FOR ANYTHING.

#43: THE BRAVEST THING IS NOT ALWAYS THE SMARTEST THING.

#45: COOPERATE WITH THE AUTHORITIES. BUT DON'T NAME FRIENDS.

#46: IF STRANGERS KNOW WHAT YOU'RE FEELING, YOU GIVE THEM THE ADVANTAGE.

#47: OUT-OF-CONTROL ANGER WILL GET YOU KILLED EVEN QUICKER THAN STUPIDITY.

#48: NEVER START A FIGHT UNLESS YOU CAN FINISH IT. FAST.

#49: WHEN ALL ELSE FAILS, JUST BREATHE.

#50: IN TIMES OF CHAOS, STICK TO ROUTINE. BUILD ORDER ONE STEP AT A TIME.

#51: THE ONLY THING YOU CAN'T AFFORD TO LOSE IS HOPE.

#52: TO BREAK THE ICE, ALWAYS COMPLIMENT A MAN'S HOMETOWN.

#53: AND ALWAYS SYMPATHIZE WITH HIS HOMETOWN'S FOOTBALL TEAM.

#54: IF YOU CAN'T BE ON TIME, BE EARLY.

#55: IF YOU FAIL TO PREPARE, YOU PREPARE TO FAIL.

#56: GIVING UP IS EASY. FINISHING IS HARD.

#57: IF YOU WANT TO KNOW WHAT'S GOING ON IN A SMALL TOWN, HANG AROUND THE BARBERSHOP.

#58: FACING THE TRUTH IS A LOT EASIER, IN THE LONG RUN, THAN LYING TO YOURSELF.

#59: SOMETIMES YOU FIND OUT MORE WHEN YOU ASK QUESTIONS TO WHICH YOU ALREADY KNOW THE ANSWER.

#60: IF YOU DON'T LIKE THE ANSWER YOU GET, YOU SHOULDN'T HAVE ASKED THE QUESTION.

#61: IF YOU WANT SOMETHING DONE THE RIGHT WAY, DO IT YOURSELF.

#62: IF YOU DON'T WANT PEOPLE TO NOTICE YOU, ACT LIKE YOU BELONG THERE AND LOOK BUSY.

#63: THE BEST WAY TO LIE IS TO INCLUDE PART OF THE TRUTH.

#65: THE DUMBEST GUY IN A ROOM IS THE FIRST ONE WHO TELLS YOU HOW SMART HE IS.

#68: NEVER SIGN A LEGAL DOCUMENT THAT HASN'T BEEN APPROVED BY A LAWYER WHO WORKS FOR YOU.

#70: WHEN YOU'RE IN TROUBLE, EMPHASIZE YOUR STRENGTHS.

#72: WHEN IN A NEW PLACE, ACT LIKE YOU'VE BEEN THERE BEFORE.

#73: LEARN THE DIFFERENCE BETWEEN TACTICS AND STRATEGY.

#74: 99 PERCENT OF THE THINGS YOU WORRY ABOUT NEVER HAPPEN. DOES THAT MEAN WORRYING WORKS OR THAT IT'S A COMPLETE WASTE OF TIME AND ENERGY? YOU DECIDE.

#75: WHEN YOU NEED TO MAKE A QUICK DECISION, DON'T LET WHAT YOU CAN'T DO INTERFERE WITH WHAT YOU CAN.

#76: WHEN YOU GAIN THE ADVANTAGE, PRESS IT TO THE LIMIT.

#77: THE SWISS ARMY DOESN'T AMOUNT TO MUCH, BUT NEVER LEAVE HOME WITHOUT THEIR KNIFE.

#78: THERE'S A REASON THE CLASSICS ARE CLASSICS: THEY'RE *CLASSIC.*

#79: DON'T MAKE ANOTHER'S PAIN THE SOURCE OF YOUR OWN HAPPINESS.

#80: GO EASY ON THE HARD SELL. PERSUASION IS THE ART OF MAKING OTHERS BELIEVE IT WAS *THEIR* IDEA.

#81: NEVER TAKE MORE THAN YOU NEED.

#82: WITHOUT A LIFE OF THE MIND, YOU'LL LIVE A MINDLESS LIFE.

#83: JUST BECAUSE YOU'RE PARANOID DOESN'T MEAN THAT SORRY IS BETTER THAN SAFE.

#84: WHEN NOTHING ELSE WORKS, TRY CHOCOLATE.

#86: NEVER BE NERVOUS WHEN TALKING TO A BEAUTIFUL GIRL. JUST PRETEND SHE'S A PERSON, TOO.

#87: MEN WANT COMPANY. WOMEN WANT EMPATHY.

#88: ALWAYS LISTEN TO THE PERSON WITH THE WHISTLE.

#91: THERE IS NOT—NOR SHOULD THERE BE—ANY LIMIT TO WHAT A GUY WILL GO THROUGH IN ORDER TO IMPRESS THE RIGHT GIRL.

#92: IF YOU WANT PEOPLE TO TELL YOU MORE, SAY LESS. OPEN YOUR EYES AND EARS, AND CLOSE YOUR MOUTH.

#94: YOU CAN FIND MOST OF THE WEAPONS OR EQUIPMENT YOU'LL EVER NEED AROUND THE HOUSE.

#96: MEMORIZE THE BILL OF RIGHTS.

#97: REGARDING EYEWEAR AND UNDERWEAR: ALWAYS TRAVEL WITH BACKUPS.

#98: DON'T WATCH YOUR LIFE LIKE IT'S A MOVIE THAT'S HAPPENING TO SOMEONE ELSE. IT'S HAPPENING TO *YOU*. IT'S HAPPENING RIGHT NOW.

#100: STAY ALIVE.

OPEN ALL DOORS, AND AWAKEN.

WILL'S LIST OF RULES TO LIVE BY

#1: IF YOU REALLY WANT TO KEEP A SECRET, DON'T TELL ANYBODY.

#2: YOU CAN'T LIVE YOUR LIFE TWO DAYS AT A TIME.

#3: IF YOU HAVE TO HIDE YOUR TRUE FEELINGS FROM YOUR FRIENDS, THEY'RE NOT YOUR FRIENDS.

#4: IF ANY TASK YOU UNDERTAKE REQUIRES YOU TO "DIE TRYING," YOU MIGHT WANT TO RECONSIDER YOUR PLAN.

#5: HEALING TAKES MUCH LONGER THAN YOU THINK. THE BIGGEST SCARS YOU CARRY AREN'T THE ONES YOU CAN SEE.

#6: THOSE WHO CAN'T DO, DON'T.

#7: SOMETIMES, IN ORDER TO GET COMPLETELY SANE, YOU HAVE TO GO A LITTLE CRAZY.

#8: DO THE RIGHT THING, ALWAYS, AND RISK THE CONSEQUENCES.

#9: TAKE CARE OF THE MINUTES, AND THE HOURS WILL TAKE CARE OF THEMSELVES.

#10: WHEN VISITING A FOREIGN LAND, IT IS ALWAYS WISE TO OBSERVE AND ABIDE BY THE CUSTOMS

OF THE LOCAL CULTURE. UNLESS THEY'RE
TRYING TO EAT YOU.

#11: IT DOESN'T MATTER HOW YOU DO IT. IT ONLY
MATTERS *THAT* YOU DO IT.

#12: IN THE FACE OF OVERWHELMING ODDS, DO
ONE SMART THING AT A TIME.

#13: READ BOOKS TO GET SMARTER. READ PEOPLE
TO BECOME WISER.

#14: BEING BRAVE MEANS BEING AFRAID AND GOING
AHEAD WITH IT ANYWAY.

#15: AN OPEN DOOR IS EITHER A GREETING OR A
TRAP. BEST TO DECIDE WHICH BEFORE YOU
ENTER.

#16: WHEN YOU REACH THE END OF YOUR ROPE,
DON'T HANG AROUND.

#17: KEEP YOUR FRIENDS CLOSE. KEEP YOUR ENEMIES
IN A BAG AT THE BOTTOM OF THE RIVER.

#18: ALL YOU NEED IS LOVE. AND SOME FRIENDS YOU
CAN TRUST. AND A LITTLE LUCK DOESN'T HURT
EITHER.

#19: DON'T EVER GIVE UP ON ANYBODY.

#20: *(from Ajay) It is our rarest possession, more precious
than any treasure from nature, God, or man. It cannot
be bought, sold, traded, or stolen. You only have so much
of it, and you never know when it will run out, so you
mustn't waste it or just let it pass or, heaven forbid, ever
try to kill it.*

IT IS TIME. SPEND YOUR TIME WISELY.
FOR IF YOU CAN MASTER THIS ONE
SIMPLE AND ELUSIVE SKILL, MY FRIEND,
YOU WILL FULLY AND TRULY BE ALIVE.

ACKNOWLEDGMENTS

Many thanks to James Thomas, editor extraordinaire, and to Barbara Marcus, Michelle Nagler, Mallory Loehr, Jenna Lettice, and John Adamo at Random House Children's Books. Thanks, as always, to my friend and agent Ed Victor, and to my wife, Lynn, for having the courage, patience, and perspective to marry a working writer.

ABOUT THE AUTHOR

MARK FROST studied directing and playwriting at Carnegie Mellon University. He partnered with David Lynch to create and executive produce the groundbreaking television series *Twin Peaks*. Frost cowrote the screenplays for the films *Fantastic Four* and *Fantastic Four: Rise of the Silver Surfer*. He is also the *New York Times* bestselling author of eight previous books, including *The List of Seven, The Second Objective, The Greatest Game Ever Played*, and *The Match*. To learn more, visit ByMarkFrost.com.